Where there had been a dot on his screen representing the nuclear-powered cruiser, there was now nothing. Six hundred feet and eleven thousand tons of guided missile cruiser, with 450 men aboard, had seemingly disappeared.

"Mitscher reports *Virginia* has exploded, sir. They say the missle probably hit the aft magazine and the forward one went off almost immediately after . . . sir, they say nothing's left . . . no survivors." The speaker's voice was incredulous.

"Submarine contact to the southwest, sir!" He saw immediately on his screen that two of Kupinsky's subs had pulled closer together, possibly for an attack on the escorts.

"Wainwright reports *John Paul Jones, Preble, Radford* and *Knox* have all been hit, sir."

Every family gives up so much in the writing of a book that I hope someday my sons, Jack and Ben, will understand why their father disappeared nights and weekends. And my wife, Georgie, soulmate when things are tough and manuscript critic extraordinaire deserves a special medal . . . but, this book is dedicated to my parents, Jack and Ruth Taylor, who have spent over forty years offering support with no strings attached while I was steaming full speed in the opposite direction. The quote on page 92 by David Charles's father was actually written by my own father in November, 1962, and that explains it all.

SHOW OF FORCE

CHARLES D. TAYLOR

CHARTER
NEW YORK

A DIVISION OF CHARTER COMMUNICATIONS INC.
A GROSSET & DUNLAP COMPANY

SHOW OF FORCE

Published by arrangement with St. Martin's Press, Inc.

First Charter Printing June 1981
Published simultaneously in Canada
Manufactured in the United States of America

2 4 6 8 0 9 7 5 3 1

Come on now, all you young men, all over the world. You are needed more than ever now to fill the gap of a generation shorn by war. You have not an hour to lose. You must take your place in life's fighting line . . . Enter upon your inheritance . . .

SIR WINSTON CHURCHILL
While England Slept, 1936

THE NAVY HYMN

Eternal Father, strong to save,
Whose arm doth bind the restless wave,
Who bid'st the mighty ocean deep
Its own appointed limits keep;
O, hear us when we cry to thee,
For those in peril on the sea.

WILLIAM WHITING, 1860

ACKNOWLEDGMENTS

I BELONG to a professional organization that provides . . . an unofficial forum for the exchange of ideas about the development and improvement of the Navy,'' the United States Naval Institute. This has given me access to a continual flow of information from both their monthly publication, *Proceedings,* and the following titles from their fine list of books: *The Ships and Aircraft of the U.S. Fleet* by Norman Polmar, *Guide to the Soviet Navy,* 2nd edition, by Siegfried Breyer and Norman Polmar, *Red Star Rising at Sea* and *The Sea Power of the State,* both by Admiral of the Fleet of the Soviet Union Sergei G. Gorshkov, and The U.S. Navy, An Illustrated History by Nathan Miller, published jointly with American Heritage.

Also of great value were *The Unknown War* by Harrison Salisbury (Bantam), *Russia at War,* 1941-1945 by Alexander Werth (Dutton), and *Supership* by Noel Mostert (Knopf).

A brief thanks to Candy's ten and a half fingers.

There are a number of close friends(whom I hope will remain so) from my own Navy days who will find themselves making brief appearances, generally in different bodies and personalities than their own. There are also three men who gave freely of their time to open up a very different world to me and many other young reserve officers. While their names are not used, they appear throughout with a great deal of respect: John C. Powell and William McDonald, former commanding officers of U.S.S. *Glennon* (DD-840) and William Morgan, former commanding officer of U.S.S. *Cony* (DD-508).

CHAPTER ONE

To everyone on the bridge of the U.S.S. *California*, David Charles offered an impression of total relaxation. He was slumped in his chair with his feet propped up on the open wing near the starboard lookout. His grayish blue eyes were open, but he squinted enough in the bright sunlight so that he could have dozed without being noticed. Actually, he had been following a cloud on the horizon, using a point on the forward launcher as a target for the cloud. Either the ship wasn't moving, or the cloud was moving just as fast as the ship, or perhaps he was moving his head enough so that the launcher and the cloud remained in line. It really didn't make much difference to him. His purpose was to simulate deep thought, so no one would bother him. What he often forgot was that he was an admiral and Task Force Commander and no one would speak to him anyway unless spoken to first.

He was thinking, too. He was digesting each of the reports on the last printout from Washington. A slight malfunction in the receiving unit occasionally turned the message into the jibberish that would appear for anyone intercepting them. But there were plenty of ensigns to put to work decoding when the unit had a problem. Most of the material he had read contained information on the Soviet submarines and their various locations. While there was one conventional-powered sub off the Gulf of Oman, the rest were nuclear and had no time limitations or dependency on supply. The reports contained the normal information: name of each boat, commanding officer's bio, number of crew and their experience, weapon load, port of departure and number of days at sea (which would be wise to keep track of), and time on station. Admiral Charles knew that there would be an immediate revision if any change of station beyond ten miles occurred. Less than that made no difference. Each of his torpedoes could find anything within that range that exhibited the same noise signature programmed into the target acquisition module in its nose. Tapes of each sub's sounds were ready to be recorded in any of the torpedoes.

Why, he wondered, was there a conventional boat out there, blatant as hell? Was it just a trick? a decoy? or would it eventually serve some purpose that the War Games people at Johns Hopkins hadn't programmed yet?

The cloud disappeared from view as the bow rose slowly on a long swell. Just as gradually, it reappeared, seeming to rise by itself as the bow slid down the opposite side of the swell. Two more swells followed until the ship gradually regained its stability. Charles looked to his left at the members of the bridge watch. None of them seemed to have noticed the change in motion. Or perhaps, he thought, so many of them have never been in a situation like this before that they're all lost in thought, too.

He tried to catch a seaman's attention, then quietly called, "Messenger."

A young boy, not really a boy but the youngest one in the section, came immediately to his side, saluted and stammered, "Y-yes, sir." He had little experience talking to admirals.

The Admiral removed his starched garrison cap, rubbing the two gold stars on his shirt. It was a habit he rarely noticed, as was the way he ran his left hand through his dark, slightly curly hair. Even though it was cut short, and there were tinges of gray around his ears, he looked younger than most admirals since most of his hair still remained.

"Son, I'd like a mug of coffee, black . . . from the forward control room, not the wardroom. And, while you're on the way, would you ask Commander Dailey to come to the bridge."

The young sailor saluted again. "Aye, aye, sir," and backed away, almost tripping over the raised coaming of the pilothouse hatchway. David smiled to himself, making a mental note to have Bob Casey, the *California's* CO, tell his senior watch officer to ease up on the enlisted men a bit. While they were in wartime conditions, taut nerves could cut down on reaction time. The crew could be sharp without being stiff. He knew no one liked having a flag on board, especially when there really wasn't room for an admiral's staff. All of them, including him, would be glad when *Nimitz* joined up and he could transfer his flag to the aircraft carrier.

After standing up and stretching, he moved into the pilothouse for a moment and checked the other ships on the radar screen. There was no reason to undergo radar-emission control since the Russians knew exactly where they were, and what they were doing. There were five other ships in an extended circle around an imaginary guide in the middle, each far enough from the other to avoid any structural damage from a nuclear attack on one of them. He glanced around at the various watch-standers, all of whom were making themselves busy for his benefit. The officer of the deck lifted his binoculars to his eyes rather than appear to be staring at the man with the stars on his collar.

Shortly after his coffee was in his hand, Bill Dailey, his Chief of Staff, appeared through the hatch on the opposite wing. David motioned with his head to come to the other wing of the bridge. Dailey, a taller and older-looking man, was starched but informal as his boss had dictated: "When you're riding a can"—even though this was far from the old tin can that David had started his career on—"there's a certain informality and I don't want my staff scaring the hell out of these people." The Admiral knew these ships were as big as the old spit 'n' polish cruisers. But he wanted to let the crew know that he still considered their ship with the same reverence as the old, expendable greyhounds that had all but disappeared years ago.

"Bill, I wanted to ask you what you make of that conventional boat they stuck up there near the Gulf of Oman? It doesn't make sense to me. The last printout didn't give a hint about its purpose as far as the War Games people were concerned," he questioned.

"Admiral," the other grinned, "I came prepared to answer just about any other question but that one. Is that bothering you, too?"

"Bill, when I was ops officer on a staff, I always offered an answer anyway, just so my boss would know I was thinking." He raised his eyebrows. "I think you're in a position where you should start asking for some answers, if you don't have any. You know that Gorenko has a reason for everything and that submarine has a purpose." Then, he lowered his brows a bit and offered just a bit of a smile. "You're getting paid to think for me, aren't you?"

"Well, sir,"—he'd served with the Admiral before—"we've worked together long enough so I knew that boat was going to get to you. So I had my boys sit down and had each one prepare a list of reasons why it was there. There were some pretty wild ones. Then we narrowed it down to fit ten items based on Games' projections over the next twenty-four hours, and I had them fire back these alternatives for the computer at Hopkins. We did that about an hour ago, and we ought to have a printout back shortly. And, since I'm still not a mind reader, I'd like it if you'd come down later and go over the response with my boys. They don't see much of you, and they'd sure appreciate having you come down and show how you operate. As a matter of fact, the more they know about you, the more they'll be able to add new alternatives to each prediction. And they're good enough that they just might end up with some answers the next day or so before you have the questions."

"You know I really wasn't checking on you, Bill." He paused and looked across the bow. "I just got tired of that damn cloud," he said, more to himself than to Dailey.

"Pardon me, sir?"

"Nothing, nothing at all, Bill. Just a cloud I was staring at . . . trying to look thoughtful to everyone." He laughed this time. "Even admirals have to look busy, and these boys don't have admirals around much." A pause. "Bill, I don't think the Russians are going to sit and wait for an answer to that speech from the President. It's not like Gorenko. He always does something for emphasis, just to show he means business. I'll give you a little side bet that he's going to do something soon, something that's supposed to jolt the President, something that's going to scare the hell out of everybody. Just a little something to put on the pressure. He probably figures if the President sees telegrams from all over the world telling him to get the hell off that island because the Russians have already made a move, he might just get scared into dumping the whole thing."

"Any ideas on what Gorenko might do, sir?"

"Not really. That's why I called you up here. What's the range of Alex's group now?"

"Alex?"

"The Soviet carrier group, Bill. The one to the east that they're sending down to play with us." He grinned at the other man. "Admiral Kupinsky is Alex. His flag is on the *Lenin*." He turned in his chair to look directly at Dailey. "Remember, he's an old friend of mine and he's bringing a task group down here to play with me and I want to know how close he is, just so I might be able to figure out what his first move might be."

"Sorry, Admiral. I'm not readling your mind again." He knew how far he could carry informality, and when he could let this man know that he was getting too withdrawn on his own wavelength, when he might have to communicate his thoughts in a second. "The sixteen-hundred-position report will indicate they're a bit more than a thousand miles off. If we continue to stream north/south in this sector, and they maintain the speed they've shown since they turned the corner, they'll be right here," he pointed at the deck, "in just about forty-eight hours, which is perfect timing according to Washington. That's when the Chairman predicted we'd be surrounded."

"Noooo . . . nope! That's not like him to wait until then." He sat up taller in the chair.

"There are six submarines around us now, sir. The closest one is out there," Dailey gestured with his right arm, "about forty miles on our quarter, near *Truxton*, keeping the same course and speed as we are."

"No. Alex is in contact with his subs, but all they can do is sink someone, and he won't do that before we have a chance to back down. And he's too far away to do anything with ships for awhile. He's become a fan of air tactics, and I think Alex will do something from the air. He's got a couple of long-range jets, those slower ones, that can stay just so far away and choose from a lovely selection of missiles. It won't be nuclear, but it will carry a message for our dear President.

"You see, he thinks this is just another bluff. I don't. If the big guns in the Kremlin feel this is an aggressive act on our part, they're going to do everything short of sinking some ships. And if the President thinks he can develop sympathy from the rest of the world if the Russians cause a little damage, he's in for a surprise."

"How much do you think they're capable of, sir?"

"Enough to turn him pasty white! Hell, Bill, the days of those phony fishing boats tracking our carriers, or Soviet ships jockeying for the same piece of water, are over when they think they've got us like this. If the President cries foul about a couple of missiles in our fantails, the Soviets will just say they were fired on first and were defending themselves. Who's going to say otherwise when we're out here in the middle of nowhere? I don't think he'll find any witnesses," he added with finality.

"War Games says damage with some fatalities is possible in such a situation, though they also wonder whether the

Russians would take a chance of hitting a magazine," nodded Dailey.

"Sure they would. Those nice shore-based sailors running those expensive computers don't have enough psychology built into their programs. Do me a favor, Bill. Have your people figure a missile range of about seventy-five miles and an aircraft, probably a Riga, that has about a thousand-mile range from *Lenin,* and tell me when we can expect a visit. I'll put a little money on it if you will. I'll bet you, right now, Alex does something in the next watch." He sat back, already having dismissed his Chief of Staff in his mind, and picked out another cloud.

The phone next to the table buzzed. "Captain here," answered Casey. David Charles and the commanding officer of the *California* were having dinner in the captain's cabin.

After listening attentively, he said, "Thank you. I'll come to the bridge shortly. Let me know any course or speed changes." He placed the sound-powered phone back in its box. "You're absolutely right, Admiral. That's my officer of the deck. Combat picked up two aircraft coming from the direction of the Russian force. Looks like your man Dailey picked everything but their wing numbers."

"He's a good man, Bob. Twenty years ago, he would have predicted the same thing without a computer." He looked at his watch. "He just wouldn't have been so damn accurate." He gestured at the dial. "About three and a half minutes off, but Alex always liked being unpredictable."

"My OOD has already notified the other ships for you. He'll sound general quarters in about ten minutes. Is there anything else we can do for you at this point?"

"Nope. There's two of them and six of us, so they'll probably split, one north and one south, and keep their distance. Dailey has already reduced their choices to six options, but I've eliminated four because I know Alex won't use nuclear weapons. He isn't foolish. He doesn't want to sink anyone at this point. I'm pretty sure they'll try the small radar-programmed missiles so that nothing major happens—just damage. Too many casualties would piss off a lot of people in Washington, and the Russians just want to show they mean business. You know and I know and Alex and all his people know the purpose of this little show of force, and they don't want to hurt anyone if they can help it. But, neither do I. Dailey already has the plan to divert the missiles after they're fired, but I want to make sure enough men on each ship see what a real explosion looks like, a Russian one. We'll try to contain it in the middle of the formation. But I want you to tell your gunboss again that I want those two planes to get back to Alex and tell him what we can do."

The two men finished their food and left the small cabin, Casey for the bridge before joining Charles in his tiny flag plot, where they would coordinate the force action.

Even *California*-class ships have a small plot set aside for visiting admirals, but the designers never really understood that a flag carried his own watch-standers, all of whom showed up for general quarters. When the Admiral arrived, passing through the ship's CIC (Combat Information Center) to get to his own space, his men and Casey's seemed crowded in a very small area. He remembered seeing the designs for this type years ago, and how impressed they all were with the space in combat for both equipment and men. Not so today. Discipline was apparently the reason that chaos would never arise, and probably the only reason in such close quarters.

"Good evening, Admiral," Dailey said without moving from his spot in front of the big board. The display showed each of the six ships, their relationship to the cause of all this, Islas Piedras, the Soviet submarines, and the two aircraft, just dots well to the right of the formation, moving toward their targets.

"Hi, Bill. You proud of yourself now?"

"Yes and no. It's pretty easy when you're tied into that big machine at Hopkins. I just hope the weapons selection was correct on our part. We received an update a few minutes ago that indicates that those Riga jets have a greater missile capability than our files show.'' He looked at the board and then at the screen to his right. ''They're at three hundred miles and closing, Admiral. Same course and speed. Estimated time to split is approximately twelve minutes.''

''Very well, Bill.'' David eased himself into the comfortable chair bolted to the deck behind Dailey's position. It gave him a clear picture of everything that was happening at a given moment. A dim glow outlined a complexity of instruments, each strategically placed in the tight space to give the officers in charge an accurate picture of a constantly changing situation. There was calm since only two aircraft were approaching the formation, but Combat had been designed to instantly clarify any tactical situation with as little human confusion as possible.

The moments ticked slowly away. Each man concentrated on his job, monitoring radar screens, updating tracking information, checking dials, and reviewing printouts on screens or from quiet printers. David noted the aircraft separating on the board and a look to Dailey, confirmed by a nod, indicated that the predicted split had occurred. Dailey, at his commander's urging, had programmed each aircraft to swing approximately one hundred and fifty miles to either end of the northward-moving formation before changing course toward its center. Analysis of strategy indicated that altitude would remain high at missile release. Both aircraft would maintain their course until the pilot's instruments indicated the weapons had locked on their targets and accepted the tracking mode. At that point, they would reverse course, taking evasive action before heading back to the *Lenin*.

Captain Casey pushed open the door from the pilothouse, stooping under the low frame, and worked his way through the maze near David Charles's position. ''My men are ready, Admiral. I think a lot of people are looking forward to this. Most of them have never been in a situation like this. They all graduated after Vietnam, so it's mostly been reading books and shooting dummies at drones.'' He looked up at the big board. ''Looks like they'll be ready shortly.''

The jets had reached the apex of their outward flight and were turning toward the formation. The captain moved over to his own position where he would con his ship and control her weapon systems.

"Bill," said the Admiral. "I want to handle that missile problem here. Assign *Virginia* and *Wainwright* as firing ships just in case, with *Truxton* and *Halsey* as backup. I want *Gridley* to handle the missile-jamming backup to us. Order each ship to break formation and undertake independent tactics. In one minute I want *Truxton* to turn down the throat of that sub on the starboard quarter of the formation and go to flank speed. Just in case Kupinsky has anything planned with those subs, I want a sonar lock-on on that boat. They should do everything to harrass that sub outside of actually sinking it. That should move them a little farther away from us, I hope."

The instructions were quickly passed over the primary tactical circuit. There was little increase in sound, though activity was increasing at each station. The staff gunnery officer turned to Charles. "All launchers loaded for air action, Admiral. *Truxton* reports forward launcher ready with torpedoes, aft launcher for air action."

"Very well." He turned to hear Bill Dailey's report.

"*Virginia* reports foreign frequency lock-on . . . identified as missile guidance . . . it's a different frequency, Admiral!"

"Northern bogey, missiles away . . . one . . . two," from another station.

"We're tracking them," from Dailey. "*Virginia* reports the missiles are now on their own program . . . still unknown frequency."

"What the hell do you mean unknown, Bill? Can't we get control?"

"Not yet, Admiral. Computer is analyzing. We may have to jam. *Wainwright* reports the same action from the south, sir. Time to missile impact *Virginia,* one hundred and five seconds . . . *Wainwright,* one hundred and seventeen."

Admiral Charles watched the beginning of the action on

the screen before him. Each ship had undertaken its own evasive action. The missiles appeared as blinking dots closing their targets. He noted *Truxton* moving to the southeast. The electronics officer to his left was visibly nervous as he awaited a solution to the new frequency guiding the four missiles. Once the target solution fed into the missile by its launch computer was complete, and the aircraft acquisition radar broke contact, it was twice as hard to search the memory core for a solution. Seconds passed quickly.

"Sixty seconds to *Virginia*, seventy-two to *Wainwright*."

"Admiral, they're on a frequency we can't control," reported Dailey. "We can't take over guidance systems. Jamming recommended. I've switched *Virginia* and *Wainwright* to local control for antimissile fire." He looked over at a screen at his right. "Those birds are moving slowly enough so we should be able to bring them down if we can't jam in time."

"Forty seconds to *Virginia*, fifty-two to *Wainwright* . . . wait one, *Wainwright* birds increasing speed!"

"That's the extra fuel cell, Admiral, the latest idea to confuse antimissile solutions. *Wainwright* has to jam now. They'll never be able to recompute for antimissile fire with the correct solution. *Gridley* will jam with her 'eye' box."

"Casey!" David called over to the *California's* captain. "Bring down that southern bogey. We can't gain control of those missiles."

The captain nodded to his own gunnery officer, seated to his left. The man spoke briefly into the headset he was wearing, pushed a button on the console in front of him, waited a moment, then pushed another. "Birds away, Admiral! How about that one to the north?"

"I want one to get back with the message."

One of the blinking dots on the screen disappeared, followed by Dailey's report, *"Virginia* intercepted one of her missiles . . . wait a moment . . . her computer reports the second one's erratic. It's tracking improperly, probably jammed by *Gridley*. It'll splash down off target."

"What's happening to *Wainwright?"*

Dailey's arm was in the air, fingers open to signify quiet. They waited. He listened, hand opening and closing. "One missile off track . . . jammed." He half-turned in his seat, arm still extended, *"Wainwright's* antimissile solution was inaccurate . . . misfire . . . they're evading. . . ." His arm dropped, along with his voice. *"Wainwright's* hit, sir."

Silence.

David Charles broke the stillness. "Casey, what's the status of your firing . . . that other bogey?"

"We had a solution when we fired, Admiral. He's climbing in a turn, but we're still locked on."

"Bill. Find out what those Rigas do for evasion tactics."

Dailey turned to see the man at the console just in front of him already punching buttons rapidly, asking the machine for stored information that would influence the next order.

"They dive, sir. They're built to fall like a rock. He'll take it right down on the deck the minute his warning buzzer tells him there's a missile lock-on."

"Put *Truxton* on local control. Bill, I want her to use her new birds. When that plane levels out after its dive, I want them to fire at ten-second intervals . . . and reload and fire immediately if they have to." He turned to one of the officers who was looking over to him. "Do you have that report from *Wainwright?*"

"Yes, sir. She had just turned her back when she was hit. Main deck. After launcher out of action temporarily . . ." he paused, listening through his headset. "She's lost steering control, but still has power . . . steering with her engines . . . fire in one of the after compartments . . . minimum casualties."

At that last statement David turned to Dailey, blanking the remainder of the report from his ears. He watched the screen, concentrating on the escaping Riga. Then, there were two new dots that appeared from *Truxton* tracking on the screen, moving toward their target. David could see that the first missiles fired by *California* had already bypassed the dot on the screen that had been their target.

"That computer was right again," Dailey muttered. "The

pilot was diving before we even had your answer. The first volley left *Truxton* before he leveled off. He's just fifty feet off the deck now, running like a scared rabbit. Our solution gives him about twenty seconds more. The second volley was kept on hold.''

They watched intensely as the dots moved toward their target, the screen unable to show the tremendous speed of both the hunter and the hunted. The Riga could only turn to its right or left. It was too late to climb away. The dots merged, flared briefly, disappeared.

"Message complete," David Charles muttered to no one in particular. The dot to the north was streaking off to the east with his answer to Kupinsky. Its pilot knew only that one of their missiles had struck, damage unknown, before his partner was gone. A tie score.

Another report on *Wainwright*—"Emergency steering rigged . . . fire in berthing compartment under control . . . no damage to launcher or magazines . . . *Wainwright* estimates two hours to rejoining under full control."

The Admiral folded his arms thoughtfully for a moment before rising. The simple show of force was getting serious. He turned to his Chief of Staff. "You can secure everyone now, Bill. Reverse formation course in twenty minutes to wait for *Wainwright* and put the action report out to Washington. As soon as they can, I want your electronics people to get those tapes on that new missile frequency into the machine for analysis by the games people. You can be sure Alex is going to be a lot tougher on us next time." He turned to the commanding officer of *California*. "Sometimes I wonder if we weren't just as well off with those old ships bristling with guns . . . and a man aiming them!"

FROM THE LOG OF
ADMIRAL DAVID CHARLES

I HAVE been reading back through this log again. As a matter of fact, I even went back to some of the earlier entries when this started out as my JO's journal. I thought perhaps that as an ensign on the old *Bagley* I might have learned something, now long forgotten, that would keep Alex and me from intensifying this game. But somehow there just wasn't anything I could get a handle on. There was too much back then about daily routine, just like the old journal that had to be turned in to your department head in the earlier days. I found entries about splicing line, diagrams of the steam cycle that I had learned my second year at Annapolis, shipboard electrical systems that I never learned, damage-control procedures, and so many more things that were stuffed into the head of an ensign. But there was nothing there I could dig into.

I did find some entries I made about Sam Carter after I decided this was going to be my journal, and that no department head was going to be allowed to read it. He hasn't changed much. He still follows a very narrow path that makes it easy to understand him. He didn't kiss anybody's ass in those days, and he still doesn't. He's no politician either, so he'll never make Chief of Naval Operations, but I'm sure he never thought he'd get this far.

I found those things he told me the day Jorge died, off Cuba, and I guess that's when I started loving him, right after I finished hating him. As an ensign, I didn't realize he was as torn up about that mess as I was, but he let me blow off steam and then sleep it off. He chose not to discipline me. And when I woke up the next day, I found a few more tears for Jorge and his men, and then I realized what Sam had really been telling me. That lesson about power and when to use it and when to hold back really makes sense even today. He's using it now and, in a way, I'm still his tool. It's almost like he was back on the bridge of the *Bagley* and I was running up

14

and down that beach in that whaleboat, except now I'm on a bridge watching the shells fall around other ensigns and I'm going to have to take my chances in losing them. Power is probably even the wrong word. Sam couldn't describe it very well that day so long ago, and I didn't begin to comprehend what he meant until the next day. People, or countries, that have power can also decide when to use it or when to sit back and let others suffer.

The other thing that's really hit home is the section at the War College on the German General Staff. Some of them never saw a battlefield. As warlike as the German nation was supposed to be, they realized that brains were the key to victory. Battles were fought daily by unknown men who either died or survived to the next battle. But victory was in the planning, the strategy, in understanding your enemy, and all that had to be done before armies met or fleets streamed into each other's range. You could almost say it was pre-determined and the forces that met in battle were just carrying out the plans of brilliant people sitting far away from the scene to determine which staff was smarter. Hell, the Germans educated their staff better than anyone else in the world. They had to think for themselves. I found the line from Prince Frederick Charles that I had written down for some reason. He was tongue-lashing a major who apparently had not been thinking for himself—"His Majesty made you a major because he believed you would know when not to obey orders." I have to keep remembering that I have more firepower in this force than any other commander has ever had before. At the same time I'm deciding how to use that power, I've got to remember that each captain and each group commander has to have his own opportunity to make decisions. If I keep them tied into the central computer, they won't have the same opportunity to protect their ships if an attack is heavy enough to exhause the computer's ability to defend the force. If there's one thing I'll have to keep telling myself every hour, it's to let them make their own decisions when it becomes evident that my own staff has reached their capacity.

I should spend more time worrying about Alex and his forces. The Russians have never gathered a strike force like this before. It is the first time they've shown that they are more than an antisubmarine navy. They are going on the attack, and Alex Kupinsky is one of the most brilliant officers I have ever known. And the Russians have followed so much of the organization of the German General Staff. I don't think they have ever had the combined brilliance of that staff, especially the one with which Hitler started the war, because the Soviets have always believed finally in sheer quantity when all else seems to have failed. No one can produce cannon fodder like the Russians. But with all the educating they have done in the very fine schools Alex has told me about, I really believe that deep down they will always be suspicious of delegating responsibility and that their lesser commanders will not be able to operate on their own. It's the same story of centralization of authority that has been the key to power in the Kremlin for so long. I'll bet Alex is following Gorenko's orders, just as they were worked out in the Kremlin, and that he'll feel me out a bit first and then come charging right across the Indian Ocean like they've been charging across open fields for centuries. They've always been able to drive out invading armies either by sheer numbers of troops or the ability to hold out until winter. No one but Russians can survive a war during the Russian winter.

But I don't think, even with all their schools, and Alex's abilities, that they understand winning in the open ocean. That's where America has a tradition and Alex has learned that lesson more than once. I'm going to read more about the General Staff, though. Perhaps there's something I haven't seen yet.

I'll stop here. I'm rambling. Too many loose thoughts, but perhaps I've come across something and just don't know it yet. I'll read this over in an hour or so.

MY DEAREST DAVID,

I think that tonight I miss you more than I ever have before. It's because Sam and Ann Carter came for dinner tonight. They're such close friends and they mean so much to me when you're away, but tonight she was quiet, always changing the subject whenever we talked about you and where you might be. And Sam was very, very quiet, and you know how he's the life of the party whenever he's had two drinks.

Maybe that's the first thing that began to scare me. He nursed one drink all night, and spent most of the time just listening to our small talk. And whenever I'd talk about you, he wouldn't look me in the eye. I even asked once if you were all right, and then he did say that yes, absolutely, you were fine. Then he got a call and had to go back to the Pentagon at ten o'clock at night. They seemed almost relieved when they left.

Before writing this letter, I went in to check on the kids. Your daughter always sleeps like a lamb, and young Sam had just fallen asleep. He was out with his friends for a while. And that's the other strange thing. You know how Sam Carter just dotes on our son because he hasn't any children of his own. Well, tonight, he didn't have much to say to him at all. He didn't ask him about school or sports, or if he still wanted to go to the Academy, or any of the things they kid each other about. And when young Sam left the house this evening, Sam went over to him and put one hand on his shoulder and squeezed it and shook hands with him, something he's never done before. It was almost like he was taking your place and saying, "Now you're grown up, son."

I don't want to sound negative or act like a hysterical wife, but I know now you're in some kind of danger. And just before I sat down to write this, Bobbie Collier called to ask if I'd heard from you at all. It seems that Bob has pretty free use of the phone at the Moscow embassy since she's been back in Washington to visit, but he hasn't called for the last few days. She said she called Sam to see if he had heard anything, and he just told her that Bob might not be calling as regularly for the next couple of days, but not to worry or say anything to anyone else. The only other person she thought she could call was me, and I told her how strange Sam and Ann were tonight.

So I think you can understand why I'm concerned. I was almost going to remind Sam of what he told me when he stood up for you at our wedding—that he'd make sure to keep you out of trouble after what you got yourself into in Vietnam, because he knew how bitter I was then about the Navy after my first husband was shot down. But then I decided that might give him the wrong idea. I know that now you're an admiral and running your own task force, you may always be near danger. I also know that something is happening out there and I wish you were here with me, loving me and watching the kids grow up. Young Sam really needs his father around, too. He's into those years when boys are becoming men, and you told me how confusing they were, and what your father meant to you. Well, Sam's right there now, and there are things you can do for him and say to him that I can't. So please take care of yourself, my love. There's three of us here that love you and need you very much. And, just in case you've been at sea so long and might have forgotten, it's getting cool at night now and I need someone to warm me up.

There's so much more I want to say to you, but I think it's better if I write again after I've had time to sort things out. I'm sure everything will turn out well and you'll be back with us soon.

With all the love you can handle,

Maria

CHAPTER
TWO

THE nest of dirty gray destroyers, four abreast, were starkly outlined against the brackish water of Hampton Roads and the gray Saturday-morning skies. They were offset even more by their larger, more modern counterparts two piers down, high-bowed frigates and guided-missile destroyers. David Charles had been here before, as a midshipman, and he knew the destroyer/submarine piers of Norfolk well. This time he was back with one gold stripe on each of his shoulder boards, ensign's stripes, and with orders for sea duty in his pocket.

The U.S.S. *Bagley* was an old ship in the summer of 1961, of World War II vintage, and she owned campaign stripes from more Pacific battles than Washington admirals cared to acknowledge for their aging fleet. A stray Jap five-hundred-pounder had destroyed her after engine room at Leyte Gulf, but they had patched her up and she had even been back to Korea after a few years in mothballs. The constant attention of tenders kept the *Bagley* and the other seven ships of her squadron in decent enough shape so they could survive the weeks of duty in the Atlantic with Task Group Alpha. Right now, she looked more like she'd been steaming underwater than on the surface.

Ensign Charles looked her over critically from the foot of
the pier. The second ship in the nest, her dented hull with the
chipped numbers on the bow pleading for redlead and paint,
the *Bagley* would be alongside the pier the next two weeks
for some much-needed upkeep. He had been waiting in the
bachelor officer's quarters for ten days for his ship to return
so he could report aboard. Usually, when the squadron was at
sea with one of the carriers, they flew new personnel out with
the mail and they then reported aboard their ship swinging
from the end of a helicopter cable. But this time the weather
was so bad that the personnel officer in Norfolk had found
another one-week school for him to attend. And then, the day
before the squadron was due to arrive, David had gotten a
message from the *Bagley's* executive officer requesting him
not to report aboard until that Saturday morning.

He picked up the two suitcases, one an extra-heavy fold-
over type with all his uniforms, and strolled erectly to the
edge of the pier to look down into the water. There was a hiss
from the steam hoses connected to the pier. The tide was low
and just beginning to change, and with no current the scum of
oil and garbage and sewage lapped gently against the tired
old hulls. The smell was as he always remembered, the stink
of the piers in any port in the world—not the rich, heady, salt
perfume of the open ocean. The bags were becoming heavier
now, and he turned up the pier toward the brow going over to
the first ship, another Pacific veteran. He turned sideways as
he inched down the narrow gangway to the quarterdeck with
his bulky luggage. A disinterested first-class petty officer
looked up, but without taking his elbow from the desk attached to the bulkhead.

The fresh-caught ensign—the shiny gold gave him
away—carefully placed each bag on the deck, straightened
immediately to salute the flag on the fantail, then the quarterdeck. The petty officer, noting the young officer was comfortable in his actions, immediately came to attention, returning the salute to the deck. "Are you reporting aboard here,
sir?"

"No. Crossing to *Bagley*."

"Yes, sir." Back to the elbow on the desk again.

Ensign Charles retrieved his bags, ducking his head as he worked his way around a winch through the midships passageway where he could see the brow over to the *Bagley*. The starboard side of the deck of the *Bagley,* just forward of the midships passageway, was scarred and dented, and some of the cable and stanchions on the edge of the deck were missing. Redlead emphasized the damage.

Another PO in a well-worn peacoat began to show some curiosity as Ensign Charles struggled down another very narrow gangway. Again placing his bags on the quarterdeck, he gave the fantail a sharp salute, then turned to the quarterdeck.

"Ensign David Charles reporting aboard as ordered," he barked too loudly, bringing his right hand to the visor of his hat. He looked the PO directly in the eyes, establishing his authority early.

David Charles did not look a great deal different from so many other ensigns that reported aboard ship each year. He was medium height, about five feet ten, with an average build. His brownish black hair was curly, and he had already learned to his dismay that it became much more curly in the humidity of the tropics. It was thick, and he kept it short to control it in the military style of the day. His face was lean to compliment the body well-conditioned from four years in Annapolis, and only his clear gray-blue eyes set him off from so many of the others. His crisply pressed, custom-made uniform and mirror-shined shoes established his military credentials, as did his comfort in arriving on the *Bagley*'s quarterdeck. He had been at sea before and was already part of the real Navy.

The PO returned his salute with a bit of effort. "Yes, sir. Mr. Donovan told me the XO had sent a message asking you to wait until this morning."

David pulled his orders from his breast pocket and handed them over to be logged in. "You don't have to wait while I log you in, Mr. Charles. I'll take care of that when I go off watch. Then I'll give them back to you and you can turn 'em over to the ship's office Monday morning." He turned to the seaman apprentice who had been leaning against the bulkhead the entire time, cold hands stuffed in his peacoat pockets. "Go wake Mr. Donovan and tell him that Ensign Charles has just reported aboard, and where is he supposed to bunk?"

"You want me to wake him if he's asleep?"

"Make a lot of noise in the passageway. Slam the hatch when you go in after officers. Bang hard on his door, like you had no idea he was back in the rack. He always wants you to think he's catching up on his paperwork. The ensign"—he nodded at Charles—"doesn't want to wait here all day."

The messenger strolled around the corner of the midships passageway and disappeared slowly, giving every indication that it would take ten minutes to find Mr. Donovan.

"Mr. Donovan is the command duty officer this weekend. He's the chief engineer." Quiet for a moment. "Been on board since he was an ensign. Started out as MPA . . . I guess." It was nervous small talk, since he really wasn't interested in talking with the new ensign until he had been sized up by the crew.

Charles looked at the damaged deck up forward. "What happened there?"

"Oh, that was last Wednesday. Hell of a storm when we were steaming back after being relieved by *Bravo*. Thirty-, forty-foot seas and half the crew barfing. The carrier decided to turn more into the wind 'cause the cans were taking such a beating—for our benefit it was! It was nighttime and no one on the bridge could really see what was coming. A big wave just caught us wrong as we were coming around and carried the whole whaleboat away. The chief said it bumped down the deak a ways. That's why some of the stanchions are gone. The first lieutenant wanted to make the repairs before we came in, but the captain said no. He wanted everyone back here to see we weren't on another Caribbean joyride . . . like they always claim we are." The PO smiled at the thought and then added with pride, "Captain Sam Carter's the CO and the best most of us ever served with, sir. You ought to like him."

The messenger returned as slowly as he had departed. "Mr. Donovan says the ensign has to bunk in his stateroom, 'cause it's the only rack left in officer's country." He bent to pick up one of the bags. "I'll show you the way back, sir, and Mr. Donovan says I should carry your bags. I'll get this other," looking unhappily at the larger one, "after I show you back." He moved slowly around the corner again, expecting Charles to follow him.

They went through the midships passageway to the port side of the ship, then toward the stern past some open hatches that went down to the engineering spaces. The messenger pulled open a heavy door, already ajar, and disappeared inside. As David stepped over the coaming into the dimly lit passageway, he barely avoided tripping over the bag that had just been set there. A few feet ahead, the sailor was leaning through a door, "This here's Mr. Charles, sir." He stepped back from the door. "I'll bring your other bag in a few minutes," and he was gone.

David stepped around the bag and moved inside the door, which had been left open. The room was gloomy with only one small porthole above the upper bunk along the bulkhead. In the lower bunk lay a form outlined by a weak reading light. The form, extremely hairy in just a pair of outlandish shorts, heaved into a sitting position. "I was just catching up on my reading." He extended a hand, which David squeezed in return. "I'm Joe Donovan, chief snipe and CDO for this our first weekend in port. Welcome aboard, for what it's worth."

"David Charles." An uneasy pause. "I've been waiting for the ship about ten days over at NOB. I've been looking forward to reporting aboard."

"So has Ensign Werwaiss," Donovan said with an amused grin. "He's been boot ensign for nine months now, and he's been looking forward to someone else taking all the shit for the last eight of them. Believe me, he's the happiest to see you come." He scratched his belly and lay back down on his bunk, yawning.

Charles looked around the small stateroom. There were tiers of two bunks on either side, separated by about two feet of standard green linoleum. A metal sink and a medicine cabinet were at the end of the room. It was hardly wide enough for anyone's shoulders if they were shaving in the mirror. Behind him and inboard were two lockers, one wide open and jammed with uniforms. There were drawers under each of the bottom bunks, no doubt overflowing. On the outboard side of the room, against the bulkhead, were what he realized were two desks, one of which had the top folded down with papers strewn across it. Above the desk were two short lockers. The bunks were covered with books, papers, clothes, and foul-weather gear.

He looked hopefully up at the bunk that was under the porthole. "Is that bunk open?"

"Nope, that's mine," replied Donovan. Charles looked at the officer stretched on the lower bunk where he had obviously been sleeping. "They're both mine," he added. "This lower one is mine in port, so I don't have to climb up there when I'm drunk, and," he pointed, "that's mine when we're at sea. My goddamn snipes tried to weld that seam,"—he pointed at a seam in the bulkhead that looked like any other one on the ship—"but it opens up every goddamn time we're in a storm, which is often. Then the water flows in, so I move up to that one." A grin and a wink. "Anyway, I've been on this can for two and a half years, so I've gotten squatter's rights to the extra one. That other lower one belongs to Mike FitzGibbon, and believe me you'll be glad he's there when we get underway the next time. He gets seasick . . . very! And he's a barfer. When you see him making love to the bucket, you'll be glad you're up there." He pointed to the inboard top bunk covered with junk. "Let me go through that stuff first, so I can sort out what's mine. Then you can dump the rest on Fitz's bunk, and he can sort it out Monday morning. He's married and he'll be happy enough by then so he won't mind if you pile it all up for him." He scratched again. "Why don't you go up to the wardroom and have some coffee and I'll get some clothes on. There's no reason to unpack anyway, 'cause I don't know where you're going to cram all that crap." He pointed at the second bag that had finally appeared. "You and Fitz are going to have to do a lot of space sharing 'cause I'm comfortable. When I leave in six months, then the two of you can fight over my space until someone else moves in.'' He stretched back out on the bunk. ''Go on up to the wardroom, and I'll be up shortly to get you started. You're going to be in my duty section anyway, so I might as well start you off right.''

"Okay, I'll see you soon, sir.''

"Call me Joe. We're going to see a lot of each other, every fourth day and every fourth weekend.''

Life, thought David, really is less formal on destroyers.

It wasn't hard to find the wardroom on the *Bagley*. They were all in the same location in *Fletcher*-class destroyers. He went back through the midships passageway, nodded at the PO of the watch who was blowing on a cup of coffee, and proceeded up the starboard side to the wardroom.

A pot of coffee that had probably been on the hot plate since the previous night simmered by the open space to the pantry. The table was covered with the standard dark green felt, bearing the stains of many unidentified spills. A beige couch riveted to the deck and bulkhead extended on either side in one corner. On the forward bulkhead, emphasized by reflections from the water outside, were the ship's plaque, photos of the ship at various stages of her life, and a photo of a white bearded man in an ancient navy uniform—probably Bagley himself. Magazines that had been waiting a few weeks for the ship's return were lying open on the couch, no doubt left there by a bored Donovan.

David Charles poured himself a cup of coffee after locating some milk in the pantry refrigerator. The milk barely changed the color and did nothing at all for the taste. He stretched out on the cracked leather of the couch and picked up a copy of a torn *Navy Times*.

Donovan made an unkempt appearance a few minutes later, tossing his cap on the table beside David and nodding. He poured a cup of coffee, taking it black, sat down at the head of the table, and gulped down half of the black mess as if he didn't notice the taste. When it finally registered, he went angrily over to the ship's phone and pressed the buzzer for the quarterdeck. When a voice answered, he said, "This is Mr. Donovan. Find the duty steward and send him to the wardroom, on the double." Turning to the new ensign, he added, "I thought I was doing him a favor last night when I said that he didn't have to prepare breakfast this morning, but the son of a bitch was too goddamn lazy to even fix a fresh pot."

"We're not the only ones on duty this weekend?" questioned David.

"Nope." Another scratch, which David thought was perhaps a habit. "The captain let me send Craig Scott home last night, since he's married, too. He decided that Paul Goorjian and I could handle everything until Saturday morning, but I sure don't know what he thought you could do. On the other hand, he's always good to the brown baggers. I'm a bachelor and that wild Armeniam, Goorjian, is a bachelor. You caught this section because you are too, and Craig was unfortunate enough to earn me because the operations officer says he wants one officer from his department in each section." He paused for a second. "You see, we're not supposed to be as horny as they are when we come into home port, and there's nothing uglier than a married officer who knows he has to wait one more night before he can pole-vault home. So the captain made a deal. When we're in any other port, my section is guaranteed liberty, and Captain Carter decided that arrangement keeps everybody happy."

"It sounds good," said David. "Does it always work right?"

"We've spent more damn time during exercises this year going into tombs like Newport, Charleston, and Mayport, Florida." He looked thoughtful for a moment. "But, San Juan was great last winter. Let me tell you what the best part is about being guardian of the brown-bag morals—the dinner invitations! We have some wives that are the best cooks in Norfolk, and they're honestly sorry that we have to live on the ship like monks—they think! But the best part of all is that the young ones all work, and they have single girl friends who show up for dinner, and sometimes it's just like shooting fish in a barrel.'' He grinned for the first time and then, thinking more about what he had said, laughed. "You play your cards right, and follow old Joe Donovan's guidance, and you'll eat good and get plenty of action, too.''

The young ensign smiled back, not quite knowing what to say. The formal training at Annapolis hadn't covered this aspect of Navy life, nor did it mention CO's who seemed concerned about wardroom sex life. Donovan was certainly not the Academy's idea of the average command-duty officer, yet he had been left in charge of the ship.

The duty steward, a Filipino in dungarees and a work shirt, stuck his head cautiously in through the pantryway. "Mr. Donovan, you call me?'' he asked in broken English.

"Damn right I did, Santo. Would you drink that crap?'' pointing at the thick mess in the coffeepot.

The steward shrugged his shoulders, maintaining a neutral expression.

''You can be damn sure the crew wouldn't touch that.'' He waved his arms above his head. "I want another pot super fast.'' The little dark-skinned man came around from the pantry to pick up the pot. Donovan looked down at his slippered feet. "And after you do that, go back down and get on the uniform of the day and report back to me.'' Turning away toward David, he muttered, "The little bastards will always take advantage of you, if you give them half a chance. And you better believe they understand English! I said last night that he didn't have to make breakfast for us, since I always let Goorjian sleep in on the weekends, and I don't eat breakfast anyway. You can be damn sure he won't do that again.''

Apparently satisfied, he sat down in the chair at the end of the green table, swinging it around toward David and stretching his legs out in front. "Now tell me a little about Ensign David Charles, other than your last four years at the barge factory.''

That day, in the second ship of a four-ship nest, Joe Donovan learned a lot about the new ensign who was bunking with him and who would stand watches with him both in

port and underway. And, David Charles learned about a new
Navy that hadn't been included in the curriculum the past
four years, one that seemed to have been forgotten by his
land-locked instructors.

FROM THE LOG OF
ADMIRAL DAVID CHARLES

I'M GOING to make this as a side entry that I might tear out later, especially if I'm going to have to turn this journal in to a department head later on.

In a way, I was kind of scared when I reported aboard *Bagley*. I've been on other ships before, during middie cruises, but this is my first actual tour of duty. I'm finally an officer, but I don't know if I want to stay in forever. When I saw this ship, as I was coming down the pier, I just said to myself, "Oh, shit. It's really a rust bucket." I guess we all had dreams of guided missile cruisers or giant carriers, as far as being part of a spit-and-polish organization, but everybody kept telling us the real Navy was in tin cans. Well, if they're right, and I'm not saying they're not, it's sure a different Navy from the one we were taught about for four years.

Joe Donovan, the CDO whose section I'm in, thinks Annapolis was some kind of prep school, and only people who wanted to give up working early went there. As a matter of fact, he's explained two or three times that when the Navy gets into a crisis they call up the reserves. And after the reserves win the war for the lifers, then they go home until the lifers get themselves in trouble again. Wow! On the other hand, deep down he really likes the *Bagley*. He knows the ship as well as the captain, and I guess Captain Carter has tried to talk him into shipping over, but Joe says there's too much to do in the real world. Maybe he's right.

Some of the other reservists are pretty good people, too. But, boy, do they ever party! After everything I was taught about Navy etiquette, I think maybe they're right. Going to sea on a Monday morning is a hell of a good way to dry out, and it also keeps you from getting too involved with the women. But some of the parties I've been to when the ship comes back are unbelievable. They work like hell when we're at sea and then they act like they've never seen the water when they get back. They rent an apartment every time they're in any port for more than a couple of weeks. Right now they've got one in Virginia Beach and they've asked me to come in with them. The hard core is Donovan, FitzGibbon, Hogan, Mezey, Werwaiss, Mundy, and Kerner. Whenever the *Bagley*'s tied up, their place is overrun with women. I think I'm going to like it, and I think I'm going to like the *Bagley* a lot more than I expected that first weekend, if I can survive the pace they set.

Even the commanding officer, Captain Carter, never went to the Academy. But he doesn't say much bad about it because he's steamed with a lot of graduates over the years, and he said he's met some pretty good ones. Right after I reported aboard the *Bagley,* the Monday after, the ship started to look like it was part of the Navy again. Captain Carter came aboard at seven thirty that morning, had an officer's conference at breakfast, and right after quarters he had a meeting with all the chiefs, too. By the end of the day, every space was shiny. All the stanchions had been replaced and the ship was scraped and covered with red lead. By Tuesday, she looked like she was ready for an admiral's inspection. Donovan explained to me that Sam Carter likes to have the fleet see that even the old buckets like the *Bagley* can hold their own with any new frigate, and that's why she always comes into port showing where she's been. And he always lets the crew off as soon as the brow goes over, and gives the duty section the chance to take it easy for a few days.

There's something special about Captain Carter. I'm not sure what it is yet, but it's obvious not only from the way the officers respect him but the way the crew looks up to him. A lot of mornings will find him having coffee down in chief's quarters instead of the wardroom, and he doesn't just wander in on his own. Apparently, they gave him a standing invitation, which is pretty rare for any officer. I wouldn't go down there unless I was invited or if I had business with one of the chiefs. And Carter sits down in the spaces and talks with the troops while they're working. He'll stop and shoot the shit with some deck apes chipping paint sometimes, and Donovan says he'll even stick his head into the firebox when the snipes are groveling around inside cleaning the boilers. Sailors don't take to any officer very easily, but I think they'd follow Carter into the middle of the Russian fleet.

One of the first things that made me more comfortable in this old wreck was the talk he had with me that Monday morning. Right after he'd finished with the chiefs, the XO told me to go up to the captain's cabin. Captain Carter told me right away that this was my formal visit with him, that he and his wife didn't need any ensigns making calls on them and leaving cards on their front table. He said I'd get to know them better at the first bash the bachelors threw at their place. Sam Carter said his first job, after the safety of the ship and crew, was training young officers so they'd find the Navy was a good job and stay in. He also wanted to sort out any that should leave. If I was serious about the Navy, I could learn more in my first year than I could learn in ten years at the Academy. He said all of his officers would have every opportunity to do everything possible with the *Bagley*, and he was just there for the ride and to train officers. He'd drive only when the ship was in danger or he felt the officers on the bridge didn't yet have enough experience.

Everything he said was exactly the way he operates. His officers get the ship underway, take it out of the harbor, con it in fleet exercises, take it alongside tankers or carriers to refuel, and just about any other possible ship's evolution. He's always there, hovering in the background, just in case of an emergency, but he never says a word of criticism until he's alone with whoever made a mistake. No wonder they love him.

And he sure was right about the parties. It's a tight wardroom in more ways than one, and Sam Carter never misses a party. Neither does his wife. After that first one, I realized why they didn't want any ensigns making social calls and leaving cards. If a war had ever started that first night, they would have had to warp *Bagley* out so the other ships could get underway, and the next day she would have caught up. His wife, Ann, is the belle of the wardroom. I imagine we all secretly love her cause she's everything a Navy officer's wife should be, lovely, charming, dances with everyone, organizes the wives, checks out everybody's date to make sure they're okay, and she loves Sam Carter.

Now that I've had time to sit down and write about the *Bagley* for a few minutes, I think I'm going to enjoy this tour after all. And I'm going to promise myself to make a lot more entries like this one. I'm finally in the real Navy, and this journal may teach me more about myself and how I want to be part of the Navy than any JO journal ever will.

CHAPTER
THREE

DAVID watched the shells hit just prior to the sharp explosions. Long shots landed in the water, throwing up great clouds of spray. But they were becoming fewer as pointers found their range. Then he saw people thrown into the air, landing awkwardly, rarely moving afterward. He had briefly known some of the ones that now lay there, although he couldn't distinguish faces through his binoculars. Only hours before some of them had been aboard the *Bagley*, nervously pacing the deck in their fatigues, chattering sporadically in Spanish with each other and sometimes joking in broken English with the crew. In such a short time the Bay of Pigs' invasion force had become a ragged gang, hiding from the withering fire behind broken palms or even the bodies of their comrades.

"Reverse your course, Palmer," Ensign Charles ordered his boatswain. By looking at the groups of palms that still stood he knew that they were near the end of that invisible line that marked his sector, five hundred yards from the beach. The sun was already high enough in the sky to make the life jackets and helmets uncomfortable.

"Op orders are like party platforms," David thought. "No one ever pays attention to them after they're written."

He had read carefully through Operation Order 8-16. After all, it had come out of the Joint Chiefs of Staff on the orders of the President. There were over two hundred pages of details, starting with designation of the task force and ending after interminable pages of detail with even the call sign of his unit—Lucky Duck. Lucky Duck, like many of the other whaleboats from the parent destroyers sitting another three thousand yards beyond the small craft, was just a number among the elements of that huge force that had set out a few days before. At sea, it was magnificent. There were carriers, cruisers, destroyers, amphibs, LST's full of marines, and aircraft of all types overhead.

And not one unit had done a thing. The order from Washington, the one that had been promised, never came. Men like David were to follow the landing force close to the beach to provide fire-support targets for the larger ships. The carriers would launch flight after flight of jets to provide close in-support after the beachhead was established. The LST's would land supplies, food, ammunition, blood for the wounded, and they would take back those who could fight no more. The troop carriers circled overhead with the trained men who would parachute behind enemy lines to help surround Castro's army. It was planned to be over in three days or less, except for mopping up in a few of the mountain areas. The Communists were said to be ill-trained and would run at the first sight of the landing—perhaps into the paratroops' arms. They were not expected to support Castro. They were said to be waiting for this liberating force, the one that would free them.

Within half an hour, David knew it was a sham. Not one shell whistled overhead toward land. Not one jet shattered the air. Not one parachute blossomed over the beaches. And Castro's army wasn't running.

"Good morning, Señor Charles, or should I start calling you Lucky Duck." It was Jorge Melendez, the commander of the troops that would be landing in David's sector.

"Good morning, Jorge," he replied. The sun was just

coloring the horizon to the east. Cuba was a darkened smudge to the north, still too distant in the early dawn to pick out landmarks. He had become close to Melendez during the three days they had been at sea together.

As soon as the *Bagley* had gotten underway, Carter called him to his cabin and introduced the young ensign and the short, swarthy Cuban. They shook hands, the jungle fighter staring deeply into David's eyes, looking for that desire that so many of his small army had. Instead, he had seen a self-assurance that was uncommon among young men. There was then no understanding of the Cuban's problems, but Melendez had been told often by the C.I.A. that few Americans knew of the plans or the part the American military would take in recapturing their island home.

"David," Sam Carter had said, "I'm going to put you in charge of a call-fire team for Colonel Melendez." At the same time, he handed over a copy of the heavy op order that was to be their bible. "The colonel and his staff will be quartered aboard this ship until we reach our position. Their men are aboard the amphibs behind us, and they will join each other only when they get close to the beaches."

"Excuse me, Captain Carter," Melendez interrupted in only slightly accented English, "Does this young man understand what we are here for?"

"He understands only what my crew has been told since we got underway—that there will be an invasion of Cuba by a trained army of exiles, that the U.S. government is in full support, and that we will likely assist, once the invasion is underway."

"Your word 'likely' makes me nervous, Captain. All our training has been built around support from your forces. It would be senseless to appear off the coast with this armada, and then send in an army with no assistance."

"You are correct, Colonel, but I can only follow the orders I have received to date. I am assigning Ensign Charles to you because most of our other officers have been trained as a shipboard team for just the type of support I hope we can give you. He also has just come from a gunnery school with the training necessary to back you up with call fire. I think you will find him a pleasant and serious officer to work with.''

Melendez found that Carter was correct. The young American was serious about his assignment, read every page of the order, asked many questions about Melendez and his army, and also became attached to the team that would go ashore.

The Cuban's hair was longer than the American sailors', and he had a thick, black moustache. His dress was casual from the Navy's point of view, and he did not look like a military man. But David learned rapidly that his friend, Jorge, as he soon called him, was very much a fighter and a leader. He was fiercely devoted to his men, whom he missed on the amphibs. He and David spent many long hours during the day discussing the invasion plans and how the necessary support would get them from the beaches into the trees where more safety was available. They wandered in various parts of the ship, sometimes leaning on the depth-charge racks on the fantail, or stretching out on the deck by the bow, watching the flying fish leap in front of the rising and falling bow and listening to the Caribbean race by through the hawse pipes.

David developed a deep respect for the Cuban. The pride in country and the determination to liberate it were something unfamiliar to his young mind. Americans were not subject to this deep nationalism, and he was just beginning to learn it through his immersion in his military life. Jorge was willing to die on the beaches of his native land, if necessary, to bring back the world that he had grown up in. He wanted it for his wife and children in Miami, and for the many other families who also waited back in Florida not knowing where their men had gone or when they would be back. Cuba became a nation to David, home of a fiercely emotional people whom one could easily become attached to. And he was suddenly worried for them.

He had gone to the bridge the night before to talk with Carter. ''Captain, is there any chance we won't help Jorge when they hit the beach? He seems to be the only one concerned. The others feel there's no problem. They're sure that Castro's army will join them within a few hours after they see us behind them.''

"I wish I could answer that, David. The orders say 'yes.' *Enterprise* is out there now with enough firepower to take Cuba without troops. *Long Beach* is joining up tonight with missiles that could knock down anything Castro could put in the air. Our squadron is ready to lay down enough five-inch gunfire so they could walk up the beach a mile undistrubed, but I don't know what's going to happen.'' He paused for a moment, picking out a bright star in the clear sky, enjoying the tropical breeze running over his face. ''The orders come from Washington.''

"I know that, sir.''

"We don't move a goddamn muscle until we're told to.''

"Yes, sir.''

Sam Carter picked out the same star again, cautiously selecting his next words. He often worked that way when he was serious, and tonight he wanted to make a point. His blue baseball cap was in his lap and the moon reflected vaguely on his bald head. Carter was one of those men who lost his hair early, and in his late thirties he had already had ten years to get used to the reddish fringe that grew around his head. It never really bothered him and at no time had he even considered the old ploy of growing it long on one side and sweeping it across his head. He was short, too, about five and a half feet tall, but that hadn't particularly bothered him either. Size wasn't important in the Navy. It hadn't seemed to concern his wife, and he had accomplished so much in his short career that most professional acquaintances probably couldn't have remembered how tall he was. His sharp, dark eyes commanded his face whether he was laughing at a party or angrily chewing out a subordinate. But he never did or said anything without thinking about it first, and he wasn't about to now.

Finally, his thoughts in order, he said, ''David.'' Carter pushed himself upright in the bridge chair and turned to look the young man directly in the eyes. ''You're now a naval officer. A lot of money has been spent on putting you through

Annapolis and graduating a young man who will learn to
make the right decisions in a time of crisis. Often, the
decisions you make will be based on orders from
Washington, from people who don't know you and don't
want to know you because they might hesitate to give those
orders if they did. Do you understand what I'm saying?''

"Yes, sir. You don't want me to say anything more.''

Carter's eyes looked back at his, glistening in the dark
night. ''More than that, David. Jorge Melendez is a soldier of
his country, and that's how he will act when he goes ashore.
You are an American sailor, and this may be the time you'll
be hurt if you don't stand back a little. I know you've gotten
attached to Jorge. This is your first real combat assignment,
and I want you to carry it out without the emotional concern
that you're worrying about now. I like Jorge, too. He's a very
brave man. I'd like to march into Havana behind him, but my
place is on the bridge of the *Bagley*. Yours will be in a
whaleboat five hundred yards off the beach, trying to help
Jorge march into Havana. But,'' and he pointed his finger at a
place above David's head, ''you must remember whom you
work for.'' The finger turned around and pointed at his own
chest. ''Me.''

"I understand what you're saying, Captain.''

"Good. Go below to your bunk and get some sleep if you
can.''

David did go below, but he found Melendez in the wardroom, and he spent time drinking coffee and talking with the
man about his home outside of Havana, and how much he
wanted to take his family back. And then, before they both
tried to sleep, they went over the plans for the hundredth
time. They discussed the circuits they would use, the primary
one for calling in fire, and the secondary one if they lost
contact. They went over each of the words again in English
that were new to Melendez, so there would be no mistaking
what he wanted when he called David. Then they went to
their bunks and slept fitfully.

Nothing was going right. David saw through his binoculars how the landing party almost made the tree line, only to fall back from what was probably machine-gun fire. That's when Jorge had first called him. "Goddamn, David. What are they waiting for? I need a couple of well-placed shells. That's all. They just have fifty calibers now, and we can move in if you'll help." He had said that word—*you*. David could do nothing but watch.

He called the *Bagley*. "Captain, Jorge says he can move his men into safety if we can just hit those machine guns."

"I can see that, David," came the response.

"Just five shots, Captain. One gun. I'll have you on target after the first two." He paused. "They're being torn apart, sir."

"Remember what I said, David." The voice was firm, and David remembered.

Overhead, well offshore and at a high, safe altitude, the 82nd Airborne sat on benches in full battle gear while the huge aircraft that carried them circled a preplanned point in the sky. David looked at the armada beginning a few thousand yards away. Squadrons of fast little destroyers, old ones like the *Bagley* and new ones with missiles pointed skyward, steamed back and forth in neat squares. Behind them were the amphibians, ungainly ships with holds full of marines, tanks, trucks, food, and ammuntion. He could see three cruisers set farther back, because their giant guns could throw larger shells greater distances to cause more devastation. And, out beyond the two small carriers they had escorted down the Atlantic coast, he could see the huge island of the *Enterprise*, whose planes could clear a path to safety for Jorge and his men in a few short minutes.

Up and down the beach he had seen the same thing happening to Jorge's comrades, the race up the beach toward the trees, the faltering as more men began to fall, the regrouping as they came together in their retreat, and then another race up the beach. David was sure some of them hardly had the chance to fire their own guns. Amid the chaos, Jorge was quiet and his calmness deceptive. "David, can you tell me what your captain has said?"

David could only explain what he was told.

"If we don't get support soon, they will have time to bring up their heavy guns, and then they will slaughter us. All I want you to do is ask for a chance. Ask Captain Carter to radio to his commanders what is happening. Perhaps that will help. Better yet, tell him we don't need planes or even paratroops. If they'll just give us some fire support, we'll move in and join with the other groups. Just tell them that."

Twice he called Carter with Melendez's requests and each time he received the same answer. Then the defenders were able to move in the larger guns. At first, their shot was erratic. They needed spotters of their own. But once they learned where their shells were falling, they became more accurate. Soon the little groups on the beach were shattered.

First it was just one man, running back to the water. David saw him race almost directly toward his whaleboat. The water was shallow and he seemed to stop for a moment when he was up to his knees, faltered and then fell forward. Others were luckier. They got far enough out so they could swim, but some were unlucky enough to have misplaced shells land near them.

Another call from Jorge: "David, I am having trouble keeping my men together. Some of the other teams have already been wiped out or are trying to get back in the water. I don't think I can keep my men together for long . . ." Then his voice stopped.

David looked up quickly through the binoculars and saw that a shell had landed near the group around Melendez. Some died in the air, others lay still where they had fallen, and David saw some get up and move quickly to another crater in the beach.

Then there was a high, loud whistling sound. Instinctively, the men in the boat threw themselves to the deck. A shell landed near enough to shake the boat as it exploded with an ear-shattering sound, more frightening than the impact itself. They were showered with water.

"Get the hell out of there, David," came Carter's voice over the radio.

"I can't yet, Captain. I've lost contact with Jorge."

"You are responsible for the men in your boat. You will take evasive action and you will return them safely to the ship," Carter responded firmly. Another shell landed near them, not as closely as before, but on the other side and close enough to bring from Carter, "Damn it, David, move that boat. They've got your range."

Palmer, who had been face down in the boat after the last explosion, returned to the tiller quickly, looking up at David. For just a second he hesitated, then said, "Turn into the beach. Make your own course."

"But, sir . . ."

He was cut off by David. "They'll expect us to turn out. Move," he shouted.

It took just a second for the rudder of the small craft to respond, and then it swung toward the beach. It had moved only thirty yards or so when another shell whistled overhead, landing this time where the whaleboat might have been had they turned toward *Bagley*. Palmer looked over at the young ensign and nodded, offering a thumbs-up approval.

After they had gone about a hundred yards, David ordered the whaleboat back on its original course so he could concentrate on the group ashore. As he put his binoculars to his eyes, he told Palmer, "They're going to keep trying to pinpoint us. Zigzag whenever you want, but for Christ's sake sound off before you do!"

He tried to call Melendez on his radio, first on the private circuit, then on the secondary, but there was no answer. He looked back to the beach where he had last seen them and thought he caught sight of the man for a second. They were that much closer so he could make out faces a bit better. A man waved out to him frantically from among a group crouched in a hole blasted in the sand. A few were firing their rifles toward the palm-tree area. But many more were not moving at all. He recognized Jorge as the one who had waved. Obviously, the last shell had knocked out his radio.

"Mr. Charles, we're not supposed to be this close," a voice called to him as another explosion bracketed their little

boat. "I heard the captain ask us to come back." It was one
of the seamen sent along in the party to assist Palmer. He was
crouched in the bottom of the whaleboat, making himself as
small as possible, a terrified look in his eyes.

David paid no attention to him. Palmer shouted just before
he threw the rudder over and the boat heeled in the direction
of the shore as it reversed course. David put the binoculars to
his eyes again, trying to see what the men on land were doing
as the boat rocked wildly on its new track. Two of the men
beside Melendez leaped up to run toward the water. The sand
around them lifted in lazy puffs as the machine-gun bullets
bit in. The one who was running the safer zigzag was the first
one to be hit. The other, probably in terror, simply raced
toward the water, somehow avoiding the bullets that became
little spurts of water as he splashed in. When he was a little
over ankle deep, he dove, landing on his belly in the too-
shallow water. Realizing he was still not far enough out, he
rose first to his knees, then stood up to run again. It was then
that the hidden gunner brought him down.

David dropped the binoculars to his chest and looked back
at Palmer, who had also been watching. They had gradually
gotten close enough to the beach so that the other men didn't
need the glasses to see what was happening.

The sailor who had first called to him now shouted wildly,
"We've got to get out of here, sir. We're not supposed to be
here by ourselves." This time he stood up, rocking the
whaleboat even more violently than it already was. David
looked back at Palmer, pointing at the sailor and mouthed
unheard words as another shell showered them with water.
Palmer simply yelled something to the engineman who
calmly reached for a canteen that had fallen loose in the
bottom of the boat. He stood for just a moment as he swung
the canteen behind his shoulder, then brought it down on the
sailor's head. He cushioned the falling body to avoid it
hitting the edge of the boat.

Palmer grinned in response to David's surprise at their
efficient method of calming the frantic man. Then he again
shouted as loudly as he could before he threw the rudder over

sharply to turn closer to the beach, and then run parallel to it.

Farther down the shoreline, one of the landing teams had managed to make it into the shattered palm trees. Now they could be seen retreating from that shelter, this time followed by their enemy. It was the first time David had seen any of the Cuban army, and he found himself glad to see some of them falling from the return fire of the pathetic little groups.

They had momentarily slowed the steady hail of bullets from the tree line, and more of the invaders now began to run for the water. They waded in up to their knees, dropping their weapons as they dove, frantically thrashing the water as they swam straight out. Many would stop to wave their arms over their heads, apparently imploring the American boats not to leave them.

Now that the invaders were turning their backs, more Cuban soldiers were moving from the safety of the palms, this time stopping to take aim as they fired at the retreating band. While the boat again rocked to a new course, David searched through his binoculars until he found Melendez. The man was on one knee, firing his BAR at a group of soldiers, stopping them in their tracks. The lucky ones threw themselves to the ground, rolling over and over, away from the hail of bullets. One in particular kept rolling until he was far enough away to come to a sitting position. He raised his gun quickly in Jorge's direction, firing rapidly at the little colonel, who was by now all but deserted by his men. One bullet found its home, and Melendez fell backward, his gun flying through the air.

David cried out as his friend rolled over twice. His assailant then turned his fire in another direction. David watched Jorge roll over onto his knees, looking in the direction of the man who had brought him down. When he found he was alone for a moment he rose to his feet, stumbling to the water's edge, wading in almost too casually. At knee's depth, he fell forward and began a slow, erratic stroke toward deeper water.

Almost at the same time David thought, We have to save them, Palmer had brought the rudder around again and was heading toward the closest swimming men.

Now the shells from the coastal batteries were more accurate. They no longer had to search for their targets. This was the remainder of an army in complete retreat, frantically thrashing the water in desperate efforts to escape certain death or capture ashore, and instead swimming among a hail of artillery shells rupturing the water around them.

My God, thought David, this is what Dunkirk must have been like! And in a way, it probably was for the ensign who had only just been born at the time the British army had fled the coast of France. His little whaleboat played much the same part twenty years later as it edged toward shore to try to save some of the men who had landed only hours earlier.

There was a sputtering in the water around the boat. Machine-gun bullets etched a pattern in front of them. Palmer, seeing the fifty-caliber gun that had been set up at the edge of the palms, again reversed his rudder away from a group of men they had almost reached. The splashing bullets paused for a moment among the swimmers.

Palmer's engineman had now picked up a BAR from the supply of weapons that had been lowered to them before they had pulled away from the *Bagley*. He handed another to the signalman crouched beside him. They ripped open the bag containing clips for the weapons, pouring them on the deck.

"Turn in again," David shouted to Palmer, pointing in the direction of the Cuban machine gun. The boat again heeled as Palmer sent it directly toward the gun firing at them, making the whaleboat a smaller target. David picked up another BAR, grabbing some clips in the same motion. Together, the three of them concentrated their fire at the machine gun. They had already passed many of the swimmers in their rush for the shore.

David vaguely noticed the water turning lighter, and then realized they were only forty or fifty yards from the beach. The water was probably only waist deep. He was looking down at Cuban sand. Palmer brought the whaleboat parallel to the beach, allowing his gunners an easy shot at their target for just a moment. The water around them was alive with bullets, some cracking into the side of the boat and others passing over their heads. They were now too close to shore for the artillery fire, which was hitting the water a hundred yards behind the whaleboat. First, it was the man beside the machine gun who half rose and began to turn before he fell. Even before he hit the sand the pressure on the trigger had stopped as his gunner fell backward.

Before David realized that his last clip was empty and that he was squeezing an unresponsive trigger, Palmer had turned the boat back to the sea. They were attracting too much attention and now sporadic rifle fire was coming in their direction.

They came upon the first two men in the water. The engine was throttled down as arms reached out to pull them in. One man almost pulled a sailor into the water as he grabbed the arm reaching down to him. The other was too badly injured to help himself and the boat had to come to a stop for a few precious seconds. Again, rifle fire began to concentrate on them.

"Don't stop next time," David shouted. "If they can't get in themselves, go on to the next ones." He was shocked at his own callousness.

Two more were picked up, but three others who were severely wounded were given a wide berth as the boat edged back into artillery range again. The big shells were coming more steadily and too close. David knew many of those in the water wouldn't survive the explosions anyway.

And then he saw Jorge Melendez's head bobbing just thirty yards away as they pulled in almost the last man they had room for into the boat. Jorge waved an arm.

Palmer didn't need to be told as he swung the boat in the swimmer's direction, motioning to throttle down the engine as they came close. Not fifteen yards away, a shell landed in the water, exploding in a deafening roar. As the spout subsided, David saw his friend's face twisted in pain. The boat ran alongside the man, and David reached out to grab his hand.

"Take my arm," he yelled to the man in the water. Jorge

just looked back at him and shook his head. "Goddamn it, Jorge, grab me."

Melendez again shook his head, this time in more agony. "Now, David," he cried, "where is your U.S. Navy?" His head bobbed beneath the surface for a moment, then rose. "Where is your Navy?"

Then he sank below the surface, not slowly, but as a dead weight. Another shell exploded in the water, this time close enough to almost upset the sturdy little whaleboat. Palmer put his rudder over sharply, at the same time making the motion for full speed, fearing the next shot would be a hit.

David turned from the side of the boat, looking back in tears at his boatswain. Palmer pointed at the *Bagley*, nodding his head that he was returing to the ship. Saving nothing, David slumped back in the bottom of the boat, vaguely aware of the noise around him and the men still in the water waving at the boat as their last chance pulled away.

The first indication he had of their return to the *Bagley* was the whaleboat bumping heavily against its hull. There was water in the bottom of the boat, and he was wet. He looked up to see familiar faces staring down at them. He became aware of many people in the boat, probably fifteen who had been lucky enough to be pulled from the water.

They edged beside the ladder. Palmer motioned for the young officer to be the first up the side. David shook his head. The few wounded they had were taken up first, followed by the still limp form of the sailor who had succumbed to the canteen. David looked up to the bridge and saw Sam Carter waving down at him, but he did not return the wave.

When just he and Palmer remained, the sailor reached down and gave him a hand, pulling him shakily to his feet. At the foot of the ladder, David motioned Palmer to step up first as he looked back at the boat, now taking on water more rapidly. "No, sir." He put out his hand and shook David's firmly. "I'd like to follow you."

The young officer nodded at the other man and stepped up

the ladder to the main deck of the *Bagley*. It was solid, a secure feeling after the wild antics of their little boat. A messenger was waiting for him. "The captain would like you to report to the bridge, if you're okay, sir."

"I am," David replied. As a corpsman handed him something cool to drink, the messenger wheeled about and headed back to the bridge to report to Carter.

David finished his drink, handed the glass to someone nearby, and strode to the ladder leading to the 01 level. He calmly walked forward on that deck and swung up two more levels to the signal bridge, nodding at sailors who stared at him silently. He moved past the flag bags at the rear of the open bridge to where Carter was waiting for him, standing beside his chair on the starboard wing. He saluted the captain.

"You wanted to see me, sir." David had suddenly become very tired. He decided he didn't particularly care what anyone else was going to say, even this captain before him.

Carter returned the salute. "You did a hell of a job in there, David, but you didn't follow my last orders."

David looked back at him. "No, sir," he said very calmly.

"Do you mind telling me why? You could have lost some good men, including yourself."

"You don't seem to understand. A lot of people were being killed. They were being slaughtered." He was very tired now.

"I know that, David. I've been there before."

"I saw Jorge in the water. He asked where my Navy was." He looked closely at Carter, tears forming in his eyes again. "Do you know where our Navy was, sir?"

"We may never know where it was, David. It wasn't out here today, and we may never know why either. But I don't ever want you to forget what I told you last night. And I think you may already have started to forget some of it. Whoever made this decision doesn't know you, or me, or even Jorge, but he or they taught you a lot about power today. And power doesn't always make the decision you think is right. But power can do that because it can do anything it wants. And if you're going to sail with me, you're going to have to remember that.''

''And can it lie to men like Jorge?''

''You'll have to decide that for yourself some day, David.'' He looked closely at the young man, and remembered another young man, a Lieutenant Sam Carter, who had had a similiar experience when he was commanding an LST at Inchon. More men had been lost then. ''You've done a fine job today, and now I want you to go aft to your room. You're tired. Get some sleep, and then we'll talk some more.'' He smiled at David for a brief second, then turned, moving into the pilothouse.

The executive officer was at the chart table. ''He was a little brusque there, Captain. I'll talk with him later.''

''No, that's all right,'' replied Carter. ''He just had to learn a tough lesson that most people are lucky enough to miss. He'll be okay.''

DEAR SAM,

You never fail to make me feel like I'm the only woman in the world. I never suspected a thing last weekend when you suggested we take a weekend in North Carolina, ''like a second honeymoon,'' you said. Now I know that I'm married to one of the world's great con men. And maybe I'm the most easily conned woman in the world, or maybe I just want to believe you'll never be in danger. Now, I can only say thank you, my love, for reminding me how important we are to each other.

And I also want to say ''damn you'' for conning me so beautifully. I had such a lovely time knowing I was the only woman in the world that had ever been loved so well, and I couldn't believe it when I turned on the radio this morning. Before they'd even finished reporting the Bay of Pigs invasion, I knew you were right in the middle of it. Now I realize part of the reason for the lovely weekend was that you had been worried enough that you might be gone for a long time—or even worse. So now you know, you con artist, that I will be forever suspicious of you whenever you decide that we should have a second honeymoon.

You know that when *Bagley* gets back, I'm going to want to know everything you did, where the ship was, everything you saw, what everyone in the wardroom did. I want it to be like I was there with you because you can't imagine how lonely it can get back here alone. I plan teas for the wives and get everyone involved over at the ''O'' Club. And the other night I even had a dinner for the wives and invited over some of the girl friends, only the serious ones, not some of those others that you get such a kick out of. It was fun, but the younger wives either work or have little children. They're all busy and talk about all those things, and that's when I worry about you the most. I can call my family, and I do sometimes, but you know how my father can get when I start talking about you. He's so pompous about the days of the ''black coal'' navy when they were gone for months at a time, and my mother stayed home and kept quiet while he took his ships all over the world. And then he always wonders whether you're going to amount to anything, even though he says he throws around so much weight for you at Bupers. I have to keep reminding him that you're one of the youngest destroyer captains in Norfolk, and that's when he makes me so mad by saying that he's part of the reason you've gotten as far as you have. You seem to take all of that so much better than I do. I just don't have the even temperament you have.

You can see why it gets so lonely sometimes. And now, I'm just waiting for the phone to ring and have Daddy ask if I know where you are or what you've been doing. He always does that just before he's ready to tell me all about it. Although maybe this time it was secret enough so that even he didn't find out beforehand. I hope so.

I guess I could keep going on, and I know you love to get letters even if you say you never have time to read them much at sea. I decided you just need someone to tell you how much you're loved, before you get too impressed with some of your ensigns' female friends. And, as long as you don't get a swelled head, you should be pleased to know that you were almost as good on your second honeymoon as you were on the first. I miss you.

All my love and kisses,

Ann

FROM THE LOG OF
ADMIRAL DAVID CHARLES

Now that I've had time to think about it, I could have blown whatever career I plan to have in the Navy all to hell yesterday. At the time, I don't think I ever hated anyone as much as I hated Captain Carter. He was the coldest, most hardhearted, uncaring, inhuman son of a bitch I ever knew. When I finally got back to the *Bagley*, I was convinced that Sam Carter was the man who had killed Jorge. There was no doubt of it in my mind.

Today, I know he didn't, and that he was probably hurting as much as I was while I was doing all the arm waving. I really came close to insulting him in front of other people, something he always avoids. As I was falling asleep in my bunk, I wondered to myself if he was going to court-martial me for disobeying orders. I could have been killed along with Palmer and some of the others, but it never occurred to me when we were in the middle of the firing. I think I decided that he might even be right if he did court-martial me.

This morning, when I got up, I knew he wouldn't. And I wondered why not, if I deserved it as much as I think I did. After all, I was literally going against the wishes of the Commander in Chief by staying close to the beach and firing back at the Cubans. For some reason, I had just figured that because we were there we would get into the fight. It never occurred to me that we were waiting to see whether the Cubans would give up and throw down their arms and welcome the invaders. And we were actually invading someone else's land, and apparently everything we've been hearing wasn't exactly correct. Maybe more Cubans are happy with Castro than we thought.

What really hurts today is losing Jorge. He was a very brave man, and he believed in what he was doing, and made me believe in it, too. He made me believe in it enough to almost go off the deep end and disobey orders completely.

What I have to learn is to make my own decisions, without letting anyone else change my mind until I know what I'm doing. Captain Carter was right about power. They never taught us that, and it's something you have to learn yourself, just like making up your own mind.

The other thing I learned yesterday was that maybe I'd make a good Navy officer after all. Once I got used to what was going on, I enjoyed it. I took charge. I was glad Palmer was there because nothing upsets him. But it was almost weird the way I felt when they started shooting at us. That was the part I didn't think I'd ever want to go through unless I had to, and there I was ordering the boat in closer and not worrying about being a target. I'd like to ask some other people about that, but perhaps they wouldn't understand. Anyway, there's hardly anyone in the Navy anymore who's ever been shot at. But I think perhaps I might know a little more about myself if I could understand why I felt that way. Maybe after I find out whether Captain Carter's still pissed at me, I'll ask him about it. If I thought I could be like him, I'd stay in the Navy.

CHAPTER
FOUR

Moscow, the Third Rome, was cold that night, very cold. Vice Admiral Robert Collier had stepped outside the embassy earlier in the evening, before the old women had swept the dusting of new-fallen snow from the streets. The snow squeaked underfoot, a sound that brought back memories of his childhood when icy cold weather made the packed snow crunchy. The first walk had been a short one, just to think. He knew that the next time he came outside the snow would have been swept off each sidewalk, piled neatly in the street, waiting for the trucks to come by to pick it up and dump it in the river. Unless there was a nasty storm, it was all very efficient. Every citizen contributed to the city somehow, and in each block there was an old woman or old man who swept the daily light dusting into the gutter. Two slightly stronger ones would then push it into piles, and shortly after it was gone. There certainly was something to say for the Party when the streets were always clean, just like the trains running on time!

Now he was walking up the slight incline from the Hotel Russia to Red Square. The residue of the light snow was gone—probably floating down the river—and he was on a midnight pilgrimage that had occurred much too often lately.

He was a walker when he had to think, and he often found himself at midnight wandering over the cobblestones of Red Square to the red marble tomb outside the Kremlin walls to watch the changing of the guard. It was just like clockwork each time. Lenin would have been pleased. At the precise moment every night—he had timed it by his watch—the fresh honor guard would appear through the Tower Gate in the great wall, goose-stepping precisely, left arms swinging as if by metronome. There was no haste. This had been practiced too often and they were chosen especially for this duty. Arms swinging, eyes straight ahead, squaring shoulders precisely without a word spoken, they would approach the soldiers to be relieved. There was no sound except the sharp crack of glistening boot heels against the pavement. Each fresh guard took his assigned place; each relieved guard left his position to join the others in exactly the same formation as those who had arrived. No noise, except the boots again, and off they went to that gate in the great wall.

Collier was always thrilled by the performance at that hour of the night. Except for a few tourists and stumbling drunks, the midnight change, the one he felt was most impressive of all, was rarely seen by others. He always enjoyed the show, but he was also there to think. This was the way he put his mind back in gear when long hours began to wear him down. All he needed was a walk, a stop to see discipline in its highest form. The crisp night air always put his mind at ease. Tonight he looked up at the spotlighted flags over the red brick walls. The hammer and sickle on the red field stood out for all to see. The flags rippled even though there was little wind—for there were blowers underneath. No fools, they. The Party made sure that the flags always stood straight out and ruffled noisily in the breeze.

Tonight there was no difference in the show, but there should have been. If Collier had worn his uniform, which he did only for official functions, the K.G.B., who he knew were following, would have asked him to return to the embassy. Actually, the Americans were close to being in a state of siege now, but it hadn't been made official. The ambassador had already received notification about the trouble, and the familiar faceless people waited motionlessly outside in case they were needed. Collier had really been challenging what was soon to be a reality, but they also knew his habits and knew where he was going and why, and since they took it as a compliment, they left him alone.

He knew of the Chairman's speech to be given in a few hours. He even knew more than most of the Russian leaders about why that speech was being given, and what would happen afterward. He knew it was time to get back to the office and call Sam Carter on the scrambler. He needed instructions, for things were going to get very hot shortly. Even the U.S. Ambassador did not have all the military facts abous Islas Piedras nor was he even aware of the new weapon to silence the Russian spy satellites. The Russians had no idea what had destroyed the one that had been taking pictures over the island. Collier was also now in charge of security at the embassy since Colonel Hamlet had disappeared. They all knew what had happened, but they didn't know if he was alive. It was an old Russian trick. They didn't want the most important people—not one that would cause too much commotion—just an intermediate who was responsible for an important segment of the embassy, the Marine detachment. If Hamlet was alive, he thought, he'd probably never be much good for anything again.

He turned after a lingering glance at the onion domes of the Cathedral of St. Basil, nodding to one of the silent men who he knew would follow him. It was now after midnight, and in a short time the satellite would be in position. This was the most secure method of contact with Washington and the only way he could converse openly with Carter. The microphone he would talk into had a built-in scrambler, and his voice was beamed to a satellite that supposedly was just for picture-taking. His words would then be beamed to another satellite thousands of miles through space that would relay it to the ground unit in the Pentagon, where it was unscrambled. The Navy had designed it specifically for a time such as now. It was almost like a telephone, with little time delay from transmission to reception. The only units in existence were at the embassy and in Sam Carter's office.

The fire that had started so mysteriously on the eighth floor had destroyed almost all communications with the outside world. The American Embassy had been effectively neutralized as far as totally secure communications were concerned. Normal business could be relayed through other friendly embassies. For some reason, all members of the staff who might have been in a position to notice or prevent the fire had been involved somewhere else. Access to the spaces where the fires had begun were so limited that there was no doubt agents were responsible, working on the staff and unknown to the Americans. They had managed to get everyone away from their responsibilities at the appropriate time—no more than five minutes—and then started a series of small, quick blazes with incendiary devices. Each place the fire had started was designed to incapacitate a valuable unit, an irreplaceable one that could only be repaired over an extended period of time or with parts from the States, which obviously wouldn't appear once the Chairman's speech was finished. Ambassador Simpson definitely had a need to know at this juncture how serious the military situation would become, and Collier needed permission to update him.

As he rounded the corner from Kalinina Prospect onto Tschaikowskistrasse, he noticed the number of figures waiting outside had increased. They weren't hiding their faces, for it was simply their job to secure embassy personnel at this time. Collier recognized some faces, some very senior ones. He nodded to a few he passed since they had met socially before at functions, mumbled a couple of vagaries in Russian just so they would remember his capabilities. He hoped it might make some of them a bit uneasy.

The Marine guard at the door came to attention but did not salute, though tempted at this point. Specific orders to the Marine detachment included no salutes, to minimize the fact that military personnel were attached to the embassy. While everyone in both countries was aware of this, protocol made it easier to accept if a civilian approach was maintained.

There were many employees up at this late hour, tidying up as much as possible, although the Moscow Fire Brigade couldn't have been nicer or more efficient. It was almost as if they had planned how to put out the fire on the eighth floor, even before it had begun. After discovery of the fire, they had waited until the right amount of damage had been accomplished, no more than a few extra moments. The incendiary devices had been most efficient. The firemen arrived with the right equipment, extinguished the flames rapidly, took care not to interfere with anything that might upset the Americans, and left shortly after cleaning up after themselves and ensuring that the embassy wanted them to leave. A very neat operation . . . well planned!

Collier exchanged pleasantries with the staff members he saw. They were becoming increasingly nervous and didn't yet know they probably wouldn't be going home for some time. You can't keep an operation like this secret from a handpicked staff of their caliber. Yet he wondered which ones he talked with on his way to the elevator were also on another payroll.

He got off at his floor and was greeted immediately by the two marines on duty. Their smiles, after formalities, acknowledged that they considered him their officer-in-charge now that Hamlet was missing. Collier looked every inch a naval officer, right out of the recruiting posters. He was tall and slender, well over six feet and almost the same weight as the day he had been commissioned. His short dark crew cut had turned white, adding to the distinguished appearance emphasized by dark eyes, white teeth, and fairly square jaw. He looked the part of the heroic captain astride the bridge of a fighting ship, though he had rarely been at sea since his early days on the *Bagley*. His intelligence and quick mind, coupled with his wife's antipathy to sea duty, had brought him seniority through staff channels along with knowledge of the power structure that came with those assignments. The major now in command was an excellent officer, but he simply did not have the charisma to dominate these specially selected men that both Hamlet and Collier had.

"Has anyone else been on this floor or attempted to get off the elevator, other than authorized personnel?" he asked.

"No, sir," the shorter one answered. "Just the change of the watch at midnight. All signatures and badges checked per your orders."

Collier had insisted that his marines be extra careful. It was just an added precaution with the confusion caused by the fire, to ensure as much as possible that the right people showed, that each one could match his signature to that on the card. Even more important, it was also to be sure no one else was missing.

He went through the motions of signing the book for the marines, showed his own badge, and then went across to the heavy metal door on the other side of the small room. He inserted his badge into the chest-high slot in the door. He then placed his right hand, palm forward, just to the right of the slot. A light glowed briefly under his palm, then the badge reappeared from the slot. He stepped back and the door opened slowly. Reattaching the badge to the lapel clip, he stepped inside, nodding to the marines who were on guard beyond the door. There were four people inside the room seated before the variety of electronic gear that glowed and blinked in the half light.

"Good morning, Admiral," one of them murmured. They continued with whatever intricate operations they were completing. The other three acknowledged his appearance respectfully, though none of them moved from their positions.

"I've just run a check with Jackson at the Pentagon, sir. He said that Admiral Carter will be available momentarily. Something big must be going on, because he said no one from his section was allowed to leave for lunch." It was now late afternoon in Washington. "He said food was sent in and that their reliefs were also called in this morning. Looks like no one's going to be going home there at the end of the day either." He turned to look at Collier questioningly.

"They're right, Cooper," Collier answered. "Before they're ready I suppose this is as good a time as any to bring you all up to date, since you're going to hear my conversation with Admiral Carter. We're already running into the same problem here." He wasn't quite sure where to start. After a momentary pause, he began, "From about now, we are all virtually prisoners in the embassy. The fires were started by parties within this building whom we can't yet identify. The reason was simple—they wanted to cut off all our outside communications and, as is obvious to each of you, they've been successful with the exception of this operation, which they're in the dark about.

"Their spy satellites over the last month have been watching the development of our base at Islas Piedras in the Indian Ocean very closely. While you all know a little about that island, it is not actually a Trident resupply base and was never intended to be."

"Well, I'll be damned," said one of them. "My brother's stationed there. What is it, sir?"

"It is a strategic base, armed with a new tactical missile that we hope to utilize to control that section of the world. One of us is going to end up on top, and it's better if it's us. The Russians have made strong inroads into control of the Indian Ocean and, from a strategic and economic viewpoint, we can't allow it, or the U.S. will be forced back pretty much to its own hemisphere. You know what that means."

"Yes, sir. We're shit out of luck!" Better than I could have said it, Collier thought.

"Before they could get accurate pictures of final installations, we employed a new weapon that has never been used before, a type of laser. Quite simply, it damages a satellite by neutralizing its electronic equipment. There's no explosion. The satellite keeps right on its programmed course, but it simply is unable to take pictures or communicate with any ground stations. There is no way they can complain to the U.N. or prove anything to any of their allies. It appears to be a malfunction of a perfectly orbiting satellite, but it's no longer of any value to them. I don't exactly know where this weapon is or how many we have, but I do know that another satellite was neutralized from another location—just to let them know it wasn't a fluke and that we can destroy their electronic links at will.'' He paused for a moment to let it sink in. They were all disciplined career people, and there was little expression on their faces.

''I'm beginning to get the message. We're not going to be exactly welcome here, are we?''

''In about six hours,'' Collier continued, ''the Chairman of the Communist Party will make a speech in the Kremlin, but it will be intended for all the world and broadcast internationally. He will state that Islas Piedras is a Trident submarine base established in a hitherto free sector of the world, that it is an invasion of the Third World, and an aggressive action that must be halted. He can't state what that island really is because their photos are incomplete and they aren't absolutely positive of what will be there when we're finished. In the meantime, he will ask that we remove that base completely. To back all this up, a huge Russian naval force left Vladivostok and Nakhodka almost two weeks ago and is now about twelve hours away from active contact with the island, although their submarines were in position two nights ago.

''It's a blockade, with a great deal of similarity to the tactics we employed in Cuba in 1962. The tactics are the same, except that they are denying us here secure contact with Washington via the fire damage. The Russians apparently feel that if the U.S. is forced to deal directly from Washington, with silence and no mediation on this end, that they'll force indecision on the part of the President and world opinion can then gain them the upper hand.''

''Wow, that's heavy stuff,'' one of the men muttered to another beside him.

''Why,'' asked another, ''couldn't we utilize communications systems from other embassies? Friends, like the Canadians or British, or even neutrals like Switzerland or Sweden? They should have secure linkage with their own people in Washington.''

"We considered that earlier this evening," Collier answered. "Ambassador Simpson even discussed this with some of his contacts at those embassies. But, if you need an example of successful infiltration of a staff, don't look any farther than right here. I'm pretty sure that fire a few hours back was started by people working here. If we have that little security on our own staff, imagine what we can expect with the others, friends or not.

"But that's a good question, Jessie. Don't get me wrong. We'll use the other embassies for general administrative messages and some direct voice contact, but we'll be damn careful what's carried. We do want the Russians to think we're going to use our friends and we're already beginning to set up a system. But that's to make them feel they've been entirely successful here. They don't know what we've got in this room, and this is the one ace we still have up our sleeves. As long as this all remains political rather than military, let them think they've been successful."

Collier looked at his watch. It was a bit after one in the morning and almost time for Carter to show up. He had been at a meeting of the Joint Chiefs with the CNO (Chief of Naval Operations) at which the President and his advisors were briefed on what had occurred to date. Collier knew that Carter would be looking for instructions to pass on to Moscow from that important meeting, for he and the ambassador might have to operate in the dark sooner than expected.

"Ambassador Simpson should be here shortly," Collier continued. "I explained most of the military situation to him this evening, and he will now be working directly with me until a solution is reached. Our job in Moscow will be to convince the Russians that what has occurred in the Indian Ocean is a *fait accompli*." He paused, then, "We want them to think it's too late for them to stop the installation at Islas Piedras and that military action will simply be a provocation to all-out war. I don't know myself how much more time we need at Islas Piedras, but I do know that Washington will be trying to convince the world that it is nothing but a replenishment base, similar to Holy Loch in Scotland."

"What are we planning to throw up against them, sir?"

"I know that we have been assembling a task force from a variety of ships that were sent out to act independently during the last few weeks. They've been in the Red Sea, off the African coast, and some were as far away as India or operating off the west coast of Australia. *Nimitz* is the flag, and I know a few of the *Virginia*-class cruisers are around, along with at least a half dozen attack subs out there. It was well planned a long time ago. There's a lot of nuclear power and not too much need for a replenishment force. But right now, I think you understand how much I'm going to be depending on you, and what you're going to have to do for God knows how long. A lot of people are relying on us."

As he finished, Ambassador Simpson appeared, visibly shaken for the first time in his life. "Good morning, Bob." He looked around the room first, then apparently realized he could talk openly in front of Collier's men. "I placed the entire staff on an emergency basis right after the fire. I would think at this point you probably have even more to tell me about the military situation. When I'm able to make a report, I'm going to mention that my position is too critical for me to have been kept in the dark about certain things that have taken place outside this country recently."

"I can assure you that a good deal of what's happened wasn't the Navy's fault, sir. I felt that you should have been involved long before, certainly when intelligence first learned of what the Russians knew about Islas Piedras. But the President, or his staff, have given us specific orders, which we've had to follow for the time being." He went on to elaborate on the details he had just finished with to his own men. Then he explained the call he was now waiting for.

The ambassador looked pensive for a moment, knitting his brows. "Bob, they've really placed me in a tough position. I've been getting indications in the daily meetings I've had at the Kremlin the past week that there was something I should know. By now, they must feel I'm either part of the whole scheme, or that perhaps I'm the dumbest ambassador they've had to deal with. You and I are going to have to work more closely together from now on, but first I'd like to talk with your people when they call. There are only so many doors you can open without me. If the Secretary of State is there, I'd like a word with him."

He was interrupted by one of the operators, "Sir, I understand Admiral Carter is about ready now."

"Thanks, Jessie. Would you find out who's there with him? If Secretary Jasperson isn't there, they should arrange for a patch right away. Tell them Ambassador Simpson wants to speak with him."

"Yes, sir." Then, a few moments later, "Mr. Jasperson is at the White House, sir. They're trying to raise him on a special line now."

"Good. How much time do we have on this call before the satellites are out of range?"

"No problem, Admiral. You have approximately . . ." some scratching on a pad, ". . . exactly sixty-seven minutes from now." The time was 1:17 A.M. in Moscow.

"No need to use the phone," Collier said. "Patch it over the speaker, so we can all hear."

There was quiet in the communications room, then, "I have Admiral Carter, sir." He pushed a button on the panel in front of him.

"Good morning, Bob." Sam Carter's voice came over the speaker as if he were in the room. There was no interference.

"Good morning to you, Sam. And how's life in the Pentagon today?"

"It's probably not as hairy as in Moscow, Bob. But I don't think you've ever seen such action in this place. The CNO briefed everyone a few hours ago, and he told me he hasn't seen faces like that since he was an ensign at Pearl. We've had our share of crises that most people never knew about, but this is the greatest shock in a long time. How are people taking it at the embassy?"

"I briefed the ambassador earlier this evening as we'd agreed. Shortly after that, he made an announcement to the people here, and the entire staff is now on an emergency basis. And when I came in from a walk not so long ago, I noticed that none of us are going to be leaving for a while.''

"I figured they'd want to do that even before now.''

"But we don't have a hell of a lot of time, Sam. First, Ambassador Simpson is here and I want someone's permission, CNO or SECNAV or whoever, to tell him everything about Islas Piedras' military installations and also about the satellite neutralizer. I believe you could say we're just about in a state of war here, and he should know everything.''

There were some words spoken beyond the microphone at the Pentagon, followed by Carter: "I've got one of my aides on the phone now, and it will only take a minute. In the meantime, what's the status of your communications? We haven't been able to raise anyone for six hours. All we've been told by the Russian Ambassador here is that some confusion would result for a while because of a minor fire.''

"That minor fire, as they call it in international politics, was a picture-perfect undercover job that negated all communications and crypto equipment—incendiary devices so small that we never knew they were brought in. Our experts here say it will be another four to six days before they can even have a proper jury rig on some of the units, but that's only if we have parts available here. And since they plan to cut us off from everything for a period, this is the only contact we'll have with you.''

"Sounds like intelligence screwed up badly, Bob.''

"Our biggest problem is that we don't know how many mistakes they've made. The ambassador, per an agreement with me earlier this evening, is telling our people only as much as we want them to know since we obviously have a major security problem. Major Hattan, who took over the detachment when Hamlet disappeared, is going over our background investigations now to see if we can find some pattern in last year's hirings, or anything that will at least give us something to go on. By morning we should literally be under siege, and then we'll have no bargaining power.''

"Just a moment, Bob. Secretary Jasperson is ready to be patched in from the White House. If the ambassador is right there, I'd like to have them talk first. The President, to be polite, is very shaken now.''

Collier looked at Simpson. Both of them knew the strain Jasperson was under now with the President. International confrontation was not part of the constitution of this small-town boy who had achieved the American dream by selling domestic issues to people. Jasperson was the President's mouthpiece and at this juncture was probably making all of the decisions for his President.

''I'm right here, Admiral Carter,'' replied the ambassador. ''I am aware of everything with the exception of some military information that I, for some reason, have not been made privy to.'' Collier noted that the ambassador's furrowed brows were probably no more furrowed than Sam Carter's at that statement. ''Please patch me in to Secretary Jasperson.''

A quiet voice came back over the loudspeaker, ''This is Jasperson. Am I speaking to Ambassador Simpson?''

''This is Simpson, Mr. Secretary. This is the only method I have available to communicate with you securely, and I'll make it as short as possible. You have already learned from the Russian embassy that a small fire disrupted our communications network for a while. Actually, it was an undercover job, an excellent one. Some very sophisticated incendiary devices were strategically placed to create destructive fires on the eighth floor. Quite obviously, our security missed something, and I suggest you have your people begin to comb all your files on us to see if they can turn up anything unusual. If they can infiltrate this embassy, they must be in every one we have. Secondly, I can assure you we will not have any other method of communications other than transfer of routine information for at least four days, and I doubt it will even be possible then. Finally, we are virtually prisoners within the confines of this building, and I doubt we will have any opportunity to assist you over the next twenty-four to thirty-six hours, when you're going to need it most. Admiral Collier has requested military permission to bring me up to date on some apparently highly classified weapons that are involved with this mess. While I don't want to belabor the point now, I think I should have been told previously what was developing, since I may have to negotiate directly with the Soviet leaders.''

There was an embarrassing silence before Jasperson came back. ''I assure you there was nothing personal involved in any decision to withhold information.'' A pause, then, ''Admiral Collier, you may take my word for it that you can tell Ambassador Simpson everything he needs to know.'' Another pause. Then, using his old friend's first name, Jasperson said ''Jack, I know you're in a tight situation and, if there is any fault, it has been right here. You know about Islas Piedras and that's the crux of the situation. If we could have completed it before all this started, then everyone with a need to know would have been briefed. As it stands now, we made a judgment error. The Russians got the upper hand on us, and it might have been worse if we hadn't stopped that damn satellite. As it was, we were using an untested weapon and we didn't even know if that would work.

''But those things aside, I suspect that we are going to need your help very badly after the Chairman's speech. You should work very closely with Admiral Collier, and I want to instruct both of you as a team.''

''I'm right here with the ambassador, Mr. Secretary. Please go ahead,'' said Collier.

''Bob Collier speaks just about perfect Russian, Jack. Since you seem to have a problem with security risks, I want Collier to act as your interpreter. Anywhere you go, he goes, and vice versa. I think the two of you will be safe, since the Russians aren't exactly sure what we have at Islas Piedras. As long as they believe they've put us out of touch, act just the opposite. Let's confuse them by acting as if we were in constant touch. As long as their information is inaccurate, you have a certain advantage. We know they'll stay in the dark for a while, although one of our agents has assured us that a new satellite will be launched within days to replace the one we neutralized. When that becomes a malfunction, I think they'll know what advantages we have on that score. However, we want to try to solve our problems with diplomacy, if possible. They know that you're handpicked by me, and Admiral Collier is a well-known student of international affairs. I want to read a list of items for you to discuss with them that I have just gone over with the President. You may tell them that the President of the United States stands firm on the following points . . ."

Silence!

The ambassador turned halfway to Collier. "Bob, what happened?" Silence. "Can you get him back? We have more time before they're out of range."

The Admiral looked at his men, one at a time. The looks on their faces were all that he required. "Mr. Ambassador, we're on our own now. I'm sure if we had any other means of communications with Washington, we'd learn shortly that our satellite was just destroyed. If it's any comfort to you, it was likely a missile. Destruction of that type will be obvious to a number of countries, and I'm sure the U.S. will learn about this provocation in the next half hour.

"In the meantime, sir, we have no contact with Washington, and I doubt we will have any for some time. As a matter of fact, if you go to your quarters and look out in the square, I'll bet you'll see there are even more guards than before."

In the aura of the dim street lights on the Tschaikowski-strasse, Ambassador Simpson saw not only more people, but they now wore the uniforms of the Red Army.

CHAPTER
FIVE

THE office was austere, much like the man who sat behind the large wooden desk. The desk and the comfortable chair he sat in were the only items in the room that signified his authority. There was a drab rug of a nondescript brownish color on the floor, and there were no curtains on the windows, only the folding wooden blinds, so familiar in Russia, that slid on squeaky metal tracks to cut out a too-bright sun. The walls and ceiling were of a pale beige color, and minute cracks showed in the plaster, which needed renewing. The only decorations were on the wall opposite the desk where he could look up at them from his work. Behind him were the normal charts and scrolls that signified various awards he had won in his long naval career. They were there for effect, for he wanted visitors to see them when he talked. There were two smallish windows to his right. He leaned back in his chair to look out at the lightly falling snow in the Kremlin yard. The air was still bright with the light crystal snow that fell this time of year from the fluffy clouds. They skittered across the sun, the one that never rose very high in the wintry Moscow sky. He pushed back from his desk, putting his hands behind his bald head. What little hair he had left provided a gray fringe around the base of his skull. This made his ears look bigger than they were, and his jowls, not large for a man nearly seventy years old, were also emphasized. He had a big head, wide, with a pronounced forehead and high Slavic cheekbones. To complete this tough-looking appearance, his eyes should have been a steely gray. But they were a soft brown instead. It might have been a handsome face, but the many hard years during the war, coupled with the sternness of a senior Russian military official, produced a perpetual downturn at the corners of his mouth.

His military blouse was open, one of the rare times he allowed himself this relaxation. He needed that comfort when he was alone with his thoughts. His chest carried an impressive array of combat ribbons, and the gold on his sleeves signified his position as the single Admiral of the Fleet of the Soviet Union. He was not only the man who had built the Soviet Navy after the Great Patriotic War, he was still in total command of it. Only moments before, he had given the order for destruction of the U.S. satellite in retaliation for whatever the Americans had done to his own.

He was well aware of the fire at the American Embassy, although that had been the work of the K.G.B. They would handle the Americans in Moscow. His responsibility was coordinating the confrontation at Islas Piedras in the Indian Ocean, working closely with both the Premier and Admiral Kupinsky aboard the flagship *Lenin*. The phone on his desk buzzed beiefly, and his secretary explained that the head of the K.G.B. was waiting to talk with him.

He picked up the phone and identified himself, then listened intently, not responding but nodding his head a few times to himself. When the caller had finished, he thanked him briefly for the information, hanging up before the other could add anything else to the one-sided conversation. It was simply formal notification that communications between the United States Embassy and Washington had been completely cut for the time being. The Americans were isolated.

There was a sharp knock at the single door to his office. An aide appeared after a respectful wait, wheeling in a chart of the Indian Ocean. Admiral Gorenko wanted nothing cluttering his office, nothing that would interfere when he was thinking. All the charts, television screens, communications equipment, computer consoles, and assorted command paraphernalia were kept in the command room next to his office. He had asked to be brought up to date every two hours, but did not care to step into the noise of the next room, where its occupants would invariably snap to attention as he entered.

The aide saluted. ''The position of *Lenin* at seven A.M. was exactly here, Admiral Gorenko,'' and he pointed to a spot well marked on the chart. ''The American force is located here,''—he pointed to another distinctly marked spot— ''northeast of Islas Piedras. They changed course in the middle of the day as you expected, bringing them to this point at sixteen hundred, about one thousand miles from our own force.'' •

Gorenko's eyes turned from the chart to the aide. ''Are there still just six ships in that formation?''

''Yes, sir.''

''Any sign of *Nimitz?*''

''No, sir. We believe she's still heading for Simonstown.''

''Don't believe. Check again.'' His eyes narrowed slightly. ''She will be turned back north, and she will be joined by all of those ships spread out on your chart. That you can be certain of, and I want to know instantly when she does.'' His head lowered back to the papers on the desk.

But he could not concentrate. He leaned back in his chair again, and found himself looking at a photograph on the wall. There were two men in the picture standing side by side, dressed in combat gear, guns slung on their shoulders. The backdrop was rubble. No buildings were standing. Written in the lower right-hand corner was ''Stalingrad, Nov. 18, 1942.'' One of the men was Gorenko, hardly recognizable today because of the strange clothes he wore then and the forty-year difference in time. The other was his friend, Georgi Kupinsky, Alex's father. And now, he thought to himself, I may be sending the son to his death.

. . . The clothes they had worn then made them look like awkward bears, but they were warm, much warmer than the

Germans or Rumanians. Their hats, with short visors to accommodate their helmets, had earflaps that encircled all but nose and eyes. The sheepskin coats were bulky and hung below their knees, and their weight made fast movement difficult, but it was preferable to freezing to death. The Volga was already filled with ice flows, and it would get much colder before the next offensive was over. They had warm gloves that were pliable enough to allow them freedom of movement, but the best part of their uniforms were their *valenki*, the felt-covered, padded boots. It was said that armies traveled on their stomachs, but since there was little food the 62nd Army managed to get by with warm feet. The Germans they were able to capture could not run because their feet had frozen in their straw-stuffed boots, worthless protection in the Russian winter.

The photo had been taken between one of the many pitched battles during the street fighting in Stalingrad. They were standing near the Central Railroad Station, a place that General Chuikov had decided would be a "must hold" position. It was near Mamai Hill, another of the bluffs in the city that had seesawed back and forth. They were not allowed to give up the station as long as they were still alive.

That was another order that had been forgotten with time. Russians in Stalingrad had to be dead before they gave ground. It had been decreed that the city would be the turning point of the war. If they did not stop the advance here, then the Germans would move on the Baku oil fields. They had been told they had only two obligations to the state— continue to fight or die. The Germans seemed to be of the same mind. They fought fiercely, giving up an attack only when there was no one left to fight. The Rumanians to the north and the Italians to the south, who were fighting for the Germans, were not as motivated. They preferred to take their chances as prisoners. They did not fear the torture the German soldiers expected if they were captured. Himmler's doctrine of Untermensch, the Commissar Decree of May 1941, order all Russian political officals and army political commissars killed on capture. The German soldiers expected no less.

The Admiral's thoughts drifted back to the early days of the war, after Hitler had surprised Stalin by striking on three fronts. Gorenko had been a young captain of his own destroyer in the Black Sea Fleet. He had been too junior to be caught up in the purges of 1937 and 1938, and the loss of so many of his superiors had created a rapid career path for him. He had then been made a commander of a squadron of destroyers, and when the Germans were sweeping into the Odessa region he had been charged with organizing the "sailor army." It was September, 1941, and his sailors had delayed the Germans until late October. The plan was to slow them down as much as possible until they were stopped completely by the Russian winter.

They had evacuated the sailors after Odessa fell. Then they became part of the Azov Flotilla, trying to keep the supply lanes open through the Azov Sea and up the Don near Stalingrad. He had organized the Kerch Landing in the struggle to save Sebastopol. The German armies were relentless and their tanks gradually drove the Russians back to the sea. But they held the city through the winter, effectively stalling Hitler's advance until the spring. It was Gorenko's sailor army that had fought the Germans so bravely, time and again throwing back the advances and taking such heavy losses. They were forced to evacuate Kerch in May of that year and in July of 1942 Sebastopol finally fell. There were few of those sailor soldiers left. The citizens never forgot the brave "five sailors of Sebastopol" who threw themselves under advancing German tanks. It was a defense of the homeland and each sailor was committed to die on land or sea.

On his wall, next to the photo from Stalingrad, was the simple message found on the body of one of his sailors at Firing Point Number Eleven:

Russia, my country, my native land! Dear Comrade Stalin! I, a Black Sea sailor, and a son of Lenin's Komsomol, fought as my heart told me to fight. I slew the beasts as long as my heart beat in my breast. Now I am dying, but I know we shall win. Sailors of the Black Sea Navy! Fight harder still, kill the mad fascist dogs. I have been faithful to my soldier's oath.

No one ever passed through his office without having it pointed out. Gorenko expected no less of his sailors forty years later.

By August, they had lost control of the Azov Sea to the Germans, and Gorenko led his small band of survivors toward Stalingrad, where the final stand would be made. If the Germans took Stalin's city and captured the oil fields, then the war was lost. Word of mouth preceded him as he led his men up the Don, skirmishing with German elements as they made their way to the next front. They did not go hungry, for the peasants brought what little they had to the sailors, whose commander was already a myth.

He lost more men at Kalach when they successfully destroyed a German fuel depot, the primary one the Panzer divisions depended on in the struggle for Stalingrad. Then, they captured a freight train and ran it along the canal to the great city. They arrived during the hardest month, October, the month in which General Paulus knew he must capture the city or face another cruel winter. The defenses had already pulled within the city limits and reinforcements from the Volga's eastern bank found themselves instantly in the front lines. The heroes were greeted for five minutes and then immediately sent to General Gorishnyi's 62nd Army, a unit already famous in its own right. Perhaps Chuikov had realized that the two heroic units should be charged with defending that part of the city that protected the supply paths over the Volga behind them. At any rate, the remainder of those sailors who had left their ships to defend Odessa, Sebastapol, and now Stalingrad would never again see the Black Sea. They died defending Mamai Hill, and a Central Railroad Station that was already unrecognizable when they got there.

There was a sharp knocking at his door. "Yes."

His aide entered, saluting as he stepped inside. "A report from Admiral Kupinsky, sir."

Gorenko nodded, not answering, as was his habit.

"Two aircraft were sent to harass the Americans. They fired missiles from long range making one hit on a cruiser. Little damage reported. One of the Rigas was brought down by a low-level missile we were unaware of. The remaining aircraft successfully evaded the others."

"Is there any sign of *Nimitz* yet, or any of her screening or supply ships?"

"Nothing, Admiral."

He pondered for a moment, then looked up to the aide. "Message to Admiral Kupinsky—continue harrassment. Sacrifice if necessary to determine any other new weapon systems."

"At once, Admiral." He wheeled and left, shutting the door quietly behind him and leaving Gorenko to his thoughts again.

Gorenko rose from behind his desk and moved over to the windows, looking into the courtyard below. The snow had stopped, and there were already many footprints through the light dusting. Soon, flakes would again drift down, erasing those prints and making room for new wanderers, though there were few in this section of the Kremlin. A brief flash of midday sun glanced off one of the domes on the Cathedral of the Archangel. He turned and looked directly at the photo.

The smells came back to him again, the gut-wrenching odor of death that hung over the city no matter where you were, and the calming blend of black bread and cabbage and makhorka tobacco in the basement command post. They had lost Mamai Hill once again and the General had been forced to move his headquarters. A fuel-shortage depot had been bombed and burning oil was running into the basements. It was quiet outside because the Germans did not usually attack during the day. Gorenko was eating a hasty meal with Kupinsky, the young sergeant who had just been made lieutenant to replace the last officer in his unit who had been killed that morning.

Gorenko decided to stay close to this man, for his troops still had a full supply of ammunition, especially grenades, which slowed any attack. And Kupinsky and his men were brave and experienced. They had been there since early September, always near Mamai Hill. Young Georgi Kupinsky had liked the Navy man, and they found that the defenders of Sebastopol and the defenders of Mamai Hill fought well together.

Their newly designated basement headquarters were by the Stalingrad Tractor Plant. They would soon try to take back the Hill.

"Tell me, Commander," inquired the young man, as he lit one of the foul-smelling cigarettes, "now that they have allowed us to finish a meal, do you think they will attack soon? Or do you think they are already aware of the counteroffensive?" It was November 18, and General Chuikov had planned a massive counterattack to take place simultaneously on each of the fronts around the city.

"It is hard to say, Georgi. And, please . . . please call me Pietr. We are friends, now." He paused to light his own cigarette. "I don't think they like the daylight any more than they have before. They like to attack at night when we can't see them as well." He stood up, motioning to the other. "Let's check with our men and see for ourselves if the Nazis seem to be curious."

As they came up onto the street, Gorenko looked for the outline of the sun through the dust and smoke that had changed it to a dull, reddish ball. It was either night and black out or a little lighter as the sun tried to penetrate the thick blanket of smoke. Few buildings existed as more than piles of masonry, an occasional wall or chimney piercing the air. Chimneys were hard to hit, so there were more of them than anything else to identify which part of town one occupied.

The rubble served as both a hindrance to movement and a boon to the foot soldiers for its excellent protection from rifle fire. The best part for the Russians was the fact that the

German destruction of the city was so complete that their tanks were unable to maneuver through much of the area they wanted to capture. German soldiers had to advance without the mechanized divisions that had led them in their sweep across Russia. When they had elected to reduce the city to mortar and ashes they had not realized that they were also halting their own most effective weapon. This gave the Russians the opportunity to pound the German positions with their artillery twenty-four hours a day, firing with accuracy from the opposite bank of the Volga.

And then, Gorenko remembered, there were the *katyushas,* those immense mortars, one of the few items in the Russian arsenal that genuinely frightened the Germans. Since they were fired from a distance, there was no warning of the impending explosion until the first shell began its descent. The great whooshing sound then announced its imminent arrival, too late for the Germans to avoid the tremendous explosions. The Russians used them effectively against troop concentrations, knowing the psychological value was worth almost as much as its destructiveness. Its intention was antipersonnel and its effectiveness justified its use, once reducing an entire advancing battalion to bits and pieces. Perhaps, he thought to himself, that's what kept us going in those days—we knew they had no *katys.*

They kept close to the remaining walls as they found their men around the next corner. Gorenko stopped to talk with one of his squad leaders for a moment, while Kupinsky moved among his own larger group.

"Georgi, has there been any movement out there?" He gestured in the general direction of the German positions.

"No, not yet, One of my scouts has just been out and has seen some ammunition carts hauling in more men. He thinks they may just be probing in the next couple of streets. They must know something's in the air."

"It's not like them to be so still during the day. Let's get ourselves a prisoner or two for Gorishnyi. He doesn't want them pulling back far enough to use aircraft." General Chuikov had ordered that his men would maintain close combat positions with the Germans, just a "grenade's-throw distance at most," so that their enemy could not utilize their air superiority. Every time the Germans moved forward they met stiff resistance, and whenever they withdrew, the 62nd Army was at their heels. Attacking was thought to be the simplest way to stay alive.

As quietly as six men could move through the remains of a pulverized building, they eased their way onto a pile of stone. Kupinsky used his binoculars to check activity behind the lines, while Gorenko and his men moved to one side to protect their post from the street. Less than thirty seconds after they had taken their positions, a German reconnaissance squad inched cautiously down the street in their direction. Gorenko communicated with his men by making hand signs for an ambush.

Looking over his shoulder, Kupinsky saw what was coming. He, too, used hand signals and his men began to move silently. But before they got there, the others opened fire. Shouts and screams, combined with the fire of automatic weapons, shattered the air. The surprised Germans had little chance to return fire. It was over almost before it began, except for the second squad of Germans following the first.

Gorenko didn't see them as he and his men jumped down from their position to locate a survivor. The second German group opened fire on them immediately, hitting one of his men. He and the other ducked behind the remains of a wall that had toppled into the street. The Germans had divided their group and, while one held down the two Russians behind the rubble, the others circled, not knowing Kupinsky was easing around behind them.

And then, from his right, Gorenko saw that the Germans had trapped them almost at the same time that they opened fire. The initial bursts killed the man beside him. He turned to fire, and found his gun jammed. The closest German came at him with his bayonet, deciding quickly that he had an opportunity to save ammunition. Gorenko rose to a squatting position, slipping as he tried to get to his feet.

Then, Kupinsky, bellowing as he ran, fired at the Germans. Two behind fell, but the one with the bayonet hesitated only for a moment when he was hit. Then he continued to chase the stumbling Gorenko. As he rushed, pointing the bayonet at Gorenko's chest, Kupinsky was there, jumping over the sprawled figure of his friend and impaling the German on his own bayonet, then firing one more round to make sure the man was dead.

"Are you hit?" Kupinsky asked, bending over the now-kneeling Navy officer.

"No, I am fine," he replied. "Only my pride is damaged, but it is better to be alive." He stood up, looking directly into the eyes of the man who had saved him. "I owe you something that is not easy to repay. I made a mistake and you saved me." He extended his hand in simple gratitude.

He never forgot the stark look on the other man's face. "No, my friend, you owe me nothing except perhaps to try to keep me alive also. I, too, want to return to my family after this is over." He smiled at Gorenko and turned away, giving instructions to his men, who had salvaged a wounded German.

They returned silently to their basement hovel, leaving their prisoner with Intelligence. They found lukewarm tea left by some officers now sleeping in another corner. Leaning against the wall, legs stretched out in the dirt and dust, Gorenko stared at his hands. They were shaking, the one that held the tea less so because it had something to grasp. He put the tea down, folding his hands to still them. Unable to calm himself, he shut his eyes and said, "I have fought both at sea and on land for almost two years and have never come so close to death, that I know of. Usually, I was behind the hand-to-hand fighting, and I never saw the people I killed or those who tried to kill me. But today, I saw that man's eyes. He wanted to kill me so badly, and I had no idea why he felt that way. Perhaps it comes with command, or the fact that the Navy does not see the people we fight at sea as human beings.

He looked over at Kupinsky, who said nothing. He went on. "I have organized and commanded a sailor's army for all of this time, when our ships were of little value to the homeland. We do not call ourselves Marines because we expect to be back to our ships so quickly. We were back to them once, after Odessa, when we were part of the Azov Flotilla. Then came Sebastopol. And I fought again with my men there, through the winter.'' He paused, separating his hands to pick up the tea. ''We fought their tanks in the streets. My men threw themselves under those tanks, with their last grenades, so that they would save one city block. And yet, I never came face to face with the men who wanted to kill me. And today, if you had not been behind me, I would have seen him do it.'' He looked over at the other man. ''When this is over, I shall go back to my ships, perhaps. But I want very much to do something for you. I feel inside that I must.''

Neither man spoke, nor did they look at each other. Finally, Kupinsky reached over, placing his hand on the other's arm. ''My friend, there is almost nothing we can do for each other in this hellhole, except try to survive. If we make it, then we are indeed lucky. What you can do for me can only be done if I die, and I think I have as good a chance as anyone else to die.

''I have a family in Leninsk. Perhaps you have never heard of it?''

Gorenko shook his head.

''It's only about forty kilometers to the east of here on the railroad. I have a small house, if the Germans have not bombed it. And I have a wife and a son, if they have not been killed in the air raids. If they have tried to write me, I have no idea. Mail hardly ever comes to Stalingrad, and they will not risk soldiers to carry mail. I have tried to write to them whenever possible to let them know the husband and father is still alive. Perhaps they have gotten some of the letters, perhaps not. As you know, there has been no mail for two weeks, because of the planning for the offensive.''

He stopped for a second to light another evil-smelling cigarette, then continued. ''My boy, Alex, is ten years old.'' He looked at Gorenko and smiled. ''He is a good boy. Very smart. Perhaps he will grow up to be a sailor like you, instead of an infantryman like me. Then, he won't have to look into the eyes of the people he kills, if there are more people who invade our homeland,'' he added as an afterthought. ''If I am killed, will you go to Leninsk? Find my family, if they are alive? See what you can do for them. I think if we are successful in our offensive, then we won't have to worry about the Germans again. If they take this city and cross the river, then we are lost. I will then try to get to them. But, if something happens to me, will you go to them? Tell my son we fought together against the Germans and that you and his father were friends. I don't want him to forget his father. Tell him why we are ready to fight to the last man. His mother understands only that we have been invaded, but not why we have to stand together.'' He smiled at Gorenko. ''Would you do that for me?''

''We will stay together, my friend, the soldier and the sailor, and we will talk about this on cold nights during the winter when we are old men at our dachas. But, yes, I will go to your family if something happens to you, if that will make you happy.''

The following morning, November 19, Georgi Kupinsky was one of the first to die leading his men at Mamai Hill. Pietr Gorenko buried the body under a pile of bricks and mortar himself, so that it wouldn't be added to the growing stacks of dead, frozen in horribly grotesque positions.

Admiral Gorenko turned from the window. So long ago, he thought. I haven't seen death staring at me since then, yet now I'm sending Georgi's son, my son, in that direction. And there are no longer invaders in the homeland as we feared then. Now, they are thousands of miles away, yet only minutes from invasion if they desire.

He became aware of what had jarred his thoughts. ''Come,'' he called in the direction of the door, caring little how long this next intruder had been patiently waiting.

This time it was not an aide, but one of the many Captains First Rank on his staff. The man was still in his bridge coat, which carried water droplets of melted snow from the outside. He inclined his head slightly in greeting, removing his hat. "Admiral, I have just come from the American Embassy. Admiral Collier came out when he saw me. He wishes to speak with you immediately. As you know, they have no outside communications."

"Did he say that?"

"No, sir. There was no need. Admiral Collier understands the situation.

"Did he say anything else?"

"Just that the ambassador would accompany him. They request the normal courtesies of a meeting. He asked you to name a time."

Gorenko smiled inwardly. There was no change in his facial expression before the younger man. "Thank you for coming to me. There is no message to return. I shall contact him when I am ready." He silently dismissed the other by turning his back and walking slowly to the window. The snow was starting again.

Gorenko had returned to Moscow before the end of the war. His first office wasn't far from the one he now occupied. After Stalingrad, he had gone back to sea and had been promoted to flotilla commander before they sent him to the staff position in the Kremlin.

He had been able to bring Alex with him. The boy's mother said anything was better than the hunger they faced in that May of 1945. The boy was then two years older than the first time they had met. He was taller at twelve but had probably not put on a pound since their first meeting.

It had been mid-January, and the icy winds sweeping down from the steppes brought unending misery to the hard-pressed peasants. Somehow Gorenko had survived the counteroffensive, Chuikov had attacked on each of the three fronts around the city and had surrounded Paulus. The Germans would not surrender, convinced that von Mannstein would come to their aid. They chose slow annihilation until Paulus could no longer accept the slaughter. When it became apparent that the worst was over, Gorenko had been released to the Navy. Medals were awarded to the leader of the sailor army and his men. There was even a celebration. Somehow the remnants of the 62nd Army had found the vodka, and they stole enough pigs from the peasants to honor the sailors in proper army style.

And then he had kept his promise to Georgi. Rather than go back toward the Black Sea with his men, he had first crossed the frozen Volga and gone east—to Leninsk. There were no trains. He had ridden partway with the army and then managed the rest of the way in the various wagons that carried what little the people still had.

Leninsk had been a poor town, but when he arrived it was a nothing town. The planes had bombed it often, for no reason he could ever determine. The major buildings were destroyed. The people lived in hovels thrown together from the remains of their homes. But he had found the Kupinsky family, still with half a house. It had suffered a near miss, and its survival justified some of the neighbors moving in with them. If it had been his home, he would have gone back to the front, he thought.

He had first seen the boy sitting on top of a dirty pile of snow. The child was dirtier than the snow and dressed in rags, but saw the military man coming and had stared at him. When the boy saw that the uniform was not quite the same as the regular infantry he had stood up, eyeing the stranger more closely. He watched the man come up directly in front of him and then saluted gravely in a little-boy manner. Gorenko returned the salute.

The child said nothing, and the man finally asked, "Could you tell me if this is the Kupinsky home?"

A shy nod was his only answer.

"Is your mother at home?" Another nod. "Are you young Alexander Kupinsky?"

The boy nodded and smiled. "Yes." He saluted the man again. "Do you know my father?"

This time it was Gorenko who nodded without speaking.

After staring at the officer before him for just a second, tears began to form at the corners of the boy's eyes. "He's dead, isn't he? I don't have a father any more, do I?''

The passing seconds seemed like hours as he looked down at the child. ''I will be your father now,'' he had said firmly, his eyes reflecting the man who had saved his life in the streets in Stalingrad.

He had taken the boy's bony hand in his own and led him into the house. He gave the woman money for herself and the child, and had sent more whenever he could during the war. Once in 1944, he was able to visit, when the trains were running again. And the following year, when the war ended, she had let him take the boy back to the capital city with him. There was nothing she could offer the child in Leninsk and she could barely sustain herself. She asked only that Alex be sent home to visit each summer if the commander had the money to do so. Each summer, he did return to his native town to see his mother, and each time he brought money from the man, who was now an admiral.

Alex became a member of Gorenko's family in those early years in Moscow. He was treated as a son, just as he had been told on that wintry day in 1943, and loved as one also, for there were no other children. He was allowed to enter one of the Nakhimov schools because of Gorenko, even though he was older than the others. When he was seventeen, he was entered in the Frunze Higher Naval School. He would not be an infantryman like his father.

Gorenko remembered the vacations the boy had, when he returned to his adopted family full of new ideas from the school. It was not an easy life, but few Russian young men his age had any idea what it meant to be easy. The two talked late into the nights of the navy and what young Alex would do when he was graduated. Many of the discussions were serious, about Russian history, and strategy, and the great military thinkers such as von Clausewitz and Mahan. Alex was not just smart. He had a brilliant, challenging mind, and the Admiral treasured these evenings.

Alex wanted to learn at any time of day or night. He forgot nothing. History was one of his favorite topics, and he sensed the struggles of the Russian people more from Gorenko than from the books. He learned of the many nations that had invaded their homeland at one time or another, and how they were always defeated by the stolid army and the Russian winters. When their armies were desperate and there was no food and they had only the clothes on their backs, then the winds blew from the north and the snow came. And the Russians had time to recoup and fight again.

Now, in the twentieth century, Gorenko taught his son how Russia would expand. No longer would they be invaded from every direction. They would expand their sphere and become a major force in the world. They would not join other countries, but they would have other nations turning to them. Always, a prime factor in this dream was Gorenko's desire to change his Navy from a homeland defense force to a blue-water fleet, commanding the oceans of the world.

He taught Alex the lessons of war. The first thing he would accomplish was the building of a submarine force. It was necessary if you were to protect your own supplies and deny them to your enemy. First you had to defend yourself, then you could take the offense. The undersea fleet would be followed by a surface force second to none. He remembered explaining to Alex that more than 20 million Russians had died during this last war, more than any other country, and never again would it happen if they could command the seas. Alex learned about *seapower* at the feet of the man who understood the American, Mahan. Each time they talked, Alex was reminded that the country that controls the oceans of the world controls the countries of the world. The necessity for intellect in the military was constantly driven home to Alex, now a young man, as he graduated from Frunze. As much as Gorenko hated the Germans, he told many stories of the General Staff methods that the Russians now emulated. It was always a good lesson to see how a small state like Germany could invade a large one like Russia. Only the best and the brightest reached the top, and that's where Alex would go.

* * *

In the mid-fifties, Gorenko became Commander in Chief of the Soviet Navy. Alexander Kupinsky had by that time exhibited this abilities both in the naval schools and on board ships. He was chosen for submarine training. He joined the fleet that his stepfather had created in less than ten years. Submarine command was Alex's dream, and Gorenko was sometimes hurt that he could not express to his comrades the pride he felt in the young man. Alex would have to make it on his own, without help from the Admiral.

It was after his first submarine tour, when Alex had returned to Moscow for a few days' leave, that they had one of their few arguments.

"I don't believe that you can extend your Navy throughout the world unless you can adequately service it. Any naval vessel should be able to survive on its own, but only if it is kept supplied. You taught me that yourself when we were reading Mahan!"

"We are ready now," Gorenko had replied. "We are thin perhaps, but our bases around the world make up for our lack of service ships."

"And if our bases are closed?"

"That should not happen again," the older man had growled. "We are too strong now. Our missiles are too much of a threat."

"We also have no aircraft carriers. Remember Mahan said you have to not only control your own seas, you must project your power, and in his time there were no aircraft carriers or even airplanes."

"That will come," was the reply. "I will not be caught like Hitler was. I will go to the oil fields and supply bases, and I will have a service force second to none."

"That is fine to say now. But how do you plan to support our submarines when they cross the ocenas?"

At that point Gorenko had risen from his chair angrily. He did not accept criticism easily, especially from the only person that he had perhaps ever loved. The conversation was cut off.

The next morning, the Admiral was his old self. He told

Alex he would have him sent to the Grechko Naval Academy for further study after his first sub command. In the spring of 1962, after an early promotion, Alex Kupinsky received his command, a submarine being made ready for a deployment to the Western Atlantic.

CHAPTER
SIX

SAM CARTER stretched lazily in his bridge chair, glancing down at the flying fish leaping gracefully through the air alongside the *Bagley*. His captain's chair had been returned to the open starboard wing after a brief tropical downpour. He looked across at *Lake Champlain,* noting activity on the flight deck a thousand yards off his port bow. The mighty elevators had already brought a dozen tracker aircraft to the flight deck, and he could see them being wheeled into position for takeoff.

"Looks like they're getting ready to launch, Bob," he remarked to his operations officer who was standing OOD watch. He looked back over his shoulder to the flag on the *Bagley*'s mast. "I'll bet we come about thirty degrees to port for launch. What do you think?" It was always a mental game.

Collier, looking up at the flag, nodded his agreement. "Can't argue with that, Captain." And to his junior officer of the watch, he said, "What will our course to station be if the carrier turns about thirty degrees into the wind?" Both Collier and the captain knew within a few degrees, from their years of experience, but every junior officer had to develop these same instincts.

"Bridge . . . this is CIC," came a voice from a pilothouse speaker. "The last flight of trackers is returning to the carrier soon. We just picked it up over their tactical circuit. I expect they'll have another launch before they retrieve. That means they will reorient the screen anytime."

The JO, who had just gone to his maneuvering board to begin plotting the solution to their assumed station, looked out to Collier for a response. Instead, Carter turned to him from his chair. "Ask Combat what the course to our new station will be." He paused for a moment, then winked at Collier. "And ask him how long it will take to get there, Mr. Stritzler."

"Aye, aye, sir," responded the JO, turning to relay the captain's query.

"Keeping them on their toes today, sir," Collier said, not expecting his captain to respond. Carter was the finest CO in the squadron for training junior officers, and he never let up on them. It was especially important now when they were in wartime conditions, standing watch on and watch off, Blue/Gold Teams as Carter called them. All stations were manned, including the depth-charge racks, hedgehog mounts, torpedo tubes, and gun mounts. The men were allowed to stand easy on these hot days—their captain was reasonable about comfort, as long as they were ready.

After a moment, "How do I know which direction the wind is from?" came back from the CIC watch officer.

Carter moved from the comfort of his chair into the pilothouse and switched on the speaker to CIC. "You have a wind indicator in Combat that is in working order unless Mr. Mezey has been gundecking the equipment reports again. I would suggest that you use that and a maneuvering board, if there happens to be one available," he added sarcastically. "And bring your solution out to me on the starboard wing within the next sixty seconds. I would hope the OTC has not already given us the signal by then." He switched off the speaker, knowing that that particular ensign would never make the same mistake twice.

Over the water came the distant roar of piston engines

warming up, preceded visually by the puffs of exhaust smoke, which quickly disappeared over the Caribbean. The anticipated signal from the officer in tactical command came over the primary tactical frequency and, after a reasonable period of time to avoid error, it was executed. *Lake Champlain* required only a change of course into the wind and increase of speed in preparation for the launch, but the little destroyers in her eight-ship screen had to scurry at top speed in a variety of directions to get to their new stations.

Collier allowed his JO to conn the ship into its new position. He knew the excitement within each new ensign when he had the chance to show his captain how he could place the ship exactly where the admiral on that carrier required it to be. Carter nodded to the young officer, acknowledging without words the smooth execution of a complicated ship's movement done well.

After watching the launch of the new flight of trackers, and the return of the previous twelve from their search for Russian submarines, Carter spoke to Collier. "I'm going below to my cabin for a while, Bob. Gonna catch up on a bit of paperwork. I may even take a nap." He looked at his watch, noting there were only twenty minutes left in the current Gold Team watch. "When Donovan relieves you, have him call me if those trackers pick up anything new on those oil traces they found this morning. I wouldn't be surprised if they had something there. The last intelligence reports indicated there were at least two subs in the immediate area, and sooner or later we're going to find one of them."

"Aye, aye, sir," Collier replied, saluting as Carter left the bridge.

Approximately forty miles from the ships of Task Group Alpha, Lieutenant Alexander Kupinsky, skipper of a Russian *Foxtrot*-class submarine, was listening expressionlessly to his chief engineer's casualty report. It had been a week of malfunctions since they had last taken on fuel and supplies from the cow that serviced them on their Caribbean station. Bearings, batteries, condensers, electronic gear—each had failed during the week that had started so peacefully and ended with alarm when they received the signal that war was imminent with the United States. There had been no further explanation, but the prearranged signal indicated that one more signal would mean that Kupinsky was to open the instructions in his safe. He had told his crew as much as he knew, but it was difficult to know what was happening when you were so far from home and so close to your enemy's coast.

There was a leak in one of the pumps. Oil had escaped into the bilges, but no one had realized the extent of damage at first. When it became necessary to pump the already over-flowing bilges, the oil had likely gone to the surface. They all knew of the search planes from the American carrier. They heard the sonobuoys dropped in the water and activated, waiting for them. They had seen the aircraft through the periscope, and they had picked up the tracker's radar many times on their electronic countermeasures (ECM) equipment.

Now there was a telltale noise in one of the shafts, a bearing, the chief had said. He didn't know when it might go, but he recommended surfacing at night. They would have to stop to make the repairs before the sub became a major engineering casualty. Kupinsky didn't think that he would have that luxury. The Americans were everywhere. Half the time when he should have been snorkeling to recharge his batteries, he was diving to avoid those planes. They were invariably in the air, and he honestly didn't know why. But he knew that this was no Cold War game. That signal indicated that the games would soon be over, and he knew his boat must be ready.

Yes, he agreed with his chief, he would try to surface at the end of the day. He must snorkel for a while in case they were driven under again, and then he would stop engines if he could for the repairs. But they must be ready to dive at any time, he insisted.

The Gold Team was relieved by Joe Donovan's Blue Team

for the first dog watch, before the evening meal. The late afternoon sun was still high in the sky at that latitude, and Donovan made his customary tour of the ship, leaving his experienced JO on the bridge. His last stop was combat, where he passed the time of day for just a moment with David Charles, the CIC watch officer.

It was quiet back on the bridge. A light breeze was cooling the day ever so slightly and the gray metal of the *Bagley* was releasing some of its heat as the sun's rays lessened their effect. The ever-present flying fish offered the only entertainment for the men on the bridge, who quietly shifted their stations every fifteen minutes to avoid the mounting boredom.

"Bridge . . ." cracked Ensign Charles' voice from Combat, "I've just copied a snorkel sighting to the OTC from Tracker Four. We have the aircraft on radar twenty-six miles on our starboard beam. We're in the best position to head there right now."

"Roger, Combat, wait one." In three strides, Donovan was at the phone to Carter's cabin, punching the buzzer repeatedly. To the captain's answer on the other end, he replied excitedly, "Tracker aircraft had a snorkel, sir. Ensign Charles was following it in Combat. Datum for last known position twenty-six miles on our starboard beam."

"Call Banker on the pritac frequency, Joe. Tell him we already have datum plotted and request permission to be released to conduct a search. We should be senior on this side of the screen. I'll be right up."

In less than thirty seconds Sam Carter was coming through the rear door of the pilothouse, buttoning the shirt still hanging out of his unzipped pants. There was no need to ask if the Admiral had responded yet. "Banker has rogered your message, sir. They probably have to call down to the Admiral's cabin. No other ships have responded yet."

Carter stepped to the speaker and pressed the button to CIC. "Mr. Charles, this is the captain. What course to datum please?"

The reply came without hesitation. "We want two eight

six degrees true, sir. The distance to contact is now twenty-five point six miles. It would take us about forty-eight minutes at thirty-two knots, sir.''

"Thanks, David." He turned to Donovan. "Have main control light off superheat. I want flank speed as fast as they can. Go on down and join your boys." He briefly checked the current course and speed. "I'll relieve you, Joe." And to the bridge watch, "I have the conn."

The hum on the primary tactical radio speaker preceded the voice by a split second. "Lucky Strike, this is Banker. You are detached to proceed to datum. Assume command of surface and air units upon arrival. Over."

As the JO acknowledged the transmission, Carter turned to the men at the helm and engine order telegraph. "Right standard rudder. All engines ahead flank. Indicate revolutions for thirty-two knots. Main control cannot answer you immediately until they have superheat. I will speak to Mr. Donovan as soon as he arrives in main control." To the JO, who was hesitantly standing to the side watching the bridge come to life, he said, "Sound general quarters, Mr. Sylvester. Tell me when all stations are manned and ready."

The ensign moved to the speaker on the bulkhead at the back of the pilothouse, depressed the switch, and announced, probably for the first time since he had reported aboard the *Bagley,* "General quarters, general quarters . . . all hands man your battle stations . . ." At the same time, he pulled down the handle that sent the alarm clanging through every space on the ship.

To the helmsman who had relayed that his rudder was right, the captain replied, "Come to course two eight six degrees true." The *Bagley* was leaning sharply to starboard as her rudders bit into the blue water. Foam bubbled around the fantail as the propellers increased their revolutions. Men, just awakened from sleep, raced from their compartments to their GQ stations, some carrying their clothes.

"My course is two eight six degrees true."

"Very well," answered Carter as the bridge-talker began to report stations manned and ready. Bob Collier came through the pilothouse door rubbing his eyes, to assume GQ OOD. The bridge watch was relieved one at a time by the special GQ team. Carter briefed his OOD quickly.

"This is Mr. Collier. I have the conn." The new men shouted back the course and speed.

David Charles relieved as JO. He checked off the remaining GQ stations as they reported over the sound-powered headphones he had donned.

Forty seconds had passed, and all reports were to the bridge except for the damage-control people, who were still checking all watertight hatches. Donovan reported from main control that superheat was rising. Thirty-two knots could be achieved within twelve minutes, and damage-control central reported ready.

Bagley was at general quarters. Carter nodded at David Charles. "I owe you a very large drink the next time we're in port, David. We were the first can to report datum on that contact. We're OTC for a four-ship search." He grinned. "You made me look awfully good out here. All we have to do now is come up with that sub," he added thoughtfully.

Twenty-four miles dead ahead of *Bagley,* Alex Kupinsky had leveled his boat off at 150 feet after their crash dive. He hadn't expected a bomb or torpedo in the water, but he didn't really know what to expect. Only in exercises in the Baltic had he ever witnessed through his periscope the fearsome sight of an aircraft diving at his boat. It was bad for the nerves at any time.

Not knowing how long the aircraft had tracked him, he changed course and speed immediately, hoping for evasion of whatever was to come. Sunset would come within a couple of hours, but he knew he did not have enough air for men or engines to stay under for the entire night. They were still leaking oil, and the bearing on one shaft was hot. He had called his men to general quarters, but neither he nor the crew knew what they could expect now. Perhaps it would be the high-speed whine of surface-ship propellers sent to hunt him down.

The squawk box echoed through the *Bagley*, "This is the captain speaking again. As I promised when I first told you about this Cuban quarantine, I will keep you informed of your ship's participation. I'm sure the rumors have circulated around the ship pretty fast in the last few minutes, so I want to make sure each of you knows what we're doing. We were sent out here to find Russian submarines, and it seems we may have one now. About fifteen minutes ago one of the tracker aircraft got a good look at a snorkel that we know doesn't belong in the area. We are OTC for a four-ship search commencing at the last point of contact. We'll be at datum in about thirty minutes to join a number of helicopters and trackers. This is an opportunity to make a major contribution to President Kennedy's challenge to the Russians. He is depending on each ship and each man.'' He paused for a moment for effect. "I want you to do your best. A lot of us have been together for almost eighteen months now, and I have a feeling we're going to show that *Bagley*'s not ready for the scrap heap yet.'' He stopped for another moment, then continued, "I want to assure you I will keep you up to date whenever I can.''

Four destroyers, each with a bone in its teeth, raced across the blue water in a ragged line abreast, two thousand yards from each other. The plan was to sweep over the sub's last position with the middle of their line. This gave Carter a mile and a half on either side of the datum, plus another mile and a half on the beam of the end ships if sonar conditions were accurate. The fringes of their sweep would be covered by helicopters just now flying by on their way to that invisible point in the ocean. Farther out, the fixed-wing aircraft had already established sonobuoy patterns in case the sub escaped the close-in search that Carter had ordered.

It was deceptively beautiful as the formation charged into a golden sun that was now settling quickly toward the flat horizon. They were too far from land for birds, and their departure had been fast enough to leave the ubiquitous garbage-hunting gulls with the remainder of the task force.

David Charles felt *Bagley* shuddering under his feet as the screws continued to increase their revolutions. Each motion of the ship was now magnified by its speed, and the helmsman had only to shift the wheel the slightest bit to feel his rudder respond. This was what destroyers were built for. The bridge was comfortable for the GQ team, even in their life jackets. The breeze sweeping across them was now close to thirty-two knots. But David knew from past experience the heat and the stench of the engineering spaces and the human smell of other groups sealed into their spaces until the captain ordered otherwise.

No air moved in CIC. Sweaty faces were outlined in eerie shades by the green reflection from the radar screens. Voices were quiet as each man strained to listen to the sonar pinging from the open compartment to the rear of their own—the sharp sound as the signal expanded from the sonar dome, and perhaps the anticipated response when contact was made.

Carter paced the bridge looking from David, reporting all-important items that came over his headphones, to the overhead speaker in the corner that Frank Welles would use only once when he reported the initial contact. But the speaker remained silent, and Carter had to be satisfied as David reported the distance to datum every thousand yards, and relayed the information from combat as Jerry Burchette resumed control of the aircraft already on station. Somehow, it didn't seem quite right; it was too similar to the exercises they participated in every month. The only real difference was the captain's pacing, which David thought very uncharacteristic of the man. The lookouts swept the ocean's surface on their 360-degree vigil, knowing that any smart submarine would be at least a hundred feet below their line of sight.

"Captain, CIC reports one of the trackers had sighted what they believe to be garbage off our port bow." All binoculars swept in that direction.

"Ask the pilot if he can identify anything it it," Carter requested.

David relayed this to Combat, waited for a moment, listened, spoke into the headset, listened again, and turned to

Carter with a grin. "Trojans, Captain! Pilot says he can identify them from any height."

There were just a few amused snickers, and then the bridge burst into laughter when Carter stopped his pacing to say, "Tell him it must be from *Bagley*. We passed through this area last night, and we're a very happy ship."

The ice was broken. The unknown for the last couple of days had been put in its place. Carter stopped pacing and moved over to his chair. The team was ready for a real target. Their captain had been put at ease by a pilot with a sense of humor.

A few moments later, David reported, "Passing over datum, sir. Combat recommends we begin a wider sweep to the northwest since the sub's last course seemed to be to the west. Mr. Bradick says the sub wouldn't keep the same course and he wouldn't reverse it. He may head toward the northwest hoping he can find some temperature gradients if he can get close to the Gulf Stream tonight.

Carter paused for a moment. "Okay. Tell Mr. Bradick to pick a course for us and have Mr. Welles recommend a speed that will maintain a good sonar range. I want to open the distance between the cans to three thousand yards. I also want to have helos dipping well ahead of us. Maybe their pinging will scare the son of a bitch right down our throats."

The four destroyers opened their formation, with *Bagley* the farthest ship to the southwest. The sun was about to touch the water's edge, preparing to evaporate in a cloud of steam. It would leave them with another two hours of light but without the blinding glare. The breeze was picking up from the south, not enough to raise whitecaps but enough to further the cooling that would gradually seep into the hidden metal recesses of the *Bagley*.

A bit less than five minutes had passed before the speaker over the captain's head erupted with Frank Welles's voice. "I have a solid contact bearing thirty degrees to port, approximately four thousand yards. No classification yet, but there's something more than a school of fish there."

There it was. Contact. Perhaps not the submarine they

were looking for, but whatever it was, it was close to where Bradick had anticipated.

Each man aboard the submarine heard the pinging of the *Bagley*'s sonar on the pressure hull. Even before they had been found, the approaching high-speed noises of the destroyer's screws were evident. In advance of that first ping, Kupinsky gave orders to change course 110 degrees, increased his boat's speed to its maximum, then took it down another 150 feet, hoping against hope for the miracle of a temperature gradient that would deflect *Bagley*'s sound beam.

Within moments, Welles classified the contact as a probable submarine, and he and Andy Bradick concurred on the submarine's course and speed at almost the same time. "Both sonar and Combat report the contact has turned almost due south, Captain. They have a port-quarter aspect . . . contact moving at eleven knots . . . he seemes to have picked up speed."

"David, ask Andy for a course to pass astern of the contact. Tell him my rudder is left . . . left standard rudder."

"Combat recommends two-zero-five at fourteen knots, sir."

"Come to course two-zero-five." Carter turned to his OOD. "Bob, I want you to set up a pinwheel around that boat with us as guide on the western edge. Add the others according to their current positions. When you're all set, I'll give the word to execute." To David, "Tell Mr. Welles that we will shortly be passing astern of his contact. When we're close, I want him to listen in the passive mode for just a minute. I want to try to classify screw noise if we can. Tell Combat to explain to all the aircraft in plain language what we're doing. As soon as we have a better classification, we'll assign them stations."

The contact did not maintain course and speed to satisfy Sam Carter, which was no great surprise since its movements seemed too well planned. Combat was tracking it step by step with a direct feed-in from sonar. As often as Frank Welles noted changes in the return echo, Andy Bradick had a new course for Carter. They had been a team for too long to be fooled by simple evasive tactics. Bob Collier was able to adjust his course and speed in tandem with the recommendations of the others As they passed astern of the contact, its propellers gave it away and a confirmed submarine was radioed back to Banker. Within a few moments the information would be encoded and sent to the Joint Chiefs of Staff, and they would interrupt Mr. Kennedy's hastily grabbed sandwich to inform him that the first Russian submarine was now being held down by units of Task Group Alpha . . . professionals in the art of sub hunting.

It was obvious to Carter that they had a diesel sub. A nuclear boat would already have raced away from the slower destroyers.

A pinwheel is an insidious scheme in the eyes of a submariner at two hundred and fifty feet. By intuition and a bit of listening, the ships above can be pinpointed, but their constant movement creates confusion. Just like a child's toy pinwheel, the ships move on the four compass points in a circular motion around their contact adjusting their position relative to each other as the sub changes its course and speed. And hovering on the outer perimeter, a couple of miles from the destroyers, were helicopters in a similar circle of their own with sonars lowered into the water below. The submarine that thought it had effected an escape from the ships would be doubly surprised to hear the familiar ping on its hull when no ship's noise was evident. And even farther off, fixed-wing aircraft were sewing lines on sonobuoys that bobbed inoffensively in the water. They relayed the movement from below to their parent aircraft, allowing cross fixes that gave the course and speed of their contact. The forces under Sam Carter's command were formidable, to say the least.

Darkness was beginning to replace the softness of dusk. "Captain," David reported, "the gunnery officer reports

that the men in the gun mounts are awfully hot and cramped
. . . request permission to open the hatches on the mounts
for a few minutes.''

"Permission granted. And ask damage control to wake up
the supply officer. I want coffee and sandwiches for the crew
before it's too dark out here . . . and have them bring some
milk, too, for some of the youngsters,'' he grinned.

The crew ate on station as best it could that evening, and
found some relief as watertight restrictions were lifted for a
few moments to receive the food that was passed in to them.
Darkness brought an increase in the force of the wind,
enough so that whitecaps would have been evident if it had
been light. A few times, Carter had sonar relay his request for
the sub to surface and identify itself according to international law. He was not surprised by the sub's silence, nor its
continuing efforts to evade his pinwheel.

Once again, Carter went to the ship's PA system. "This is
the Captain speaking again. As you've no doubt heard, we
are circling what we believe to be a Russian diesel submarine. Two of them were reported in the area in the last
couple of days. Neither of them was able to refuel from its
cow, since our carrier planes were escorting it. Our orders,
which have been relayed from Washington, are to stay with
the sub until it is on the surface. I do not expect anything
other than a peaceful surfacing. We are not at war, and God
forbid that we ever have to be. There will be no forceful acts
on our part unless we are provoked. Each of us is responsible
to Mr. Kennedy in his own way to ensure his orders are
carried out peacefully. If it becomes necessary, we will wrap
grenades in toilet paper, the same as we've done during
exercises with our own subs, to make our point. I don't
expect him to get away. As a matter of fact, I hope we'll be
steaming alongside him tomorrow morning, though I don't
think there will be time to exchange souvenirs.''

He was interrupted by David Charles. "Sub's dead in the
water, sir. Wait one . . . funny noises in sonar. Mr. Welles
believes he's increasing his depth. He may be trying to find a

temperature layer down there.''

"David, tell the gun boss to have some grenades brought down aft. The least we can do is make it uncomfortable for him.''

A few moments later, when David reported the grenades ready, Carter ordered. "Tell them to drop the first one in thirty seconds and then two more after counting to fiteeen each time, as we pass over him. And make sure Welles knows when we're dropping them. I don't need an ASW officer or sonarmen with punctured eardrums.'' He turned to Collier, "Tell the other units over pritac what we're doing. I don't want to have some other CO trying to deck me in the "O'' Club the next time.''

The noise of an underwater explosion is compounded since water tends to hold that sound, as opposed to air, which rapidly dissipates it. A grenade going off underwater may sound like a cannon shot to those nearby. Within a submarine, the explosion is magnified to the point that an untrained crew, or one with little experience, will think they have just been hit. The purpose of the toilet paper is to ensure that the sub's crew is kept as nervous as possible. The paper will gradually disintegrate as the grenade floats down until the handle releases, still taking a bit more time before detonation. A light wrapping of paper will bring an explosion at about 100 feet, while a gunner's mate with experience can wrap the grenade so that it might go down as far as 250 to 300 feet, or more. The deeper the water, the greater the pressure, the louder the bang . . . all that effect for the price of a grenade! Welles estimated the sub to be at about 300 feet, and the grenade was wrapped by an expert.

It was extremely humid in the cramped submarine. The water temperature outside was cool enough so that heat wasn't the problem. But the combination of humidity caused by the always leaking water, and the increasing closeness of the air, made comfort of any kind impossible. Alex Kupinsky had no concern about his crew cracking under the strain. They were all hand-picked, as was he, and they offered no complaints. The most difficult problem for all of them was the fact that they didn't know yet what had brought about the apparent conflict with the United States, nor were they sure of the intentions of the American destroyers. The unknown was their greatest enemy.

The chief engineer had just reported that the fuel pump was acting up again, and that the air supply was good for a little more than five hours. And the bearing on the shaft was heating up again. He could not guarantee to his captain that it would last the night. If it reached a certain temperature, then they would have to shut down the shaft or risk it warping at 300 feet. Each of those problems were considered separately by Kupinsky. The fuel pump could be a problem later. He would try to keep his speed down except for a couple of rapid changes, especially if he could find a temperature gradient. The air supply was his major concern. While they could stay down for another five hours, the greatest problem was that the men's efficiency would decrease at a certain point, and then he might just as well surface. Since he was the only one aboard the boat with any knowledge of English, he understood the Americans on the underwater telephone saying they would hold him down until he had no choice but to surface. Then the grenades, which were indeed expertly wrapped, began to explode at the same depth as his boat. It was the worst of times to be facing the unknown.

"Tell Frank to request them to surface again. They've had time to think about those grenades now," Carter nodded to David. The whitecaps had now grown into waves that were large enough to make the many course changes uncomfortable. One advantage, David knew, that a submarine had was the smooth weather underneath, but he decided he'd rather be on the surface at this point.

There was no answer to the grenades, nor to any of the repeated requests to surface. The night drew on and the men grew tired. They had been at their stations since before 1800, and it was now almost midnight. Six hours . . . any response would have raised their spirits, but it is difficult to perform consistently when there is no evidence that your efforts are having any effect.

"It's tough for them down there now," Carter began to nobody in particular. "It stinks in that sub, a lot worse than in CIC or main control. The air has been breathed by too many people too often, and it doesn't taste good at all. And I understand from submariners I've known that you get a headache after a while, a throbbing one that doesn't go away." He knew everything he was saying would be relayed by the various talkers on the bridge to the other stations. "And can you imagine what it's like when those grenades go off? Which reminds me, David. Have them drop five more this time. Same precautions as usual." After he was satisfied that his orders were being carried out, he continued, "I don't mind telling you . . . the noise those things make when you're inside one of those boats . . . No, sir, friends have told me when they came back to Pearl from a mission that half the stink in the boat was the shit in their skivvies." He went on and what he was saying passed through the ship, and he knew that shortly the men on the *Bagley* would stop worrying about themselves. They would respect their enemy's position.

The men on the other ships were just as itchy. Carter noted that the signalmen were talking more often with their lights. Once or twice, the other CO's mentioned the possibility of using stronger methods to convince the sub to surface. The captain of *Bartlett* had even suggested that he would be happy to roll one or two depth charges. He hastened to add that, of course, he would ensure that the depth and location would be far enough away so that there was no danger of damaging the enemy. Carter thought to himself how easy it was for the hunter to always consider a weapon larger than he needed.

Frank Welles had picked up an occasional screeching sound on his sonar, which he finally identified as submarine machinery rather than playful porpoises. The other ships heard it, too, and all agreed that their quarry was experiencing some mechanical problems. He'll try a few more tricks and then surface, Carter thought. He won't do anything rash unless he's provoked.

"Pinwheel Leader, Pinwheel Leader." The voice was urgent over the primary frequency. "This is Backfire. Un- identified device in the water bearing two eight five my position." It was *Bartlett* again. "Initial identification . . . torpedo," the voice bellowed. "Taking evasive action."

Before Carter could question sonar, the speaker over his head, the one that was used only for contact reports, answered, "We copied that transmission, Captain. It may be a noisemaker." Carter ordered a turn toward the object.

After another fifteen seconds, Welles's voice came again, "Recommend emergency . . . negative! Forget that . . . We've got a noisemaker definitely, repeat definite noisemaker . . . He's just turned again, and he's picking up speed. That's his decoy." There was a pause for a moment while Welles kept the key down on the speaker. "And what a wail in his machinery, Captain. He's got problems." After another moment's hesitation he added, "Oh, sorry, Captain. I forgot the speaker was right over your head." A click, then silence.

But *Bartlett* was not satisfied. "Pinwheel, this is Backfire. Contact precipitated action first. I am preparing for a torpedo attack. We have a firing solution based on their new course and speed after torpedo release."

"That stupid son of a bitch!" Carter grabbed for the mike himself. "This is Pinwheel Leader. Break off all attacks. I repeat . . . break off all attacks. Device is identified as a noisemaker. Acknowledge, over."

"Like hell it is," *Bartlett'*s CO came back. "We know what a goddamn torpedo sounds like. We're no sitting ducks."

"This is Pinwheel Leader. I say again, break off attack. I am running down the bearing of the device in the water now. I will pass over it in ten seconds. It is not a torpedo . . . repeat, not a torpedo. All ships prepare to reform pinwheel. Contact has just broken through our circle."

And at that moment, David was repeating the words as

they came over his headset; ''Combat reports submarine has broken toward the west. Sonar reports lost contact . . . he's in the baffles. Mr. Burchette is moving the helos into position now. Mr. Welles thinks he may have gone deeper, but says he has to be close to his maximum depth now.''

As the ships scurried back over the black, tossing water to reestablish their stations, Carter murmured, ''He's smart. He knew he couldn't outrun us, so when his chances were down he used the trick he'd saved for last. Mitchum would have loved that.'' He turned to David, ''Ask if the helos are in position yet.''

''Captain,'' asked Bob Collier, ''Did you really feel that was a noisemaker when you gave that first order to the helm?''

''No, Bob, I really didn't know for sure. But put yourself in that sub's position. None of us want to start war, except maybe *Bartlett*. That boat down there is in serious trouble. If he was to attack, which we don't believe he's authorized to do, he knows he'd get sunk. It's likely his orders are just to keep from getting caught on our turf, and you know as well as I do that he was due to try anything to get away. He's tried every evasive maneuver he knows, but he didn't once try a noisemaker. I've been waiting all night for one, but he was smart enough to wait until we were all tired. What I really had to do was show *Bartlett* that we were sure it wasn't a torpedo. People will do crazy things and what I wasn't sure of is whether *Bartlett* might not just have fired that torpedo if we weren't in the way.''

''Helos have contact, sir,'' David reported. ''Combat says he's about twenty-six hundred yards off the starboard bow heading away from us at nine knots.''

''Okay, Bob, I think we'll have him in a while. Take us in there and calm down the pinwheel. It won't be long now.'' Carter got down from his chair and stepped out onto the bridge wing nearby, staring into the dark waves, then up at the stars.

''David, have Mr. Welles tell the sub that we know he has an engineering casualty. Tell him we will make room for him to surface safely, that we don't intend to harm his boat in any way . . . tell him we stand ready to render any assistance he may require . . . and tell him to speak slowly and repeat it. I know someone down there has to understand English.''

There was no answer to Welles's carefully stated plea, but the elapsed time and the screeching sound that was occasionally picked up over the sonar told them that the sub's time was limited.

At 0122 on the morning of October 24 the first confirmation of human life below the surface was heard by the four ships. In barely discernible words, sometimes breaking off completely, they were told that the sub intended to come to the surface.

"Tell him we will stand away for safety," replied Carter. "Request that he fire a flare to mark his location before surfacing, and we will then give him clearance to surface."

The destroyers rapidly expanded their circle until there was no doubt that the boat would know there was room. A flare appeared toward the middle of their circle, flickered briefly in the wind, then rose straight up to mark the position of the sub.

"Tell him all clear," Carter's voice rang out happily. "As soon as CIC has the first mark on him, I want an immediate course and speed. We'll adjust to where he wants to go." As an afterthought, he added, "Make sure we have the fire-control radar locked on him. I'll want mount fifty-one to fire illumination."

Frank Welles reported sounds of the sub surfacing at almost the same moment Combat reported radar contact. *Bagley* gradually moved in to take station five hundred yards on the port beam of the sub. It could not be seen clearly from the bridge. A black submarine on a dark night at sea is outlined only by the phosphorous from the waves breaking against its sail.

"Gunnery reports mount fifty-one loaded and ready for illumination."

"Very well, David." He turned to Collier, "Have the

signalmen ask the sub if they require assistance. When they say no, have them explain in whatever international signal language there is that we're going to illuminate, that there are no shells in the guns. I don't want them pulling the plug!''

Signal lamps flashed back and forth for a moment. Then, after a brief period, flashing began again, followed by even more flashing.

''Captain, we don't seem to be able to explain about the illuminating shells.''

''Oh, for Christ's sake! David, ask if any of those aircraft have flares they can drop without scaring the pee out of that boat.'' What a hell of a note, he thought. We've just spent seven and a half hours committing the power of the U.S. Atlantic Fleet to chasing that sub around the ocean, and we can't find a light!

''The trackers each have ten flares, sir . . . forty-five seconds duration. They'll commence their own runs in one minute to try to keep everything lit up for the time being. If their timing happens to be off and the lights go out for a moment, their CO says he apologizes in advance, and it won't happen again. And he also sends his congratulations for a great job.''

''Have Jerry roger that and tell them we couldn't have done it without Navy air.'' He stepped out on the wing to stare into the darkness where his prey was supposed to be. *Bagley* was rolling heavily on its present course, and he had to hold on to the railing. The lookout next to him was straining through his binoculars for a glimpse of the sub. ''Don't think you'll see him for a few minutes, son. We've got to wait for the airdales to light him up.'' He looked more closely at the sailor, who was probably no more than eighteen or nineteen years old. ''How long have you been standing this watch?''

''I've been here since general quarters, Captain, except for being relieved from time to time.''

''Were you worried?''

''No, sir. We all know that we're safe here. No one ever expected that you wouldn't get that sub, Captain.'' Realizing that he had taken his glasses from his eyes, he quickly began scanning wherever the horizon might have been. "What are you going to do to him now, sir?"

"Nothing, son. It's already been done." He turned to move back to his chair, then thought better of it. "You all did a good job, son . . . a great job. You be sure to tell that to everybody on your circuit." Then he moved back to his chair.

"Illumination in about thirty seconds," David reported.

"Start to take her into about two hundred yards, Bob. I want to get a good look at our friend."

The illumination began sporadically, with the flares going out a couple of times just as the bridge personnel were getting their eyes adjusted. As the light became steady, Collier brought *Bagley* close in. It did not look at all like they expected their elusive quarry to look. Instead, they saw a black hulk, indistinguishable from any other submarine they had seen tied alongside the piers in Norfolk. It wallowed in the heavy seas, as helpless as any other machine that has been built for the depths. Somehow, it didn't look like an enemy should have looked. It seemed neither dangerous nor frightening.

"Captain, the carrier is sending out aircraft to begin taking pictures for identification. They should be here in about twenty minutes."

The ultimate humiliation, thought Carter. "David, come on over here. I want you to see something. Take a good long look at that submarine, then remember he may be your real enemy someday. He looks pathetic there with the waves breaking around his sail, doesn't he? After all he's been through, he's probably got men barfing their guts out in this heavy sea.

"We won today, so to speak, but don't ever forget that he's lost not only to us but back home, too. They'll probably send him to the salt mines, wherever they are, because now we can prove that Russian subs are patrolling the Caribbean to back up all those missiles in Cuba. But, even more important, they'll be punishing the wrong man. He did the best he could without his cow or a base to return to for repairs. He drove us six ways to Sunday and back again, and did more than I would have thought possible with that thing he's riding. And then, to top it all off, he had the audacity to try to escape when he should have given in . . . and he almost got away with it.'' Carter looked over his shoulder to where the other ships were steaming nearby.

"He could have gotten sunk for his troubles if that nut on *Bartlett* hadn't been just a bit unsure of himself, enough so that he called me before he fired.'' He pointed at the sub, where two figures could be seen guiding their craft as best they could. "David, you're going to be a fine officer some-day, and I want you to remember this night. That captain set an example we should never forget. And I'll bet he's no more than eight or nine years older than you. They really didn't start building that class until a few years ago, and then they had to go out and train a new set of officers to drive them. I'll bet he's only a lieutenant, or whatever they call them in Russia, and I'll say he's not more than thirty. How old are you, David?''

"Twenty-three, Captain, almost twenty-four,'' he grinned.

"See what I mean. Maybe he's only six or seven years older than you. He's accomplished a lot in his short life, and I sure hope they're not too rough on him.''

Soon the planes came from the carriers for the next step, picture-taking. The Navy was taking no chances on the sub diving before dawn to avoid photos. They dropped longer-lasting flares from higher altitudes, and when they came in low for their pictures, they used flashes that lit the air like daytime. As well as anyone could see from the *Bagley*, the two men on the sub's bridge never looked up once. General quarters was secured shortly after, and the Gold Team relieved to complete the watch. David Charles stopped for a moment on the main deck to look over at his enemy outlined against the artificial lights, and saw only a black, dented hull that still looked strangely like every other sub in Norfolk.

The watch had been relieved for breakfast. The crew was now completely awake, ready for another tedious day after the excitement of the previous night. The ship's PA system clicked on. "This is the Captain speaking again. First, my sincere, personal thanks for the contribution each of you made. You made *Bagley* a ship of war to reckon with again, years after a lot of people would have junked her. Ships are important, but the Navy can never replace the men who sail them.

"Of course, I have received a message from the Admiral that I will have distributed in each compartment. But even more important is the message that was handed to me a few minutes ago. It's addressed to *Bagley, Bartlett, Payne,* and *Kerns,* and the helos and fixed-wing squadrons that worked with us. It is from our Commander in Chief, Mr. Kennedy, and says, 'My congratulations to all units of Task Force Alpha and especially those of you who participated in the surfacing of the Russian Foxtrot submarine on the nights of October twenty-three and twenty-four. Though I personally reviewed your units with admiration last year, I can now truly say you have served your country more than your loved ones at home will know for some time to come. And today, I say with pride I was a sailor, too.'

"I want each of you to hear that now," Carter added. "This operation is classified, and you will be unable to relate your accomplishments to anyone when we finally return home. But, we can all have confidence in our ship and our Navy in the future, for we will have that sailor at the helm of our country for many years to come." There was a long moment of silence throughout the ship after Carter switched off the PA and returned to the open bridge.

FROM THE LOG OF
ADMIRAL DAVID CHARLES

CAPTAIN CARTER told me yesterday that I'd make a fine officer some day. Coming from him, that's the finest compliment I guess I'll ever hear. I've been watching him pretty closely, trying to learn how he commands a ship. Now I'm beginning to think it just comes naturally and you have to be like that from the beginning. Maybe if he feels I can be a good officer, I'll be able to command like he does.

I'm pretty sure that last night the United States came about as close to a major war as it has for a long time. Even Sam Carter was scared, enough so that he was ready to take some chances to keep it from happening. The captain of the *Bartlett* must be some kind of nut or else the Navy's making some big mistakes with some of its CO's. The man really wanted to fire torpedoes at the Russian submarine. I don't think he was really concerned about what would have happened on a national scale. He just wanted to kill a sub, maybe to show someone how tough he was. But Sam Carter talked him out of it and used our ship to do it. It was taking a big chance, but I know today that the odds were worth it. Captain Carter's making me an expert in hindsight, but maybe that's the way you train ensigns.

Last night was also a good lesson in seapower. That was something they pounded into our heads for four years, and maybe you have to see it to understand it. If that's true, it's too bad they didn't have all the politicians around to watch it, too. The captain was right in telling me to look at that sub closely. It was black, dented, slippery like ours, and pretty damn lonely out there by itself being forced to wallow in a sea it really wasn't built to ride on top of. The sub was supposed to be in the Caribbean for a reason, to protect their shipping to the Cuban bases, I imagine. It was a projection of seapower by the Russians, but they sent that sorry son of a bitch halfway around the world almost by himself. He had no access to food or fuel or ammunition unless he either went into Cuba, where they really aren't equipped to help submarines, or else used those cows they send over to service their boats. But Carter was right again. I went up to the radio shack and looked at the fleet scheds, and every one of their cows is being escorted by a destroyer, sometimes even by a couple in case a submarine tries to show up at a meeting place on the ocean.

So that poor submarine was helpless. He couldn't project the power they'd sent him here for because the Russians just aren't ready to do that yet. I think that if they were going to the trouble of bringing missiles all the way over here, they should either have been able to protect them or else made up their mind to fire them if we challenged. It doesn't make any sense to do something like this halfway and then be made a fool of. Now I know why we spent so much time reading Mahan and some of those other military strategists. What he had to say seems to be ageless, as long as we keep the size of the world and the new weapons in mind. Someone's still got to be in charge.

Captain Carter got me to thinking about the CO of that sub, too. He really probably isn't a hell of a lot older than me, and I imagine he's going to be in a lot of hot water when he gets back. The Russians are pretty tough when someone makes a fool out of them, although Captain Carter's right. That captain wasn't really a fool. He tried almost everything he could to get away, and he almost made it once or twice. Carter said that anyone that can keep all those destroyers and aircraft so busy for most of a night must be pretty damn smart. And that sub was sick. Frank Welles said the sounds coming out of that sonar were something else, and that if our engineering plant sounded like that, Carter'd have Donovan living in the reduction gears until he figured out what was wrong. But a sub that's being chased has a pretty rough time finding spare parts or getting to the surface for air so the crew can even breathe.

I hope the Russians don't send that sub captain to the salt mines, or whatever they do to them there. I wish there was some way we could meet him and find out what really happened. I learned a lot yesterday, but getting the other guy's side must be a good way to learn, too.

DEAR DAVID,

I can't tell you how thrilled we were to receive your recent letter and at last get some word of where you are. The letter took almost three weeks to get here and, of course, everything has quieted down where you are now. When everything suddenly happened, the worst thing was not knowing where you were. We knew you had gone down to the Caribbean for those exercises, from your letter early in October, and we had expected to hear from you when the *Bagley* returned.

You can't imagine the shock when President Kennedy announced on television about the Russian missiles in Cuba and how the Bavy was already in position to set up a blockade. You know we have never experienced anything like this since the Korean War (you were only twelve then), but the real fear was that it was happening in our own backyard. And when we think of blockades, your father said there hasn't been anything like that in this country since the Civil War. The whole country really lived in a state of terror for three days before we were a little more sure that there would be no missiles fired or bombs dropped. And we can all imagine what Mr. Kennedy must have been going through.

Since you have been at sea all this time and probably haven't seen a paper, I'm enclosing some clippings you all might like to see of what it was like back here. One of the most frightening things to us here is seeing the pictures from down south where the marines and paratroops are walking around the streets in fatigues and battle dress. Apparently they didn't have time to pack before they were flown down south to be in position. Again, we just haven't seen anything like that in this country for so long.

Another clipping that I hope you'll especially like is one that your father wrote that's going to appear in the local paper after Thanksgiving. It's about the meaning of Christmas, and they asked some of the local business leaders to write what they thought was most important after we were so close to war. I'll tell you the parts I like the best:

Most of us . . . take for granted the air we breathe, the water we drink, the friends we cherish, the delightful countryside we live in. It is only when we are faced with the specter, however tenuous, of our separation from such things or their very loss that the realization is brought home to us that many other items heretofore high on our list of "wishes" are really quite inconsequential. And so it may be with what, we fervently hope, may be referred to by the time this appears in print as "the recent Cuban Incident." If it has served to remind us that material assets, however desirable in normal life, are as nothing when weighed against those that really matter, it will not have happened in vain. If it has prompted us to give thanks that the blessings of peace are still ours, it will not have been without profit. And if it has brought home to us anew that there are those principles we hold so tightly that we are willing to exchange even the priceless boon of peace for them—because without them there can be no peace—then it will have served some constructive purpose.

He goes on to say some nice things about Christmas and fellowship and the things you'd normally expect to read about at Christmas, but I thought you might understand better how everyone at home felt while you boys were out there. Knowing where you are and what you're doing, I guess, would have made us all feel a lot better.

We have sent you a separate package with the sports section out of the Sunday *New York Times,* as you asked in your letter, and we'll send anything else you need if you'll let us know. Perhaps this will all be over soon and you can be here at Christmas. As soon as you get into port anywhere, please call us, and make it a collect call. We want very much to hear from you.

We do hope the *Bagley* has been far away from any trouble and that you haven't been involved in anything dangerous. Again, please call collect as soon as you can.

Love from all of us,

Mom

CHAPTER
SEVEN

"You're not really going to write yourself orders to go there?" It was a question asked with a tone of incredulity, backed by a facial expression of absolute disbelief.

"You bet your ass I am."

"Hell, David, you won't have one left to bet. Some little yellow man in black pajamas is going to blow it off for you." The speaker was a young, happy-looking lieutenant with a brush cut, about David's age, looking freshly pressed in his tropical whites. But he also looked somewhat undressed to many of his companions. He lacked the colorful chest ribbons displayed by the many returning Vietnam vets.

"Well, they didn't last time, and they're not going to have any better chances this time either. Look outside," he gestured toward the windows that looked out on the crowded streets. "Saigon can't be any hotter than Washington this time of year. And I'd much rather be cruising on one of those Swift boats than commuting to Virginia in that damned traffic." His friend gazed back at him uncomprehendingly.

"I'll tell you what," David Charles continued, "I'll cut some orders for you right now. We can go over together, be in the same squadron together. Think of the extra combat skins, the leaves in Bangkok, Taipei, Hong Kong, Sydney," he waved his arm toward the other. "You're just going to waste away here chasing secretaries and drinking too much and wishing you could have some excitement. You can't say no.''

''No.'' It was emphatic.

''Okay. It's your choice. Right here,'' he pointed at some papers on his desk, ''right here, I've picked out my billet. XO of a riverboat squadron. I know the CO from my last tour, and we had a great time there. As a matter of fact, that's who convinced me to go. Old Phil Mezey called me a few weeks ago, 'cause he remembered I'd gotten orders to Bupers, and asked if I could fix him up with a riverboat squadron. When I found one and called him back, that's when he asked me if I'd like to be his XO. Boy, was he happy to be going back over.''

''Who the hell is this other crazy man?''

''He was one of the officers-in-charge with me during my last tour in the PT boat squadron. Nastys they were called. We bought them from the Norwegians. Phil and I used to race them up and down the coast after these junks that used to smuggle weapons, people, anything they could get their hands on.''

''And you really want to go back?'' The other officer, Dan Mundy, leaned back in his chair, hands behind his head, the same quizzical look of disbelief in his eyes. ''You lifers are all the same. You don't know how to relax.'' Then he looked over at David more seriously. ''You know, things are a hell of a lot different than when you first went over there. That was 1965 when everyone wanted to get there before the war was over. Remember, you had to go get a little combat under your belt if you were going to stay in. Now, you know, there's more people getting killed in a week than got killed in six months when you were there.''

''That's the chance you got to take if you're going to make CNO in this man's navy,'' David grinned. ''You would have loved it if you'd been on those Nastys. Damn,'' he emphasized, ''we could wind those things up to forty-five knots. Just skip over the surface. Get up a little sea, and you could just about leap all eighty-five tons of them out of the water at full speed if you hit a swell right. We figured those little yellow people used to fill their pants seeing us coming in at them. Of course, that was part of the idea, according to our squadron commander. Psychological warfare, he called it. He said it would scare them enough so that we'd control those waters and cut off all the arms shipments from up north.''

''And did it?''

''Nope. Not really.'' He folded his arms. ''You know we caught an awful lot of them. But I think even more of them got through, 'cause we never heard of gooks running out of ammunition. Those little mothers were always well armed, and they knew how to use those things. It makes me awful glad I'm not a marine,'' he finished.

''Jesus Christ. That's just what I'm saying, David. That's a real war over there. You seem to think it's just another firefight. Do you realize you'll have to go back through combat training again for six weeks, just like a goddamn marine. Because that's what you're going to get into. Didn't you see in that ALNAV the other day that they're going to name one of those new *Knox*-class frigates after some lieutenant who got himself killed in those riverboats? Do you want to have your mother break a bottle of champagne over the bow of the one they name after you?'' As an afterthought, he said, ''I'd much rather drink it if it's all the same to you.''

David's face became more serious. ''I know you're right, Dan. But I think I really belong there. And like you said, I'm a lifer. This is my career, and I don't want anything else. I'm still single. And I guess there's really a hell of a lot I've got to learn over there.'' He thought for a moment back to the days when he and Phil were racing their PT boats up and down the coast, burning diesel fuel like it was water. Christ, he thought, we figured we were just like the cavalry charging in there to break up all those Indians. And that's just the way it is, he said to himself. Not so long ago we were chasing the Indians, and now we're chasing the gooks out of their own country.

''I guess you're right, Dan. I wouldn't want you to go with us. You could get hurt, and there's probably no reason for you to take the chance.'' He stretched and smiled. ''But I don't have much choice, even if I didn't want to go. Hell,'' he grinned again, ''that's why I conned myself into this cushy detailing job—so I could write my own orders! Do you know what I mean?''

The other man was suddenly more serious too. ''Yeah, I suppose so. That's why the hell I want to get out after this tour. I extended to get to D.C. And I want to make sure none of this rubs off on me before I get out. You guys are so serious sometimes, I feel like I ought to see a shrink and find out why I don't care to duck bullets. Then I remember. I went to a normal college, a civilian one—not the Baltimore Boat and Barge Company.''

''Wrong town,'' David said, amused. ''You mean Annapolis, not Baltimore.''

''Like hell I do. I mean Baltimore. In my last wardroom we decided Baltimore was the shittiest place any of us ever saw, and we decided anyone who went through four years of that shit you did must have thought they were in Baltimore. Hey, I shit you not. I was just over there to see a chick a couple of weeks ago, and it was so bad, I thought I'd taken a wrong turn into the Academy.'' He stopped. ''Hey, David, what am I into this for? You are writing those orders, aren't you?'' He looked at the papers on the desk.

''Right here.'' David waved some papers at him. ''But first I'm going to give myself a week back home, and then three weeks of sin in San Francisco. Followed by those six weeks with the marines, and then off to dear old Saigon in time to help them celebrate their New Year, and in sixteen months I'll be back here with a chest full of fruit salad. And by then, I will have gotten another stripe and be Lieutenant Commander Charles, and our esteemed boss, Captain Kehs, will have written me orders to go out to Monterey, and you take it from there, my friend.''

''Okay, my friend. If that's the way you want it. I will look forward to the day when we can sip martinis and celebrate your still being alive.'' He paused and thought for a minute.

"Did you say you're going to be there in time for their New Year—parties and all that stuff?"

"Yup. They call it Tet."

Mundy had been right. Thank God he's not here. I can just see that "I'm always right" look of his, thought David, looking at the water and mud. It wasn't a normal rain compared to what anyone back in the States would call normal. It was a cloudburst, with the exception that it had been raining just as hard since the previous night.

And Mundy had been even more right about another thing. He had received all that marine training because that's what they were doing—acting like marines! The main effort since they'd been there was to protect their added squadrons of Swift boats and river-patrol boats by building a fortress around the base. They laid minefields around the perimeter, dug trenches, built fortifications, went on patrols to cleanse the area, and on and on and on. And when they weren't doing that, they were cleaning weapons and practicing maneuvers in the river. But they were definitely not going out on missions, at least not the type that David had dreamed they would. Their weapons were rifles, grenades, .50-caliber machine guns, mortars—just like marines.

And the worst part was that they looked like marines, right down to the fatigues, flak jackets, and helmets. The sailors in the squadron looked like marines with hair, and he suspected some of them were even beginning to act that way.

Nothing had been like he expected. Their welcome was already in progress when they managed to land at Ton Son Hut shortly after the Tet Offensive began, the New Year's party that had amused Mundy. As they came in low for their approach, he could see sections of Saigon burning. The only information they had was the pilot's comment over the speaker that there was fighting near the airport and there was a possibility they might come under fire on their final leg of the approach, but he hadn't seemed concerned. He was probably a marine, too, David thought.

The moment the door to their plane opened, he knew they had arrived at the war. There was the smell of smoke in the air, and artillery explosions in the distance. Closer to the airport, they could hear small-arms fire, occasional shots for a few seconds, followed by rapid fire from a number of weapons. Well, he said to himself, I cut my own orders, so there's no one to blame but myself.

Inside the main building in the reception area it had been business as usual. Military and civilian personnel, both American and Vietnamese, went about their business seemingly unaware of what was going on outside. His processing was similar to landing at Kennedy after a European vacation, slow, methodical, disinterested—no one cared that Lieutenant David Charles had returned once again, this time as second in command of a riverine squadron.

There was no time for sightseeing. They were expected to report immediately to the base camp on the Mekong, where their headquarters were located. As David learned later, the Navy planned reliefs very tightly and there were two officers very much looking forward to their arrival. When one was that short in Vietnam, after twelve months of surviving, they wanted to be relieved immediately, if not sooner, and turn-over of command required a day or two of familiarization.

Once the Navy agreed that they really were who they said they were, a helicopter took them to their base camp, north and west of Saigon, well up the Mekong toward Cambodia. They flew over lush, green tropical forests, perfectly laid-out rice paddies that sometimes extended for miles and little clearings that signified villages. This was the part he had rarely seen during his last tour. Previously he had been on the ocean, always returning to the coast, but rarely inland unless they had a few days off. And, then, they usually went no farther than downtown Saigon. Now, he realized, he would see the real Vietnam.

But up until now, he'd seen very little of the country. He had spent his time assisting Lieutenant Commander Mezey in setting up the camp as he wanted it run, which was one eighty out from the way the previous officer had set it up. The new

CO figured that the Vietcong would know almost immediately that new management had come in and they would try a few night attacks to see how they were doing. Mezey simply didn't want his defenses set up the same way, since he assumed the Communists had probably memorized them. The second night after they relieved, the attack came. He had been right.

First came the mortars. Those were always the first warning of an attack. There was no noise until the first shell landed within the compound. Then all hell broke loose. Mortars from half a dozen different sites came roaring in, followed by the flares to illuminate the compound. Then, accompanied by the chatter of small-arms fire, the VC came running up the free paths between the mines they had previously charted. And the thing that saved the compound from much damage that night was that Mezey had made sure the first change was the location of the mines. Half a dozen mines were tripped, cutting through the attackers and stopping the second wave in mid-charge. Mezey, unfortunately, had been in the latrine at the time of the attack, and one of the early mortar rounds had landed nearby, close enough to jam the door. He began to rock the wooden structure to attract attention to his plight. Finally, it tipped over on top of its door. He later pointed out, to David's amusement, that the mortar shell had cleaned him out for at least a week, but it was a hard way to solve a problem. The attack was over as fast as it had begun. There were few casualties to the defenders and part of their luck, as Mezey had commented, was that they acted just like marines.

Each day they made a point of changing the defenses. It was just enough so the VC knew there were safer places to attack, and within a couple of weeks they decided they had a secure base. In the meantime, while the weather still held, they spent hour after hour learning their boats and running through exercises, until they finally passed the boring stage and became automatic.

Now he was staring out through the screening around their tent, watching the cloudburst that wouldn't stop. The monsoons had begun, and the dust turned to mud in no time. The only saving grace here was that even though they acted like marines, they really weren't. And he wouldn't change places with those poor bastards sitting in muddy trenches or slogging through inches of mud on another of their incessant patrols.

The rains continued, and with them the tedium. VC movements were limited, and the Americans were just as happy to spend more of their time patrolling the river and searching native craft for weapons, or anything else that might be smuggled.

Their PBR riverboats added little to personal comfort, since they were essentially open to the rain. They were developed for high-speed combat in shallow waters. They had fiberglass-reinforced plastic hulls and ceramic armor, and carried a 60-mm. mortar, a grenade launcher, and three .50-caliber machine guns. When they were traveling in excess of twenty-five knots, they were impressive to any VC they happened to be chasing, but they provided little protection from the elements, not to mention enemy fire. If David managed to board a boat dry, he found himself wet before they were away from dockside.

He and Mezey generally rode one of these open PBR's. On occasion they went in one of the Swift boats, which were even faster and had enclosed cabins. But more of the latter were being turned over to the South Vietnamese Navy, and the Americans took what they were allowed. So far, it was not the type of tour he thought he had written orders for.

"I think maybe we've got what we've been looking for, David." It was Phil Mezey's voice calling over the water, just returning from a conference downriver.

"Anything could be better than what we've been doing so far," David answered. He had been supervising ammunition storage, and had found himself wondering why the hell the Navy was bothering to send them ammunition. David stepped in front of the sailor waiting for the line from Mezey's boat. He caught it easily as it snaked through the air, and looped it around the forward cleat. As the boat swung its stern in David took that line also.

"Right here. I think the answer's right here." Mezey swung off the ugly little PBR onto the dock, waving a sheaf of papers. "There's some heavy troop concentrations up toward the border, and the Big Z thinks maybe they're building up for an offensive north of Saigon. Believe it or not, he thinks the best way to search for them is from the river. He's warned the generals that if they start sending reconnaissance aircraft and ground patrols in, all they're going to do is convince the VC to stay low until they're good and ready. And Washington can't stand any more surprises."

"And he picked us?"

"Well, not really. I kind of volunteered our services. I explained that we hadn't lost any boats. Our squadron was full and in excellent condition, and we knew that territory near the border like the back of our hand."

"Shit," David laughed, "we're in such damn good shape because we haven't seen any action. We haven't even scraped any paint. And, Christ, Phil, we haven't been within twenty miles of the border. That's a maze up there."

"You're right each time, David, my boy, but there has to be a first time for everything. We saddle up at first light tomorrow." He slapped David on the rump. "Come on, we have a bit of organizing to do," he said gleefully. "And by the way, they're even loaning us a little fire support, our very own ASPB, the battleship of the Mekong," he laughed, "to do whatever we want with it, as long as we return it in the same shape as we get it." They were slower, heavily armed boats used for fire support for other small craft, such as the PBR's, and they wallowed along looking very much like the Civil War *Monitor*.

A very hot sun hung high in the afternoon sky. There was almost no breeze in the stifling air, and the helmets and flak jackets were increasingly uncomfortable. The group moved at the speed of the slowest craft, the heavily armed ASPB. Two Swift boats patrolled ahead. They were looking for any sign of the ambushes that the VC favored when they knew the riverboats were on the prowl.

The thick green jungle was set off by the brown water of the river, which moved ever so slowly toward the rich delta, far to the southeast of their little group. The river was a bit narrower upstream, though it would sometimes just as surprisingly open up as they came around a bend. Smaller rivers entered the main stream from under the dense vegetation. But, as some of them had learned in the past, these little rivers were sometimes just estuaries that went back a short distance and ended abruptly with a wire stretched across to stop unwary boats.

They were now in unfamiliar territory, and David spent much of his time memorizing passing landmarks. This would help a good deal if they found themselves going the other way at high speed. If trouble occurred ahead, they would just have to take their chances.

David had just lifted his binoculars to his eyes to scan the jungle forward and to his left when the river erupted. The sound of the actual explosion came after the mine had detonated. A nearby PBR was lifting into the air. Water was hurled up around the craft, but he could still see the bow separate as it began its descent, almost in slow motion. The .50-caliber in the bow and the sailor manning it went in another direction. The other members of the crew were not to be seen as the remains of the boat settled back to the brown water.

It must have been shallow there to cause so much upward force, he thought. The boat he was riding immediately cut out of the formation to close the wreckage. "Scatter," came the order from Mezey over the radio, almost at the same time that the boats were independently changing their courses and speeds to confuse enemy gunners. The most important thing was to be one step ahead of the VC, who were likely ready to set off the next mine.

"We have two of the crew, Phil," David called over the radio.

"Don't hang around. There's more than one of those mines in the water if the VC have been doing their homework." And at his last word, another was set off just ahead of one of the forward PBR's, not quite close enough to damage the craft severely. Water cascaded down on the little craft as the wheel was thrown over by a frightened sailor. "Look out for each other," called Mezey instantly on the radio as a boat almost collided with the one that had just missed being sunk.

Another mine exploded, this time twenty yards behind David's boat. Mezey called for speed and the small craft lifted their bows perceptibly as the General Motors geared diesel engines forced the waterjet-powered boats through the water. Another explosion, no mine this time, went off near his boat. David was at the radio instantly, "Mortars," he shouted, "from the starboard bank, I think."

The water came alive with exploding mortar rounds. The air was also filled with machine-gun and rifle fire, all of it from starboard. The boats now were on their own. As they came under fire, each helmsman followed his own nose, paying attention only to where the other boats were. The gunners poured their fire in the direction of the enemy, at the same time trying to avoid hitting each other.

"I'm heading five hundred yards upriver with half the squadron," Mezey called. "You take the others down, and we'll try to get them in a pincer. Get that battleship here as fast as you can. They've got some heavy stuff in there. We're catching bazooka fire." And he began ticking off the numbers of the boats that would stay with him. David didn't need to say anything to his own group. They all heard the order and their numbers at the same time, and they would pick their own way back around the bend.

As they rounded the corner below the ambush area, the ASPB was moving toward them as fast as it could. David gave the hand signal that would turn his boats back. They roared back upriver again at full speed, resuming fire as they came into range of the jungle hideout. Mezey was doing the same from the opposite direction.

They sped into even heavier fire this time, obviously from a large group on shore. They had not seen a human being yet, and had no idea whether or not their return fire was effective.

Now that both groups of the squadron had taken the time to settle down, their guns were concentrated into one narrow section of the jungle. The battleship now began to fire its 20-mm. shells into the undergrowth at a rapid rate, cutting out trees where the .50-calibers on the small boats had only been chopping down limbs.

And as suddenly as it started, the water around them was free from explosions and bullets. How long they had been firing with no return they didn't know. "Cease fire, cease fire," came Mezey's voice over the radio. He called out the numbers of two of the boats. "David, you and the rest cover us while we go in to check them out. That seemed to be a company-sized attack with all those weapons. They can't get away that fast."

David watched the shoreline until half a dozen men from the three craft had disappeared into the undergrowth. When he surveyed the group of boats, only one other was inoperable. It had taken a mortar round that had slowed it long enough for a second one to finish it off. The PBR was floating on the other side of the river, smoking, the holes in it gradually filling with water. Many of the other boats, including his own, showed the effects of multiple small-arms fire, but they were all effective. Casualties, with the exceptions of the two sunken craft, were relatively light.

It wasn't long before Mezey returned to his boat, moving it out in the water next to David's. "You wouldn't believe it if you saw it. Christ, we chopped up everything in an area the size of a football field and there's not a body in there. We found some blood, so there must have been some hits, but there wasn't a soul there—just vanished." He shook his head, "Everything we've heard about them is true. Hit and run. Hit and run. The little buggers sure know how to scare the hell out of a man, though." He paused for a moment, a finger to his lips. "What's that?" He cupped his ear and turned his head slightly.

David shook his head. He didn't know what to listen for.

"Listen." There were some muted sounds, engines. It

was coming from upriver. "That sounds like diesels." He listened again. The sounds were no louder, but it seemed there were more engines. "Son of a bitch! I'll bet they've got boats up there. They were just sent down to see how many we were and scare us away at the same time." He nodded at David. "Let's go. They must have had something bigger to hide if they wanted to chase us away that bad."

It was a loose formation, at best, that moved cautiously up the river. Mezey had probably been almost upon them when he feinted upriver before turning back for his attack. There had been a couple of sharp jogs in the river's course at that point. They could have been either farther on or under camouflage at the edge of the bank, but they were certainly gone now. The air was as still as it had been all day, but just a touch of diesel smell lingered.

They had no idea how many boats there were, or how well they were armed. They did not want to fall into another ambush, no matter how little time the VC would have to set it up. So, Mezey had them move at about the same fifteen-knot speed as the *Monitor*-style battleship. Not a word was said over the radio between the boats. Mezey had called into his headquarters to report VC contact and asked for aircraft on standby in case they caught up to anything worthwhile.

David Charles had spread his charts out on the deck of his boat. He noted they were getting closer to the border, the no-man's area that they weren't supposed to cross. Too often, it served as a hiding place for their enemy. Less than ten miles ahead was Cambodia. He also noted the river would widen in less than a mile, a good place to fight the VC if they could catch them.

Their enemy had the same idea. They were greeted by two native-style boats as they rounded a bend and entered the wide shallow section of the river. They were shallow craft, motorized vessels moving at a slow pace as if on the way to market. But at approximately two hundred yards, after each had fired initial mortar rounds, their sterns settled back in the water and their engines opened up to full speed. They came directly at the Americans, still firing the mortars inaccurately, but pouring streams of machine-gun fire into the nearest boat.

As the wheel of his own PBR was thrown over, David briefly saw more of the craft going away from them. This attack was intended to slow them just long enough to make good the escape of the main VC force.

The VC boats actually came up to and passed the lead boats in the squadron, raking them with small arms, their machine guns maintaining fire directly into the PBR's. Only the closest boat could return the fire, for the ones in back were afraid of hitting their friends. Now, the forward PBR's began to concentrate their own .50-calibers. Both of the attackers were zigzagging as best they could, their fire limited to tail gunners as they passed the rear PBR's.

One of them slowed, obviously damaged by the machine-gun fire from half a dozen American boats. At this point the lumbering battleship picked it up with the 20-mm. shells, and the craft began to splinter before their eyes. Smoke lifted from its stern as it lurched sideways, presenting a perfect target. Then flames began to spread across the decks. Its remaining crew leaped over the side through the still intense machine-gun fire, hoping to reach the safety of the shore. Then the guns of both the battleship and the PBR's concentrated on the other. It also had begun to slow down. As the 20-mm. shells again found their mark, a thunderous explosion rocked the river, tearing the VC craft apart, flinging large chunks through the air. When the water settled, nothing remained to indicate that a boat had been there just seconds before.

This second time the squadron wasn't as lucky. The inability to concentrate their fire until the VC were far enough from friendly craft had taken a toll. Two of the boats were rapidly taking on water and two others had been seriously damaged. Personnel casualties required the squadron to bunch up for a moment.

As he came close to Mezey's badly damaged boat, he saw his friend stretched out on the stern, two of his crew hovering over him. David brought his own boat close enough to jump onto the other.

Mezey looked up at him, face contorted with pain. "Damn it, David, they've done just what we didn't want. The main body's heading for the border, and we're licking our wounds." David knelt beside him as a corpsman from another craft bandaged both wounded legs. "Take half a dozen boats in the best shape and enough men to handle some extra weapons and go after those mothers. They've got something they're hiding to pull a stunt like that."

"Right," David responded, without questioning the orders. "Are you sure you're going to be all right on the way back?" he queried.

"Yeah. I'd love to go, but you're going to have enough problems without a goddamn cripple on your hands. I'll go back with the damaged boats." He looked at his ragged fleet, the one he had so willingly volunteered only the day before. "Keep the rest a mile or two behind you, along with the battleship. You may need them if you run into any more of this shit." He grinned up at David. "Remember, this is what you cut those orders for. Get your ass in gear and get out of here."

It took only minutes to sort out the six least-damaged boats and exchange enough of the weapons and men to make them a more formidable force than they had been previously.

They moved out at high speed, each one cranked up to maximize the twenty-five knots they were designed for. This time David had little opportunity to study his charts or memorize the landmarks for a return trip. Each boat was on its own until they discovered their quarry. The first item in his plans involved calling headquarters. He asked directly for the Task Force Commander for their region.

"This is Victory Garden One," the Rear Admiral answered after a short delay. "Go ahead. Over."

"This is Bugle Boy." He wasted no words. "Have encountered heavy riverine resistance near the border. Two attacks. Bugle Boy One is returning with damaged craft. XO now in command. Two craft sunk. Two badly damaged. Half a dozen in poor condition. Eenemy escaping over water toward border. I believe they are covering for a large force, possibly the heavy troop concentration we were sent out to look for. I am closing with six well-armed PBR's. We have a secondary force of damaged boats and the ASPB is a rear guard. Request airborne assistance. Over.''

"Roger, Bugle Boy. What is your estimated range from the border? Over.''

"Estimate three to five miles. We are moving at flank speed, and it's hard to tell our exact location. Over.''

"This is Victory Garden. Roger your location. We believe the troop concentration may be close to your present location. Do you require the aircraft for your own protection? Over.''

"This is Bugle Boy. Negative. We believe there is a larger force ahead because of the nature of their attacks. If they lead us into it, the airdales can take it from there. Over.''

"This is Victory Garden. We are scrambling Phantoms for you now. Call sign Playboy. Time on station twenty minutes. They will contact you on this channel. However, do not cross the border. Repeat, do not cross the border. We will monitor this channel. Over.''

"This is Bugle Boy. Roger and thank you. Out.''

They were rounding a bend of the river in a ragged formation when the water in front of them belched upward. The lead boat was not with them when they appeared on the other side of the wall of water. It had likely been on top of one of the mines and had simply disappeared. Ahead were the VC, the ones who had detonated the mines strung across the river, and this time they were waiting for the Americans.

As the PBR's came through the wall of water, the VC opened fire from both the boats and the shore. David's boats answered, this time with the increased firepower he had acquired from the other boats. The Communist craft, realizing they were offering too easy a target near the shore, moved out into the river. But it was too late for two of them. Both bazooka and .50-caliber fire ripped into them. They began to smoke.

There was no place for the PBR's to seek cover. The smaller VC boats were moving across the river. "Take them head to head," David shouted to his boats over the radio, and the little PBR's maintained their twenty-five-knot speed right into the middle of the enemy.

At this point, David realized that the fire from the shoreline had been heavier than from the boats. They must have been off-loading troops, probably the ones that had ambushed them downriver. The fire from shore could not keep up with the speeding boats, and was minimal once David's PBR's were among the enemy. The VC craft were not as fast or as maneuverable as the PBR's. The latter boats had the advantage of speed and firepower as they swept by. Reversing their direction, they made a second run on the VC boats, only two of which now showed much fight. The others were aimlessly floating in the middle of the river, abandoned by their crews. One of the remainder took two bazooka hits simultaneously, drifting toward the shore. With all the fire now concentrated on the remaining boat, it was literally lifted out of the water.

David's five remaining boats had been raked continuously by small-arms fire but none of the heavier weapons from shore had touched them. With only superficial damage, they were still fully operable, and he turned his attention to the sporadic fire from shore. They're going to disappear again, he thought. He picked up the mike, calling to his meager force, "I'm going in to shore to see where they're off to now. Number four boat come with me. The rest of you cruise offshore, covering us. You're going to see a bunch of Phantoms coming in low soon, and that's when we can all relax."

They beached their craft right where the VC boats had pulled out from the shoreline to stop them. It was just like Mezey had said about his previous trip ashore that day. Not a soul remained. Spent shell casings gave evidence of weapons having been fired. There had obviously been many people there at one time, yet they had disappeared as if by magic.

Then, on the opposite side of the huge clearing they had entered, he saw the vehicle tracks, many of them. Since there were few roads through the jungle, the VC used trucks and other large vehicles only when they were carrying heavy equipment. The docking area they had landed at indicated it was well used, probably to land men and supplies. This must be the staging area the generals and admirals had been hoping for. He heard the roar of the jet planes at the same time the first call came over the radio, "Bugle Boy, Bugle Boy, this is Playboy. Do you read me. Over."

"This is Bugle Boy. Welcome. Over."

"This is Playboy. Request your coordinates. Over."

David studied the chart he pulled from his pocket. He found it hard to convince himself that they weren't already in Cambodia. "This is Bugle Boy. You are passing directly over me now. Can you see anything to the west of this location. Over."

There was silence on the circuit for a moment as the five Phantoms swooped low over the jungle not too far from where the staging area existed. "Wow! I have trucks, artillery, and many troops in sight. Bugle Boy, what are your coordinates? It looks to us like we've got a problem. They're in another country, my friend. Over."

"Playboy, Playboy, you are cutting out on this circuit. Switch to channel seventeen. Out." And the circuit was suddenly dead. He had to take the chance. He knew that headquarters would be listening on that circuit, or at least they could hear the talking from the Phantoms' end.

He had the coordinates he wanted as he attempted to regain contact with the Phantom squadron leader. "Playboy, this is Bugle Boy. How do you read me now? Over."

"This is Playboy. You're loud and clear. You can bet that Victory Garden is going to be unhappy about not being in on this conversation. They want to make sure we were playing by the rules. Over."

"Roger, Playboy. I understand. I have our location now." And he had bought the time to give them the coordinates that would have placed them about three miles to the east. Now, he didn't care if Victory Garden had also switched to channel 17. "You're safe to make your runs, now. And give it to them good. They tore apart our squadron, and we'd like them to know how it feels. Over."

"Roger, Bugle Boy. We are commencing our first run now. And I also think you're lost, but I never saw such a great target. We were told to follow your orders. We thank you for your assistance. Out."

They could see nothing through the jungle that surrounded them, but as they returned to their boats they could hear the multiple explosions well above the roar of the mighty jet engines. As the five boats slowly pulled out onto the brown water they were greeted with an earthshaking explosion in the distance. It was followed by billowing clouds of black smoke, then continuous, thundering explosions.

After the Phantoms had made the last of many runs at the unseen target, and were climbing for their return home, the same voice came back on channel 17 again, "Bugle Boy, this is Playboy. We thank you. That goes down in the books as one of our best targets. That lovely cloud of smoke you see probably represents both a fuel and an ammo dump. They were up to something big. Hope you see it when our film is developed. Have a safe trip home. Out."

The court of inquiry was said to be an informal one, but David noticed there were more stars than he had seen in one room in Vietnam for a long time. The reason for the announced informality was to make sure none of the correspondents appeared. The less they knew about the purpose of the inquiry, the better for all involved as far as the Navy was concerned.

The films taken from the Phantoms had shown not only the largest staging area they had come upon in a long time, but they also confirmed the fact that it was in Cambodia. The inquiry was to determine how such an error could have been made. It centered on Lieutenant David Charles, who had called for the air strike after inflicting heavy casualties on what apparently had been an effective water route for one of the largest VC forces in the area. The five petty officers in charge of David's remaining boats each indicated that their acting commanding officer had checked his charts earlier but had no time afterward to pinpoint his location because of severe enemy fire. As a matter of fact, they stated, only by his taking the enemy under fire at full speed and sinking the remainder of their riverine force, had they been able to pinpoint the location of the VC forces that were finally destroyed.

The findings of the court of inquiry were not made public. However, for the sake of form, the court found Lieutenant Charles guilty of negligence in going over the border. On the other hand, they recommended only an official reprimand be placed in his service record since his personal efforts were responsible for destroying an exceptionally large enemy force. They further decided among themselves that the Admiral also ensure that a commendation be placed in his service jacket for individual initiative. They felt that they could not award him a medal since that could become public acknowledgement. Lieutenant Commander Mezey received the Silver Star, the five petty officers each were awarded the Navy Cross, their crews the Navy and Marine Corps medal, and the entire squadron received a unit citation. The final recommendation was that Lieutenant Charles be transferred back to the States. They intended to make it as difficult as possible for the press to learn about his special day in Vietnam.

Lieutenant Charles was sent to Treasure Island on temporary duty to await orders to his next billet. Upon arriving in San Francisco, he got in touch with his old friend at Bupers and asked if they could arrange to send him to Monterey to Russian language school. Ken Kehs was glad to cooperate, especially since the stories had already reached Washington. The senior officers were more than happy to have the young man in Monterey, a quiet, out-of-the-way place where he would be far away from the cocktail circuit stories of his Cambodian escapade.

Captain Kehs was also happy to inform him that a special board had recommended him for lieutenant commander, an early promotion.

At his wetting-down party at the Officers Club, he also met Maria Springer, whose husband had never returned to his carrier from a mission over Hanoi. The other pilots in his Phantom squadron reported that a missile had sheared off his left wing. No parachute had been seen. He was declared officially dead, and Maria had said to herself that she would never again go out with a military man. But the Navy takes care of its own, and her friends had stayed close to her. They wanted her to get out and socialize.

She hadn't intended to go to anyone's wetting-down party, especially with the noise coming from that lounge. But one of the people in her group had been a classmate of David's and insisted they should join the party. Before they had gone in, the friend had told everyone of the rumors that were preceding the young man. The next thing she knew she was being introduced to the officer who had supposedly performed the daring feats. She wanted to hear nothing of Vietnam and found that he had nothing to say about it.

She assumed he must be quite drunk at his own party, and she made a point of not smiling. The new Lieutenant Commander Charles was having a good time, but he was not too drunk to look twice at the pretty girl he was introduced to. She was quite tall for a woman, probably only two inches shorter than he was, but he reasoned that he was fairly short for a man. Her figure was obviously full, even with the conservative clothes she still chose to wear, and her high cheekbones and green eyes were set off by long dark hair.

David decided she would be even more attractive when she smiled. Having had enough to drink to remember old jokes that could be told in front of women, he finally made her laugh and found that he was absolutely right. Her green eyes sparkled when she decided he wasn't so bad after all, and crinkled around the edges, staying that way even after she had stopped laughing. She accepted the drink she had at first refused. She also found his conversation interesting, even when she realized he had adeptly sidestepped her polite questions about him and had her talking about her own Midwestern background. Maria stayed until the party broke up and then accepted a ride home.

David Charles called her the next day and asked her to dinner, and that was the beginning of her new life. In less than a month, even before he was scheduled to arrive in Monterey, he had asked her to marry him. After arguments with herself about propriety and another Navy husband, she agreed, and the Navy allowed him to take an extra few days for a honeymoon. They had both begun a new life that neither had been looking for.

FROM THE LOG OF
ADMIRAL DAVID CHARLES

I THINK I know exactly when I decided that my life would be the Navy. It was when we realized those bastards were hiding over the border and using Cambodia as a staging area for killing Americans. I never thought much of the war one way or the other and kind of thought that we were wasting our time in Vietnam, but as long as there was an American being shot at, I always thought we ought to stand up for ourselves. When I decided to send those planes in, I made a commitment to myself to stay in the service. Perhaps I decided there has to be someone around to make up their mind when American servicemen are being killed. I have no doubt our government is going to get me and a lot of others in the same position again, and I want to be sure someone like me is going to be there to protect the troops. That sure looks a bit foolish on paper, but I had to get it down so I'd know why when I start asking myself what the hell I'm doing in the Navy six months or six years or sixteen years from now.

If I had the guts, I'd fly back to Washington right now to talk this over with Sam Carter. But he might say I'm wrong, and I'm not ready for that yet. He is a strong believer in maintaining the separation between the civilian and the military, regardless of the way the politicians keep committing lives without giving the poor grunt the opportunity of all the protection the country has to offer. There's a question of objectivity there that Sam and I could argue about, but perhaps all my ideas aren't ready to be punctured quite yet.

I won't make myself available for any combat assignments again for a long time. Not only was Mundy right about taking such chances, but now that I have Maria, there is suddenly more to live for than I ever imagined. And she's taught me so much, beyond just how to love. Perhaps it was some of the things she's said to me that made me come to the decision I mentioned above. She told how she stood out on the rocks near the Cliff House the day *Enterprise* left for Vietnam. She watched the ship pass under the Golden Gate, her deck empty except for the plane-guard helicopters. Then she heard, before she actually saw, the Phantoms passing low overhead, only moments after their takeoff from Alameda. They swept ahead of their carrier in formation, then circled as *Enterprise* turned into the wind to take the air group aboard. She thought one of them had tipped its wings, as he always said he would whenever they went to sea, but she was never sure. She told me how hard she cried, so hard she couldn't drive home for more than an hour afterward. Somehow, she knew he wouldn't come back.

What hurt her the most after he was shot down was his attitude, that he always felt he'd get through, that it would be the other guy who wouldn't bail out. I think that's why I've changed my attitude about my own survival. The other reason is simply that she wouldn't agree to marry me at first if I stayed in the Navy, and then she relented when Sam promised her he'd always be looking over my orders to make sure I stayed out of trouble. I think perhaps the fact that the Navy made it quite clear that they wanted me to keep a low profile for quite a while helped change her mind. Now, I have a responsibility other than myself.

The other thing that Sam and I did discuss again before he went back to Washington was his old concept of power. Since that first time he talked about it, I've done a lot of reading and a lot of thinking. Use of power and abuse of power are hard to differentiate sometimes. And power doesn't always have to come from sheer might. The VC proved that to me. Power can be ninety percent in your head, and I suppose that goes right back again to the German General Staff. The VC used their heads to take advantage of their land and our American egos. When that happens, you can create the biggest bang in the world, but you're not going to impress anyone other than yourself if the enemy is simply waiting for the smoke to clear so they can get back to the business at hand. That's what they always did, whether they were slipping into camp on a hit and run, disappearing during the day, or hiding on the other side of the border. And they made more use of American stupidity than anything else. The concept that you allow your enemy to shoot at you and then let them cross an imaginary line where you don't go after them is the dumbest idea any civilian ever thought up, and I think even Sam agrees with that. The politicians constantly let us beat ourselves. Clausewitz spent a lot of time writing about that, so I guess that proves wars don't change much in a hundred years, even if the weapons do.

I need this time at school. Monterey is a lovely place. I'm married and happier than I've ever been before. I have time now to learn more about myself and maybe grow up a little bit. No more of the American warrior for a while. I'd much rather be a professional military man in the intellectual sense. Perhaps if there are enough of us, we can keep the civilians away from wars. Maybe what bothered me more than anything else over there was that while I was practicing being good at my job, a lot of people were dying to satisfy politicians' egos and academics' theories.

CHAPTER
EIGHT

THE sailor on the small flight deck raised his arms to signify over the noise that all was clear. A helicopter lifted slowly from the deck, rotors cutting the air with a whistling sound to compete with the roar of the engines as *California* moved away from under it. Then, obviously clear, it hurtled rapidly upward before swinging out and away from the ship. Already another of the choppers had appeared, hovering behind the ship, waiting its turn to land and retrieve more of David Charles's staff for their transfer to *Nimitz*.

Inside the cabin of the first helicopter it was much quieter, enough so that the occupants could hear themselves talk.

"When we're about halfway there, have him take her up to five thousand feet," said David. "I'd like to take a look at the others." He was referring to the additional ships that had joined *Nimitz* and her escorts moving northward after her feint toward South Africa. Knowing that the Russians followed each move of the U.S. carriers, he had sent *Nimitz* on a supposed visit to Capetown as soon as he had been made aware of the situation surrounding Islas Piedras. He hadn't actually expected Gorenko to believe he would permanently shift his flag to a cruiser and send his airpower off to spread goodwill at a time like that, but he wanted to keep them guessing. The Russians were almost paranoid about American movements that did not fit into their way of doing things.

"Approaching five thousand, sir," came the voice from the pilot's cabin.

"Hover," he casually said as he leaned to look below him. "Or slow circle . . . or whatever the hell he wants to do, as long as I see the whole damn force," he added.

Below, the Indian Ocean stretched out before him in a blue, shimmering expanse in whatever direction he looked. It was broken only by the sun's reflection on the whitecaps that twinkled back at him incessantly—and the outlines of the mighty ships cutting through the water. To the west was *Nimitz,* the mightiest warship afloat, tremendous even from that altitude. Scattered in every direction were the smaller cruisers, destroyers and frigates, each scurrying for a point around the carrier now that the two forces were joining. The Admiral for whom the carrier was named would never have dreamed that a formation could actually exist when each of the ships was at such a great distance from the others. His great task forces of the forties were composed of many more ships, but they never had to fear an atomic attack.

Further to the west and south were the service forces, ready to provision those non-nuclear-powered ships that would require fuel or perhaps even munitions if it became necessary to use weapons. And even farther away to the west, off the east-African coast, were the amphibious ships with their marines going through the exercise that had been so carefully planned the previous year. It had been announced the year before to assuage the fears of the other nations that Islas Piedras might be the reason for the Marines' presence. Only the attack submarines were not in view.

They circled for a few more moments as he counted the ships again, checking over in his mind what his flag lieutenant always had on his clipboard—the description of each ship. He noted that Frank Welles, *Nimitz'* CO, had placed the Aegis-equipped defensive vessels ahead of their line of movement, reserving the smaller frigates for whatever might be required later. Then he noticed the bigger ships reversing their course. He finally pointed down with his thumb, nodding that he was ready to land. The moment he was there the joyride would be over. He would go inside the great ship to an aritificial world of darkness, air conditioning, red light, and no visible change in time. There would be no day or night unless he allowed himself to stroll for a few moments on the flight deck or kibitz on the bridge between flight operations.

They set down near the carrier's island, by the aft elevator. Even before the rotors had stopped, six sailors in dress whites scurried out from the main hatch and positioned themselves at attention at the foot of the helicopter's steps, three on either side. At the same time, Frank Welles, in freshly pressed tropical whites, also came across the flight deck, accompanied by his executive officer and department heads.

Frank Welles would greet David with all the respect due a flag officer from a junior officer. The sea was in his blood and, since his divorce, had become his life. Once senior to David Charles, they had first met on the *Bagley*, and David had remained as close a friend as Welles ever had or probably ever allowed. His talent was immense, and his devotion to duty was almost devout. But his one limitation seemed to be working closely with other people. While he got along well enough with the enlisted men, he would never have the leadership qualities of Admiral Charles, that special something that cannot be taught. It was for that reason that David had been jumped over his peers since his days in Vietnam. Yet it was that devotion to duty that allowed Frank Welles to accept the situation, and keep his minor failings within himself. Welles's appearance, as usual, was exemplary. He radiated confidence in his uniform. His sharp features and slightly graying temples beneath the gold-encrusted visor presented a leader of uncertain age in command.

Admiral David Charles's right hand snapped a salute to the flag, as the sailors in the quickly prepared honor guard piped him aboard. His hand dropped partway from his visor before returning again to acknowledge the welcoming salute from Welles. As Charles was about to greet them, the ship's speaker echoed, "Task Force Fifty-eight arriving."

Noting quickly over his shoulder that the Admiral's pennant had been hoisted, Welles extended his hand. "Welcome aboard, Admiral. We're sure happy to have you back with us." His smile was warm, though his eyes were as expressionless as David remembered them. Welles was as professional a naval officer as there was, but his personality was still hidden, David noted. He had been aboard *Bagley* for two years when David reported to that first ship, fresh from Annapolis. Now, David Charles was not only senior to him, but the Task Force Commander.

"Thank you, Frank. It's good to stretch our legs again after life in those little fellows." *California* was half the length of the carrier, but to them the escorts would always be referred to that way. "And thanks for piping me aboard. It's nice to hear the 'Task Force Fifty-eight' associated with his name again." When David had received his orders, he had immediately contacted Sam Carter in Washington, asking if they could carry that designation aboard the great carrier named after the Pacific Fleet Commander. It had been approved not only to honor Fleet Admiral Nimitz, but to cause that much more confusion for the Russians, who wanted a reason for every odd American move.

Welles stepped quietly to David's side as he finished shaking hands with the other senior officers. "We have a report of a flight of Backfires heading this way from Mogadishu. They've been in the air for about an hour already. I've taken the liberty of reorienting the Aegis ships to the west, though it'll be better if we change course that way also."

"No, Frank, let's not give Kupinsky that advantage right now. You've already done the right thing. We'll let the aircraft come right up from the rear. We can still tell exactly what they're going to do." He turned just before entering the superstructure to look at some fighters near the stern, their pilots watching him from their cockpits. "Have you scrambled any Tomcats yet?"

"No, sir. Been waiting for you."

"Send 'em out. Have them keep their distance until they

receive orders from us." He waved to the pilots, then turned to his operations officer. "Bill, get on up to flag plot and set GQ for the force. You can get on the pipe and tell them what's happening. I'll be up in a few minutes."

David Charles's office, next to flag plot, was large and comfortable, as it should have been for an admiral of his position. He and Bill Dailey were seated at a typically green-felt-covered table, scattered with papers. His steward had just brought them iced tea, and David leaned back in his chair. "So Alex is farther away than I would have thought."

"Not so far really, Admiral," Dailey answered. "We've been steaming toward each other the last few hours at about twenty knots. That's forty knots an hour, nine hundred sixty miles if they hadn't slowed for replenishment."

"He's very careful, Bill, very careful."

"Pardon me, sir?"

"Oh, just a comment on life, Bill. Alex is very careful. He'll never allow himself to get caught with his pants down again. He learns well, and once was enough."

"I'm afraid I don't follow you, sir."

"Oh, it's nothing really, Bill. An old war story that's probably improved with age. But you should always remember those stories, too." He raised his eyebrows. "Not so long ago, the Russian Navy lacked the service force they have today. They tried to be a blue-water navy long before they should have, and we spanked them for it, or President Kennedy did. Alex was there, and his stepfather was running the Soviet Navy even then. Alex says he has always reminded the old man about that since he was a lieutenant. They used to fight about it. But Alex insisted that Gorenko couldn't ever achieve supremacy at sea until he could back up all those fancy warships they were building. That's one reason that service force of theirs set sail the other day from India and is hovering east of the Maldives. Gorenko ensured that any task force of his anywhere in the world could replenish whenever needed, and Alex is so damn paranoid about that that he'll have every damn ship topped off with

everything he can think of.'' He looked again at Dailey and
smiled. "He doesn't want to get caught with his pants down
this time."

"When you said he was an old friend, I didn't realize
you'd actually met Admiral Kupinsky before, sir.''

"Met? Hell, yes. I'll say I have, both formally and infor-
mally." He shut his eyes for a moment, stroking his nose
with a thumb and forefinger. He remained quiet for a moment. He finally looked up at Dailey again, a saddened
reflection in his eyes. "Yes, I certainly do know him. He's a
very fine man.'' He stood up, finishing the iced tea as he
stepped back from the table. "Come on, Bill, it's time.''

"You're sure these Backfires are going to fire at us, aren't
you, sir?''

"I don't know why not. They're controlled from the
Kremlin, not from Kupinsky's group. Those ships coming
toward us are a show of force, just like we are. Their orders
come from Moscow, but the decision at a given instant to use
weapons will be from the force commander. But these planes
are probably in direct voice contact with Gorenko's staff
right now.''

"Use of weapons would be a direct provocation to war.''

"It would be any time, but less so out here, Bill. There are
no land masses to be concerned with, no civilians to worry
about, no one's territory invaded. We're just two military
forces up to no good as far as the people in Washington or
Moscow are concerned. It's our job to be here and take our
chances. Right?'' He continued without waiting for an answer. "The Chairman's speech makes it quite clear that the
United States has already engaged in an act of war, and
therefore stronger methods than usual are justified to warn us
off. Now the U.N. or just about any other country is going to
figure it serves both Russia or the U.S. right if we start
shooting at each other's military forces as a warning. But, no
one expects war. It's just that some bully drew a line across a
point on the playground and said, "Don't anyone cross it or
I'll beat you up.' So now we've crossed it, and I think they
probably want to make us go back to the other side. They've

already announced that certain actions may be justifiable. And, after all, remember they say they're defending the Third World nations out here. What more do they need?'' He nodded toward flag plot.

The Russian AS-7 cruise missile, launched from a Backfire bomber, has a range of almost five hundred miles. Its advantage is simply that it can be launched at a surface target, preferably a carrier, beyond the range of most of the carrier's flight umbrella. Then, it becomes the job of the protective surface screen around the carrier to stop the missile. The Backfire may then turn for its land base, avoiding the opposition's fighters completely.

On this particular day, as Admiral Charles and his staff operations officer entered plot, the Russian bombers had just released their missiles. But they didn't have the opportunity to return to their base immediately. The Navy Tomcat fighter is a bit faster, by about two hundred miles per hour. Since the Russian planes were bigger and heavier and could not change course until their missiles were released, the fighters were literally upon them at a distance of two hundred miles. And when the Backfires had completed their mission, they didn't simply turn around. At their speed of approximately two thousand miles per hour, they made a very long turn. By that time, the Tomcat's radar had locked on to their targets and their own Phoenix missiles had been released.

None of the planes ever saw each other beyond the display on their radar screens. However, four of the six Backfires were brought down by the American missiles. The other two were able to evade and managed to escape, since the Tomcats did not have the fuel to continue pursuit.

All of this was noted in the flag plot on *Nimitz* and relayed immediately to a computer outside Washington. In the meantime, the Admiral's anti-air-warfare officer was busy in front of his console, giving orders to people connected to his speaker and occasionally pushing buttons. There were twelve cruise missiles speeding toward them.

''Admiral, we have a solution. We've assigned *Virginia*

and her division for the forward air defense. Each ship is
radiating carrier characteristics. Impact time . . . .'' he
looked at a dial on his console, ''. . . fourteen minutes.''

"Very well. Let me know when they're locked on and
ready to bring them down.'' David Charles had a great deal
of faith in the Aegis system. It had been designed specifically
to counter such a threat, and its Standard missile had a range
of three hundred fifty miles, if they ever had the opportunity
to fire when a Russian missile was that far away. He felt that
the combination of the antimissile system and the electronic
equipment, which confused the attacking radar system into
thinking that all ships were carriers, would protect *Nimitz*
sufficiently.

He turned to Bill Dailey. "There's no longer any doubt
about their intentions, Bill, and we're going to retaliate. I
want a squadron of A-7's with some Tomcat protection out
after Kupinsky.'' And, in answer to a question that never left
Dailey's open mouth, ''Nope. Conventional armament for
now for the leaders. Drop two behind about four or five
minutes with nuclear warheads. We won't use them until we
explode one of those cruise missiles and see what it's carrying. And send orders out to the two submarines closest to
Lenin. I want them to harrass the hell out of that screen
around *Lenin,* but stay the hell away. Their long-range antisubmarine weapons aren't that good, so there's no reason to
get up close to test their new ones. Have them pick out one of
those *Kresta-* or *Kara-*class cruisers if they can.''

He turned back to his status board to hear a report.
''Fighter launch from *Lenin* now within radar range. Twelve
aircraft. No identification yet.''

''That makes sense,'' David remarked to no one in particular. ''Land-based Backfires from Africa and those short
range Riga fighters from the other direction. They've got to
find out what we've got too, before they start anything really
big.''

Frank Welles's voice came from the speaker to his left.
''Admiral, I've got some aircraft on deck if you want me to
send them up to coordinate the antimissile firing.''

"Negative, Frank. I believe"—he looked up at one of his staff who was giving him a thumbs-up sign—"the Aegis system has taken over now. Just a second." He called over to the officer controlling the Aegis computer and received a nod. "Right, the computer has control now. And we've already fired. In a moment they ought to be close enough to lock on. We don't really have any time anyway, Frank, with that strike I'm sending to the east after their surface ships."

He turned off the speaker switch, and his eyes returned to the screen in the front of plot where the Russian cruise missiles were being tracked. *Virginia* and her division were now monitoring their tracking equipment to ensure their missiles were locked on to the incoming ones. While the electronic equipment took over, men were activating the automatic machinery that would reload the launchers for the next firing. Secondary computers had already picked up the track of the attacking missiles and were feeding information into the close-in Phalanx system, the secondary defense should the Standard missiles fail to complete their mission.

"Four minutes," replied the AAW officer at his air defense console.

"Rigas closing from the east, sir. They apparently had no contact with our own launch."

"Very well," David replied. "Is there any submarine movement near us?"

"They've been active, sir," Bill Dailey answered. "But nothing to make me think anything's being coordinated."

"They're always independent. Send a couple of those frigates out to fool with them. We're not ready for that sort of game yet." His eyes returned to the screen displaying the Russian and American missiles closing in on each other.

"Computer predicts that Rigas will stay to the north and fire their own missiles before the cruise missiles impact."

"Thank you," David answered. "What ships are to the north?"

"*Wainright* and *Josephus Daniels* are the two cruisers and . . . the cans are *Dewey, Preble, Semmes,* and *Ricketts,* and a couple of smaller FFG's, too."

"Okay, Bill, I want you to make sure we bring down all those aircraft. They already know about that low-level missile of ours, so let's make the best of it now. The less planes they have later, the better." He followed the action on the screen before him as it became clearer exactly what the Russians were doing. It was obvious that Gorenko in Moscow had ordered the flight of Backfires from Mogadishu, and that Kupinsky was coordinating the air attack from the north.

"Ninety seconds to impact cruise missiles . . . *Virginia* reports lock-on to four of them now . . ." There was a breathless pause in the darkened room. " . . . Confirmed explosion of conventional warheads . . ." an audible sigh of relief, "lock-on to two more . . . Computer reports all cruise missiles locked-on to western escorts . . . *Nimitz* is not a target. . . ." Another sigh of relief.

"Bill, hold those two trailing Tomcats behind. I don't want anyone making mistakes with those warheads."

"I have already, sir. Recommend we send them up north to pick up any of the Rigas that might get away."

"Good thinking, Bill. I . . ."

Two more of the curise missiles had just blinked out on their screens when a speaker cut in: "Six cruise missiles through the barrier. Targeted ships have their own control." This was the test they had been afraid would come. The Vulcan/Phalanx weapon system had been devised as a last-ditch effort for a saturation attack by cruise missiles, but twelve hadn't been considered saturation. It was activated when the missiles were within one mile of their target and consisted of no more than rapid-fire 20-mm. shells sprayed in a Gatling-gun effect. The fire-control radar constantly tracked the incoming missiles and corrected the direction of fire. It was a last-ditch, protective shield of metal.

"Rigas are within missile range of the northern force. *Wainwright* is controlling ship. They have assumed control for the twelve northern ships. They are under fire." On his board, David could see new dots of light appear between the Rigas in the air and their surface targets.

He looked back to the left side of his screen, where the six remaining cruise missiles were now reduced to two, but were merging with dots that David knew were his own ships. "Four more missiles down," he heard the report. But each person in the room was watching, horrified as one of their own ships disappeared from the screen. The voice continued for a moment, then broke, "*Harold Holt* hit amidships . . . she's broken in half . . . after section sinking rapidly."

But the second hit was even worse from the Admiral's viewpoint. He knew from the early part of the battle which spot on his screen represented *Virginia,* and that one of the missiles had merged with her dot also. "What is the report from *Virginia?*"

"Nothing, sir.. We have no communication with her."

A click from the speaker on *Nimitz*' bridge drew their attention to Frank Welles's voice. "Terrific explosion over the horizon to the west, Admiral. Something besides a missile."

"That's the *Virginia,* Frank. Can you see anything? We know she's been hit."

Silence, for just a moment, even though the speaker button was depressed. They could hear the exclamations in the background. "Oh, my God." It was Welles's voice again. "There was a second explosion in the same location, sir. . . ." He paused for a second, likely using his binoculars. "There can't be anything else left!"

Where there had been a dot on his screen representing the nuclear-powered cruiser, there was now nothing. Six hundred feet and eleven thousand tons of guided missile cruiser, with 450 men aboard, had seemingly disappeared. One of his few Aegis-equipped ships had gone as if by magic. The voice brought his mind back to the present: "*Mitscher* reports *Virginia* has exploded, sir. They say the missile probably hit the aft magazine and the forward one went off almost immediately after . . . sir, they say nothing's left . . . no survivors." The speaker's voice was incredulous.

"Submarine contact to the southwest, sir!" He saw immediately on his screen that two of Kupinsky's subs had pulled closer together, possibly for an attack on the escorts.

They had to get through them before they could get to *Nimitz*, and that was why he had sent some of the frigates off in that direction.

The board in front of him told the story to the north as missiles that had been fired by the Rigas either blinked out or continued on toward their targets. These were not as big or as fast or as sophisticated as the cruise missiles, but they could do enough damage to any ship. As he watched, a number of the Rigas disappeared from the screen, victims of *Wainwright*'s coordinated firing with its small northern force. And some of the missiles that had been fired at the ships were now merging with their targets.

"*Wainwright* reports *John Paul Jones, Preble, Radford* and *Knox* have all been hit, sir."

"How serious?"

"No report yet, sir."

David could see another Riga wink out on the screen. The new Mongoose missile system was proving effective. Like many of their other weapons, it had never been tested in battle, but much of its development had been based on the Riga fighter, a jet that Kupinsky had originated to complement the new VTOL carriers, he had created for the Soviet Navy. He wanted a jet that could fire low-level missiles, difficult to track on radar. Sam Carter had known for quite a while that the Riga would have to be developed. The Russians had no long-range threat from their *Kiev*-class carriers until a VTOL jet could be built that could land and take off on the smaller decks, carry enough fuel to prove itself as a long-range fighter, and still have a weapon system that would make it worthwhile for air/surface attack, in addition to protecting itself in the air. Carter had simply made that aircraft a priority-one project for the C.I.A., and he had developed a missile to counter it as the basics of the Riga were made known to him in bits and pieces. The Mongoose was up to expectations.

"*Wainwright* reports three Rigas still in the air but turning to the east. She's breaking off attack to assist in fighting fires on *John Paul Jones*. Heavy damage to the other three ships, but none are in danger of sinking.''

"Okay, Bill." He turned to his operations officer. "Send a couple of those Tomcats after them."

"No problem, sir. We already have the target information relayed to them and they're in the last approach phase now. Our only difficulty is that there's three of them, each on different courses and at different altitudes, and only two of ours. I think you're going to have to settle for one of them getting back to the barn."

"Shit!" He looked at the screen, then back at Dailey. "How many Rigas in that flight?"

"An even dozen, sir. Give *Wainwright*'s ships credit, Admiral. They got nine of them. The Mongoose tears a plane apart when it's hit. And, please remember, they were countering a missile attack at the same time, Admiral. It was no turkey shoot, but that's almost half *Lenin*'s complement of fighters. They're going to have to borrow the air group from *Minsk* before they get any closer."

"You're right, Bill. I know. Perhaps I should be sending another flight out now to try to finish off *Lenin* while she's weak."

"Let's wait out the first strike, sir. They should be on target shortly. And *Lenin* still carries Forgers for close-in air protection."

Another voice broke in. "Tomcats have fired on the remaining Rigas, sir." David looked up at the screen, but found it was taking him a moment to reorient. He saw the two dots representing his own aircraft, and three for the Rigas, but there appeared to be missiles fired from both groups. At about the same time that two of the Russian planes were obviously hit, one of the Tomcats disappeared from the screen. As if in answer to his next question, he heard, "Pilot in the water. *Josephus Daniels* has helos out for recovery."

"Bill, I'd like to get a feedback from War Games as soon as possible on their tactics. As far as I can see, their naval air just doesn't have enough experience, but then we're not so hot in defending ourselves against their damn missiles.''

"Yes, sir." Dailey bent forward slightly and picked up a sound-powered phone, speaking briefly for a moment. He waited. His eyebrows knit together. He spoke briefly and replaced the instrument in its cradle. "Problems with computer relay, Admiral. Computer officer is checking it out again, but our equipment seems okay. He says the only other problem could be in their equipment at John Hopkins, but they have backup. Unless something's happened to the satellite relay." He raised his eyebrows in question.

"Call him back, Bill. Tell him not to worry about his computers, if they check out. And you might tell him it's probably not Hopkins either."

Admiral Alexander Kupinsky leaned forward, cradling his chin in his hands and resting his elbows on the deck railing of the signal bridge, one level above the pilothouse. He surveyed the maze of radars, missile launchers, and antiaircraft guns before him. *Lenin* was as well equipped to fight off an attack as a cruiser, with her array of surface-to-air, surface-to-surface, and antisubmarine missiles. She also carried torpedoes and rockets in case of close-in attack, but her main armament was still her aircraft. Built as his flagship, she now carried 24 long-range Riga fighters, 12 short-range Forger fighters, and 25 Kamov helicopters, and she still maneuvered like a destroyer. Kupinsky had literally designed her himself, or rather he had designed the first of her class, the *Kiev*. There had been more than enough time.

His mind drifted back over twenty years. After his return from Cuba, where his submarine had been ordered after the Americans tired of playing cat and mouse with it, he had been given a formal hearing in Moscow. No submarine commander in the Russian Navy had been so humiliated before. Only Gorenko's personal intercession had kept him from a court-martial. As it was, the Commander in Chief of the Soviet Navy had taken a great chance. He was not a strict Party member, and there were many who would have been happy to see him go. But he had Khrushchev's ear. The two older men had much in common, and thus there was a hearing first.

The Admiral did not involve himself in the formalities, but Alex found himself with a highly efficient defense counsel, another Party member much like Gorenko. He was polite, nodded at all the details that were presented, declined to ask any questions, and gave every indication of being there just to ensure that Kupinsky received fair consideration. However, when his turn came, he had both the quartermaster's and engineer's logs in hand, and presented details from each, exactly in order as each engineering casualty occurred to the submarine. By the time he got to the American quarantine operations, the senior officers conducting the hearing were beginning to appreciate the problems of the captain of a diesel submarine in foreign waters, with a minimum of support from the homeland.

Then began the story of his longest night, the discovery by a carrier aircraft, the American destroyers, the helicopters, the sonobuoys in the water, the grenades, the incessant pinging on the hull, and the pinwheel fence that was literally thrown around him. Then there was the inadequate air supply, the leaking oil, the shaft with the hot bearing that was about to seize. And, worst of all, there had never been any instructions from Moscow. There were no effective communications systems to explain what was happening to them. They knew that something was up with the Americans, but they had no idea whether they would be sunk or not or even if they were to fight. And finally, the man read from the log about the hours of maneuvering in Kupinsky's attempt to escape, and, after closing all the logs, he related the conditions of the boat and the men when their brave captain finally had no choice but to surface.

They could not court-martial him. No Soviet submariner had ever undergone such an action before. Gorenko had built a new fleet after the Great Patriotic War, but they had yet to take those boats into battle. They decided that Lieutenant Kupinsky had responded admirably considering the limitations he was forced to work under. However, too many senior officers knew of the surfacing. It was one of many insults heaped on them over a ten-day period by the U.S. Navy, and some action had to be taken. They sent him inland, to a university for further education.

Alex had the opportunity, before the hearing, to spend some evenings with Gorenko, discussing the quarantine and exactly what had gone wrong, and the older man had listened. Gorenko had always publicly ridiculed the American aircraft carriers, but he knew the advantages they offered in antisubmarine warfare, and suspected that a future Russian blue-water navy would need them in some form. The other point of discussion was one that Alex had always felt strongly about, and now he could speak personally about the lack of an effective service force. "All right!" Gorenko had offered. "I'll build the service force, after we have the missile submarines. You study your aircraft carriers and come back to me with an answer. But," and he had leveled a finger at Alex, "don't bring me a big expensive American carrier."

Life at the university, five years of it, had been difficult for Kupinsky. He had been brought up as a youth in a sailor's home, he had been educated as a sailor, and he had truly become a man of the sea. He was sent far from it. There was no choice but to immerse himself in study.

The most important gain of the homeland was his research. It was during this period that he accepted the challenge to develop the aircraft carrier—but not an American type. What evolved was a challenge to the American submarine fleet. While he had been humiliated by a particular destroyer, he had been found by a carrier-based aircraft. For a submarine, there is no knowledge of an aircraft's proximity until it has you. It doesn't matter whether it is a fixed-wing type or a helicopter, because it does not come in contact with the water until it is reasonably sure a sub is there. And then there is no longer any element of surprise, which is the submarine's greatest advantage! Then there is only escape.

So his aircraft carrier became an antisubmarine force in its own right. It would carry many helos, which were easy to store, launch, and recover from any platform. But of even more importance was the VTOL aircraft. Intelligence provided the latest in research from the British, the leaders in the vertical takeoff and landing aircraft. With the information passed on to him via Gorenko's office, he was then able to plan a ship that was three hundred feet shorter than the American carriers, and half the tonnage. With the limited space required for flight operations, he was able to add the protective and offensive weapons that American carriers depended on their escorts for. The carrier would bristle with missile launchers to counter attacks from the air, surface, or subsurface, and it was especially built as a sub killer. The *Kiev*-class aircraft carrier became a reality on paper. The air-strike capability would come later, as long as the planes could be adapted to the available platform.

After returning to Moscow and presenting his detailed plans to Gorenko, he went on to Leningrad for leave, and that was where he met Tasha. In a renaissance city, one savors the culture, especially during the winter when everything is frozen. He first saw her in the Hermitage, leading a class of her students from room to room in the standard-issue Russian slippers. There was so much to see that she was barely giving them enough time to survey each painting before she hustled them to the next room.

She didn't look like a native to him, though she seemed to be quite comfortable in the Hermitage. She was slimmer than many of the Russian women and her clothes were more stylish. She wasn't dressed in the manner of the European or American tourists, but she carried herself in a special way, and her clothes had more color than one normally saw in Leningrad.

It was her face that had first caught his attention, her eyes. They were a lovely green, and he noted that they crinkled at the edges and seemed to smile by themselves when she was smiling at the children. When she began a lecture about a certain painting or an artist, her round face would become serious again. But she was still pretty to him, especially her eyes. When he decided to talk to her, he noticed she was speaking another language, but perhaps she was a guide.

His introduction to her failed miserably. ''Your students

won't be able to tell you tomorrow what they saw today at this speed. Perhaps I could assist you.'' He smiled at her serious face. ''I'd be happy to escort some of your children.''

She looked first at his uniform, then at his face. She did not smile, nor was there even a change in her expression. She shook her head, ''You are the military. What do you know of art?'' And she had turned her back, having barely broken the running lecture she was giving.

He saw her again that night when he went to the rooftop bar in the Leningrad Hotel. This time he was not wearing his uniform and she was not with her students. He carried his brandy over to her stool at the bar. ''I'm sorry if I upset you today. I really do know my way around the Hermitage. I go there whenever I am in Leningrad.'' Alex wanted to apologize before she could put him down again.

She turned in her chair, staring at him, not quite realizing that the short, quiet gentleman in the dark suit was the same officer that had interrupted her class. ''I beg your pardon.''

''Today. You were in one of the seventeenth-century rooms with your students. You were moving and talking so fast, I didn't think they'd ever remember what you were saying.'' She tilted her head, looking more closely at him. ''I was wearing a naval officer's uniform. I don't believe you liked it.''

''Ah, yes. I remember now.'' There was no smile on her face, nor even a sign of recognition that he had offered to help. ''Why would a military man be in a place of culture?''

''As I've said, I go there whenever I am lucky enough to be in Leningrad. Doesn't everyone who comes here?'' He smiled again at her, trying to make her believe he was harmless. ''Haven't you ever seen military people there during your visits?''

''Perhaps they have appeared. I never look for them. I am always too busy with my students.'' She began to turn to the bar.

''Where do you and your students come from?''

''Nisula.'' She looked over her partially turned shoulder at him. ''Over the border. In Finland.''

"I see." Silence. Finland. Many of the Finns hated the Russians for the centuries of invasion of their peaceful little country. On the border, he knew they were constantly harassed. "And has your family been there for a long time?"

"Yes. A few hundred years, I suppose. Whenever it was called Finland. When it wasn't, they were Russians." She looked back at him again. "I really don't think we have anything more to talk about." Her voice was quiet and soft, now that she was no longer lecturing students, and her accent was not as heavy as many of the Finns who spoke Russian only when it was required.

"I'm sorry," he responded quietly. "I meant no offense. I am just here by myself, and I plan to spend another few days at the Hermitage before I return to my university."

He was from a university, polite and quiet, and, she decided, even a bit shy. She turned around in her seat again and smiled for the first time. He extended his right hand and introduced himself, and he never had any doubts about his life after that. The Navy could do what they wanted to him, but he would be happy. And for Tasha's part, he erased the evil memories that had passed down through her family for a few hundred years. She found at least one Russian military man who was gentle and kind.

They were married in Leningrad late that May, when the snow was gone and the canals flowed once again. The wind from the Gulf of Finland filled the air with the warm smell of apple blossoms. They honeymooned in the city, taking day trips to the Summer Palace and Lake Ladoga and the seacoast, and even boated on the Neva with the tourists. Too soon it ended, and they were back at the university, more work already waiting for Alex from Gorenko. The plans for the carrier were acceptable. Now he was to design it piece by piece with the naval architects that were being sent to assist him.

It takes as long to design a new class of ship as it does to build it. His duties consisted not only of development of the carrier but of advising Gorenko in building his blue-water service force: tankers, ammunition ships, repair ships, and full-line replenishment ships. They must be capable of handling a variety of warships steaming together in a task force.

He was promoted in line with his peers, but he did not get back to sea. While the Commander in Chief of the Navy was literally his patron, there were enough senior Party members who had not forgotten the dark days of Cuba. Gorenko was not about to antagonize them further. Kupinsky traveled freely about the country, visiting shipyards and discussing his plans with both military and civilian builders. He was allowed to attend a variety of schools, including the staff and command schools that he had been scheduled to attend earlier in his career. He was also allowed a brief tour in the embassy in London, where he learned even more about aircraft carriers from the Americans.

Gorenko was ensuring that Alex would catch up with the officers in his own age group, yet satisfy his detractors at the same time. The Party sometimes worked in strange ways, and in that massive country one individual could not avoid the continual observation of his seniors. When the keel for *Kiev* was laid in 1971, Kupinsky's job was finished. Now the supervision would be turned over to the shipbuilders at Nikolayev, and he would only return irregularly to review progress, especially when alterations were introduced.

He was now able to convince Gorenko that he must go back to sea. But the major problem was that his seniority demanded an advanced position onboard, and he had been away from the water for almost eight years. In the Russian Navy, an officer spends a great deal of time, five years or more, aboard the same ship, learning his specialty. He may even assume a department head's rank and then become an executive officer, if the captain and the political officer deem him fit. Unless he makes too many mistakes, he will often become commanding officer. It was therefore most difficult to find the right ship for Alex. His future was in the surface force now, and he was almost too senior for command of a destroyer. Gorenko again dipped into his purse of influence and found an executive officer of a guided-missile cruiser in disfavor with his political officer. Captain Second Rank

Kupinsky became executive officer of the *Admiral Fokin*, a *Kynda*-class cruiser in the Red Banner Northern Fleet.

Alex was able to reverse the natural distrust of an outsider into respect in a short time. He approached his new job with the same determination that he had found to create the first carrier. He was not hurt by the fact that Gorenko had interceded for him. His knowledge of submarines and antisubmarine tactics were invaluable to the *Admiral Fokin*, more attuned to surface and air warfare but often finding itself involved in antisubmarine maneuvers. When the captain was transferred to a senior command, Alex became commanding officer and captain first rank. He would be ready for flag rank after this tour.

"Excuse me, Admiral." Kupinsky's thoughts shifted quickly back to the signal bridge of *Lenin*. He straightened from the railing, turning quickly, and returned the salute of the young staff officer who had interrupted his dreams. "Sir, Captain Svedrov reports that our Rigas have inflicted heavy damage on surface units of the American forces. They left at least four ships, one of them a large cruiser, burning."

"Were any of them sunk?"

"I do not believe so, sir, although a guided-missile destroyer was severely damaged."

"And what of our own casualties?"

The young man hesitated. "The American missile system was very accurate, Admiral. Three of our Rigas escaped, only to be set upon by fighter aircraft." His voice dropped almost to a whisper. "Only one is returning, sir."

"I see."

"Also, he wishes me to inform you that the American attack aircraft are only ten minutes away. We have sent our helicopters south to assist the destroyers with the approach-, ing submarines. He respectfully asks if you will join him and the staff shortly."

"Yes. Inform Mr. Svedrov I will be down in a few moments." The young man saluted, then wheeled about to carry his message, even before Kupinsky had returned the salute.

He hated the idea of going down into the dark flag plot where he could see nothing of the action taking place. It was simply moving dots on screens with no size or shape or animation. He would have much preferred to be on the signal bridge watching the effect of the various weapons. But he realized that most of the action would take place beyond his eyesight anyway, and they needed him to coordinate the action once they had initiated his battle plan.

Plot in *Lenin* was similar to that in *Nimitz*. It was a bit smaller, since the Russians often sacrificed human space for weapon space, but it performed essentially the same functions. Many of the weapons were different, yet they had been devised for the same purposes. As Alex entered the room to assume his position next to Captain Svedrov, his Chief of Staff, he quickly reviewed the status of operations. He saw the flight of A-7's approaching his force, the American submarines to the south, and in another corner of the room, a board showing the dispersed American force.

As he seated himself, Svedrov reported, ''All ships have expanded the screen in preparation for any nuclear attack, sir. Our computers indicate that the American planes are not armed with atomic weapons at this time, but I felt it better not to take any chances. We have already dispersed high-level chaff to counter their missile radar, and our escorts are radiating large-ship signals. I doubt they will be able to select *Lenin* unless they are willing to come within visual range.''

''The lead aircraft will fire Harpoon missiles, and that should be any minute now. Their range is over fifty miles,'' remarked Kupinsky. ''Once those are locked onto a target, they will then send the secondary flight in with their Bullpup missiles. Do not let anyone be fooled when those first aircraft turn back after firing. I know that is just what David Charles would like to see.''

''Who, Admiral?''

''Admiral Charles, their commander. He believes quite strongly in the dual-strike method.'' Svedrov looked quizzically at his commander. ''I know the man well, Svedrov.

Remember my explanation of the other day? He is a brilliant commander. I can also assure you that his submarines are maneuvering to position now to fire at about the same time as those aircraft.''

It didn't happen exactly the way that Admiral Kupinsky predicted, but it was close enough to satisfy his staff. The submarines anticipated the A-7's by just half a minute, but David Charles had expected that would be possible. All of his fleet units were instructed to act independently when they were going into action, unless they were tied into the master computer. In this case, he wanted his commanders to shoot when they were in the best position.

While *Dallas* sped off underwater to the east to draw off some of the helicopters, the captain of *Mendel Rivers* simply went full ahead for a few moments, directly toward the center of the Russian force. It was relatively easy to evade the helos in the vicinity for long enough to confirm a solution in the computer and fire the Harpoon missiles. The formation had been adequately plotted by satellite earlier in the day and *Rivers'* sensors were able to maintain the locations of the larger Soviet ships.

The missile broke the water approximately forty miles from the southernmost cruiser in the extended screen. After igniting and orienting itself, it raced toward the target in full view of the helos already warning of its approach. The CO of *Rivers* had chosen his target because of its name and importance to the Russian people. He had a perfect solution for the missile, and it was fired too close for the captain of *Marshal Timoshenko* to consider evading. There was no time for a solution for his own antimissile weapons, and his men vainly fired their 76- and 23- mm. guns at a missile that could barely be perceived at that speed. The ship also tried to maneuver. The explosion on impact literally ripped the stern off the 7,500-ton ship, completely destroying the after engineering spaces and detonating one of the magazines. The secondary explosion tore a hole farther forward from the main deck to well below the waterline. She was dead in the water in less than thirty seconds, the fires providing an excellent target for any aircraft that cared to finish off the long sleek cruiser, but she soon sank of her own accord.

Just moments later, as the lead aircraft from *Nimitz* were launching their own attack, *Dallas* successfully fired two missiles, one at the lead destroyer of a group of four heading in her direction, and the second at another cruiser in the rear of the formation. An instant before the missile exploded, blowing the bow off *Bodry*, one of the newest destroyers in the fleet, the Russian ship fired its own antisubmarine missile, based on a quick solution in tandem with one of the helicopters. The missile from the fated destroyer did not land in the water as close to *Dallas* as it had been planned, but that was of no help to the American boat. The torpedo carried by that missile locked on to its target immediately. Seconds before *Dallas'*s pressure hull was shattered, each man heard the whine of the high-speed propellers overtaking their boat. The destroyer, racing forward at thirty-two knots, ripped itself apart. With no bow, its weak interior bulkheads collapsed from the forward motion.

The second missile from *Dallas* removed the bridge and the three top levels from the giant cruiser *Nikolayev,* named after the yard that had built so many of the ships in that task force. *Nikolayev* was also a target of the air attack. Just as she regained control in after steering, with her executive officer now in command, two more missiles hit, one amidship at the waterline, destroying main control, and the second in a torpedo magazine. The dual explosion, and the water rapidly filling the starboard side, rolled *Nikolayev* onto her beam. Secondary explosions completed the job, and she turned turtle.

As far as Admiral Kupinsky was concerned from his position in flag plot, the exchange was weighing in favor of the Americans. While the latter did not have as strong a defense against airborne missiles as his own force, he decided that his own antisubmarine protection was not as effective as it appeared on paper. Though their ships carried enough weapons to sink each American sub three or four times, they had to catch them first, and the rapid acceleration of a nuclear attack boat easily confused his own helicopters. He needed the long-range standoff capability to fire on the subs before they fired on him. The loss of one cruiser and one destroyer convinced him that it was time to send his ASW units away from *Lenin* to keep the subs at a distance. He would have credited *Dallas* with a second cruiser, but that had actually been finished off by the Americans' planes.

Just as he had predicted to Captain Svedrov, the American aircraft first launched their long-range missiles from enough distance to protect them from shipboard missiles. Then, right behind that attack, came more aircraft with the shorter-range weapons. Their ploy was to hide behind the Harpoons, assuming the Russians had their hands full just bringing down the first flight of missiles. The less maneuverable Forgers that *Lenin* had launched earlier were no match for the American fighters. The Tomcats flying shotgun had been armed with Sidewinder missiles. These easily brought down most of the Soviet jets, which had been designed as bombers anyway.

The Russians' electronic deception equipment was the equal of the Americans'. The missiles fired at the Soviets had locked on the best available targets. They wanted *Lenin*, but only visual contact would suffice. As the second flight came in more closely with their Bullpups, they saw the destruction caused by the submarines. They had unknowingly assisted *Dallas* in the sinking of *Nikolayev*, but many of their Harpoons had been picked out of the air by antimissile fire. One had streaked in past the defenses to explode on *Sevastopol*, a guided missile cruiser, but now this secondary attack was necessary to inflict maximum damage.

The Bullpup missile has a range of about ten miles. The Soviet antiair missiles have a range of about fifteen miles, and the latter were fired first. The A-7 pilots spent their time evading these missiles while their men in the rear coordinated their own firing. First one, then two, then three of the attacking planes were hit. The remainder were able to complete their attack, turn, and head back for *Nimitz*. As they turned, two more were brought down, and a third was hit and began immediately to lose altitude, desperately struggling for that long glide toward safety.

Kupinsky watched the boards before him anxiously. *Nikolayev* was lost—a combination attack. One of the Harpoon missiles had exploded aboard *Skory,* one of his older high-speed destroyers, leaving her dead in the water. A total of twelve Bullpups were fired by the surviving aircraft.

"Svedrov. Are our destroyers using that new countermeasure equipment, the one that radiates false targets to their missile radar?"

"Yes, Admiral. Only two of the forward ships have it installed, but they are radiating now."

Kupinsky watched the progress of the American missiles, two each fired at six targets. He noted that two of them winked out seemingly before they reached the lead ship. He turned to his Chief of Staff, who smiled and nodded before his Admiral could even ask the question. The missile had convinced itself to explode on a target that never existed. The destroyer *Razitelny* was not so lucky. Built in the late 1970's, her captain had been personally selected by Gorenko to command this powerful little destroyer. Capable of traveling at speeds in excess of thirty-eight knots, they had felt this ship could be the prototype answer to the American high-speed attack submarines. But two missiles easily got through all the defenses, one exploding just behind the forward launcher. It detonated the missiles just then being loaded, and blew off the front of the bridge. The second hit, amidships near the waterline, exploded in the engineering spaces. Immediately she was enveloped in flames and the damage-control parties found themselves unable to control the fires.

Many of the ships were successful in exploding the missiles before they got to their targets. One hit the after launcher on Kupinsky's first surface command, *Admiral Fokin,* putting her stern weapons out of action. But she was still able to maintain her position in the screen. The only other missile to get through found *Lenin* and exploded in her starboard elevator. There was no fire, but the elevator, so important in bringing the remaining Rigas to the flight deck, was jammed in twisted metal.

"How long before that elevator can be repaired, Svedrov?" Kupinsky inquired. "If we can't have it in operation by the end of the day, I want to turn away. Their reconnaissance aircraft will easily be able to spot that hit, if the satellites haven't already photographed it."

"Commander Kalinn has reported that his damage control people will need at least twenty-four hours, sir. The hydraulics are not damaged, but metal must be cut away and it will take time to complete repairs to make it operational again." He paused in his report, then said, "But I wouldn't be overly concerned about their satellites, sir. We believe that Admiral Gorenko has seen to that. My assistant is checking now, but he believes a message we received an hour ago stated that our missile satellites may have neutralized theirs."

"Is there some problem with your communications?"

"Yes, sir. We aren't sure what it is, but the last messages were badly garbled, almost as if our own satellites were malfunctioning."

Kupinsky leaned back in his chair, his chin resting in his left hand, waiting for Svedrov to look up again. "Captain, I suggest you have your man try to establish direct contact with Moscow right now. It is just as conceivable for them to do the same thing to our own satellites. It is important to me and our tactics over the next twenty-four hours to determine if we are alone here or not."

Captain Svedrov, an understanding look on his face, rose immediately to join his communications staff. Kupinsky returned his attention to the boards before him. The last of the American aircraft were disappearing to the west. He had lost two cruisers, one of which was new, and two high-speed destroyers. *Admiral Fokin* was badly damaged, but her forward launchers were operable. One destroyer was so badly damaged by explosion and fire he would probably sink her. His own carrier was operating with only one elevator, and that meant that he would have to move the Rigas to the other side of the hangar deck if he needed them soon.

The Americans were not much better off, he noted, although the major victory had been the sinking of *Virginia*. A U.S. frigate and one attack sub had been sunk, and the Rigas had left four ships badly damaged, a cruiser, two destroyers, and a frigate, and *John Paul Jones* had been reported burning so badly that she, too, might have to be sunk.

"Admiral." It was a concerned Svedrov. "Admiral, we are unable to contact Moscow at this time. We are in the process of checking all the equipment step by step. We are not in contact with the satellites."

"Svedrov, you may let your officer make sure his equipment is in working order again, if you like. Then you can tell him to stop worrying about it. The trouble, I am sure, is in the sky, and there is little we can do about it. We are on our own for the time being." He looked first at the now-blank screens in front of him, and then back at his operations officer. "You may signal the force that we are turning to the north until *Lenin* is fully operational again. I want a report on *Admiral Fokin*. If she is unable to contribute or protect herself adequately, I want to send her to the yards for repairs. If *Razitelny* is as bad as I think she is, sink her. You may also schedule rendezvous with the service ships. Since we have no communications with Moscow and we can see nothing by satellite, I want you to try to contact the submarines in the American area to learn what they are doing. At this point," he grimaced, "I am operating with about the same information that our commanders had during the Great War forty years ago."

Captain Svedrov saluted him and left. The plot area was back to its normal operation status again. Few men were present in comparision to the recent crowd. What, he thought, did we accomplish today?

In his stateroom on *Nimitz* Admiral David Charles stretched out on his bunk, turning off the wall light. He rubbed his eyes, and yawned, hoping he might be able to sleep for a while. But his mind was still too active. He reflected on what they had seen from the new weapons that day. Many—no, most—of them had never been used in anger before, not against ships or people. It had been awesome, really a new era that they weren't prepared for. Men on a ship never saw who or what fired a weapon at them, nor were they aware of the vehicle of their destruction. Submarines now could stand off so far that they were never known to be in the area. Aircraft and most ships launched missiles well out of visual sight. And there was no noise of action or warning of impending doom, just an explosion. The power of the new warheads was so great that there was no longer as much opportunity for a damaged ship to fight again. Most were simply destroyed. The personnel casualties were the most shocking. There were few survivors. The magnitude of the warheads saw to that. Often, ships were hit so hard and went down so quickly that there was no opportunity to search for survivors. Modern sea battle was impersonal, even more so than they had ever anticipated. He hoped the future would bring ships requiring as few people as possible.

I wonder what great events we have accomplished today, he thought. With the wrecks we will sink, Alex and I have lost eight ships and seven more are damaged. Both of us will probably sink the wrecks. He sighed audibly. And we've lost a lot of men. He hoped that Dailey would find some way to reestablish communications, since he did not like the thought of placing more of his ships in battle without the understanding of Washington. He would maintain his present position until he knew what Alex was doing. It would give him time to reprovision.

DEAREST MARIA,

There's a flight taking off *Nimitz* shortly for land, I'm told, and I wanted to make sure this letter was on it. I've been very, very busy the last few weeks, and my letter writing has suffered a great deal. As a matter of fact, before I forget it, please tell the kids that the next plane that leaves after this one will have a letter for each of them.

You know me well enough by now to know that I'm not a worrier. But I've decided that when I get back home we're going to have a good, long vacation and I'm going to think about retiring. I never thought I'd be CNO anyway, and now I don't think I'd want it if Sam said it could be mine for the asking someday. What I guess I really want is two vacations, one for you and me so we can get to know each other again after all this sea duty, and then one with the kids so they know they really have a father. I'm sure you will be able to convey to them better than I will how much I miss them, too.

I'm not much of a writer, and never will be, especially letters. You've spent a lifetime, it seems, wondering when I would write the next one, which I would do only if I couldn't phone halfway round the world. Well, I'm no better now than ever. I have been reading back through my log, the one I told you I've been keeping since I was an ensign. There's some good things in it (the writing is awful), and I think part of what I've written over the years has affected what I'm doing now, enough so that I may want to retire and apply it outside the military. I want so much to tell you everything I have inside me right now, but I'd have trouble writing it, and I do have to go.

You know how you and the children are in my thoughts all of the time and how much you all have my love,

David

My dearest alex,

Your father didn't want me to write you today, but I wanted to more than ever after talking with him. Maybe in my old age I'm getting more able to stand up to him. Please don't take me wrong. I love him almost like my own father, and you know that even fifteen years ago I didn't think I'd ever be able to say that.

But the reason I'm writing is more important. I wanted to tell you how much I do love you. I know you'll say I never have to do that, just like you always say whenever you come home from sea. But I know something is desperately wrong wherever you are, and sometimes it's just nice to know someone far away is thinking about you and needs you. I told your father that, after he wouldn't tell me where you were (he said he really didn't know, but he can't fool me anymore) and he said you learned how to be alone a long time ago. Perhaps learning how to be alone is the first step in learning how to love someone. I was going to tell him that, but then I decided he wouldn't understand. You know what I mean.

I planned to have your son write you also, but he went out in the fields to hunt this afternoon. Yes, that's right. He's home from his naval school. I don't know why, but your father (he brought him) said he was doing very well but studying too hard, so he thought a few days at the dacha would do him well. After Pietr comes in from hunting, I'll try to have him write you. Maybe he'll even bring back some birds for dinner, if the snow's not too deep for him to move around out there.

And now for the exciting news! I received a letter from Maria Charles yesterday. Apparently David is also at sea, and she has decided that we should all plan to get together this summer. In London! Isn't that wonderful? She said that all of us could afford a trip like that since you're both admirals now, and she said you both have such fine contacts (your father and his Mr. Carter) that we shouldn't have any trouble getting permission if we ask soon enough. Maria said maybe it would improve the spirit of détente, since it's been dragging a bit lately, if everybody knew we were going to get together. Do you think if I ask your father now he might see if he could arrange to let us leave the country and go to London for a week without having to take one of those horrible tours with the Intourist people? And she and I both agree it would be good for the two of you to get away for awhile. She said David's responsibilities are wearing him down, and I couldn't agree more as far as you're concerned. I know I shouldn't worry about you, like your father says, but each time you go to sea I worry a little bit more.

If you're not going to be home to celebrate the New Year, then I've asked your father if he can arrange to let me go back to my village in Finland for a good, old-fashioned Christmas. I miss that holiday so much, and he claims he understands. He said he was very busy the last few days and didn't know how much longer he'd be tied up, but he said he'd try to make arrangements as soon as he had time, because he thought you might be away.

There's so much more I want to say in this letter, but I don't know how many other people might read it before you do. But I don't care how many people know how much I love you and miss you, as long as you know it. I hope this letter might find you safe and on your way home.

With my deepest love.

                                                            Tasha

CHAPTER
NINE

Not knowing quite what to say, the staff communications officer simply listened to the tirade.

"I don't give a shit if you have to tie a long string between two tin cans. We had to talk to Admiral Collier a couple of hours ago!" Sam Carter rarely gave visible signs of losing his temper, but this time there was no doubt about it.

"Sam, we've got to give those boys time. They can't just send up satellites on demand."

"Sorry, Mr. Secretary," Carter nodded his head, grimacing. "It's just that we're losing ships and men, and our strategy's shot to hell if Collier can't lay it on the line to the Kremlin." He looked at the Secretary of State for some support. "We can't afford to lose this one or we might as well pack our tents."

"First of all, Sam, enough of the formalities. It looks like we're going to spend some time together on this. I'd sure appreciate it if you'd start calling me Tom." The older man had grown quite fond of the naval officer in front of him in a very short time. Unlike so many of the others, this one didn't mind making his own decisions. He was no politician, probably the reason he'd never be CNO. "That's what my close friends have all used, and I hope you and I will remain friends long after this is over.''

"Yes, sir," replied Carter automatically after so many years of dealing with superiors.

"Tom," the Secretary corrected.

"Right." Carter smiled, still not quite able to use the man's first name. He would next time. He liked Jasperson also. The Secretary of State had been introduced to him a number of times since he had begun working under the Chief of Naval Operations, and he had known for quite some time why those in the know referred to this senior statesman as the "closet president" whenever things got tough. Jasperson was always there when experience was needed and a decision maker was required. He rarely attracted the headlines nor did he like publicity, but he wanted to ensure that his President mouthed the right decisions. Thomas Jasperson looked very much like the paintings of the man many compared him to—Thomas Jefferson. Jasperson was a scholar, a statesman, a framer of treaties, a painter in his own right, and an author. Now he was a military strategist since he had a real one to work with.

Sam Carter had found himself with complete responsibility for the tactics in the Indian Ocean. His boss, the CNO, had decided that his own responsibilites were purely administrative. He felt his place was with the President, another man who was now unwilling to involve himself with a potential war, or the avoidance of that war. And Jasperson had found himself working with Carter. The President, rather than negotiating as planned, was now talking of withdrawal from the carefully planned installation at Islas Piedras. It was the last chance the Americans had to protect themselves as a world power. Now should have been the time that Admiral Collier and the Ambassador to the Kremlin presented themselves to the Russians. They should have instructions from Washington to explain the situation tactfully in an effort to avoid further bloodshed, backed up by a firm President. But it was already too late. The Russians had learned too soon of the missile installation at Islas Piedras. Quickly they determined the reasons for the U.S. strategy. World leadership was basically seesawing between Russia and the United States. The many nations in the immense Indian Ocean sphere, most of whom were either just-emerging countries or in the throes of revolution and counterrevolution, were easily swayed and looking for leadership. The Cold War romancing by the two giant nations had lost touch with the reality of new countries caught between socialism and capitalism. Economics and protection was the name of the new game. Whichever country offered security would become the suitor. Military protection was paramount.

The end result would be American missile control over Africa and the oil states, and an obvious shift to the United States of support from the Third and Fourth World nations. The Russians destroyed communications between the American Embassy and Washington as quickly as the U.S. had done with the Soviet communications and missile satellites, and the President was unable to carry off the supreme bluff.

Now it was a stalemate. The Americans either had to go through with their plan, or withdraw, shamed before the world. While their leaders attempted to gain the upper hand by enforced silence, two great fleets unavoidably became engaged in a death struggle in the Indian Ocean.

Admiral Carter resumed his instructions to the lieutenant commander in front of him, a communications specialist on the CNO's staff. "All right, son, we won't use tin cans." Jasperson, now standing behind Carter, smiled in the direction of the other officer. The latter gave no indication that the silver-haired Secretary had won a point with the Admiral. "First, let's consider communications with Moscow. Do we have any satellites of our own, or any owned by private companies that can provide us with secure contact with Admiral Collier?"

"No, sir. Even if we did, it would have to be one that had a direct space/ground line to the embassy. We feel that if more than one relay is used when the scrambler is in operation, there is the possibility, even probability now, that the message would be recorded each time. That greatly increases the odds of starting to compromise our scrambler system if they have the same message recorded twice. It is communications policy, Admiral, and I would need your written orders to do otherwise.'' The junior officer stopped for a moment, thinking better of his explanation. ''I didn't mean that exactly the way it sounded, sir. Those are just my orders, and I thought you should be apprised of them.''

''No, no problem,'' replied Carter. ''We're just trying to determine our next move.'' He turned to Jasperson. ''What does State have in its grab bag . . . Tom?'' The use of the first name of this distinguished man didn't come easy.

The Secretary raised his bushy white eyebrows as he often did when thinking, wrinkling his forehead. ''Nothing impressive, I must admit. I guess we've always figured there'd be one more satellite at a time like this.'' He nodded briefly in the direction of the younger officer and said, ''I guess you wouldn't be here now if you didn't have every clearance in the book.'' Then back to Carter, ''We have a type of hotline to the embassy, similar to the President's hotline to the Kremlin. But it was set up primarily for direct communications between my office and the ambassador's, mostly for lesser affairs of state. I doubt it's very secure and I'm sure it's tapped right now.'' He smiled. ''It probably rings in the Chairman's office in the Kremlin.''

''But if we used, say, a onetime code, at least someone at the embassy would be able to relay to Collier, wouldn't they?''

''Oh, no problem with that, sir,'' offered the communications officer. ''We just have to be certain we don't use any that were aboard the ships sunk today.''

''It sounds rather like our Civil War systems,'' mused the Secretary. ''We seem to be going back to conditions of more than a hundred years ago. It's kind of ironic, isn't it, that in an age of satellites and instant relay we might be reduced to reading coded messages over a telephone. But,'' he decided grimly, ''it's better than nothing at all.''

''I also have no secure method of communicating with

Admiral Charles, Mr. Secretary . . . Tom,'' Carter faltered.
''I have a task force on the other side of the world that's
essentially fighting blind now. It's the fastest, best-equipped
force the U.S. Navy has ever had. Its sophistication makes it
purer and more effective than the Russian force, and its
computers are tied directly into the War Games Center at
Johns Hopkins. The tactical situation can constantly be fed
back to the center, which can then evaluate every strategic
possibility and relay possible decisions to Admiral Charles in
seconds. And, if he decides to take the computer's advice, all
that need be done is to push a couple of buttons. The system
controls air, surface, and subsurface units and can unite the
proper weapons in any of the three dimensions to stop the
enemy . . . without ever seeing them,'' he emphasized.
''And that system is absolutely useless right now with the
loss of the satellites that unite War Games and the flag ship.
You're right for the time being, Tom. Maybe David Charles
isn't quite back to a Civil War level, but he's making decisions on his own with no backup from the system that was
developed for a crisis such as this.''

The Secretary of State, who with his wavy, neat, silvery
hair looked every inch a man who should have been in that
position of authority, paced across the room a few times, his
hands clasped behind his back. He finally stopped in front of
the nervous young communications officer. The younger
man was feeling the strain of being in the same room with two
who were making decisions that would effect global strategy.
Jasperson smiled at the officer, and said rather loudly, ''I
don't give a shit if you have to tie a long string between two
tin cans,'' and then he laughed heartily.

From a former distinguished senator, a Vice-President, a
onetime candidate for President, a former Ambassador to the
Court of St. James, and now the Secretary of State, the
pronouncement broke the ice. ''Now, my friend,'' he said to
the youngest officer, ''how would you suggest that Admiral
Carter and I get in touch with Admiral Charles?''

''It's not going to be easy, sir. We already had another
satellite on the pad for just this problem. My boss had

planned for something like this months ago. But before we can send it off, we have to ensure that the Soviet offensive satellites are neutralized, or the same thing's going to happen again. And my Admiral says he sure as hell doesn't have any more satellites in his back pocket.''

''Of course not,'' Carter responded. ''When will you be sure about the safety of this one?''

''As soon as the people at Hopkins get back to us, Admiral. Their intelligence indicates that our initial laser firings got all of the offensive satellites, but they have to check what may have been launched by the Russians since then. They've got a hell of a lot of them in reserve.'' He paused for a moment. ''And we can't just push a button and put another satellite up, sir. We have to wait until we have enough information on the position of Admiral Charles's forces, so we have a direct relay.''

''Fine, son. Why don't you find out the status of that satellite, and the onetime code system, and get back to us just as soon as you can. And if the people over at Hopkins hesitate, remind them that some very fine men and some very valuable ships need their help immediately.''

''Yes, sir.'' The communications officer saluted quickly, turned to the Secretary of State and half-saluted him, not knowing what might be expected, and left the room.

Jasperson used the phone for a few moments to contact various aides. Finished, he turned to Carter, who was relaxing calmly in an easy chair, seemingly unconcerned. ''My people don't seem to know much about your Admiral Charles, just that he's not only one of our youngest admirals but that he's been promoted very fast for his age. And they say that's all quite surprising for an officer with a letter of reprimand in his official file.'' The Secretary sat down also, his eyebrows raised, waiting for a response.

Carter's eyes narrowed every so slightly, and Jasperson noticed just a slight edge to his voice. ''That letter of reprimand was a necessity as a result of a court of inquiry. David was responsible for saving an inestimable number of lives during that incident in Vietnam. He took command of a

badly battered riverboat squadron, after his CO had been
wounded, and fought a VC force back to a base camp that had
been hidden for weeks from intelligence. Not only did his
men put up one hell of a fight, but they went ashore and found
the enemy staging area prepared for a full-scale offensive.
Most of that was destroyed when he called in aircraft and
personally directed the strike from the ground.''

"That's a very impressive action to merit a reprimand."

"The staging area was just over the border in Cambodia,
Mr. Secretary. We were under political instructions not to
cross it. David made a decision based on his duty and the
lives of his men."

Jasperson smiled, noting the returning formality, and nodded, ''I remember it now. I was in a junior position at the
U.N. then. I can remember the hell that raised for us. The
President was so damn mad because he finally was forced to
come out and admit it was an illegal act. But he told me later
how proud he was of whoever that boy was. He just asked us
to get him the hell out of there before he marched into Hanoi,
but he wished he could have personally decorated him.''

"As it was," remarked Carter, "he also got a letter of
commendation for his initiative. But I would have given him
the goddamn Medal of Honor,'' he added vehemently.

"You know Admiral Charles pretty well, don't you,
Sam?"

"Yes," sighed the Admiral, "I guess I know him like a
son. His first assignment out of the Academy was to my
ship. He wasn't a student, no MacArthur or Nimitz or Ernie
King. As a matter of fact, they had to kind of push him
through. But what a leader! He could use his head, and he
handled his men beautifully.'' Admiral Carter smiled to
himself. ''Even as an ensign he had that initiative. And he
wasn't scared to stand up for himself. I had a couple of battles
with him even then, but he always learned from them, even if
it was the hard way sometimes.''

"I didn't mean to cut him down a few minutes ago, Sam, if
that's what you thought.''

"No, no. That's okay." Carter waved his hand in acknowledgment. "He is like a son, and he's a good friend, too. As a matter of fact, Tom, I gave away the bride when he got married after Vietnam. Maria was the widow of a Navy pilot shot down over there, and I remember convincing her the night before the wedding that I'd make sure he stayed out of trouble."

"And now, he's right back in the middle of it." The Secretary paused for a moment. "Well, we'll see what we can do to help him from here, Sam. I don't think the President's going to do us any good. One of my aides said he's thinking about going to the U.N. to see if they'll mediate for us."

"And let everything go down the drain?"

"I'm afraid it's possible, Sam. He's never really wanted to worry about anything other than medicare, and grain, and social security. That's how he got elected. I was just informed by my assistant secretary that we have another twenty-four hours to work this out our way, or he'll call the Secretary General at the U.N."

"And is my boss with him?"

"Yes, but perhaps that's the best place. He seems to have had the President's ear long enough to convince him that you may know what you're doing, so I'm going to need you and your young Admiral pretty badly in the next few hours."

Sam Carter was very proud of his assignment as Vice Chief of Naval Operations. He had come a long way for an officer who had never seen the grounds of Annapolis until he received his first orders to Washington. He had been one of the thousands of officers churned through the V-12 programs during the latter days of World War II. He had been a twenty-year-old ensign when he proudly sailed into Tokyo Bay on his first ship, and he decided at that point he would make the Navy a career.

Promotion was slow in those days, and would have been even worse because of his non-Annapolis background if he had not married Ann. She was the daughter of an Admiral who had graduated from the Academy at the turn of the century, when classes were small and those who were good enough to survive looked after each other. The old man made sure Sam got the right orders, and Sam made sure he carried them out superbly. He was always in the right place. He was in the amphibs, commanding an old LST during MacArthur's landing at Inchon. He was executive officer of a DE in the Mediterranean when the Marines landed in Lebanon. He commanded the *Bagley* when that first submarine was surfaced during the Cuban quarantine.

Between his tours at sea, he managed to obtain his masters degree at Monterey, and there was little problem getting to Washington twice, where you had to go if you were going to shake the right hands. He was never a politician, but he had that advantage of being in the right place at the right time. And Sam Carter gained a reputation as a comer. He could drive a tin can through a knothole in a hurricane; he was a fine leader of men; he gained a reputation for brilliance so that he made it to the War College; and he was probably called by his first name by more senior officers than any other man as he attained each rank. But, because he never went to Annapolis, he knew he would never become CNO. And now, according to the Secretary of State, he was functioning in exactly that position.

* * *

The phone on Admiral Carter's desk interrupted his thoughts. He snatched it off the cradle. "Yes."

He listened for a moment, nodding his head occasionally. "I see. Can't you launch in less than thirty-six hours? . . . What can you do if we can't wait that long? . . ." He listened for a moment and then remarked, "Why don't you just come out and say tough shit? No need to avoid it if the answer's going to be no. We'll simply have to take a different approach. What about the onetime codes? . . . Good, stay close. I'll need you when Secretary Jasperson comes back . . . and would you please also see about someone getting some food up here?" He added, "For you, too!"

The one bit of good news was that they could get through to the embassy in Moscow with a onetime code that was secure, if they could get to Collier before he decided to move on his own. Carter silently thanked God that it was Bob Collier in Moscow, a man with an intellect respected both by the military and civilian people at the upper levels.

Collier wasn't a sailor on the same terms as Carter or David Charles. To keep his wife and family, he had acceded to mostly shore duty, even though he had deeply loved the sea since his days on the *Bagley*. After leaving that ship, he had asked for the Russian language school in Monterey, mostly to keep his wife happy and still remain in the Navy. He quickly became the top Russian scholar in the school, and his next assignment was in Washington on the CNO's staff. This solidified his career, for he was in the proper place for senior officers to recognize his abilities. After that, it was a matter of the right staff positions as he was educated at a variety of schools, culminating in early orders to the Naval War College. There he distinguished himself among some of the foremost military scholars in the nation. He was the perfect man to be at the embassy in Moscow.

Carter looked up from his desk as Secretary Jasperson quietly let himself into the office, unannounced. He stood up in greeting but was immediately motioned back into his chair. "Relax, Sam. Like I said before, we're going to be together for a while, so we might as well get used to it." He looked briefly around the large office. "You have a better communications system here, and I know you want to be here when you reestablish contact with Admiral Charles, so I'm having my phone hookup to Moscow transferred here." He sprawled in an easy chair, pointed at the floor, and smiled at Carter, "and I'm going to make myself at home."

"Fine, Tom. I just ordered us something to eat. I'm afraid it may take as long as thirty-six hours to contact David, maybe less if the experts can try something they've only been experimenting with up to now. But I'm told we can try out a onetime code if you can raise the embassy yourself."

"We'll give it the old college try." He smiled at Carter for a moment, then straightened up from his slouch in the chair, his face turning serious. "Sam, I've had a chance to talk to the President for a few moments, and things aren't very good over at the White House. He just doesn't understand what's going on, or he doesn't want to.'' He sat even higher in his chair, staring directly into Carter's eyes. ''He seems to think we're installing offensive weapons . . . getting ready for an attack. He says he'll be damned if he'll order one.'' He paused for a moment, rubbing his left eye. ''Just what is there about this new weapon on Islas Piedras? Does he know something I don't?''

''It's simply an advanced missile system. You may remember that it was determined during the last administration that the Indian Ocean had become the most strategic of international waters. It covers an umbrella from the tip of Africa through the oil states, India, Southeast Asia, and all the way down to Australia. Since the Russians have been trying to use Africa as a jumping-off point to the South Atlantic, and the Arabs have become increasingly frightened about who they want to jump into bed with, we felt we had to do something.''

''I remember quite well, Sam.'' Jasperson had been Vice-President at the time, but had lost on his bid to run for President.

''We've been trying to set up Islas Piedras as a major base since the Russians moved into the Maldives. At the same time the laser system was being developed to neutralize Russian offensive satellites, we were also able to create a missile that was sort of a combination between an ICBM and a Cruise missile, long range and low level. We didn't need the range of the ICBM, and the SALT agreements made it difficult to justify, but this one just seemed to be the right one to protect our African interests and keep us on top of the oil states at the same time. I think you can feel comfortable in emphasizing to the President, if necessary, that this weapon is still purely strategic, and has not been established on Islas Piedras as an offensive weapon to start another war.''

''I know, Sam,'' mused the Secretary, ''they never are. But what would you think if you were a Russian?''

''Jesus, would I ever be pissed off. It's literally the same thing as their missiles in Cuba over twenty years ago. We don't plan to use them against Russia. We just want to grab their sphere of influence by the balls.''

"Exactly. Remember, this was supposed to be a *fait accompli*. The missile system was going to be completed by the time the landing exercises were over. The President had authorized the use of the lasers for exactly the opposite reason you think—expecting they would never have to be used, and assuming no lives would ever be involved.''

"But, damn it, Tom, they always are.''

"I know, Sam. But I've been in this political business a long time, and I can tell you that Presidents don't expect things to go wrong or get delayed—because they don't want them to. And he wanted this only as his own *fait accompli*, to make him look good, not to get caught with his pants down. Your people used the lasers because that was the next step if the Russians got word of this, and now you've scared him. Now, if you'll pardon the expression, he sees the Navy making him a prime asshole in the eyes of the world and the Russians forcing him to give up what he had been told is our most strategic base—not to mention control of the seas.''

"So what next?''

"How long will it take to finish off the Islas Piedras installation?''

Admiral Carter thought for a moment, folding his hands in his lap, placing the index fingers together, and finally resting their tips on the bridge of his nose. "A week, maybe two if we have trouble getting the warheads there. One thing to remember, we didn't want to have warheads on the island, especially nuclear ones, until we were damn sure it was secure. Can you imagine how foolish we'd look if the U.N. were to supervise us in removing nuclear-tipped weapons from an island in the middle of the Indian Ocean?''

"How long can Admiral Charles hold off the Russian force?''

"Tom, it's not a matter of holding them off. Remember, this started off as a show of force. They've already shown they're willing to fight. In a while, news of the first big sea battle in forty years is going to be spread all over the world. The Russians can figure on a battle of attrition with our forces, and if they keep them busy, their submarines can get to our supply ships. By that time the President will have either gone screaming to the U.N., or even worse, he might have picked up the hot line and surrendered a war that never started.''

"How well do you know the Russians, Sam?''

"Do you mean the party Chairman, or Gorenko, or Alex Kupinsky?''

"I have met the people in the Kremlin, Sam. Who is this Kupinsky, the one you call Alex?''

Admiral Carter drew a deep breath, again resting the tips of his index fingers on the bridge of his nose. He exhaled slowly, ''Alex Kupinsky is in command of the Russian Indian Ocean fleet. He is also Gorenko's adopted son. And not only is he a brilliant naval strategist who we know influenced the expansion of their support forces, but he was the brains behind their blue-water carrier task forces.''

Secretary Jasperson whistled quietly. ''That's a lot of horsepower.''

"If your aides found that letter of reprimand in David's service record from more than fifteen years ago, I'm surprised they didn't also tell you that he was reassigned from the embassy in London because he developed a friendship with his alter ego in the Russian embassy.'' He stared directly at Jasperson.

"They did, Sam. I was just waiting to find out from you,'' he admitted. ''Are you leading up to what I think you are?''

"Yes,'' he replied quietly. ''It was Alex Kupinsky. If you put two people from different worlds in the same room, and they found out they had mutual interests, they'd spend some time together. They are both highly intelligent people, committed to the study of seapower. Alex knew his Mahan, and David had read everything that Gorenko wrote about the development of the Soviet Navy. And,'' he added thoughtfully, ''Alex was in command of that submarine I surfaced off Cuba in 1962.''

"Oh, my God! Now, I see!" was all that Jasperson said.

"That's right, Tom. The positions are reversed now. I don't think there's any way Gorenko or Kupinsky are going to give. David has to win, and you have to hold off the President."

The Secretary of State nodded his head in understanding, not saying a word. He understood perfectly well not only the stakes they were playing for but, now, the players.

Their personal thoughts were interrupted by a knock at the door. A word from Carter allowed the young comm officer to enter, followed by a cart with food for all of them and the necessary technicians to install the Secretary's phone to the Moscow embassy.

They ate in a silence punctuated only by the sounds of the men completing the phone system. The communications officer was relieved, as they neared the end of their meal, when someone finally spoke.

It was Jasperson who broke the silence. "I assume this onetime code of yours is simple enough to learn."

"Yes, sir. There's a simple code word to let them know on the other end which one you'll be using. Right now, you want to prepare your message in as few words as possible, and I'll translate it to fit the code. As you prepare it here, you destroy the system. As they translate it there, the same thing happens. We'll simply have to read it to them on the landline, and that's why I suggest as few words as possible." He then took a few moments to instruct the Secretary.

Together, while the other men gave instructions over the phone for placing the call, Jasperson and Carter prepared their message. In as terse a statement as they could make, they attempted to inform Collier and the ambassador of the status of Islas Piedras, David Charles's task force, and the attitude of the President.

"I have the embassy on the line, gentlemen."

Secretary Jasperson reached for the phone, prepared to give his message as quickly as possible. "This is Secretary Jasperson. I have an urgent message for the ambassador and Admiral Collier."

A distant voice at the other end replied, ''I am very sorry, sir, but they received word that Admiral Gorenko would talk with them and left only a few moments ago . . .'' and then the connection was broken.

Jasperson'e earlier statement was true. The phone had also rung in the Kremlin.

FROM THE LOG OF
ADMIRAL DAVID CHARLES

COMMUNICATIONS. They're something the Navy takes for granted and something I have always accepted as a natural adjunct to my job. Communications were provided by other people. I never had to worry. In a whaleboat off a Cuban beach, in a riverboat in Vietnam, wherever I've been, I've never had to worry about them. I've always been able to communicate when it's necessary.

Today, I continue to be out of touch with my seniors and my country via any kind of secure channel, voice, teletype, even the old Morse code system. And the computers that my command ship carries that are supposed to be in contact with War Games are as useless as a kitten. I'd always been made to understand that when it became evident in the sixties that our sophisticated electronics could easily be disabled by a single bullet, that everything was protected. There were simple methods of armoring, equipment placement in the ship, cross-connected circuits that could bypass any failures, any number of methods that I could never understand. But no one ever considered the relay source of the signals themselves. The computers are useless unless they receive some input to generate information. A computer is only as good as the information provided for it, and the Russians have made sure that the source is useless by simply zapping a few satellites. The millions, maybe billions, of dollars spent to have instant access to anything War Games might be able to provide for a tactical situation are so much chewing gum on the sidewalk. I hope that right now someone back in Washington is thinking of a better mousetrap for the next war.

At least I have some advantages over Farragut and Dahlgren and some of the others. I don't have to rely on signal flags and line-of-sight communications. But my captains and I are as much on our own in making decisions as a company commander in the field. Our lives are dependent on our wits. We're back to making our own decisions again. That's what Sam has been pounding at me for years, and he couldn't have been more right. He is probably grinning right now in Washington, knowing just what the situation is. But now, he's part bureaucrat and he's probably tearing his hair out trying to get hold of me. If you ever read this, sorry for the inconvenience, Sam.

I don't like the situation I'm in either. Perhaps it's a bit of age showing, but the idea of meeting Alex in battle doesn't appeal to me. That belongs with King Arthur's knights or the old western gunmen. This showdown with friends, regardless of the situation, just isn't attractive to me, but I know both of us will continue. We've both been trained for this, and we'll do our jobs, but I wonder if he knows any more than I do why he's ''gunning'' for me?

Islas Piedras is a mystery to me. I don't absolutely know what it means to us or why the Russians are so anxious about it. And I'm sure not the type to question orders. I wouldn't be here unless there was a reason. John Mack told me the Navy always has a reason, but I just hope that damn island is important enough to make it all worthwhile. Perhaps the reason I need to know what it means is so that I can pass it on to my men. Most of them haven't been around as long as I have, and a lot of them need to know why they might die before they really have their heart in it. Sam Carter used to be so good about that, telling the troops what was happening from day to day, and they loved him for it. I don't need to be loved, but I sure do know what's going through their heads. Silence can be terrifying.

CHAPTER
TEN

THE international damage was complete. The Party Chairman had made his speech. Enough preliminary ground-work had been laid so that it was distributed world-wide by most press syndicates within hours. The seeds of further distrust of America were germinating. The Chairman had shown proof that the United States was finishing a base for Trident submarines at Islas Piedras that would be a threat to not only the Asian subcontinent but Africa as well. Of even more significance, he saw a greater threat to the integrity of the emerging Third and Fourth World nations. Little more need be said. It had proved effective beyond even the Chairman's wildest hopes.

Now, Bob Collier knew, the Russians had bought time. The advantage was switching to their side. They didn't know exactly the stage of launcher completion on Islas Piedras, but they knew it wasn't anything as simple as a sub base. The Americans saw the value of the Indian Ocean and its sphere of influence in a world grown miniscule. Gorenko had explained it briefly and to the point to his inner circle of decision makers, and they had given him the authority to protect their interests.

World opinion was to the Russians' advantage now, too, and they would not release any information about the clash of the opposing fleets off Islas Piedras. Since the U.S. needed time to complete their installation on the island, the Russians would now use the rest of the world to force the Americans to bargain, while their task force under Admiral Kupinsky kept the United States at bay. Although the Russians were unable to communicate in secret with their own forces, they had successfully compromised the American communications with both Task Force 58, and the embassy in Moscow.

The chaos created by the inability of either Washington or Moscow to contact their surface forces securely was a boon in other ways. Neither American nor Soviet officials cared to make public the clash in the Indian Ocean. For almost forty years, the two superpowers had been threatening each other on land and sea, matching missile for missile, ship for ship, atom for atom. Yet for all their posturing, there had been little damage or loss of life between them. While the rest of the world had feared the worst if the two countries should ever begin to shoot at each other, mutual understanding of the destructive forces in their stockpiles negated the possibility.

So, it was better that this show of power that had already advanced into a contest of weapons and wills was being fought in a remote part of the world. And the fact that communications were nonexistent kept knowledge of the struggle between the contestants for the time being. The two nations could survey the flow of battle via photo satellites or high-flying spy planes, with no foreknowledge on the part of the other nations of the world.

Collier knew what he and Ambassador Simpson had to do. It would be a bluff that Gorenko might or might not accept. But they had to make the Russians think that there were still some communications with Washington. His aide had contacted Gorenko, and they had been granted an appointment with the Commander in Chief of the Soviet Navy. But the terms were his. While they were not officially under house arrest, which the Russians would never openly admit, the K.G.B. was ensuring that no one from the embassy would leave unless the Russians wanted them to go. They were to be picked up by one of the long, black limousines with shaded windows that were forever passing through the Kremlin walls at all hours of the day and night.

When Ambassador Simpson stepped out of the elevator onto the ground-floor lobby of the American Embassy, he found Bob Collier already waiting for him, seated in one of the many cushioned chairs in the corner farthest from the main entrance. "I didn't mean to keep you, Bob," he remarked, seating himself next to the Admiral. "I wanted to spend a few minutes with some of my people, just to review what we think the Russians might know at this stage of the game."

"That's something we're just going to have to bluff our way through, sir. They know damn well there's no Trident base going in down there, and I'm sure Gorenko doesn't think we believe that speech either. This meeting is going to be based on how much he thinks he can bluff us."

"One of the concerns my men mentioned was Colonel Hamlet. We know they've had more than enough time to make him talk."

"I don't think you have to worry about that aspect, sir. He was in charge of the Marines here, and he was an intelligence expert whose prime mission was to gain as much information as possible about weapons development. He can probably tell them more than they want to know about their own weapons systems, but he knows nothing about Islas Piedras." Then he added gravely, "Which could be unfortunate for him."

"Um . . . yes, too bad," replied Simpson, aware of the interrogation that Hamlet might still be under. "Bob, I guess what bothers me most at this point is simply that I don't speak Russian well. All my life I have been able to hold my own because I can talk directly with my opposite number. Facial expressions, intonation, all of those little signs are things I've taken advantage of. And now, when I think I'm correct in saying that I'm involved in the most crucial challenge of my career, I'm going to be sitting next to you, waiting for your translation, hoping I can put expressions and voice changes together." He looked over at the naval officer beside him, dressed now in the Admiral's uniform, which he rarely wore in the Soviet Union. "The other thing my aides were doing was something I should have done myself when you first arrived for duty, study your background." He leaned forward in his chair. "Bob, I'm going to have to trust you implicitly in Gorenko's office," and he raised a finger for emphasis leaning slightly forward toward the other man, "not because I have no choice, but because I am as sure as I'll ever be that you can function as well for me as I could myself."

Collier said nothing for a moment, then, "I thank you for your confidence, sir. But," he hastened to add, "I've never been in a position like this before regardless of the language they're speaking. I'm a naval officer, not a diplomat."

"Bob, whenever an attaché is assigned to an embassy as critical as this one, we know he has been specially selected, and we are forwarded reports by the man's superiors. Before I was given this job, I had the opportunity in the late seventies to spend a few days at the Naval War College in Newport. It was probably the best three days I ever spent as far as understanding my own military. I attended lectures . . . rubbed elbows with a lot of brass," he mused. "But, more important, I was able to talk with some senior officers. They really changed my mind about the so-called military attitude being all-pervasive throughout the service. There were some men I talked with, some of whom are running the military today, who were well-educated and capable of independent thought. And the man who was president of the college at that time was Vice Admiral Stockdale, who took the time to explain what his students were doing there."

He paused and looked thoughtful for a minute. "He was probably the man who impressed me most. You know him. You were there about the same time. He was a senior navy pilot shot down over Vietnam and a prisoner of war for years. He continued to lead men regardless of what the VC did to him. And he came back and started his career right from where he had left off, stronger mentally than most men. While I was impressed with his mind, I guess I was more impressed by his inner strength, his convictions about the country . . . about moral values. He made a speech there that was later published in the *Review* about personal responsibility and moral principles that I never forgot. And I decided right there and then, Bob, that he was influencing men I could respect.'' He paused. ''The strongest recommendation on that record of yours is from Admiral Stockdale.''

''I didn't know about that, sir.''

''Well, you do now. I just want you to know that you will speak for both of us, for me, for the country,if you will, and you need not hesitate in your discussions with Gorenko. I want you to translate when you feel you should, but perhaps it's just as well if he is unsure of our relationship in these talks. Let's start out by having him think we may need some moments of privacy to talk, and then let's surprise him by you making a decision on the spot if you desire.''

''Thank you very much, Mr. Simpson. I think I know Gorenko well enough so that you can trust me.'' He smiled, looking first at his hands folded in his lap, then back at the ambassador. ''This isn't quite what I expected when I thought I was going to become an old sea dog, but I guess it's the best way I can help David Charles right now.''

''I take it you are acquainted with Admiral Charles?''

''David and I served together on the same ship, over twenty years ago.'' He paused for a moment, then looked up, ''Sam Carter was the CO.'' He grinned at the ambassador. ''We all left the ship at about the same time . . . must have been a vintage year.'' He nodded in the direction of the front entrance, where a marine was motioning to him. ''It looks like our car awaits us.''

''Okay, Bob. Remember, straight faces and strong tongues.''

The black car was waiting right outside the embassy doors, facing south toward the Moscow River. Blockades set up by Russian soldiers held back the crowds of curious civilians who had begun to collect since the Chairman's speech. More than likely, Collier thought, the K.G.B. collected them for the occasion, probably take pictures of them to put on the

photo wires for worldwide distribution. He could imagine the
captions that would be provided.

The car swung rapidly onto Tschaikowskistrasse, following another black, more official-looking car with flashing
lights. They turned left on Kalinina Prospect, racing past the
Gorki Museum that Collier had enjoyed so much during his
frequent walks. Then, much faster than he had expected,
they were past the Lenin Library on their right, across Marx
Prospect, which had been kept open for them, and through
the gate by the Alexander Garden facing the Church of the
Assumption. The car halted before the building where
Gorenko's office was located, probably braking for the first
time when it stopped there. The door was yanked open
instantly by a guard standing at attention, right hand at his
visor. Ambassador Simpson stepped out first, and as Collier
followed, the salute was dropped without ever being returned. So much for protocol, thought Collier. Their rank
and privilege had been acknowledged. Further respect had
been dropped. The tone of the meeting had been set.

As they began to climb the rounded, time-worn steps, a
senior officer fell in step beside them without a word. Collier
had mounted these cold stone steps many times and knew his
way down the dark, hollow ringing corridors from many
visits. Each time he had always been politely escorted as they
were now. They were led through the massive wooden doors
of the anteroom to Gorenko's office, where they were
motioned to sit. It was next to the operations room, where
Gorenko preferred that his aides work. That served as a
communications and command center, and also provided an
entrance into Gorenko's office from a side door. That was
how they would be announced.

Within moments, their escort appeared from another door,
the main entrance to Gorenko's office, and announced in
perfect English, "The Admiral will see you now." Collier
responded in Russian, drawing the man's eyes to his own for
just a split second.

Admiral Pietr Gorenko had prepared for this meeting. He
moved from behind his desk to greet his guests, extending

both hands in greeting, a slight smile on his hard face. "Ambassador Simpson, I'm so pleased you could join us." And then, turning to Collier, "And Admiral Collier, I thank you for requesting this meeting. I'm sure you have been feeling as uncomfortable as I have with the current events." His English was halting, and he pronounced his words with a heavy accent, but he had made an effort to soften his guests. As he moved behind his own desk, he gestured them into chairs on the opposite side.

"We appreciate the opportunity to discuss these grave matters with you, Admiral," replied Simpson. "However, I'd like to suggest that the conversation be in your native language. You are aware that Admiral Collier speaks Russian almost as well as English, and I feel that will make it easier for all of us. If necessary, he will stop to translate for me on occasion." He paused for a moment as the smile left Gorenko's face. The Russian tilted his head slightly to one side, as if to ask a question, but Simpson held up a hand. "Oh, don't worry about me. I understand enough of your language to get by, and Admiral Collier has been authorized to act in my behalf." Again he paused, to make sure the Russian understood, then added, "He has my complete confidence."

Gorenko's brows furled together. He stared first at the American Ambassador, then at the naval officer in full uniform, including medals. This was not the way it had been planned. They had felt that Ambassador Simpson, without instructions from Washington, would be dealing blind. While they knew he was strong, they thought he might be essentially ignorant of Islas Piedras and the military situation, thereby making statements or commitments that could be to their advantage. After all, he had been appointed by a President they had little regard for.

On the other hand, they respected Collier. He had impressed both military and civilian personnel he had been in contact with since he arrived in Moscow. They were pleased he spoke their language and that he did not hesitate to say what he thought. But it quickly became evident that he was a difficult man in both political and military discussions, a hard-liner.

"All right." Gorenko's face softened. "I thank you for this courtesy since your Russian is better than my English." He smiled and nodded in the direction of Simpson, who nodded back and mouthed a few words of acknowledgment in Russian.

"Let us be honest with each other," Gorenko began. "You cannot communicate with Washington at this time. I don't begin to know what may have passed during your earlier conversations via your satellite, but you haven't been able to talk in confidence with anyone in Washington since after midnight. You know exactly how these communications were interrupted, and that it was done in retaliation for interference with our own satellites."

"Admiral Gorenko. I have no information concerning anything that might have happened to your satellite systems," began Collier, "nor do I know if anything has. I cannot say necessarily that you have any reason for retaliation, but we are officially protesting interference with our normal communications. That is a factor that could eventually come before the U.N."

"It's nothing you can back up, I'm afraid. I assure you that your own country was the provocateur, and I'm sure we both have a similar attitude toward the U.N. But if you are so upset, I will pick up this phone," he gestured at one of those on his desk, "and ask that a special phone system be set up at the embassy immediately."

"There's no need to be condescending, Admiral Gorenko. We both know that's not what we are looking for. We will restore our own contact with Washington in a short time, maybe a few hours," Collier added. "What we are really here to discuss is your Chairman's speech concerning Islas Piedras." He stopped, waiting for Gorenko's reaction.

"Your Trident base, Admiral Collier," and he also nodded in the ambassador's direction, "and Mr. Simpson, is a mattter of concern to the Soviet Union as the leader of the Asian countries, and in respect to our many allies on the

Indian Ocean. In simple terms, if I might, we consider it bordering on an act of war. You are establishing a base for nuclear submarines . . . warships . . .'' he gestured with his right hand, index finger pointing in the air, ''. . . with nuclear missiles where you aren't wanted. The United States does not now, nor in the future, belong in the Indian Ocean for reasons other than commerce. Quite simply, you have been asked by the Chairman, in a speech before the countries of the world, to admit your error in judgment and remove yourselves from Islas Piedras, first dismantling your Trident base there.'' His pointing hand dropped back to his desk, grasping the free one.

Collier paused for a moment, not willing to respond to the other man's language until he had collected his thoughts. He first had to condition his mind to think in Russian, so he asked Gorenko's patience while he translated to the ambassador. Then, before Simpson could respond, he turned to Gorenko. ''May we ask why you failed to contact the embassy before that speech was made? Simple diplomacy would have been all that was required.''

''Admiral Collier,'' Gorenko began, ''if you were in a crowd of people, and one of those people raised a shotgun toward your head and cocked it, would you call attention to your predicament or ask that man with the gun to sit down and reason with you?'' No response. ''Would you not also assume that if the man fired at you, it would be likely that he then might turn his weapon on others? And that they, knowing this could be the end result, might offer you assistance immediately?''

Very quietly, Collier replied, ''We are not holding a gun to your head.''

It was Gorenko's turn to say nothing. After a moment's hesitation to assure himself there would be no answer, Collier continued. ''Islas Piedras is an American possession. There is no doubt about that. The world knows that we have Trident submarines operating in the Indian Ocean. It offers an excellent base for replenishment of those craft, not to mention any of our surface forces operating there. That is no more of a threat to you than the base at Holy Loch, Scotland, is to the British.''

Gorenko's face was rarely anything but passive, an expressionless visage that never hinted what he was thinking. Now color crept into his cheeks. His eyes narrowed slightly. His lower lip quivered just a bit. "Do you take me for an idiot, Admiral Collier?" His right arm had slowly been lifting into the air, and now it came down with force, the slap of his hand echoing through the room. "Do you, Ambassador Simpson?" He half-raised himself from his chair. "That is no Trident supply base on Islas Piedras." His hand slapped down on the desk again with even more force. "You didn't believe that part of the speech any more than I did. And,'' his lower lip shook just a bit more as he made a great effort to control his rage, "you did not come here to ask us to retract our statements, either." His hand went once more in the air, this time stopping to level his finger at the ambassador. "What are you pointing at our heads, Mr. Simpson?"

In answer to Simpson's questioning look, Collier responded in English, briefly explaining the gist of Gorenko's tirade. It allowed enough time for the Russian to regain his seat and a certain amount of composure. And it gave Collier that necessary few seconds to again comprise his thoughts.

"I see we understand each other, Admiral Gorenko.'' Collier wanted the Russian to have a bit more time to relax himself. When the man inclined his head slightly in acknowledgment, he continued. "Our base on Islas Piedras is a strategic one. We feel quite strongly that we must protect our merchant shipping in the Indian Ocean. After all, we are talking about lanes that follow the coast of Africa, have access to the Mediterranean, the oil states, all of southeast Asia, and even our ally, Australia.''

Again, he had apparently misread Gorenko, for this time the man stood straight up, pounding his fist on his desk. "That island is not strategic. I repeat, not strategic. We know it is tactical. Admiral Collier, that island is a weapon, and you are aiming it at us.'' With each point he made, his fist beat upon the desk for emphasis.

Before Collier could react, Gorenko pressed a buzzer on his phone that instantly brought an aide to the door from the adjacent room. "The photographs," he growled. "Bring me those photographs." Then, to the Americans, "I will show you"—he looked first at Collier, then at Simpson—"that you have not fooled us. That island is a weapon."

Neither of the Americans responded, deferring to the other man's temper. It was obvious to both of them that half of what they had to say was already known to the Soviets, but they hoped the other half was still uncertain.

The aide returned with a number of large, glossy photos that Gorenko snatched from his hands, shooing him back out the door with a wave. Slowly, with a sudden calmness, he lay each of the pictures on the desk, seemingly to avoid wrinkling them. Collier realized they were being put down in order and instinctively knew that a lecture on the meaning of the photos would be forthcoming.

"For Ambassador Simpson, I will use a few words of English." He leaned slightly toward him and said, "These are photographs of a missile installation, a very large one. They were taken by one of our satellites . . . before it was destroyed. The launchers that you see," he indicated with his fingers, "are on Islas Piedras." His eyes glanced in the direction of Collier, then returned to Simpson to finish his short speech in English. "You will note the numbers on the corner of each picture. Let me refer you to this slightly larger one, where you see each of those numbered ones placed together like a puzzle." His diction in the strange language was remarkably clear, though he spoke quite slowly to emphasize his words. "That is your Islas Piedras." He sat back in his chair, calm now, arms folded resolutely, not smiling, but a look of satisfaction on his face.

The ambassador had never seen such aerial photos before, and did not realize how clear they could be. He studied them self-consciously before looking at Collier. The naval officer had only glanced at them for a moment, and then only to ascertain if they were detailed enough to show the state of completion of the installation. It could be questionable, he decided, but it was time to test the waters.

"What we are looking at"—Collier gestured toward the photographs—"are Wolverine missile launchers. The Wolverine is a bastardized version of the best of our ICBM and cruise missile knowledge. It is long range, can carry single or multiple warheads depending on the purpose, and can fly so close to the ground that it is almost impossible to pick up on radar until it is too late. The launchers are retractable. They can be drawn into the surface of the island for complete protection. It would require a direct hit by a nuclear weapon to cause damage, but you have noted that there is more than one launcher. It is not intended for launching against the Soviet Union. I repeat, not against the Soviet Union. It is intended to protect against any attacks on our shipping or in defense of any U.S. allies within its range that ask for our help."

He paused for emphasis. "You are correct that the island is a weapon, Admiral Gorenko, but it should not be used against you. And at this point, sir, the fact that it is already installed should make the situation obvious. We cannot remove it once the many countries in its range know it will defend them." That was the clincher, the reason they had asked to see Gorenko. Would he accept it?

Gorenko said nothing, calm now after his earlier rage. This was the time he should have been pounding his fist. He looked both of them in the eyes, nodding his head in thought. Then he spoke, carefully weighing each word. "You are insinuating to me, Admiral Collier, that you are offering the lesser countries in the Indian Ocean sphere protection from the Soviet Union." His eyes narrowed. "Is that assumption correct?"

"Not protection from you specifically, Admiral, but freedom to make their choice." It was a weak answer.

"I see." Gorenko's head had begun its nodding again, agreeing with each assumption his mind silently came to. "And I would like to know—or perhaps this is a question for Mr. Simpson—might this not be considered aggression, rather than protection? Aren't you delivering an ultimatum that might possibly . . . just possibly," he leaned forward to look deeply into the ambassador's eyes, "create a world war?" He tilted his head slightly to one side. "A nuclear war?"

His sudden calmness after the desk pounding was unnerving to Collier. "No, I don't think that is necessary. We have not talked to any of the countries in the sphere about this yet. I'm sure you'll appreciate that fact."

"Certainly. We thank you."

He's too cool, thought Collier, too comfortable, and added, "On the other hand, you are leaving us little choice at this point. The destruction of communications with my country does create a serious problem, one that could lead to the threat of the use of those missiles if we are unable to regain contact. And that fleet that has entered the Indian Ocean—"

He was unable to say anymore. Gorenko reared straight up now, his face a mask of fury. "Enough!" His eyes blazed. The one word he had uttered in English jolted Simpson, who was beginning to sense that something was going wrong with the conversation. "Those launchers are inoperable on Islas Piedras." Each word came out clipped, spit out independently by his fury. "Your bluff is too late. We know your launchers are not complete, and," he leaned forward, his hands on the desk for emphasis, toward the still-sitting Americans, "your missiles are not yet on that island." His voice softened, with just a note of triumph in it. "That is just one of the reasons I have sent that fleet into the area."

Collier made a motion to say something, but Gorenko stopped him with a wave of his arm. "There is nothing more to say. When we are ready, we will address your aggression to the world . . . and we will force you to remove everything from Islas Piedras, or we will turn it into glass!" He sat back down in his chair, his eyes moving from one American to the other, waiting for a response.

Collier translated what Simpson already suspected. This time they could say little. With no contact with Washington, they were not in a position to bluff. Gorenko knew exactly where he stood, and he was an intelligent man who knew how to use power.

"It is *our* turn to force the United States to see reason." He pushed a buzzer on his phone, which brought an officer to escort them back to their car.

A light snow had begun to fall again on the streets of Moscow.

CHAPTER
ELEVEN

DAVID CHARLES struggled upward, recognizing the sharp knocking this time. It can't be Maria, he thought . . . Maria's not here. The sound came again, more distinctly. "Good morning, Admiral," came from behind his cabin door. They weren't in London . . . he'd been dreaming that he and Maria were back there again, celebrating one of the happiest times of their lives. "Admiral, are you awake, sir?" It was Bill Dailey's voice.

"Yes . . . yes, I'm awake, Bill. What is it?"

"It's zero six hundred, sir. You asked to be called now. Our current position is approximately two hundred miles east of the Seychelles, course one eight zero, speed sixteen knots. The officer of the deck has been maintaining the north/south course change every hour, sir. Do you have any additional orders?"

It was a normal wake-up report, as usual hard to assimilate when coming out of a sound sleep. "No, nothing, Bill. I may go to the bridge for a constitutional before breakfast, but just let them continue the same orders. If you'll have my steward lay down breakfast for two at zero seven hundred, I'd appreciate it. And, Bill, would you please join me?"

"Aye, aye, sir. Thank you."

He was gone, his duty done, and David stretched in his
bunk, trying to awaken muscles that had been so taut only a
few hours ago. For so long, he had been unable to sleep more
than an hour or so at a time. Too many thoughts raced
through his head: strategy, Maria, lost ships, his old friend
Alex who was now his enemy, London . . . . He had finally
fallen asleep when he thought back to those wonderful days
in London, when he had been ordered there on embassy duty.
He shut his eyes again, trying to bring back those lovely
dreams that had brought momentary relief.

It had been summer when they first arrived, a somewhat
rainy summer, but the people in the embassy had said it was
something you had to expect in London. Sometimes the
summers were hot when you least expected it, and other
times they were just an extension of spring, the cool damp
becoming a lukewarm damp as July and August came. But
autumn turned gorgeous. The sun stayed out, the days were
always pleasant, the nights cool, like San Francisco in the
spring, he remembered.

It was a second honeymoon, too. He had just finished
another tour at sea, and they had missed each other so very
much. Perhaps absence does make the heart grow fonder,
they had decided, but they also agreed maybe age added a
little bit to their individual loneliness. The opportunity for
eighteen months together in London seemed like a romantic
interlude.

The work was easy. There were few demands other than
being a duty officer, representing the Navy at appropriate
functions, and assisting the more important VIP's as they
passed through from Washington. Together, they loved the
receptions they were required to attend. There were fascinat-
ing people to meet among all the dull ones who turned up at
each party. There were formal dinners, strange languages,
even stranger customs in that international city. He was glad
other officers didn't know how good this duty was, or they'd
have to rotate them every six months, and he and Maria had
never wanted it all to end.

David Charles's mind drifted back to that party at the

Iranian Embassy, a delightful one, he remembered, as he shut his eyes tighter, trying to make reality stay away for just a few more minutes. There had been fountains of champagne to wash down the ever-present caviar, a national treasure of Iran. Maria loved the caviar and found that the more she ate, the thirstier she became. Champagne did the trick and assuaged that thirst. She was having a wonderful time. He was too, though he cared little for the too-salty fish eggs and made sure to drink lightly at official functions.

"Oh, David . . . David." It was Maria calling him, her voice high, her hand waving as she worked her way across the crowded floor, green eyes smiling, hair down her shoulders. He excused himself from a group he had been passing the time of day with, and turned to meet her halfway. "David, I've just met someone I want you to meet. She's a Finn, just like me . . . only she's a real one, from Finland, a native." Her voice was happy and excited. "She can speak the language . . . and she's so cute. Come on over and meet her." She linked her arm in his and led him through the crowd to a woman standing slightly apart from those surrounding an hors d'oeuvres table. "Tasha," she said to the other girl as they approached, "this is my husband, David . . . . David, this is Tasha Kupinsky."

The other woman spoke not a word. She simply stared at his uniform, her mouth slightly open as if she were about to say something, her eyes wide. Finally, with a slight accent that he would not have been able to identify, she said, "Good evening." She extended her hand to his. "I'm pleased to meet you."

"And it's a pleasure to meet you." He took her hand, squeezing it gently, and smiled, noting her nervousness. "I'm very pleased to meet someone from Finland. Maria has just been dying to talk with someone from your country. She's wanted to try out her Finnish since we arrived in Europe. We've even thought of going there on leave this fall to see if she can find any relatives." The woman was still staring at his uniform. "Oh, you're wondering about my uniform. Maria should have told you I was attached to the

embassy. Naval attaché. We have to wear these outfits at all
these formal parties . . . show the flag,'' he grinned.

She nodded slightly, acknowledging his feeble joke.
Maria began to speak to the other woman in very halting
Finnish. But David noticed her new acquaintance was looking over his shoulder at someone else. Very casually, he
reached for something on the table behind him, turning
gradually and saw a Russian naval officer, in full uniform,
approaching them.

"Excuse me, just a moment,'' Tasha requested, looking
first at Maria and then David, then back at the officer now
only a few feet away. She moved over to him, saying a few
words they were unable to overhear. Then she locked her arm
in his, turning back to them. ''I would like you to meet my
husband, Captain First Rank Alexander Kupinsky . . .
Alex,'' she added almost protectively as she continued to
hold his arm. ''This is a new friend of mine, Maria Charles.''
She turned to David. ''And this is her husband.'' She stut-
tered slightly, ''I . . . I'm afraid I don't know your rank.''

He saved her further confusion by extending his hand to
the other man and replying in his best Russian, ''David
Charles. I'm pleased to meet you.'' And to Tasha, ''It's
captain, much like your husband, but it doesn't matter.
Please call me David.'' He smiled, trying to put her at ease,
knowing she was uncomfortable. The table, loaded with the
many delicacies the Iranians had little trouble finding, and
the flowing champagne made small talk easy. The two
women were once again able to make their transition to
Tasha's native tongue, Maria forgetting the men as she
struggled to recall the language used in her home so very long
ago.

Others at the reception that night couldn't help but notice
the strange sight of the American naval officer and his Soviet
counterpart deep in conversation. After the first two difficult
moments, when they realized they must talk together as their
wives again became engrossed in each other, they were able
to relax. David Charles spoke Russian within reason. Alex
Kupinsky's English was much better, and they found com-

mon ground as they toyed with the meaning of new words.
The sea was the mainstay of that first evening, for it was
something they both understood. And like so many sailors
that had gone before them, that common bond of the sea
became a union that knows no boundaries of language or
ideology. Much more also became apparent to the two men
that night. They both were serious students of seapower, and
it became important to compare notes. They left each other's
company that evening with promises to meet again soon, the
men shaking hands formally as they once again acknowledged each other's uniforms, while the women walked to the
door arm in arm.

David's eyes flicked open for an instant as he heard the
familiar bosun's pipe followed by the bugle for reveille
sound throughout the giant carrier. Then he squeezed his
eyes shut, reaching back again to those happy times, fighting
the new day for just another few moments.

It was a sunny, warm Sunday in London, the kind that
brings Londoners out in droves to stroll, listen to the speakers
in Hyde Park, visit Regent's Park Zoo, feed the ducks and
geese at St. James, or just stretch out on the green expanse of
Kensington Gardens. The Russian Embassy is on the northern fringe of the Gardens where Bayswater becomes Notting
Hill Gate. It is a forbidding building behind high walls, a
satisfactory design for Soviet politicians, but it was less
appealing to Tasha Kupinsky. She had ensured, shortly after
their arrival for Alex's embassy duty, that they be allowed to
take a flat not far from that uninviting building. Often there
was a bobby on duty outside to keep an eye out for fringe
types who might want to embarrass the British government.
She didn't want her son, Pietr, named after Alex's stepfather,
to be brought up under guard. The flat was close to the
embassy, but still far enough so that she had to approach the
building only when Alex indicated they were required officially. Instead, she found a new place just off Bayswater
where she could see the park and take young Pietr for walks.

She loved to wander over to the sunken gardens by the
Kensington Palace or sit on the grass by the flower walk, or
just stretch out with the other mothers and nurses as the
children chased the birds by the Round Pond or the Serpen-
tine.

This Sunday, Maria Charles had called her, and they had
agreed to meet at another of little Pietr's favorite spots, the
Peter Pan statue by The Long Water in Kensington Gardens.
It was a lovely warm day, one of those rare days when there is
not a cloud in the London sky, and each person in the park
smiles at strangers. Pietr and young Sam Charles, both about
four, were unable to communicate in each other's language,
but they were satisfied to chase the pigeons together or
marvel at the high flying kites. While Maria and Tasha
happily renewed distant ties, the two men found themselves
much more at ease with each other, dressed now in casual
clothes. Leaving the others for a while, they wondered
through the vast park, discussing the naval history and theory
that they both knew so well, but not yet comfortable with
discussion of each other's navy.

By the time they had returned to a picnic and some wine
their wives had brought, mutual respect was loosening their
tongues. In every relationship, whether between husband
and wife, parent and child, or very close friends, there is a
certain tie established, and the two men found it that afternoon almost by accident. David had questioned casually,
"Have you always been in the surface navy, Alex?"

"No," Tasha answered for him, patting her husband's
knee. "Before I knew him, he was a submariner and we
almost lost him. It was a good thing for me they chased him
out of those frightful things, or I never would have met him."
She looked over at Alex. "I would have always been afraid
when you went off in those things. But you didn't hate them
like I do, did you?"

"No. I loved them . . . And I was very good at them
also," he added, an earlier trace of a smile gone from his
face. "I miss that duty." He nodded toward David. "I think
you understand. Did you have a first love?"

The American remembered also. "Destroyers. The old ones. My first ship was an old bucket from World War II days, one that we used to say turned into a submarine in a storm. It was old as hell and badly dated, but it was just as fast as the day it was built, and we had a captain that could sail that ship around the moon if he had to, Sam Carter."

"I have heard the name," said Alex.

"You'll hear it even more in the future. He'll go a long way in the Navy. He might even be Chief of Naval Operations someday." He shook his head, "But what a sailor. I'll tell you a story, Alex, one that may hurt a bit because some Russians were involved, but that will give you an idea of why I loved that ship and Sam Carter."

He went on to describe the period before the Cuban quarantine, the endless training they went through, the time Carter spent personally with him to help in the young ensign's qualifications, the lessons on how it was more important how you handled that ship than how modern it was. He explained the part *Bagley* took in the Cuban operations, how one of the aircraft spotted a Soviet sub, and how *Bagley* became a major part of that night when the submarine was finally surfaced.

David became so involved in the story that only the women noticed the change in the other man's expression, his eyes also looking back to that same time long ago that David was recounting. At the same time, Tasha dredged her memory to try and remember the story that Alex had told, only once, years ago when they had first been married. It was this same story she now remembered that had frightened her so much. Then she knew. She had only to look deep into her husband's saddened eyes.

David had just arrived at the part of his story where the Soviet submarine had been forced to the surface and he had found himself wondering what the commander of that boat had been thinking when Tasha interrupted, "Why don't you ask him, Captain?" She held out her hand in mock introduction. "Meet Captain Lieutenant Alexander Kupinsky."

Her statement was followed by silence. No one wanted to

speak. Finally, Alex looked steadily at the other man. "She is correct, David. You have described the action exactly as it happened." Silence again.

Then David said, "We could have killed you." He shuddered visibly, as if chilled. "You don't know how close you came that night." His voice echoed his shock. "There was one captain who wanted to fire torpedoes. It was so close." He paused for just a second, then said, "Captain Carter turned our ship right down your bearing to prove you had not fired at us."

"The way I felt then, he might just as well have sunk us." Alex added, "But I had my men to think about. There were about seventy others for whom I was responsible. Can you imagine what my country might have done if you had sunk us?"

"I hate to think about it, Alex. One night, not so many years ago, Sam and I were drinking together and he brought that up. Thank God he was there."

"Thank God," echoed Tasha. Her mood had changed. "I think I would like to go home now," she said to Alex. She turned to the others. "It is not because of you. We were all much younger then, and none of us knew the other. But tales like that scare me. I do not like my husband to go near danger, Maria . . . to become involved in war," she added. "Let us meet again soon. I would like that." As they stood up, she put her hand on Maria's. "Please do not be insulted because I leave so quickly. I just want to be alone for a while with my husband."

"I understand," replied Maria. "It means the same to us to be here. London is almost like an island." She squeezed the hand that engaged her own. The two men quietly shook hands, that long-ago night unexpectedly relived, a certain allegiance forming through a shared experience.

Admiral David Charles was seated at his mess table, dreams of London behind him. After spreading jam on his toast, he used that slice to push some scrambled eggs onto his fork. "Looks powdered to me," he remarked to Bill Dailey.

After tasting them, he unhappily agreed with his analysis, "They are. We've been at sea too long." He made a sour face, then grinned at the other, "I learned to hate these as an ensign, along with grits, shit on a shingle, and every other goddamn thing the Navy decided belonged on a breakfast table. Sam Carter said I'd never be a good officer if I didn't learn to like them." He slid another forkful into his mouth and added, "I can't stand black-eyed peas either or some of the other crap the South has inflicted on us under the general term of military tradition. But I eat them all, and every once in a while I remind Sam of what he said."

His operations officer said nothing, eating quietly and waiting for the decision he knew was coming. The ships that could be relied upon with minor repairs had taken care of themselves and reported ready that morning at zero seven hundred . . . whether or not they were completely safe, Dailey thought to himself. But they wouldn't disappoint their leader. Task Force 58 would fight again, and no sailor wanted to miss it. They wanted to avenge their losses in this undeclared war.

Radford and *Knox* had been sent for repairs to Capetown. *Preble* would fight again. Repairs had put her stern missile launchers back in action, although her after engine room was badly damaged. *John Paul Jones* had been sunk by torpedoes during the night, after her survivors had transferred to *Wainwright*. She had been capable of floating, but her weapons systems were inoperable and her engineering spaces had been too badly damaged. And much of her crew had been lost when the wind shifted just at the time of an explosion, sweeping sheets of flame back through two fire-control parties.

"Our recon aircraft have Kupinsky up near the Maldives," David began. "Wish to hell we had access to those satellites taking pictures to see what shape they're in. The zero-six-hundred report indicated they were reforming to the southwest of the islands."

"I expect they'll be heading back in our direction, sir. Their recon has been just as active as ours."

"Alex is as careful as I am, Bill. If you have the time, don't commit yourself until you know the exact strength of your own forces. Plus, we're both working without instructions from home, at least I believe he is, according to our last report."

"That's correct, sir. My intelligence people have been monitoring their satellites, too. I think we got them all."

"That just backs up my reason, Bill. Neither of us is officially at war, at least we aren't aware of it. And I think both Washington and Moscow would break radio silence in plain language if we were." He looked thoughtfully at the younger man. "They're just sitting back, I guess, waiting to see which dog kills the other."

"I assume we're going to turn to the east soon, Admiral."

"Right." With a wry expression, he pushed the remainder of the chalky eggs away, nodding in agreement to his steward, who was pointing at the coffee steaming on the hot plate by the pantry. He gestured toward Dailey's cup also. "I know what I want to do, and I'll lay it out now, step by step. I know Alex better than your intelligence boys, but I want you to try them out on these ideas with their fancy computers."

Dailey put his notepad on the table as he stirred sugar into his coffee. "I'll try them, sir. But I think you're wise if you rely pretty much on your own instinct at this point. Their best work is done when they're tied into the big fella at Hopkins. That's where all the war gaming and tactical input takes place. When they get out here on their own, they're limited to what's already stored in their own equipment."

"I know that, Bill. I've never had any trouble making my own decisions. I can match Alex blow for blow, but your people have the background on the other ships he has with him, their engineering characteristics, weapons capabilities, commanding officers' backgrounds. That's what I want." His eyes brightened. "I'll put a sawbuck on what Alex is going to do, though."

"Done. It's worth it to keep you honest," Dailey grinned.

"He's under orders to make sure that no more supplies get into Islas Piedras and that we are denied access to it. He can't allow us to protect the island so that construction can continue or allow missiles to be off-loaded. And the only way he can stop that is to keep us on our toes and sink ships.'' He stopped for a moment to sip his coffee. ''Truism number one, Bill,''—he held up the index finger on his right hand—''he's on his way right now in a direct line for the island. Two,''—he held up a second finger—''he's going to have his new Rigas in the air, the ones that he's picked up since last night, but he's not going to chance losing them all again until they figure out our new missile systems. So they won't be involved in any massive attacks.'' A third finger was added. ''He's going to challenge me head on. Maybe we'll even sight one another this time. The idea is to put us on the defensive. As long as Gorenko thinks we're scurrying around the Indian Ocean with our heads inserted, they're going to make more speeches about those aggressive Americans they're trying to save everyone else from, not to mention scaring the hell out of the President.''

''I'd have to agree with you so far.''

''And, number four, we're going to steam right into the middle of them if we have to.'' Dailey said nothing, just nodding in understanding. ''That's why I want the printouts on their individual ships, Bill. I want our submarines to play with them. When you have all the info, relay it to the subs. We'll put together their orders later.''

''What about *Nimitz,* sir? Are you going to sail her into the middle also?''

''I'd love to, just love to. Just to show the flag. But I'm afraid we'll have to keep her in the rear of the screen. Alex will do the same with *Lenin.* We can't afford to have a capital-ship battle just yet, Bill. Maybe some brilliant politician will figure out how to call off the dogs before that happens.'' His face became suddenly serious, more so than Dailey had ever seen it. ''Alex is my friend, Bill. Right now, I don't think I'd ever be able to live with myself if I killed him. We've trained for this showdown all our lives,'' he was staring at the overhead, ''and now I feel like I'm sparring with my brother.''

Dailey said nothing. He knew he wasn't expected to respond, and he waited until David spoke again. "Turn us east, Bill. Probably just about due east. I want to intercept *Lenin* head on. Want to bet on a course?"

"No, sir. I expect you're right."

"Aw, come on, Bill. You're going to take away my last little bit of fun if I don't have someone to bet with."

"Okay, I'll take zero nine one."

"You're on." Mockingly, he held his chin in his hand, eyes shut tight as if thinking. "Can't be exactly due east. I'll take zero eight seven. What're the stakes?"

"Good bottle of brandy at the next port. Winner's choice."

"Perfect." The Admiral was out of his chair and on his way to the bridge, his operations officer right behind. As they raced each other to the chart room, both appeared to a surprised crew as if they were heading for the first liberty boat.

Alex Kupinsky had not slept at all that night. Captain Svedrov was a bit worried about this man he had learned to love almost as a father. But he was not as concerned as he would have been about other admirals he had served with. He knew that Alex could go for long periods without sleep and still exhibit perfect reactions. And, sometimes, he would doze for short periods, in his cabin, or even in his bridge chair where he was now. His eyes would be shut, but Svedrov knew he could be awake instantly, ready with an answer as if he had overheard a question. So he was not too worried this morning as they regrouped to the southwest of the Maldives, *Lenin* having taken on a fresh air group. The sky was just turning bright to the east, and his Admiral's eyes were shut again. Svedrov went from man to man on the bridge, a warning finger to his lips.

Alex might not have been able to answer a question out of this sleep. His dozing had brought Tasha to him, and he was subconsciously sending his mind far away from his body, where it could warm him with treasured memories.

Their happiest times together had been when they were away from the Motherland. That occasionally troubled him but never concerned Tasha. But she was not Russian anyway, he always justified. He had loved their time in London. Gorenko had sent him to the embassy as part of his training. He must get out of the country to meet other people, he had been told. The best defense is to know your enemy. But they had not met enemies. Every place they went they were treated politely, even deferentially by those who wanted to learn more about these Russians. And their flat off Kensington Gardens was a paradise. It was in the city and was not as beautiful as his father's dacha outside Moscow, but they were totally at peace with themselves, and apparently with those around them, he was surprised to learn.

Tasha adapted readily to the new social life, much more so than he, for he had never known anything but the military since he had gone to live with Gorenko's family. There were parties that she especially loved, for her life in Moscow had been very private. It was at one of those that she had met Maria Charles. He remembered the look on Tasha's face when he had come over to meet the couple she was talking with. She had been so afraid he would be upset because the man was in the American Navy. But he had told her afterward that he had been instructed to meet some of them. And he had liked the other man. David Charles was almost as old as he, and of an equivalent rank. They found that they had much in common. Tasha and Maria had arranged those early meetings in the park. The two boys had a wonderful time, adapting to their differences as only children can, teasing with each other's language until they had invented a middle language of their own.

He had been told to learn more English and, with David's Russian lacking, Alex was able to practice on his new friend. The sea had become their mutual language, and it was while they searched each others' minds that they also became closer friends. He remembered the day they had decided to have lunch together. He was to meet David outside of the American Embassy. He remembered Tasha teasing him about Gorenko's reaction if the older man knew he had extended his study of English to dining with American naval officers. He had told Tasha that Gorenko would know anyway.

He had jumped into a cab on Bayswater and said, "American Embassy, please," in his accented voice.

The driver, realizing the man he had just picked up in front of the walled building was probably Russian, turned back through the window of his cab, eyes wide. "Did you say the American Embassy, Guv?"

"That is correct," he had replied with as straight a face as possible. "At Grosvenor Square." And then he added, "Do you know where that is?" realizing the driver's surprise at a Russian going to the American Embassy. He had considered telling the driver he was going to ask for asylum, but knew that would just start something Gorenko would never have understood. No sense of humor. The driver had pulled right up to the front of the Grosvenor House, its glass front so rich and powerful, and deposited him with a curious look. David had been waiting outside, and came over to shake his hand as Alex dug for change to pay for the cab. The driver, openmouthed, had not even checked to see if there was a tip. He had probably driven off dreaming of this wild story to tell his missus about the Russians and Americans when he arrived home that night. Those days had been wonderful. They had unearthed his sense of humor.

A radio speaker on the other side of the bridge briefly interrupted Alex's reverie, but it was quickly silenced by a wave of Svedrov's hand, and he forced his mind back again to those days. He remembered best that Saturday the four of them and the boys had gone to Greenwich to visit the Royal Naval Museum and the Observatory.

They had met at Marble Arch and decided right then that they had a talent for picking superb days. They walked over to a nearby Bakerloo underground station and took one of the lovely old trains that were left over from before the war, the ones with the wooden cars and velveteen seats with armrests. It wasn't like the underground in Moscow that was so clean and efficient and modern, he remembered, but it was a symbol of the British love of tradition.

They got off at Charing Cross, walking the short distance over to the Embankment, and then down the steep steps, worn by time and the feet of people dead for centuries. One of the riverboats was just leaving for Greenwich and that left them near the head of the line for the next one. When it pulled up to the pier, they were able to easily find a seat in its bow. They had grandstand seats for the Thames riverfront as the boat slid under the Waterloo bridge heading downstream.

Adults want to point out all the sites to children on such a trip, while children want to watch the sea gulls and the tugs and the variety of garbage afloat in the river. So while each family used a map to dictate history to their child in their own language, each boy pointed out for the other the gulls, and the garbage, and the tugs sliding past.

Wistfully, Alex thought in his semi-dream how lovely it would be to take Tasha back to London, even to have David and Maria join them. The boys were so much older now, they'd probably want to go off by themselves rather than tag along with their parents. The dream persisted as they passed HMS *Discovery* on their left, resting calmly at her last mooring. There was always one more bridge to pass under, black with the soot of times gone by, once witness to armadas of sailing ships heading down to the Channel or returning from faraway ports of call.

And then, they were passing HMS *Belfast* on one side and the Tower of London on the other. The old cruiser had seen action in the second World War, but he and David both agreed that she seemed so ancient now compared to the ships they had both served on. And on the opposite side from the old ship, they remembered their visit to the Tower, once a seat of government, home of powerful kings, a forbidding prison, the end of life for the two young princes, and guardian of the crown jewels. All four of them embraced London's history, seeing the great places that had been serving man for more than six hundred years.

They passed under the Tower Bridge, the most beautiful in

London, they thought, and then it was only a short distance to the landing at Greenwich, with Christopher Wren's low marble buildings of the Naval College built right to the edge of the bank. With the tide out, they climbed the steep stairs to the land.

Cutty Sark, resting now on her permanent mooring far from the water, caught the boys' attention for a while. But it was the *Gypsy Moth* that fascinated Alex and David. They both marveled at the skill and daring of that one old man, willing to face unknown dangers in vast oceans to sail around the world single-handed.

The women made sure they were on the lawns behind the Maritime Museum to watch the red ball descend at the observatory at thirteen hundred. "Time has begun," laughed Maria Charles, and they joked about how time had managed to begin every day for centuries in that very spot. They lay on the grass and watched the boys play for a while. No need to drag them into the museum.

The flowers in the gardens surrounding the museum were magnificent at that time of year, as if it were spring. "What do these gardens remind you of?" asked Tasha of the three others. "I'm just being curious." She looked to the other woman. "You first."

"It takes me back to spring, back in the Midwest," answered Maria, "when the fields are growing, just tall enough to start waving in the wind. That's when my mother's flowers looked like these. I don't think I'll ever forget that, even if I never get back home."

"When I was in Washington, my favorite part of the year was the cherry-blossom season, and I even used to walk along the Potomac by myself." David added, smiling at his wife, "Maria will tell you I'm not much of a fan of the cold, and when those blossoms came out, I knew winter was gone."

"That's like Leningrad," remarked Tasha. "Can you imagine that's what I remember more than my own home? In spring, when the apple blossoms came out in Leningrad, that's what I loved most. The ice was off the canals and the boats were on the Neva again, and we could put away those heavy clothes for another season. It was glorious.''

They turned to Alex, stretched out on the grass, his eyes closed, one hand resting under his head, the other absentmindedly pulling sprigs of grass. "There's not much to charm you in Moscow," he said. "But at my father's dacha outside the city, I remember spring, too. After those cold winds whipping down from the steppes, there was spring, with leaves in the trees, and birds singing.'' He paused. "I guess the reason I love it so is because we hardly ever get out there. My father loves it too, but he spends so much of life working that he can never enjoy it as he should. When we do go, we walk in the woods. He knows the flowers and the trees and the birds, and he taught me. That's one part of him that only I know. He doesn't let anyone else inside of him. It's about the only time we're ever by ourselves when we aren't working or talking about the Navy. I'll never forget him that way.''

They were all silent for a while, lost in those private, personal thoughts they had exposed for just a few moments, memories that you relate to only your closest friends. Yet they knew they were still worlds apart, and that made these moments so much more unusual.

"Why don't you two go into the museum for a while if you want to look at all those paintings," Maria had said. "Tasha and I will stay out here with the boys. They won't understand those old pictures about sea battles and places they never heard about.'' Alex and David had agreed, and they wandered through the high-ceilinged rooms examining paintings done hundreds of years before of naval engagements between sailing ships in wars forgotten by all but scholars.

Then they were trooping back down the streets of Greenwich to the landing to get a boat back up the Thames. This time, they were near the end of the line, and they found themselves in the stern, looking back upon the sights the boat had passed. The youngsters found that the best part of a return trip was being left alone to watch what they really wanted to see. Their parents talked among themselves, while young Sam and Pietr counted birds and tried to be the first to see something strange floating by.

Those had been wonderful times. It came to an end too soon, for their friendship was looked upon with regret by their superiors. It happened to both couples almost at the same time, as if the two embassies had compared notes and decided to take the same action. They had been able to get together only once more after their orders came through. They had dinner one night at one of hundreds of Indian restaurants in the city. David had been told that his relationship with the Russian officer was looked on suspiciously by some of the senior people in the embassy, once it became known. Quite simply, they felt it was bad for his career and he was being reassigned to Washington to await further orders. For Alex, it was simply orders to return to Moscow right away. They would help Tasha to close the flat, but they wanted him to leave immediately after his papers were in order. He knew the reason, but it was confirmed by Gorenko when he arrived in Moscow. But it had been a time to dream about forever.

Lenin had just completed her turn, coming right to a southerly course as the remainder of the force took station on her. The bright, early morning sun had shone directly in Alex's face, just for a moment, enough to awaken him fully. He didn't know how long he had been asleep. It had originally been a desire to close his eyes and rest until they were formed up, but he knew he had slept hard.

Svedrov was at his side, arms behind his back, watching like a mother duck as the last of the smaller ships scurried into their stations. He was aware, almost at the instant, that his Admiral was awake. He saluted, "Good morning, sir. The last of the early morning replenishment has been completed, and I have the force just coming to one eight zero at sixteen knots." He briefly explained why he had assigned each ship to its current position, and their readiness status. Kupinsky had yet to say a word, but Svedrov knew he was totally alert.

"Thank you, Captain Svedrov." He looked for one of the

bridge messengers and motioned with his arm when he saw
one. The sailor bounded rapidly across the bridge, his salute
slapping his right eyebrow, the fingers remaining right
against his forehead until his Admiral asked him to relax.
"Please find my steward. Ask him to set breakfast for myself
and the captain here. We will be down in fifteen minutes."
Again the sailor saluted, turning to carry his message before
dropping his hand.

The ever efficient Captain Svedrov had been up very early,
ensuring that every little item was taken care of before
Admiral Kupinsky awakened. Unlike his brother, who was
captain of the missile destroyer *Boiky,* Svedrov preferred to
be an administrator rather than a leader. He would be satisfied with the remainder of his career as Chief of Staff for an
admiral, especially this one. This Admiral was by far the
finest he had ever served with, and Svedrov would happily
remain with him as long as he was wanted. Alongside his
leader, he appeared even shorter and stockier than he really
was. His face was heavy, his thick dark beard requiring him
to shave twice a day if he was to set an example for the rest of
the staff. Whether he was taking orders or giving them, his
face remained expressionless. It wasn't totally impassive, for
he could change it to anger instantly when his Admiral's
orders weren't being executed properly. He was a natural
buffer between Kupinsky, whose feelings and sensitivity
might become apparent to those under him, and other members of the staff and ships' captains. He was also a friend to
this quiet leader, whom he revered without question. Captain
Svedrov was a necessity for Admiral Kupinsky.

"Before we have our meal, sir, I should give arming
instructions to the air group commander. Do you wish to
have them carry nuclear weapons today?"

"Not at all. We do not know if we will ever be forced into
using them, nor do we even know whether we will have to
use weapons today. Perhaps," he sighed, "this will be over
before we have to face each other again." He turned to look
at his aide more closely. "I understand your concern for the
ships and the men, Captain. I feel that same way, but I cannot

allow us even the slightest chance of incinerating the Americans, even the mistake of firing the wrong weapon, or a malfunction that would cause it. Because then all the work that Gorenko is doing to establish the Americans as the aggressors will be lost." He paused. *"And* I do not want such a thing on my conscience, either. Arm the outbound flights with conventional warheads and keep enough aircraft in reserve with special weapons should we have to use them after all. Where are the Americans now?" he added as an afterthought.

"Their last position was approximately two hundred miles east of the Seychelles. Intelligence believes they have already turned to the east. They have sent their crippled ships away to the south."

"I'm sure David Charles will head directly to the north of his island, and place himself between it and us. Ask the navigator to set a course for interception with his Task Force 58 based on the next intelligence report."

"If the computer is correct, sir," answered Svedrov, "I expect we will want to swing just a few degrees to the west and increase speed to about twenty knots. That would mean that we would meet them at about noon tomorrow."

Alex Kupinsky smiled. He was very attached to this captain who seemed to anticipate his questions. "Very good, my friend. You read my mind well. I want to see how they react to our meeting them head on. I'm sure you will agree that we are outmatched in an aircraft battle."

Svedrov's brow became a frown. "We damaged many ships yesterday, Admiral."

"That's right. But they have almost literally knocked every plane out of the sky that we have sent at them. We have been able to hold theirs off also, within reason, but I think the only way we can keep the Americans from Islas Piedras is by meeting them directly. Please order the group commander to keep his aircraft out of range and to fire only if they are engaged. I want to have accurate intelligence on their units and their movement. Then you can put your computers to work later today. And Svedrov, we will make maximum use of our submarines also." He climbed down from his bridge chair, stretching as he did so. "I'm going to have a quick shave. Join me in a few minutes, and we will work out our plans over a good breakfast."

Task Force 58 looked tiny on the radar screens in the Soviet aircraft circling well to the north. Admiral Charles had sent out his own intelligence planes on much the same assignment, and he had no more taste for aerial battles than his Russian counterpart did that day. The pilots avoided each other, much as they would have in Cold War exercises, both under orders not to engage unless fired upon. The two commanders were uncomfortable with the lack of communications with their superiors. Fighting a war was unpleasant enough, but, in the electronic age, it was almost impossible without direct contact with their leaders. They had unknowingly agreed that nuclear weapons would not be used without direct orders, the one comfort provided by a lack of communications. General messages and information still flowed into comm centers, but nothing a Task Force Commander could use to assist himself in tactical decisions.

The second problem inherent to both sides was the inability to use their master computers for the job they had been designed for. The Americans had a specially designed unit at Johns Hopkins that could advise each tactical group through its own computer as a battle was in progress, revising assignments as ships or aircraft were lost or achieved a superiority, often before those on scene could make such a judgment themselves. The Russians had a similar setup.

Each ship had its own computer that could function to fight alone intelligently. In addition, it was tied into the command unit, which could better assign each ship to act in whatever dimension best suited its weapons system and location within the force. But at this point, both master computers were limited by the information that had been fed to them up to the time the satellite war had started. Now all the data amassed by the master computers during many fleet exercises were unavailable to them. After the billions of dollars and rubles spent over the years by geniuses who had been educated to install the sophisticated equipment in these weapons platforms, they were essentially going to fight blind.

David Charles was as uneasy as Alex Kupinsky. He had spent the better part of the day analyzing the information about the other force that had been available in *Nimitz'* computer. He knew every ship in the Russian force, its performance characteristics, the effectiveness of its weapons systems, even each individual ship's captain, along with the man's education and career pattern.

He had been able to come up with few revelations. The Russians had more ships and certainly more weapons individually, but the facts seemed to be that they might not be as effective as his own. The smaller Soviet ships bristled with detection systems and a variety of weapons. On the other hand, it appeared to him that these systems took up so much space that the ships might not have the capacity to carry enough backup ammunition. Their first-strike capability was awesome, but they did not have the storage capacity to maintain a fight for long. In addition, only the submarines had a long-range missile to attack surface ships, but to do this the subs had to be on the surface also. Their surface-to-surface capabilities were mostly line of sight rather than over the horizon. David also noted that the Soviet fleet was now a bit older than his own. With the problem of quality control that the Russians seemed to have, this could also be to his advantage. But he needed more input, of the human kind, and he called Captain Dailey back to his cabin.

''Bill, what have your young geniuses come up with today that I don't already know?''

''Well, sir, I've got a couple of men who are rather disappointed that they're out of touch with Hopkins, and they didn't know what to do with themselves. If they were on the bridge, they wouldn't know which end of the binoculars to use, but they know how to dig. They came up with a couple of ideas you might like, things that the computer doesn't have stored.'' He took a deep breath. ''Number one, the Russians have a very rigid command-and-control system, probably the result of mistrust of each other. Command is centralized, and there is a distinct possibility that on-scene commanders, or an individual ship's captain, might hesitate in making a decision if it doesn't come down from above. In other words, one of my boys said we ought to take a lesson from the Indians. Hide behind trees and pop them off one by one.''

''I assume they meant using my submarines.''

''I think so, sir, but I've learned never to ask them such direct questions. It confuses them,'' Dailey answered drily.

''I hadn't thought too much about that idea, Bill, but they may be right. When I sent those submarines off this morning, maybe it was just dumb luck. But I figured we ought to try to cut that force of theirs down as much as we could, since they've got a lot of firepower face to face.''

''Another thing one of them remembered was a statement made a few years back when we didn't have the cruise missiles available. Someone said that the Russians had a great advantage because all they had to do was hit a ship with a missile, but we had to hit a missile with a missile. So, if we keep them busy with what seems like superior airpower, this limits their ability to fire surface to surface. And if we can keep their submarines down, they can only fire their cruise missiles about thirty miles when they're underwater. In other words, if we keep them busy enough firing missiles at our missiles, and keep their subs from surfacing, then our subs can go to work on that one-to-one basis, from behind the trees.''

''Bill, I think you may have lost this morning's bottle of brandy to your brain children. I like the idea of using our subs to best advantage, but you might also ask your experts how they expect this perfect surface battle. Explain to them the first-strike capability Alex has, and ask how I'm going to keep them busy with all those missiles of my own. Tell 'em I'll end up an Indian with an assful of arrows.'' He grinned. ''Don't make them feel bad. I'll buy a bottle of brandy for them if you won't.'' He was thoughtful for just a second, and then he shuffled through a sheaf of printouts, finally finding the one he was looking for. ''Here, give this to them. It's the details of the Russian missiles and their ranges. If they can figure out what I can do with those Aegis ships to counter that first strike, I'll take back what I said about that assful of arrows."

Dailey looked at his watch. He hadn't been outside to see or smell the ocean since morning, and now he knew the sun was setting. "We'll be close enough to each other to probe by dawn, Admiral. Are you going to keep going or stand off?"

"I'm going to go right at them, Bill. We have to find out more about that first-strike capability and then see what their staying power is like. I'm going to use my subs like Indians at first light, and try to knock a couple of them off. Create some confusion. And I'm sure I could take another bet with you that that's just what Alex will do."

"You seem pretty sure of that, sir."

"The old central-control idea again, Bill. Alex is one of the few commanders they have who is willing to strike out on his own. He knows a lot of his captains are going to be hesitant, and I'll bet he's going to try the cavalry approach, too—show them that they can steam right into the enemy. I think he's got too much confidence in that first strike." He cocked his head to the side. "What do you think?"

"Well, if he heads right at us, I hope you're still around to collect that brandy."

"We will be, I think, Bill. The Russians are going to waste a lot of aircraft trying to sink *Nimitz,* and we're going to have a screen of metal around this ship. They'll try to neutralize the force by sinking the carrier, and this is the one thing I can't afford to lose."

By 0700 the next morning the two forces were within two-hundred miles of each other. Within six hours they could be crossing each other's screen. If the Americans increased certain of their leading ships to flank speed, they would fire surface-to-surface missiles by 1000. It was also important to hold down the Russian submarines to minimize their missile range. Both *Nimitz* and *Lenin* had dropped to the rear of their groups for additional protection and to launch their first air strikes.

While this was taking place on the surface, there was an entirely different strategy taking place under the sea. David Charles had given his attack-submarine commanders the autonomy they needed to carry out his orders. His Indians moved to positions on the southeast and northwest quadrants along the Soviet line of approach. If there could be wolfpack tactics in the nuclear age, this was it. On each side of the approaching force they had staggered themselves for both missile and torpedo attack. The idea was for the boats at a longer distance to fire missiles first, creating havoc among the Soviet ships on the outer perimeter. Then, the two subs that were lying silent on either flank would make a rapid final approach and fire torpedoes into the cruiser-size ships that remained untouched. With luck, they might even close *Lenin*.

Before the satellites tied into Hopkins had been destroyed, each Russian surface craft had been identified and the memory bank of each submarine computer had been checked to ensure they contained the sound characteristics of their enemy. Passive listening devices could isolate a target, identify it, provide a solution if the captain chose to attack that particular target, and fire a missile that would be well within lock-on range before the surface ship could take evasive action.

Bluefish positioned herself well away from the Soviet fleet, keeping deep enough to avoid any type of airborne detection. At precisely 0630 her commanding officer sent his crew to battle stations. His sonar operator had identified the antisubmarine cruiser *Kronstadt,* a sister ship of *Marshal Timoshenko,* which had been sunk two days before. The computer, of course, had analyzed the sound that had traveled almost two-hundred miles underwater to the listening devices aboard the submarine. The surface ship's sounds were isolated by the computer for the attack console, which fed continuous information concerning the course and speed into the number-three torpedo tube. That tube contained a Tomahawk missile.

At 0700, exactly as Admiral Charles had ordered, *Bluefish* ejected the missile from number-three tube. Upon breaking the surface of the ocean, and righting itself, the engine ignited. The missile climbed to its selected altitude and achieved maximum speed, leveling its flight according to the information previously programmed into it. It knew exactly where *Kronstadt* would be in the less than ten minutes it would take to reach its target.

Fifty miles to the northeast, but much closer to the enemy ships because of her shorter range Harpoons, *Philadelphia* was following the same pattern of target acquisition. She selected a guided-missile destroyer, *Boiky,* one of the outer circle of ships defending against possible air attack on *Lenin*.

On the opposite side of the Russian fleet, *Los Angeles* and *Archerfish* were accomplishing much the same, although *Los Angeles* was much closer to her targets, since she, too, was utilizing the shorter range Harpoon.

The electronic warfare unit aboard *Grozny,* a Soviet cruiser selected by *Archerfish,* gave the initial warning. A bored technician had been quietly scanning the frequency bands when he happened on to the acquisition radar of the approaching missile. He quickly flipped the switch that started a computer to identifying the source of the enemy signal. Within a split second it had identified the Tomahawk missile. Alarm bells went off at the same time *Gronzy'*s radar automatically began searching on the assigned sector for the missile. But it was too late. The launcher that was selected was unable to fire before the Tomahawk warhead's one-thousand pounds of high explosive detonated slightly below and abaft the bridge level, destroying the starboard side of the bridge, and ripping a jagged hole into the room where the no-longer-bored technician unfortunately still sat. For an instant, he realized that the early warning system was not as fast as he had been instructed it was at school. But before he could even cry out this injustice, the force drove his equipment into his body, tearing him from his seat and hurling him the width of the small room that was shattering as he died. Torpdoes in the tubes forward of the bridge exploded, lifting the forward missile launchers clear of the ship. In less than two seconds, *Grozny's* bow was a mass of flames, sweeping back to midships as she still plunged ahead at twenty-four knots.

Kronstadt was luckier. It was taking just enough longer for the missile fired in her direction to arrive. She was able to locate the incoming weapon and direct both antimissile and 76-mm. fire at the attacker. A shell explosion close by the Tomahawk caused its direction to deviate slightly as it dove, enough so that it exploded twenty yards off the beam of the great cruiser. The impact buckled the bulkhead in the forward engine room. The chief of the watch was just making his entry in the log following the bridge's order for all the steam he had. The noise behind him was one he had never heard in all his years in an engine room. He turned to see the bulkhead tearing inward, steam lines closest to the impact already bursting. For an instant, the blast held back the ocean. Then, as the first traces of superheated steam touched him, he saw the water filling the great hole, rushing into his beloved engine room. The high-pressure steam scalded him to death before his feet were even wet. Shrapnel from the explosion set off ammunition in one of the AA gun tubs, destroying the mount and its crew.

Boiky, being much smaller, was unable to survive the direct hit of the smaller missile. Her commanding officer, Nikolai Svedrov, helplessly watched the last couple of hundred yards of the Harpoon's approach. The weapon grew bigger as it fell, and his last thoughts were not about his ship but of his brother. He could not imagine that the Americans could possibly hit *Lenin,* and at least his brother would be able to tell his family that he died in battle. It occurred to him at the last moment that they might learn that Boiky never had time to fire a single gun in her own defense. The five-hundred-pound warhead detonated at the waterline, lifting the ship enough to break its back. The captain was thrown into the side of the pilothouse, his neck snapping instantly.

Her stern rapidly lifted into the air as the forward section filled with water. The bow section, streaming burning oil, lost speed while making a slow erratic circle to the left as her crew abandoned ship.

The fourth missile exploded in the after crew's quarters on the cruiser *Vladivostok,* causing a fire but little damage to the ship's ability to maneuver or fight.

The explosions were the signals for the close-in submarines to commence their attack. Their torpedoes had ranges of over twenty miles. At forty knots, submerged, they presented a difficult target to a force already taking evasive action, and that was their greatest advantage. *Cavale* fired four torpedoes, two at a cruiser they had been tracking for some time and two more at what later was identified as *Kronstadt*. The first ship picked up the torpedo noises immediately, turning down their path, offering as little target as possible.

Kronstadt was not so easily maneuvered nor able to hear the torpedoes in the water. The combination of the water still coming into the forward engine room and the damage-control crews' desperate efforts to stem the flow were her death knell. Those sailors in her after engine room at the instant the torpedo entered probably recognized for a moment what few ever know, the source of their death. The explosion, which is always magnified on a ship from the weight of the water behind it, tore a tremendous hole in the hull, ripping upward to buckle the main deck, and downward to rupture fuel tanks. The ocean now became a part of *Kronstadt*'s engineering spaces, creating an automatic list of almost ten degrees. The fuel from the ruptured tanks caught fire instantly. The second torpedo struck aft of the engine room, disabling the giant steering gear and adding another five degrees to the list. Again water did the rest. *Kronstadt* was dead in the water, burning, and the fires quickly found their way to one of the magazines in the after section of the ship. Before the first report was made to the bridge, her captain knew he would stay with his ship, but gave his crew the order to abandon.

The submarines dove immediately after firing, their job

done. By chance, *Mendel Rivers* was the last to fire. With
their attack commencing at 0700, the missile-firing submarines were allowed a full ten minutes to make their departure. Those close in were to take advantage of the confusion
that always follows a surprise attack. However, at 0700
Lenin had also launched her first flight of Rigas, and she had
helicopters in plane guard station. At the first alarm, the
helos left those stations and were vectored to the attacking
subs by those ships lucky enough not to be targets.

The sonar operator on *Rivers* heard the sonobuoys hit the
water and reported them immediately to his captain. The
attack could not be halted. *Rivers's* CO, having no more
combat experience than any of the others, completed his
attack but was late in taking evasive action. The attack
console in the Soviet helicopter quickly located the undersea
craft and two homing torpedoes were dropped into the water
at close enough range so that little fuel was expended before
locating their target. *Mendel Rivers* her fish launched, turned
and was already diving at the sound of the splashes, but she
could not escape the torpedoes closing in on her. The first one
exploded against the sail, causing enough damage to disable
and eventually sink her. But the rest of the hull was intact
enough so that death would have been prolonged. The second
explosion, forward of the sail, ruptured the pressure hull,
mercifully making *Rivers's* final dive a rapid one.

The attack by the American submarines was quite different
from that planned by Admiral Kupinsky, but the purposes
were similar, to pick off as many of the forward element as
possible and soften the opposition's protection of the carrier.
The Soviets did not have the missiles that could be fired from
underwater at as great a range as the Americans had. They
did not take the chance of firing from the surface because the
reconnaissance planes from *Nimitz* would have spotted them.
In addition, as with the American attack, the element of
surprise was crucial, especially since they would be firing
from a much closer range.

Admiral Gorenko had learned a great deal from the Army

during the Great Patriotic War, and one of the lessons he learned was sheer power in numbers. He built submarines as often as his budgets would allow, for he had learned that submarines were expendable and you could never have too many. There were an even dozen that attacked that morning, waiting on either side of the approaching ships, much like the American attack. One of them silently hovered at maximum depth, waiting to surface in the midst of a group of ships it hoped would be vulnerable to an interior attack. They also hoped they might be able to surprise *Nimitz*.

Truxton was the first ship to sense something ahead. The night orders from Admiral Charles warned against the possibility of a submarine attack, simply because he had planned one himself. So *Truxton'*s CO had left his own night orders for sonar to switch to the passive mode every five minutes, just to listen. With the variations of water conditions and sensitivity of the new sonars, it was a wise idea, boring but wise. The first indication of something other than schools of fish off her port bow came just before 0700. The sonarman on the phones reported unidentified engine noises to the bridge.

The captain was in the wardroom, having joined his officers for breakfast, when the call came from the bridge. The OOD was ordered to signal the flagship and to sound general quarters. If the captain had been in sonar as he raced up the ladder outside the wardroom, he would have heard the telltale sound of the missile leaving its torpedo tube. Perhaps, if he had been at the top of the forward lattice mast with a pair of binoculars, he might have seen the missile engine ignite after breaking the surface. As he passed CIC, where the radar strobe was making its incessant sweep, he might have seen the approaching missile painted on the scope for the first time. By the time he arrived at the bridge, a worried OOD had already received reports from sonar and CIC and was reporting the attack on the primary tactical circuit. It was not really necessary, since CIC had already ensured that the information on the missile they were tracking was being fed into the master computer on *Nimitz*. The task force was warned.

Truxton was not properly equipped for antimissile defense. She depended on the other ships. But this time she was alone, for a single submarine had picked her out, rather than a flight of aircraft that she could defend. Her captain turned her in the direction of the missile to present as small a target as possible. The fire-control radar did manage to lock on and her five-inch gun did fire some token shells at the intruder. But that type of defense was like throwing stones at a tank. The detonation was well behind the forward gun mount, and just under the bridge. The ship nearest to her decided that it must have hit her torpedoes. It seemed the only answer, for the explosion was so powerful that they could not tell the missile detonation from the secondary explosion of the torpedoes. The bow was left attached to the rest of the ship, but that was only visible at the waterline. She was well enough built so that her forward motion didn't rip the bow off. But her bridge was another matter. It had simply disappeared, the forward lattice mast crumpling over the side. Her nuclear engineering spaces were still intact, as was her missile launcher in the after part of the ship, but much of her crew had still been forward at the time of impact. Many of the officers and men had been on their way to general quarters. Few of them were now visible on the decks. Some were able to begin swimming, but the majority were dead before they hit the water. When the closest ship moved in to assist, *Truxton*'s appearance was almost surreal. The damage was devastating, but there were almost no blood or sailors evident to show the human effects of the explosion.

O'Bannon wasn't as fortunate. The missile that pierced the helicopter flight deck, a bit forward of her deck gun, continued down into the engineering spaces before exploding. Two of her powerful gas turbine engines were disabled by the blast, and she lost steering control. Flying metal also damaged her main electrical board, and power was lost throughout the ship. Both of the men assigned to correct such a loss were killed at the same time. To an observer, there was no smoke and little apparent damage, but *O'Bannon* was crippled.

Turner Joy had been retained by the Admiral because of
her guns. He had anticipated that her three five-inch guns
might come in handy at the right time. And the Admiral had
an affection for this old ship that went back more than twenty
years. Howard Bivins, her gunnery officer, was a mustang,
enlisted for many years before he became a commissioned
officer. He had been a seaman aboard the *Turner Joy* the
night she had been attacked in the Gulf of Tonkin. The
gunnery officer at the time was Lieutenant David Charles.
Bivins had later served with Lieutenant Charles on the PBR's
on the Mekong. When Bivins had been encouraged to apply
for OCS, it was his old exec whom he had called in the
middle of the night for advice. Commander Charles had
written the recommendation that sent him to Newport, and it
was Admiral Charles who had sent him the first letter of
congratulations when he heard Lieutenant Bivins had received orders as gunnery officer on *Turner Joy*.

Just as fast as her newer sister ships, but much smaller, and
without the sophisticated weapons systems, *Turner Joy* was
really not worth the two torpedoes that sank her. The first
exploded in her hull well below the forward mount, setting
off the magazine, which in turn accounted for most of her
bow. Lieutenant Bivins had just been adjusting his helmet
while talking with the captain, when the wall of fire from the
magazine wiped out every individual in the bridge area.
Neither man knew that the ship they both loved was already
lost. The second torpedo, set for an even deeper run, went off
in one of her fuel tanks. Very little remained between her
stacks after the ensuing explosion, and the fires could not
possibly be controlled. *Oldendorf* moved in as quickly and as
closely as was safe and lowered her boats to recover those in
Turner Joy's crew who were able to escape the flames.

Nimitz had also been launching aircraft at the time of the
submarine attack, and her helos were vectored toward the
underwater contacts that the forward ships found all around
them. One of the pilots watched fascinated as he saw missiles
breaking water in two locations. Helpless, he watched their
flight paths approach two of the forward ships. The first

descended between the stacks of *Mahan*, but there was no explosion. Later that day he ferried two weapons demolition experts back to *Mahan* to defuse the warhead nestled in the after officer's head.

As he gave orders to his crew chief to release the sonobuoys along a line his copilot had devised, he watched the cruiser *Gridley*'s close-in weapon system bring down a missile bearing down on her with a shower of rapid fire 20-mm. shells. *Gridley* then swung to starboard and raced directly down a torpedo wake. The fish passed down *Gridley*'s port beam at approximately the same time the pilot heard the positive contact report on the attacking submarine.

Almost mechanically he swung the helo toward the drop point, still in awe of *Gridley*'s luck in surviving both a missile and a torpedo attack. His copilot's arm, in the air with fists clenched until they reached the right spot, dropped. The pilot released the homing torpedo, feeling his craft lurch up and sideways from the sudden loss of weight. They were close to the water and went into a hover at two hundred feet, hoping for evidence of a hit. It was not long in coming. The high-speed torpedo had found a slower conventional sub, likely the one that had fired the fish at *Gridley*. The sonobuoys recorded the explosion, probably at a depth of 250 feet or more. It took longer than they had expected for the oily, roiling waters to begin bubbling to the surface, discharging those remains that had not followed the sub to the bottom. The pilot swung his craft back toward *Gridley*, hovering near her bridge for just a moment, exchanging the thumbs-up signal of victory with her captain.

The frigate *Barbey* had been well to the north of the other ships, positioned there for early warning and a first line of defense with her Harpoon missiles if Soviet ships attempted to swing north. One well-placed torpedo was all that was required to immobilize her. It hit aft below her helo flight deck. The attacking submarine then moved in slowly like a cat to position itself for a second shot that would sink *Barbey*. The torpedo was fired, and it did break *Barbey*'s back, but the Soviet captain's mistake was to take too much time in preparing a perfect solution for his second torpedo. *Meyer-cord,* five miles astern of *Barbey,* had launched her LAMPS helo at the first indication of submarine attack. When the pilot sighted the first explosion in *Barbey*'s hull, he had flown directly north of the damaged ship. The sonar contact that *Meyercord* located and fed to her pilot was confirmed by his MAD detector, and his Mk-46 homing torpedo hit the water less than five-hundred yards from the Russian craft.

The Russian attack from the flanks had been moderately successful, considering that the Soviet subs had to fire from a much shorter range. The fact that Admiral Charles assumed his counterpart might plan the same type of attack provided enough warning to prevent more danage than occurred. The forward element was now scouring the ocean for the remaining attackers with both LAMPS and *Nimitz* helos.

What they had not anticipated was the Soviet attack submarine *Frunze* surfacing in the middle of the screen between the cruiser *Belknap* and the guided-missile destroyer *Joseph Strauss*. Both ships had been tracked for long enough to plan an effective attack. The captain of *Frunze* had decided to fire his forward torpedoes point blank at *Belknap,* since he would be only five-hundred yards off her beam. No console solution would be required. The after bank of tubes had two torpedoes reserved for *Joseph Strauss*.

Frunze maintained absolute silence, hovering below a temperature layer that protected her from the searching sonar of her quarry. When he knew the two ships were close enough so that the sound of water escaping his tanks would cause confusion rather than evasion, he drifted up to one-hundred feet, firing first at the larger cruiser, then at the destroyer.

The first indication of a submarine in their midst was *Belknap*'s sonar. The operator couldn't believe the sudden strong return from the object off his starboard bow. He was alert enough to punch the contact alarm, but waited for three successive echoes before classifying it as a submarine.

It was too late. *Frunze* shuddered as it fired first two torpedoes from its forward tubes, and then two more from the stern. The running time to *Belknap* was insignificant. The two explosions, one following the other by only seconds, shook the already diving submarine as it maneuvered under the roiling waters around *Belknap*. The cruiser was aflame aft and fore. Fires astern quickly found the magazines below the after gun mount. The water invading the forward engineering space brought on a rapid list. Damage-control parties were too late to keep the rushing water from buckling weakened bulkheads. The ocean advanced too rapidly. She was sinking.

On *Joseph Strauss*, the damage-control party was checking watertight fittings in the forward section when they heard the sharp explosions roll across the sea. They turned in unison to stare, horrified by the water spout from the first torpedo, already higher than *Belknap*'s bridge. Some of the men may even have seen the spout emerge from the second one. Openmouthed, they watched in silence as the flames followed, billowing clouds of black smoke and flame engulfing the cruiser. There were a few muttered comments about the chances of the crew of the other ship, then more about how lucky they were to be on the right ship. They were moving aft when *Joseph Strauss* took the first torpedo slightly forward of midships. Her commanding officer had been on the same side of the ship, his binoculars on *Belknap*. He had briefly noted his DC party on the main deck just before his own ship had been hit and he had been thrown backwards. When he got up from the deck after the blast, his first thought was to look over the side to see what had happened to those men. He saw only a hole in the deck where he assumed they had been. As the spray settled, he saw two motionless forms near the torn metal of the deck. None of the others seemed to exist.

The torpedo hit was shallow, causing more damage above the waterline than below. The second torpedo for some reason veered away from the ship as the first detonated, running its fuel out and sinking. The ship was able to drop back, and her damage-control parties found they could minimize the amount of water entering the boiler room. Welders from one of the larger ships joined them to prepare a patch that would suffice until they could get back to port.

Unfortunately for *Frunze,* water conditions improved for sonar ranging. The noise of the sinking *Belknap* protected the submarine for only so long. Both *Forest Sherman* and *Ramsey* located the evading submarine and tracked her long enough to provide solutions for their ASROC torpedoes. Both weapons were fired at approximately the same time, and both torpedoes, though traveling independently, found *Frunze* changing course frantically at her best possible speed. It made no difference to her crew that the explosion of one torpedo as it pierced her hull probably caused the other to go off also. The combined detonation of both torpedoes was sufficient to shatter the brave little submarine.

The element of surprise had worked. Old-fashioned wolfpack tactics had been successful beyond expectations. Both forces had suffered heavy losses again, yet they steamed directly toward each other. Neither knew exactly what was expected of them, nor did they know if they would ever regain secure communications. They both knew that high-altitude intelligence planes or spy satellites had likely photographed the actions of the last forty-eight hours, but they had no way of learning whether they were strengthening the bargaining powers of their leaders. Eventually, one side would have to establish voice contact, knowing the other would be hanging on every word.

For some unknown reason, the air strikes that had been launched as the submarine attacks commenced did not come in contact with each other. The American planes had gone to the south, planning a sweep north at the last minute. The Russians had planned exactly the opposite. But this time they came in at surface level, hoping their Rigas wouldn't be picked up on radar until they were on top of Task Force 58.

David Charles was seated at his general quarters station, watching the status boards, waiting for the attack they knew was imminent. *Texas* was the first ship to give the warning.

"Local control," David ordered, releasing computer control to the Aegis-equipped ships at each point. The cruisers

Texas, South Carolina, California, and *Arkansas* each had three guided-missile destroyers under their control. "Designate Sectors Red and Green to *South Carolina* and *Arkansas*. I want *California* to serve as backup." He called to one of Bill Dailey's assistants, "You're sure there are no other aircraft outside those sectors.?"

"Correct, sir. They're coming in low, trying to avoid radar contact. We got them at about sixty miles."

"Thank you. Have *Texas* tie into *California* with her ships for anything coming through toward *Nimitz*." He casually referred to the giant carrier as if he were on another ship. His flag controlled all ships, yet had to function as if it rode none. The captain of *Nimitz* was ultimately responsible for his carrier, not the Admiral, who was merely hitching a ride.

The Rigas kept their low altitude, confusing fire-control radars as long as they could. Antimissile solutions were difficult with the radar screens cluttered with surface return, unable to pinpoint the attackers. "They're not going after the perimeter ships," said Bill Dailey.

"They're going to try to get through to the cripples and the carrier," answered David Charles. "Bill, have the inner screen put their guns on local control. They don't need solutions to fire."

"Yes, sir. You don't think there's any danger of hitting some of our own ships with gunfire?"

"No more than with missile fire. The Rigas have to slow down to pick out the cripples and climb a bit to fire their own missiles. Our guns aren't going to be any more dangerous than the Rigas are to our own ships."

Truxton was the first to be hit. They picked her out easily, her bridge gone, no guns to fire in her own defense, fires still burning forward. There was little opportunity for her to bring her stern launchers to bear. Two missile hits left her burning fiercely and dead in the water. It was even worse for *O'Bannon,* her men working desperately to regain electrical power. Her remaining turbines gave her enough forward motion, and she was being steered by hand, but there was no power available to her mount or launchers. She, too, was helpless against the aircraft that got through. *O'Bannon* disappeared in less than five minutes, leaving no trace of an eight-thousand-ton destroyer, and few survivors.

While the open formations allowed the ships enough room, in case one received a nuclear attack, they also invited single-ship attack by the aircraft. The Rigas were excellent planes, highly maneuverable and reasonably able to avoid missiles in a crowd. But coming in low they were able to pick out only one target, fire, and get away as quickly as possible. They had learned in only one day not to cluster together, inviting the Americans to a turkey shoot. This caution limited their firepower. Longer range and speed forced the designers of this VTOL jet to limit the weapon load. So they were able to make only their one run and then head for the barn.

The only other ship to be hit was the frigate *Robert E. Peary*. The smaller ship exploded moments after taking a missile near the after magazine. The explosion and fires left few survivors, and only those in the forward section escaped serious burns. Four Rigas were brought down, but only one of them got near the sector guarded by *Texas* as a backup. The new strategy saved Rigas for a later attack, but caused little damage. *Nimitz* was still unscathed.

The American planes also found a better organized defense when they came upon the Russian force. Sensing that the attack would come from the south, Alex Kupinsky had weighted his air defense ships in that direction, reversing enough defense for his carrier as David Charles had done. The Americans coordinated a two-pronged attack, similar to their first one, holding back some of their power to confuse the defenders.

The cruiser *Grozny* was still burning furiously in the rear of the formation when the two Intruders dropped out of the sky to finish the job the submarines had started. The attack on the cripple brought a hail of missiles as the two planes then turned toward *Lenin*. Neither was able to release the remainder of their payload before they were brought down.

Svedrov coolly assigned sectors as his American counterparts had done, and then ensured that each AA ship received local control only after it was given a target. The American pilots found they were under attack on an individual basis, and they had no choice but to evade missiles rather than finish their initial attacks. Only one Intruder was successful in completing its first run, placing one of its missiles in the hull of a *Kashin*-class destroyer, *Slavny,* and leaving it sinking. The second flight fared better, deciding to come in low to take advantage of slow Soviet rearming and the confusion caused by confirmed tracking of some of the escaping first flight. When their cockpit alarms remained silent, indicating to the pilots that no fire-control radar had yet locked onto them, they became bolder, closing the ships for ease of attack.

The cruiser *Admiral Nakhimov,* on one of the points, had been designated by Kupinsky to fire chaff rockets with minimum charges. This created a variety of targets, making it difficult for missiles to lock on the ships. The outer perimeter of Kupinsky's ships then fired both guns and missiles at this second flight, under the coordination of Svedrov's individual assignment plan. He gave the targets one by one to his ships, and they, in turn, were able to fire missiles that locked immediately on their targets. Again, the attacking planes were forced to evade, only one getting through to hit another destroyer. This time four of the Corsairs were brought down.

To Kupinsky's delight, his ships had survived what could have been a devastating air attack, after the heavy damage inflicted by the submarines. "You were correct in your assumptions, Captain Svedrov. We have only one sunk and one badly damaged ship as a result of the American airplanes." And, as an afterthought, he said, "I doubt *Grozny* would have made it anyway."

"Thank you, sir." Svedrov changed the subject quickly. "But we have already lost a great deal today. Do you plan to maintain this course to intercept the Americans?"

"We have little choice. Our orders are to keep them from

completing the installations on that island, and David Charles has placed his Task Force 58 between us and Islas Piedras.''

The younger man leaned forward, his elbows on the table in front of him, massaging his closed eyes with a thumb and forefinger. ''We will be there in a few hours.'' He stood up, looking very tired. ''Let me go to the bridge and check with the navigator. We will want to reposition some of the ships forward.''

''Just a minute, Svedrov.'' Alex gestured him toward the chair he had just left. ''Sit down, please. You are still bothered by something, I am sure.'' The room was almost cleared out, leaving them to talk privately. Svedrov sat. ''This is the time I need you most. I trust your judgment a great deal, and I cannot do all this myself. Tell me what is troubling you.''

''Futility, Admiral.'' He spread his hands, his bushy eyebrows rising. ''We are ordered out here to be an extension of national policy, but we have no idea whether we are doing right or wrong.'' He shook his head. ''We have lost many ships, planes . . . many men. For that matter, the Americans have, too. And this is all over a little island in the middle of the ocean. What is so important about that island that so many people must die?''

''Svedrov, I know you well. And I know you will do your job as long as you are still able to draw breath. That doesn't concern me. What you must understand,'' and he pointed his finger at the other man, ''is that Admiral Gorenko knows what is on that island and that what we are doing is important. You are a much younger man than I am. You remember nothing of the Germans sweeping across the Motherland . . . to Leningrad . . . to Moscow . . . to Volgograd. I don't remember a great deal, but I grew up in Gorenko's house, and he taught me from the day I arrived there that no one must ever be able to bring Russia to that point again. So many wars have been fought on Russian soil, and so many innocent Russians have died, peasants, not soldiers,'' he emphasized, "that he will never allow it again while he is alive."

The other said nothing, and Alex continued. "If he is asking us to die out here, near an island we shall both probably never see, then we are in some way protecting the Motherland." He paused, drawing a deep breath. "If you had been there when the Germans came, then you would see there is a meaning."

"Will you attempt to contact Admiral Gorenko?"

"No. If he feels it is important to chance the Americans intercepting our messages, then he will contact us. I have no doubt they have all the photographs necessary of our engagements from the spy planes."

Svedrov forced a weak smile. "I am sure I have understood all along. Sometimes it is necessary to hear it spoken." He had grown to love his Admiral. He stood again. "Let me go to the bridge to determine our latest position. There is a great deal to do in the next few hours, and we have so little time to plan it all."

"Yes, and we must plan how we will deliver *Nimitz* to Admiral Gorenko."

Admiral David Charles was on the wing of the open bridge, his binoculars to his eyes. "Can we save her, Bill?"

"I doubt it, Admiral." Bill Dailey was also peering through his binoculars at the smoke from *Turner Joy*. He noted the Admiral was especially disturbed. *Oldendorf* and *Cochrane* were standing off, upwind of the stricken ship, their hoses playing on her twisted decks as volunteers gingerly searched the smoldering wreckage for other wounded. Dailey finally had to report to the Admiral there was no sign of his friend, Lieutenant Bivins. There was little that could be done for the old ship.

"Have them get everyone off. Sink her." The Admiral had shouted it out at the open ocean to no one in particular.

In less than ten minutes, the boats had returned the searchers to the protecting ships. *Cochrane* left to resume her

station. *Oldendorf* turned her stern to the battered destroyer
and stood off a thousand yards. They didn't have to wait long
for the first torpedo from *Oldendorf* to leap from its tube,
entering the water with a splash. They followed the shallow
path, then saw, before they heard, the explosion that cast a
great wave of water above the midships section of *Turner
Joy*. A second torpedo followed closely behind the first,
going off in what was left of the bow. She listed more heavily
to port. A third torpedo was fired, hitting just to the rear of
where the first had hit her.

"She doesn't want to go down," David murmured.

"Pardon me, Admiral?" answered a lookout nearby,
thinking the man had spoken to him.

"She doesn't want to go down, son. She's an old bucket,
but she had a grand story to tell." He dropped his glasses to
his chest and turned fully to the sailor. "I was her gunnery
officer at one time. She was a hell of a ship." His eyes misted
over from old memories. "I left her before that night off
Vietnam."

"What night was that, sir?" the boy queried.

"I guess it doesn't matter now, but that was a night that got
us into a war we sure shouldn't have got ourselves into." He
smiled at the lookout, nodding toward *Turner Joy*. "Every
ship has a story to tell, son. Perhaps her passing will end that
Vietnam night for good."

They all watched as the fourth torpedo finally did the job,
opening up the bow. She began a long, graceful dive toward
the bottom, her screws arched toward the sun for a brief
moment. David moved back to his bridge chair, avoiding the
eyes of the young sailor.

So much death, he thought. I hope the spy planes have
been taking lots of pictures to show the politicians back in
Washington. I just hope to hell this means a lot to them.

"Admiral . . . Admiral?" He had heard Frank Welles's
voice, but he hadn't responded. Without answering, he
turned in his chair toward the captain of the *Nimitz*. The
chaplain was with Frank. "Admiral, Captain Loomis has

requested permission to take a helicopter to some of the other ships. He'd like to assist with the burials at sea.''

The chaplain, unlike so many of his peers, had become an accepted member of the wardroom and a friend to many of them. He was reasonably tall, dark and had black hair that was rapidly graying at an early age. It was always a bit too long, and the jokes in the wardroom were based on the chaplain's habits when ashore, which were also much unlike his peers. He could often be found drinking with the other officers, and his Monday morning hangdog appearance made him the brunt of many of the wardroom jokes. Of even more amusement to the others was his fondness for the women in whatever port they happened to be anchored in. Since he never set himself above the crew, David noticed that they paid more attention to what he had to say. Chaplain Loomis was one of a kind. When he had somehow managed to graduate from divinity school, they had definitely destroyed the mold.

Goddamn, David thought, at a time like this he's worried about saving souls. No, that wasn't it. He was just trying to do his job. ''I'm afraid I can't allow that, Tom,'' he said to the chaplain. ''It wouldn't be very safe for you. It seems that the Russians aren't going to take no for an answer. They'll be here in less than two hours, and I'd have my tail in a sling if your boss ever knew I had you dangling from a helicopter in the middle of a battle.''

''I realize that, Admiral. I just feel I should be doing something for the other ships. *Nimitz* hasn't been touched, and so many of the others have been in the middle of it all.''

''You're right, Tom, of course. But I still can't let you bob around on the end of a helicopter. I'll tell you what I will do if you're willing to compromise. We'll put you out over one of our radio circuits.'' He nodded at the chaplain. ''If you'll offer a few words of inspiration beyond just a service for the dead you might make a lot of friends, too. Times like this a lot of the men suddenly find they're not so suspicious of people like you.''

The chaplain grinned. After so long at sea, his eyes were totally clear. He'd heard it all before. He'd offered religious services for every denomination in so many ways that it would have left his teachers at divinity school shaken. He knew he'd never make it as a civilian again. "I'd be happy to, sir, but do you mind if I ask why the hurry?" He'd served with David before, and knew this admiral well. They had even had some lost nights together in the past.

David pointed straight ahead, off the carrier's bow. "Russians," he answered. "Every size and shape you want. And they're coming in carriers and cruisers and destroyers and submarines and God knows what else unless you've gotten the word. And in about two hours we're going to be right in the middle of them."

"Pretty stubborn, huh?"

"Pretty stubborn," David agreed. He pointed to the chair next to him. "Hop up for a minute, Tom. Make yourself comfortable."

Loomis settled into the offered chair, saying nothing, waiting for David to talk as he knew the Admiral wanted to. Finally, Charles said, "I sometimes wonder, Tom, why the hell any of us make a career in the military." The chaplain knew he wasn't finished. "You know, we all talk about preserving the peace, which is very honorable in time of peace. But I don't feel I'm preserving anything right now except some goddamn island that some goddamn politicians have decided is very important." He looked at the other man. "Do you know how many men we've lost?"

"Too many."

"Right. Too many. I guess somewhere between fifteen hundred and two thousand already. And that doesn't account for all those Alex has lost."

"Alex?"

"Admiral Alexander Kupinsky, commander of the Russian force, Tom. An acquaintance of mine, you might say, a very good one, as a matter of fact. We knew each other in London not so long ago." He went on to relate parts of the story of those happier days when they had found affection for each other in the similarities and the strangeness of their backgrounds. David kept the story short, answering a few of Loomis's questions that were intended to draw him out, talking as the other man knew he must before the next engagement.

"Admiral." It was Bill Dailey interrupting his monologue. "I've just about completed the orders for the task force, sir. We're ready to hold down their subs, but I have a couple of things that just can't wait."

"No problem, Bill. We were just trading lies here." He looked over to the chaplain. "Got to get back to work, Tom. Duty calls," he added with a grin.

As he made his way to the ladder at the rear of the bridge, he turned back. "And thanks for the small talk. Stop by again when you're making the rounds." The chaplain waved in acknowledgment and smiled. "And you'd better get off your rump there, Tom. There's a lot of souls need saving this morning. And how about playing 'The Navy Hymn' over the circuit after you give your pitch to the troops. That's always been one of my favorites."

Alex Kupinsky was in a familiar place, leaning on the railing near the rear of the open bridge, when Svedrov came up to him. "Something very unusual, Admiral. The Americans are using one of their tactical frequencies for some type of speech. Our interpreters do not understand exactly its purpose."

Kupinsky moved toward the front of the bridge wing and gestured to a radio speaker near his chair. "Patch it in there." Svedrov saluted and was gone.

A few moments later the speaker suddenly blared through the quiet with a too-loud American voice. He turned it down in an attempt to make out the words, but they had stopped. As Svedrov returned to the bridge, the music began its slow cadence. He looked at his Admiral, shaking his head in bewilderment.

It was "The Navy Hymn."

FROM THE LOG OF
ADMIRAL DAVID CHARLES

WHEN I was in plot early this morning, there were so many notes I wanted to write down for this log. Now I know it's not necessary. The history books will take care of that. They don't need my scratchings. I wonder what they will call what's happening here. Will it be the Battle of the Indian Ocean or the Battle of Islas Piedras? We have seen the ocean, but I don't think anyone on either side has seen that goddamn pile of guano that caused all of this. Will they lump all the fleet actions together, or will they separate the individual segments? I'd call this the third battle myself, although this day's just starting. We're going to meet head on in a few hours, and then will that be the fourth battle or part of the third?

What have I learned from this confrontation? Maybe that's what I'll want to look back on most, or tell my grandchildren sometime. What I know without having to be told is that I'm chasing around the Indian Ocean on the foremost target, the *Nimitz*. Gorenko wants this ship because once our air-strike capability is gone, that island will be theirs if they have to squander ships in vast numbers to get it. Never before at sea has the awesome power of the air strike been so evident to me. And never before have I realized that we have a huge problem with just one giant carrier when the stakes are so high. If I had the chance to do it all over, I'd want half a dozen little carriers all over the ocean, fast little jobs that could get their air groups close enough to the enemy to strike from one direction while another carrier did it from the opposite side. And if we lost one, or two, or even three of those bird farms to the enemy, we'd still have more to throw back at them.

That, I think, is what we need the most. And we have to develop those VTOL planes like the Russians have. If we only have so much money to spend on ships, we need little dual-purpose carriers with planes that don't need much space

252

for takeoff or landing. Then we wouldn't mind the expense so much if they get used for antisubmarine purposes one time and this type of battle the next. They'd never dream of using *Nimitz* for ASW after the bundle they dropped on this ship.

And since these carriers can't protect themselves from missile attack very well, I'd just as soon have a bunch of those little frigates chasing around me, as long as they had plenty of antimissile gear on them. I used to think that offensive power on these little ships was so important, but now I think I want to have defense instead and project all my power with carrier aircraft.

All the missiles are carrying a bigger bang than ever before. When a ship is hit, especially a little one, I think that may be it for them, more often than not. So maybe they don't need that expensive engineering plant after all. If they've got to be expendable like they've been in the past, then why spend too much money on engines and double screws when the first hit will probably be the last. They're not going to steam back for repairs like they did forty years ago.

Alex isn't going to win. I don't know if we are either, but he's not going to get that island. There are more of them than us, but he doesn't have the carrier strike that he needs. His ships are bristling with weapons, too, but that fierce look doesn't do a hell of a lot of good if they aren't as reliable as ours. I think that's another place I may have Alex beaten. Our technology is supposed to be more reliable, and if it is, we'll hold out.

After everything that's happened this morning, I should be able to write a book, but I know Bill Dailey needs me now and I feel so tired.

My dearest David,

I know I wrote you only yesterday, and that it's very unlike me to worry about you or even to write more than once a week. But I know something is desperately wrong and you may need these letters very much. I called Ann Carter today, and she was strangely quiet. Sam had never come back after he had left from dinner here the other night, and she says he has returned only one of her calls and was very abrupt even then. I've noticed other little things, too. Last night, when I was coming home from Bobbie Collier's (and she is sure something's up), I noticed that a lot of military cars were not in the driveways where they belong at that hour. I'm sure they're all at the Pentagon working late, or not planning to come home at all.

I might be getting too old for these Cold War crises, but I looked in the mirror the other day, and the face didn't look too ancient to me. So maybe I'm not imagining things after all. And by the way, I heard on the morning news that the White House is tighter than a drum since yesterday afternoon. I guess all of this meandering of mine keeps coming back to the same point—I worry about you these days. I'd always thought admirals kept to their desks and stayed out of trouble, but I have this horrible feeling you're steaming right into it like you used to. Please remember, admirals aren't intended to go in harm's way. I don't remember who used that phrase before, but the statement about admirals is purely mine.

Now, the news is just beginning to talk about some speech by a leader in Russia that was very threatening and then there are reports that merchant ships in the Indian Ocean are sending signals about fighting at sea. That's why I'm worried now, just in case you're anywhere near whatever is happening. You did your share when you were younger, and now it's time to let someone else do it. And that's not selfish, David, that's just good sense!

I just went back and read what I'd written down so far. I thought about ripping it up and starting over because I was rambling so, but then it seemed to me that maybe you'd better get to know me when I'm worried and act like this. Maybe it will bring you home sooner. It says what all the other letters I've written have ever said, though. I miss you and I love you, and I want you home with me. Take good care of the man I love.

All my love.

Maria

TASHA, MY LOVE,

I have thought of many letters I would write you over the last few weeks at sea, and I have written only two, both too formal, neither saying what I really want to say. I didn't know how to say it, and I didn't want to be a fool by saying it wrong.

Something has happened to me on this trip. I can't be sure what it is. But I do know that when a naval officer spends more time wishing he was in Leningrad at the Hermitage or listening to a group of women play their balalaikas and sing peasant songs, then maybe he should think about changing his job. Does that surprise you? I have felt that way often over the last year or two, and so much more now. We've been married long enough, so I'll bet you are surprised by this little revelation of mine. Please believe me. I am serious, and I want to do all of this with you.

It may be that I am afraid time will pass me by and then we will be too old or too sick to do all these things. I want to travel with you. I want to take you back to the village where I was born, and go south into Georgia to sip the wines. I want to see Sevastopol where my father fought with his sailor army, and I want to take you to the places we've talked about on the maps, the Caspian resorts, Tashkent, Samarkand. We should take the train across the country, right through Siberia, and stop at all the little villages along the way and eat the strange foods of the natives. I don't want us to miss these things, and you are the only one I want to do this with. It sounds a lovely way to live, doesn't it?

I have spent all my life in military schools, and ships, and universities, and I fly over these faraway places, but they offer no romance in the air. Maybe that's what we need, a little romance in this life of duty that I have led and brought you into. When I think of the years of our marriage that you have waited so patiently at home, then I know I have to make some decisions. Does the way I said it sound romantic, or did I go about it all wrong? I want so badly for you to understand what I mean, and to understand that I have thought it for a long time even if I haven't said it out loud.

But this letter is my promise that our life will mean so much more in the future, that we will be together much, much more. I'm sure you realize I am upset by the requirement of my current orders, but please believe that is not the reason for this letter—perhaps it is a little. But what I have to do now simply made me understand what I have kept in the back of my head for so long.

I count each day until we can be together again and plan all this.

With love,

Alex

CHAPTER TWELVE

"I find that very hard to believe." Sam Carter shook his head, in dismay as much as sheer wonder that such a statement could be made by one of the most powerful people in the world.

"On the contrary, Sam. He vacillates from one side to the other when you least expect it. At one time, I thought it was caused by the latest opinion polls, but that theory didn't work either." Secretary Jasperson wiped his brow in exasperation, then used the same handkerchief to clean his glasses. "When he asked just who in the hell ever authorized that damn fool island in the first place, his sidekick, the one who hires and fires, gave him the high sign. Then, after they talked for a few minutes, he requested a detailed report of the entire plans for Islas Piedras from its inception to ensure he had been given full access to all information prior to giving his approval."

Carter shook his head again, sadly this time. "You told me a few minutes ago you were taking me into your deepest confidence, Tom, which I appreciate. But I thought you probably had received some earthshaking decision." He smiled wistfully. "You don't have to worry about my confidence. If any of my staff heard that story, I'd have a hell of a time keeping them from going over to the other side." He put his hand to his mouth. "My lips are sealed. No doubt about that."

The Secretary of State had come back to Carter's office, where they had established their command post, in a high state of anxiety. Never in his brilliant public career had he been so shocked. When things got tough in Washington, crises were usually met head on by strong people, each contributing their special talents to see the country through a time of stress. Personal and party suspicions usually took a back seat to problem solving. Not so in this administration.

Jasperson had described the meeting in the Oval Office in detail. The President had spent most of the time sitting behind his desk, almost as if it were a barrier between him and the problems they mutually faced. Occasionally he got up to pace back and forth behind the desk, sometimes stopping to look out on the south lawn and the gardens. Perhaps, the Secretary of State interjected, it was the only peaceful vantage point the President had, and he was a man of peace, little able to conceive of the responsibilities of confrontation.

It was the man's hands that Jasperson noticed most. They were in constant contact with each other, wringing, folding, picking, squeezing. Whenever they let go of each other, they were in motion in the wrong place, wiping his brow, scratching, fingers drumming on the desk, scratching again. His nerves were nonexistent at this point. He had lost control of the most important visual aspect of a President, the ability to exude calm before his underlings. Each man knew it. Nothing was said.

The President was very tired. His eyes showed it. The sagging, non-smiling face showed it. But most of all, the hands radiated that loss of confidence. At such a time, he had determined to surround himself with his closest advisers from his earlier political days, the ones that had helped him to the top and now were not about to be dislodged from the good life they had worked for. Bright men, they had known how to bring their man along in politics, package him properly and deliver his liberal ethic to the people. The voters sent him to the highest office of the land. When he got there, he found his cohorts were unable to readapt to the realities of a world grown much smaller, one that hadn't affected them in their halcyon days at the local level.

Now the man, a decent man, was caught in the middle. His own people were trying to tell him the easy way out, the one that would get him elected again, the one that would keep their jobs. The Chief of Naval Operations told him that his Navy could put the Russians in their place and he would stay beside the President. The CNO had high ambitions after this final tour of duty. The Ambassador to the United Nations was scared to death of the situation and openly preached giving in. The other members of the cabinet had ambitions of their own and offered advice that neither confirmed or denied their personal opinions, but left them open to agreeing with the President if his decisions later proved correct.

The Secretary of State laid his cards on the table and told the President exactly what the odds were for each situation. He explained how Islas Piedras had been conceived, by whom, and what the purposes were at the time. He backed up the logic of the situation with hard facts. Secretary Jasperson left the Oval Office as the closet leader of the country, though he had already known that when he had stepped into the room.

The President did not want to accept the severity of the situation, and his advisers were looking for someone to blame. Their leader's initial reaction had been to pick up the hot line to Moscow. He said he was ready to negotiate before one more American life was lost, especially since history would hold him responsible. At that point, Jasperson had been able to take aside the President's adviser for international affairs and explain what he felt would happen if the red phone were used. The Secretary understood and respected the adviser and knew it wouldn't be hard to convice him of what would follow.

Jasperson, noting that the news media already had wind of something, outlined what he and Sam Carter had planned, and asked only for twenty-four more hours before the President admitted defeat and used the hot line to open negotiations.

"Did you show him the aerial photographs?"

"And the estimated casualty lists, Sam. Regardless of his strengths or weaknesses, he has to know everything."

"What did he say about the ship losses?"

"They were all stunned, Sam. The thing that got to your boss the most was the loss of the *Virginia*. It just didn't seem possible to him that it could blow up. The U.S. has never lost an atomic powered ship in battle before, and a nuclear cruiser just astounded him."

"He was her first CO, Tom. He got his first star right after that and was golden boy from then on. But give him a little bit of credit. Sea commands are like mistresses. You always have a special place in your heart for them."

"Oh, I know he's nobody's fool, Sam. He knows how to play politics, and he just hasn't made up his mind which side he wants to join yet. He knows exactly the state of construction on Islas Piedras, and he knows it's not quite a viable weapon yet. If he finally makes up his mind that we can't hold it, he wants to make sure the President remembers it was the CNO who told him when to throw in the towel."

Carter laughed, a full hearty laugh. "I suppose that's why he told me I'd reached my pinnacle in the Navy. One evening when we were discussing the facts of life in Washington, he jumped on almost everything I said. He told me that I couldn't decide just to be a naval officer once I'd reached this position, that I had to be a politician just as well. I told him I didn't think I'd know where to start, and that it didn't sit well with my oath. I think I said something about the military handling the military and the civilian sector overseeing the military. That convinced him that I should never replace him." Carter's eyes twinkled. "Now I suppose if he makes himself look good this time, he'll be looking for a cabinet post or maybe he'll even want to run for senator."

"Don't be too surprised, Sam. Crazier things have happened. Anyway, you should have seen the look on the Presi-

dent's face when he saw the picture of the *John Paul Jones*
being torpedoed by our own ships the first day. By that time,
he could tell the difference between ours and theirs and he
was really upset to see us sinking our own ship. We showed
him closeups to explain why Admiral Charles probably had
to order it sunk, and I think that's when I felt a little sorry for
him. It really hurt him to see that ship with that grand name
reduced to a smoking, twisted hulk.

"I think he wanted to be a President of peace. He didn't
want any of these confrontations. The loss of all those men is
really hurting him."

"Christ, it hurts all of us!" answered Carter.

"Agreed, but you're trained to accept a certain loss to
achieve a goal. He's a man of ideas. He, and so many people
like him, believe sincerely that their academic theories will
succeed in the real world even though their enemies have
been operating for centuries on just the opposite. When they
see reality, it hurts. Because there was fighting, I really think
it was hard for him to accept the fact that an order he gave a
few years ago has finally led to something of this magnitude.
He still hasn't, and maybe never will, accept the fact that he
has to fight for an island in the middle of the Indian Ocean to
preserve a way of life in the United States."

"Better there than here!" Carter spit the words out.

"Spoken like a true military man, Sam." The Secretary
raised his eyebrows, acknowledging Carter's earlier point.
"You said, yourself, you weren't a politician." His face
changed completely then. "That's why you and I have to
work this out together, Sam. My whole life, other than a few
mistakes of running for office, has been playing the middle
man, and your boss in one of his apolitical moments assured
me you were the man to work with. So he'll come out
smelling like a rose anyway, and you and I are going to have
to play games for a little longer."

Carter nodded, looking at his watch. "It looks to me like
we have a little more than twenty hours to play that game."

"Less than that. We have to show results in that time, not
plans. As long as that man's President, he's going to make

decisions on what he sees, not what we project. He doesn't give a damn how many Russian ships your David Charles sinks. He cares about how many American lives are lost. So we've either got to have a striking change in affairs in a very little while or else have secure communications with the task force.''

''We're sure as hell not going to have secure communications by then, at least not by satellite. In forty-eight hours maybe, but not less than twenty-four.''

''We should try the land line to Moscow again, Sam.''

''No problem. We can use the onetime codes. You're familiar with it now. Personally, Tom, I believe, it's more important to get through to Moscow. Admiral Charles is simply following orders to fight a holding situation until we can achieve a political victory. The important part is to get to Bob Collier. He'll be bending Gorenko's ear.''

Jasperson's face took on a hurt look. ''Don't say that to the President, please. He doesn't see things that way. It's his ambassador who's supposed to be negotiating. Remember?''

''Right.'' Carter paused thoughtfully for a moment. ''The one thing I haven't been able to pick up here,'' he gestured around his Pentagon office, ''is world opinion about the Chairman's speech. You have people who spend all their time assessing opinion, I'm sure. What do they say?''

''That is one of the aspects that scared hell out of the President. Everyone has an opinion, almost none of them on our side.'' He paused, putting his ideas in order before continuing. Then he moved over to the large map on the Admiral's wall. ''If you want to be remembered as a popular President on an international level, you have a lot of people around the Indian Ocean to please. Start here at the tip of Africa.'' His finger was on Capetown. ''You have here one of the last of the really conservative governments in the world. Most everyone has it in for them.'' He half-smiled. ''Good place to start because they're one of the only ones to support us, for good reason. Then take yourself north. Most of the countries you pass through are pretty tenuous as far as their stability is concerned, Third World if you will. Heavy

Russian influence. Mozambique, Tanzania, Kenya, Somalia—Malagasy Republic, out here getting more valuable to whoever maintains influence—then the Arabian Sea leads into more goddamn oil than you can shake a stick at, and a must source to support our conventional ships out there.''

He then pointed to the Gulf of Oman. ''And here is what the Soviets want the most. The key to Iran and its oil. And if they can complete that takeover, then they've finally completed their charge through Afghanistan and Iran to a southern ocean port. That's probably got something to do with that damn submarine of theirs that's just sitting there in the Straits.

''Then you've got India and the Pakistans, Third World again.'' He turned to point with his other hand so that Sam Carter would have a better view of the Southeast Asian countries that he had been covering. ''Each of these countries is Communist of its own making, but the Russians don't want the Chinese to get any more foothold than they already have.'' In almost an aside to himself, he said, ''They'd probably rather have us get them than the Chinese.

''These island nations''—his hand was sweeping down the archipelago of the Malay peninsula to the Indonesian island—''are so rich in minerals, oil, and what-have-you that the winner isn't going to have to worry about imports into the next century. And last but not least, our old ally Australia, who loves us.'' He shrugged, ''They're on our side, too, but I think they'd stick with us even if we invaded Perth.

''Now, the most important point, Sam, is that not one of those other countries or just about any others in the world will come out and support us now. We didn't take them into our confidence earlier about Islas Piedras, and their only information at this point is that speech from Moscow. They can only believe what they're told, and they got a bellyful about aggression, oceanic hegemony, capitalism, Soviet love of the Third and Fourth Worlds, and a lot of the standard bullshit, too.''

''No choice,'' Sam interjected.

"If you were to listen to the President, you'd believe they were all correct in their initial reaction," exploded the Secretary of State. Then, more quietly, "No, they really don't have any other choice at this point. They've got to stick with a winner, and right now they think the Russians have us by the balls. You remember our position over Cuba. We were talking about it not too long back?"

"Too well."

"Remember, right was on our side. We invoked the Monroe Doctrine, God, everything Kennedy and his boys could think of, and laid it out nice and neat for the world to look at before Khrushchev had a chance to respond. Made him look like an asshole, too," he added with a smile in an un-Secretarylike way. "I was there, too, at the time. Too junior to do much but listen in awe in the corridors of power, so to speak. Well, now that's where we are, Sam. Hardly a friend in the world."

"I would think we could have attracted the same support if we could have finished the construction and gotten the base operative."

"Oh, no doubt about it. All those unstable countries looking for the right superpower to tag along with would have jumped right on the bandwagon. Then we would have had control of one hell of a lot of property."

"I take it the concept still doesn't wash up at the White House."

"What the White House doesn't understand yet is that control of the west coast of Africa will lead to control of the east coast, and then the Soviets have an easy shot at South America. It hasn't necessarily worked that way for us in the South Atlantic, since control of that ocean has always been ours and we still don't have a lot to show for it. And, I guess the same goes for the Pacific. We've had the western Pacific since the end of the last world war, but it hasn't done much for our influence in the communities that border the Indian Ocean on the other side." He stopped and took a chair across from Admiral Carter, waiting for a response.

Finally it came. "Tom, the Soviets are claiming Islas

Piedras isn't finished and therefore it's easy to force us off. But, there's no way we can finish before they call that bluff.''

"That's where the President and I disagree wholeheartedly. It took a hell of a lot to het him to give us even twenty-four hours to try to pull it off. We have to convince each bordering state, not to mention Russia who may not be absolutely sure, that the launchers are complete and armed, and that we stand ready to protect the entire Indian Ocean sphere. If our ambassadors in each place can get that idea across, all we need is one or two countries to change their minds, preferably at least one that's been leaning toward Moscow for a while, and I think we'll be able to get the rest.''

Admiral Carter leaned back in his chair, sighing deeply. "If only I had a chance to talk to David now, to explain it to him that quickly, I'd feel a hell of a lot better now. With the battering he's sustained he must be wondering just what in the hell it's all for.'' He peered intently into Jasperson's eyes. "David's not a simple man, Tom. He's a very complex person. A hell of a warrior when it's necessary, but he always needs a reason. He's no damn-the-torpedos-and-tell-me-why-later type.''

"I realize that, Sam.''

But Admiral Carter hadn't finished. "It would be a hell of a lot easier if he was facing an obvious enemy, someone of a different color, or someone out to conquer the world. He needs someone to hate!'' He was warming to his point. "Tom, Alex Kupinsky is just like David in a lot of respects. Same color. Same intelligence. Same interests. Their wives are like sisters. They've been writing each other since that tour they had in London together. For that matter, you might as well consider David and Alex friends. They know each other's minds so well, they don't need any computer to tell them what the other may do.''

Jasperson said nothing. The two men looked at each other and then at their hands for a while, looked out the window, then back at each other.

"Perhaps Gorenko's thinking the same thing we are—time! Whatever, your Admiral David Charles has to hold out for the next twenty hours. That's all the time I have to sway a little world opinion and get the President on my side. Otherwise, to borrow a Navy expression, we're going to be ten feet lower than whale shit."

"Let's try to get on the pipe to Admiral Collier again."

"You mean Ambassador Simpson, don't you?" the Secretary smiled.

"Yes, if that'll make the President happy."

Shortly after Carter stepped from the room to ask the anxious comm officer to try the Moscow embassy, they were told that Collier was on the line.

Admiral Carter spoke into the phone. "Is that you, Bob?"

"Right here, Admiral. Ambassador Simpson's with me also."

"Let's not waste time, Bob. Admiral Gorenko's probably listening to us with his hand over the phone." It was a weak joke. He explained the reaction around the Indian Ocean to a certain point. Then, he gave the code words to identify the onetime system they would use.

In as few previously well-chosen words as possible, he covered the status of Islas Piedras, the losses on both sides, and the necessary tactics they wanted Collier and Simpson to undertake.

It took less than thirty seconds. Carter knew it would be recorded in both the embassy and the Kremlin, but only the Navy would be able to decode it.

"Secretary Jasperson would like to say a few words to Ambassador Simpson, Bob. Good luck."

Jasperson began, "I just wanted to assure you that everything's going fine on our end, Jack. How about the repairs at the embassy?"

But there was no answer. The circuit was dead.

Admiral Gorenko was furious, literally unable to speak. But he had enough presence of mind to give the signal to break the American land line. He had expected to hear more, and knew they would attempt to use some type of code. And he knew they would both record it. Unfortunately, he had not expected it to be so short, a factor that would make breaking it that much harder. He was not familiar with the American onetime system, or he might not have let the conversation last as long as it did. But what had upset him the most was the attitude of both the Secretary of State and that Assistant to the CNO. He had them where he wanted them, and yet they sounded so damn sure of themselves it angered him.

The Americans were guilty of every type of aggression in the Indian Ocean, and then some. Yet they were acting so cocksure even when he was positive his intelligence photos showed the launchers were still incomplete. They could not let any other country in the sphere even so much as think that perhaps the installation was already done and that the Soviets instead of the Americans would be held at bay.

He must have Alex press on, he thought. They must get on to that island and show the world that Islas Piedras was not yet complete, that it was time for the Americans to shrink back within their own continent. He would hazard a direct voice contact with Alex, and make his point quite clear. Plus, he wanted the *Nimitz* sunk!

But first, he would call Admiral Collier back. He could not let the Americans buy any more time. He would show Collier the newest photos of Islas Piedras, proof that the Russians knew there was little left for the United States to bluff with. And he would control his temper this time. His explosive reaction had had little effect on the obviously cool American naval officer.

Bob Collier was surprised when Gorenko called, requesting him to return to the Kremlin for further discussion. The Russian had spoken to him directly, preferring not to leave the phone call to an aide. To Collier that meant only one thing. Gorenko was disturbed by the direct contact with Washington. Even with conclusive proof, perhaps Gorenko had just the slightest doubt that he was missing something from the earlier photos, or from his intelligence network. Lack of trust was a Russian weakness, and Collier wasn't about to let on that their intelligence was superb.

Again the black car was waiting by the embassy door for

him. This time, on the assurance of the Soviet Admiral that the ambassador needn't come, Simpson remained with his staff, agreeing that now one of them should always be within the building. The crowd outside was larger than before, and uglier. He had to assume that other American embassies in other foreign cities were experiencing the same problems by this time. Possible nuclear confrontation frightened people of any nationality, frightened them enough to exhibit violence. And the world had to be aware now of the great battle being fought in the Indian Ocean. With the merchant shipping in that sector, fantastic reports of sea battles must be filtering back from the neutral ships escaping from the immediate area.

His reception within the walls was no different than earlier that day, but his greeting by Gorenko was decidedly changed.

"I must thank you for returning so soon after your last visit, Admiral Collier," beamed the other man, extending his hand in a too-confident manner. "It is an inconvenience, I am sure, but then we have a problem that is not easily solved by avoiding each other."

"Thank you, sir," Collier replied, taking a chair offered to him with a grand sweep of the hand. "Anything we can do to reach a meeting of the minds is certainly of prime importance."

Gorenko touched a button on his desk and almost instantly the door opened from the operations room to admit an aide pushing a cart containing a large, highly polished samovar. "Tea, Admiral?"

"Thank you."

The aide served the tea in magnificently engraved glasses bearing the Admiral's seal. There was delicious black bread, the mainstay of the Russian diet, a meal in itself, that was offered by the aide, with another smile and a take-one-please gesture from Gorenko. When the service was complete, the aide left, never having uttered a word nor having received a command from his Admiral.

The tea was strong and black, as Bob Collier expected it

would be. It and the bread reminded him he had hardly eaten since dinner the previous day. There was little conversation for the first few moments, only pleasantries between two strong individuals sizing each other up after the earlier meeting.

Gorenko hoped the guard around the embassy was doing its job satisfactorily.

Yes, they seemed to be.

Was the crowd being held back far enough?

Yes, they would prefer they weren't there, but there seemed to be little inconvenience to the American marine guard.

It was hoped the Russian armed guard could be dismissed soon.

Yes. Collier was sure they all felt that way. Too many niceties, Collier decided, but he'd play the game. The bread was excellent, he remarked, and he was disappointed the cooks at the embassy couldn't bake that way.

Gorenko would have some sent over.

"I'm sure," continued Gorenko, "we might enjoy tea together again sometime, or even a stronger drink, for I have no doubt we could find a great deal to talk about of mutual interest. Right now, we both have many brave sailors dying far away from their homelands. It is unfair to our nations that this tragedy should take place. However, I must place the blame at your country's feet. It is you who have attempted to establish a military presence where you are not wanted."

"Perhaps I could correct you somewhat, Admiral Gorenko. You have made the first move as a result of your Chairman's speech. We Americans may not be wanted right at this instant, but you are incorrect in your usage of the word 'attempted.' We have established this military presence on Islas Piedras, but it is for the protection of peace in this sphere and not for aggressive purposes. We will shortly assure all nations at the U.N. of this fact."

Gorenko smiled as he shook his head in mock sadness. "You should be the ambassador here for your persuasive manner and, of course, your diplomatic approach. Also, you are unlike many of your naval officers. However," and he reached into a desk drawer to pull out, then spill, a number of photographs on the desk top, "I have evidence that precludes your statement. These pictures tell much now." He stood. "Perhaps you have never seen this Islas Piedras of yours as clearly before, as if you were reading a travel brochure."

Collier stood to get a better look of the photos. "I've never had the pleasure."

"This is what it looked like when it was peaceful and undisturbed and"—he looked directly at Collier, the earlier smile gone, the eyebrows raised—"this is what it looks like now." He dropped one of the new photos he had been holding in his hand next to the first one. "I'm sure you see the difference."

"I don't deny it." He returned the icy stare. "We never have."

"Let me put them in perspective for you." The photographs were again each numbered in the upper right corner, and Collier noted the well-scheduled shots of the island through its development, both from a high scale showing the island expanse, and then closer to show individual launching sites. The older photos were often of poor quality, which was probably the reason the Russians hadn't caught on earlier.

They both stood there, on opposite sides of the otherwise clear desk, examining the pictures, Gorenko saying nothing, waiting for Collier to force the discussion. The photo considered most recent showed a close-up of a launch site that any expert would feel was incomplete, regardless of a lack of familiarity with the equipment itself. Collier sat back down.

"I assume you find these pictures of your Islas Piedras of interest?" Gorenko sat in his high chair, his head resting against the back, returning the other's stare. "Let's not fool each other, Admiral. I don't know what kind of missiles you are installing, and I don't particularly care whether you call them Wolverine or whatever. And I don't have to, because the launchers that are installed are not only not ready to fire, but I see no evidence of missiles of any kind, nor have we observed any ships delivering such a cargo."

"I think it should be quite obvious that our intentions were not to lay everything out for your cameras. Your intelligence gathering is as good as ours . . . almost," Collier added, "but we certainly were not performing for your satellites or your spy planes." He stopped for a minute to fold his arms. "You determine quite correctly that you are not familiar with that particular installation, and I imagine that may be the major reason your experts have told you that Islas Piedras is not complete. Admittedly, you almost caught us off guard, but not quite."

"How so?" It was a direct, disbelieving question, delivered with utmost confidence by Gorenko.

"As you have also obviously perceived, the majority of this system is underground. Only the sensing devices and certain guidance equipment are in plain view. Perhaps our experts in Washington were trying to make you think we were building a navigation or weather station." Gorenko blinked, but said nothing, seeing no humor in the previous statement. "I think we've done an excellent job of camouflaging the entire thing, so well that we were able to confuse your intelligence people."

"And the missiles, Admiral. Tell me about them."

"Underground, of course."

"I suppose you want to tell me that they arrived in little pieces and then were rebuilt underground."

"No. By submarine." Collier's answers were brusque and confident, and would have given the appearance of absolute authority to almost any other person but Gorenko.

"I don't believe you, of course, Admiral Collier. But you do have what my son, through American acquaintances, calls a big set of balls." Gorenko smiled at his Americanism.

Collier smiled, but said nothing.

"As a matter of fact, I am so sure you are lying to me that we have deployed submarines around your island to ensure your ships do not land the missiles."

"We are aware of that, but I think you will find there are no ammunition ships about to penetrate that barrier."

"We also plan to land on that island and show the rest of

the world exactly what your country has been planning.

"Admiral Gorenko." Collier sat forward in his chair, squaring his shoulders. "That would be direct aggression on American territory. Not only would we take every step to prevent that, but I warn you that it would be a grave mistake. You would be proving to the world, the hard way, that we have completed an installation to protect the countries of the Indian Ocean, and I think perhaps you would be doing a good deal of the convincing that we had already planned."

"As I said, you handle yourself like a diplomat. Your bluff is excellent, but I believe the world will respect us more for our willingness to sacrifice some ships and men to maintain a balance of power."

"Admiral Gorenko, you know as well as I do that it's no longer a matter of a few ships and men. My talk with Admiral Carter established that fact."

"I will grant you that. I have been saving these," and he threw more photographs on the desk in place of the others, which he swept to a corner, since I'm sure you haven't seen what's been happening to your precious ships."

The new photos were no better than the others, worse, he noted in examining them, since they were taken from high-altitude spy planes in place of the inoperable satellites. Gorenko had selected the most gruesome of his collection. Collier saw American cruisers, guided-missile destroyers, frigates, all damaged, burning, or in the process of sinking. Even knowing that he would not see anything of Soviet ships in the same condition, he was shocked. It appeared worse than Carter had said.

"We, too, have suffered some damage, Admiral, but not so devastating as your own. Do you still want to continue with this charade?" No answer. "I don't think your Navy would suffer this damage to prevent us from getting to your island if those launchers were already installed and armed," he asserted.

"The United States has as much a proprietary interest in the Indian Ocean as the Soviet Union. We have a base on Islas Piedras that has been threatened by your government.

The initial attack was predicated by Russian aircraft. Our ships did not fire until they were fired upon, and I have no doubt aerial photography will substantiate that fact.''

''I appreciate your coolness, Admiral Collier, but I'm sure you will also agree with me that the last shot fired is much more important than the first.''

Collier knew enough about Gorenko to accept the fact that the man obviously had no intention of backing down. He had read everything about the man that was available and had read translations of his books. Gorenko had been the architect of the Soviet Navy, and his reputation from the days of Sevastopol and the sailor/soldier until now had been one of perseverance. He had survived the Germans against tremendous odds. He had managed to continue a steady career pattern in the face of purges from within his own government. He would not back down from this greatest challenge of all.

''As long as you do not underestimate the willingness of the U.S. Navy to protect that island to the last man, I'm sure we both value the importance of that last shot.''

Gorenko appreciated formidable opposition. He smiled widely, this time as a boxer looking across the ring at his opponent would. The smile said ''Let the better man win.'' The American returned the smile in the same manner. The feeling was mutual. So much was at stake that they would slug it out toe to toe.

''Since we seem to have come to the end of any negotiating we might have become involved in, would you answer a question for me?'' Without waiting for an assent, he continued. ''Your messages to your Admiral Charles refer to Task Force 58. That is no task force. It is not large enough. There has been no similar designation recently. What does it mean?''

''No doubt you are familiar with our Pacific War about forty years ago?''

''Of course.''

''Nimitz established Task Force 58 at the end of 1943 to sweep the ocean of our enemy.'' He paused for dramatic effect. "They did just that." He gazed directly at Gorenko, trying to look beneath the blank stare returned to him. The other man said nothing.

Finally, Gorenko said, "You Americans mystify me sometimes." With nothing more to say, he stood up. "Our meeting must end, Admiral Collier, for there is really nothing more we have to say to each other." He came around from behind the desk and extended his hand. "I cannot be absolutely sure, but I think we might have been friends at a different time. I will allow you to use your connection to Washington for the next thirty minutes, in the event you would like to report this meeting to Admiral Carter."

"I may. Thank you."

Gorenko paused at the framed pictures on the wall of his otherwise austere office. "I don't believe I showed you these on your earlier visit." Again not waiting for an answer, he continued. "That was taken at Stalingrad, at the worst of times. You likely don't recognize me as the one on the left, do you? That was more than forty years ago also. We were young then, but we looked very, very old, didn't we? We were half starving then, but we continued to fight the Germans. The man on the right is Admiral Kupinsky's real father." He turned slightly to look directly at Collier. "He was also my friend. He saved my life. He died. I lived. I continue to fight on. But we Russians do not forget those sacrifices, even after so many years."

Gorenko pointed to another picture, something in the Cyrillic alphabet. "Do you read Russian?"

"I did once, years ago in Monterey. But it's been so long that I'm afraid I couldn't begin to translate that."

"Then, by all means, I will be happy to read it to you." He paused for just a moment, then began, never looking at the writing, but directly at Collier.

"Russia, my country, my native land! Dear Comrade Stalin! I, a Black Sea Sailor, and a son of Lenin's Komsomol, fought as my heart told me to fight. I slew the beasts as long as my heart beat in my breast. Now I am dying, but I know we shall win. Sailors of the Black Sea Navy! Fight harder still, kill the mad fascist dogs. I have been faithful to my soldier's oath.''

He looked back at the old photograph again, then at Collier. ''I used to read that to my son, Alex, until he could read it himself. Now he has a copy of that on the bulkhead in his stateroom, and he ensures that all of his people see it, too. We do not give up, Admiral.''

''Then, sir, I believe we must both come from the same sturdy stock. I thank you for your time.'' As Collier stepped through the doorway, the same unspeaking, unsmiling aide was waiting to escort him to the car.

Gorenko went to the door on the other side of the room, calling in one of his aides. ''I want you to send this message in plain language to Admiral Kupinsky.'' On a piece of paper, he scrawled in large letters: GET *NIMITZ* AT ALL COSTS.

And back in the American Embassy, before reporting to Simpson, Admiral Collier went first to his communications room to take advantage of the circuit Gorenko was allowing him to utilize for a short time. But rather than make a report for the benefit of the listening Russians, he simply informed Sam Carter that the Soviets were steadfast and brave and then he made an unusual request, ''Sam, do you remember the message CINCPAC sent to Halsey, the one that enraged him, after the Battle of Leyte Gulf, when Nimitz was inquiring after Willy Lee? If not, look it up and send it in plain language to David. He'll understand.'' And that had been all he had to say, for they both knew the Russians would not turn back from the path they had chosen.

When Admiral Gorenko was shown the meaningless message sent by Carter to the American task force, he lost his temper. He raged first at the communications officer, who was equally puzzled, and then at his whole staff. The message read: WHERE IS RPT WHERE IS TASK FORCE THIRTY-FOUR RR THE WORLD WONDERS.

Dear sam,

Since I haven't seen you for two days (almost), and I
thought you were finally desk bound and my days of waiting
for ships was over, I decided I'd better write you this note if
you came home. Since you're always so good about turning
out the lights, I knew you'd find it here.

I want you to wake me up when you come in. Maria
Charles talked with me for a while today about what you're
all involved in, and she's awfully worried. I know if we could
talk about it for a few minutes, I'd be able to put her mind at
ease. There I go again, back to being the wife of the ship's
captain and taking care of the flock while the wardroom goes
off the briny.

I've heard enough on the radio and the TV this evening to
know that something very big is happening halfway around
the world, and Maria's afraid David's right in the middle of
it. She even reminded me of that dumb promise you made to
her at the wedding when you said you'd keep him out of
trouble from that time on. I think you had to be flying high to
make that promise, but she's sincere about it, so I said I'd talk
with you. Before you fly off the handle, I didn't promise
anything. I said that sometimes, as wonderful as she thinks
you are, you can't control absolutely everything the Navy
does and that even you might not have control over everything David does. I hope that made things a bit easier for her
to take if he is there, but you better not let us down too much!

Now I didn't intend to write a letter since you're just
downstairs reading it, but I got carried away since you've
become a dry-land admiral and come home most every night.
See, I haven't forgotten how to write. You'd get some great
love letters from me if you were still at sea. As a matter of
fact, once you wake me up, there's other things to do after
our little talk.

All my love and kisses.

                              Ann

CHAPTER THIRTEEN

CAPTAIN SVEDROV wasn't absolutely certain whether he was concerned more about the coming battle or about the priorities Admiral Kupinsky had established. He knew of the short, simple message Gorenko had sent and realized there was nothing Alex could do but make *Nimitz* the number-one priority.

Svedrov sat before his desk in his cabin, a place he had rarely visited in the last forty-eight hours. He was tired, but he knew sleep would not come, not when contact with the American forces was imminent. He had read and reread the order of battle they had promulgated only thirty minutes before. The airwing commanders had joined in the briefing in flag plot, while the captains of the other ships had taken part by direct TV hookup. Electronic access was so simple that they were literally present.

Svedrov had to agree with the commanding officer of the *Azov*. Admiral Kupinsky's presentation was one of the most stirring any of the senior officers had ever been privileged to witness. He had quietly begun the meeting with a moment of silence for their fallen comrades, an action with almost religious overtones that most Soviet officers wouldn't have dared do. Then he reviewed the purpose for their being in that section of the Indian Ocean, and the reason that the Americans were there. There was no doubt in his mind, he con-

tinued, that Admiral Charles and his people were probably
having the same type of conference at this time and that they
intended to persevere just as the Russians would. It would not
be an easy day. Quite obviously, more ships and men would
be lost. Then he stopped for a moment, just long enough for
them to hang on to his next words.

It was a story that many of them were not familiar with, but
Svedrov had heard it before. It was about a young Soviet
submariner back in October of 1962, a time when most of
those listening had not yet crossed the brow of their first ship.
Admiral Kupinsky assured them that it was just as well, for
October 1962 was one of the darkest periods for the emerging
Soviet Navy. Russia had been in the process of becoming a
blue-water naval power, the only way a major nation could
survive as a leader in the twentieth century. But, and this was
an important point, she did not then have the sophistication of
the U.S. Navy. Many of the ships were not ready for the
challenge, and suddenly they were facing an America with
the determination to drive them out of Cuban waters. The
Soviet subs had neither the fuel nor repair facilities necessary
to project this power. As a result, the United States had
dominated.

Then he finished with the story of the Russian submarine
that had been surfaced by an old wreck of a destroyer, a relic
of World War II, and the resultant humiliation. He rose from
the long table, pacing back and forth before them as he
spoke, their eyes riveted attentively. He kept his hands
locked behind his back, looking each man in the eye, even
gazing directly into the cameras that carried this meeting to
the other ships. And finally, he announced to his listeners
that Admiral David Charles, the commander of this Task
Force 58, had been on that destroyer that day the Soviet
submarine had been humiliated before the world. And now,
he explained to them both as individuals and as a group, it
was their opportunity to turn the tables.

Svedrov looked over his notes of that meeting, but he
didn't need them now. He had written the order of battle for
his Admiral, and he had explained it at that meeting. Im-

mediately on completing his speech, Kupinsky had turned
the meeting over to Svedrov. There was nothing complex
about what he had explained to them. The main objective was
to sink *Nimitz*. That would curtail American airpower and
allow the surface ships a better opportunity to close and
engage their opposite numbers with missiles. And to
everyone's surprise, he called upon three new service ships
of a rather unusual design to move up with the main force.
But no one felt privileged enough to ask the reason for these
noncombatants to hazard themselves.

Captain Svedrov folded the papers neatly and placed them
in the small desk safe, twirling the wheel a few times to make
sure it was locked and secure. He changed into a clean
uniform, as he knew his Admiral would be doing at this
point. They would present a fine, almost urbane appearance
to their staff, and the word would spread through the force
that Admiral Kupinsky and his Captain Svedrov looked as
though they were on holiday in Leningrad, preparing for a
stroll through the Gardens of the Summer Palace.

He found Admiral Kupinsky leaning on the railing on the
portside catwalk about the flight deck, watching the launch.
Lenin was unlike an American carrier, for the VTOL planes
simply lifted off the deck vertically, pointing their noses first
down slightly, then upward as their powerful single jet engines increased thrust for takeoff. It was noisy but had none
of the drama of the American launch, with the planes being
flung violently forward, steam hissing and catapults slam-
ming into their stops.

But Alex Kupinsky saw drama in this event. Two mighty
oceangoing forces were about to engage each other for the
first time in forty years. The previous engagements by aircraft or submarines were simply softening-up exercises, feeling out the opposition. This would be truly a three-
dimensional battle, air, surface, and undersea all at once.
Continents were at stake. One country should emerge a victor
without a land battle. Men and ships were immaterial in the
face of national goals. It was sad in a way that time had

brought this disregard of human life and that political ambitions overrode human consideration.

"We should be in flag plot now, Admiral. They are so
close that we could be under attack at any moment."

"Ah, Svedrov, you have found me." He turned, clapping
the younger man on the shoulder. "Stay here for a few
moments with me and watch the last of the planes take off.
They know I am up here, and they have waved. It will be
good for them to see you, too."

They saw the last of the Forgers and Rigas head skyward.
This time the aircraft were near enough to their target so that
they could stay close to their stations for awhile. This was
preferable to the earlier long-distance quick run and return to
avoid running out of fuel. Now half of the aircraft were
armed to protect the other half. The latter would be making
attacks on the surface ships. With the submarines and the
surface ships in the area, the Admiral felt that the coordinated
attack would require less air-to-surface missiles, and he
wanted these pilots to have a better chance than the last air
group. But he feared there would be a ring of carefully guided
steel surrounding *Nimitz*.

"All right, my friend, let's join the others in plot. I'm sure
David Charles is planning much the same things we are, and I
need you to coordinate our defense today. We must save
Lenin at all costs, and I'm sure they do not have the surprise
for us that we have been saving for them. We have a superior
air defense, but they have a great many more aircraft to
sacrifice."

Svedrov paused with his hand on the door leading into
plot. "You may be sure I will do everything within my
power, even to sacrificing the little ships if necessary, as you
said." His face was sad and serious.

"I know. That's why I picked you. We will stay close for
the next few hours, for they will be the most important in our
lives." He extended his arm courteously to his aide as the
other man pulled open the door, politely gesturing for him to
enter the darkened room first.

"Attack and fighter aircraft launched from *Nimitz*, sir."

He saw the appropriate dots on the board in one color, the approaching submarines in another. Soon a third color would show the cruise missiles he anticipated from the surface craft leading this Task Force 58.

"*Lenin* has launched aircraft, sir." The announcement redirected David Charles's attention for a moment as he saw the dots move out from *Lenin*. Right now, however, he was more concerned about the Soviet submarines. They had to be held under by the antisubmarine groups or they would have the opportunity to fire missiles from beyond the surface force's range of detection. Once the subs got closer, the smaller ships could handle them.

"Admiral, those Russian planes are doing pretty much what we're doing ourselves. They're heading for high altitude."

"I was fairly sure that would happen, Bill. The logical thing for the Soviets to do is wait until they can fire simultaneously from three separate geometric locations. Their weapons are designed to do the same as ours are, and their countermeasures are similar also. We'll have less opportunity to identify individual missiles, select a weapon, and bring them down if they come from the air, the surface, and from underneath all at the same time. With each one operating on a different frequency, thank God it doesn't confuse the computer."

The ships around *Nimitz* had been stationed with exactly that assumption in mind, and they were assigned sectors for each type of potential attack. The decision of whether to coordinate each sector defense from the master computer or to assign local control to Aegis-configured or even individual ships would come from Bill Dailey. David planned to keep as far from the individual details as possible. He had to evaluate the flow of action, planning his attack around the success of his defense, releasing a ship for total offensive capabilities only when he felt it was not needed for defensive purposes.

"Fighters in contact, sir. They're being fired on by Forgers."

"Remind them their primary targets are the Rigas." He knew the Rigas had been armed to attack *Nimitz,* and his Tomcats couldn't waste all their missiles on the fighters as Alex wanted them to. Charles's advantages was more aircraft in reserve to attack the Rigas once the Forgers had expended their missiles. But he couldn't ask the pilots to dodge missiles without firing. He had told them in the ready room what they had to do, and they were brave men. "Remind the group leaders to conserve their ammunition. Wait a minute, belay that. Don't tell them a thing!" They were grown men who knew their profession. He would let Bill Dailey do his job and stay out of it. "Sorry, Bill, I always get excited on first contact. Go ahead."

"Yes, sir." He picked up a speaker phone resting near his left arm. "Relax all EMCON. They're on top of us now. Designated ships commence radiating on enemy frequencies." Now those ships he had just directed would begin electronic warfare procedures, emitting signals to distract enemy radar. It would show carrier-size targets in place of an actual destroyer, creating false targets. They would also jam guidance radars attempting to lock on American ships, and fire rockets filled with metal foil that would confuse acquisition radars. The first step had been to meet the attacking aircraft halfway. The second was to confuse those that got through. Now the computer would take over the air attack, assigning targets to perimeter ships, identifying missiles fired at the surface force and assigning ships to bring them down, and finally releasing a ship in extremis from computer control.

Bill Dailey's next move was to check remaining time on station of the helos assigned to hold down submarines. It was important to ensure that relief was at the site before the first helo left. Otherwise, the subs could surface, fire cruise missiles, and dive again in a short time. The responsibility for this phase was turned over to the staff ASW officer, who accepted control with the flick of a switch on the panel before him.

The surface-picture responsibility was retained by the

master computer and displayed for Admiral Charles and his Chief of Staff on the huge boards before them. The Soviet force had changed little since the display had been set up more than an hour before, although it was evident that some of the ships in the flank had moved up well ahead of *Lenin*.

What are those ships moving up, Bill?''

''I'm not sure, sir. They were originally identified as service force, but they seem to be moving too fast for that, don't they?''

''Request that one of the spy planes take some pictures and relay them back here.'' He looked up at the array of TV screens before them. ''Put it on number-three screen.''

''Right.'' Dailey pointed at a nearby officer whose job was to carry out such orders with as little noise as possible. In a moment, the picture flickered on, the screen a snowstorm. There was a change in the background as the spy plane brought its camera into focus on the force eighty thousand feet below. The automatic lens was activated to bring the Russian ships closer, though even after thirty seconds, they were still ants on a vast screen. Gradually *Lenin* swam into view as an identifying ship.

The Admiral picked up a radio phone. ''Have that circuit with the pilot patched in here.'' He nodded at the comm officer, who was looking over his shoulder at him, holding up the phone with one hand and pointing at it with the index finger of the other. The young officer nodded.

Lenin was becoming clearer on the screen, her island on the starboard side identifiable, as were the circles painted on the deck for aircraft positions. The close-up lens halted when they could identify a figure on the flight deck. There was static from the earpiece of the phone David Charles was holding. ''What's his call sign?''

''Spy Two, sir.''

Out of habit, he keyed the mike a couple of times, then spoke into it. ''Spy Two, this it Top Dog One. Do you read me? Over.''

''Roger, Top Dog One, loud and clear. Over.''

''Spy Two, there are some large surface craft that have

moved from the rear of the formation ahead of *Lenin,* probably midway between the carrier and the forward cruiser. Can you pick them up for me? Over.''

The lens was already rapidly moving from the carrier over open water. ''Roger, Top Dog One. Wait.'' The picture on the screen was a blur of ocean. An object appeared for a moment, left the screen, then returned as the camera centered on it. The lens brought the ship closer. ''How's that Top Dog . . . One. Over.''

''Perfect, Spy . . . . Hold it for a second.'' It appeared to be a type of tender, huge, but it did not move as a heavy ship of that size should. The bow wave was higher and the stern from the rear of the deckhouse was of unusual construction. ''Spy Two, can you get a closer look at the stern? Over.''

''Roger, how's that?''

''What do you make of it, Bill?''

''Never saw anything like that.'' He turned to one of his assistants. ''Get a photo of that down to my boys in the Rumpus Room.'' He turned back to David. ''We'll see what my experts have to say. It has a hell of a high stern, like an amphib, but there doesn't seem to be any well deck.''

''Nope, no sign of doors either. But I sure don't like that.'' He picked up the radio phone, ''Spy Two, this is Top Dog One. Thank you for your effort. We have some photos for analysis . . . take care of yourself. Out.''

''Five Rigas through the intercept.'' It was a report from another officer. ''Looks like they just jammed the stick forward and dropped like a rock.'' On the screen, Bill Dailey could see that they were also separating, each now independent as they moved into five different sectors.

Dailey punched a series of buttons. The screen in front of them identified the firing ships defending each of those sectors. Even now electronic information was flowing from the acquisition radars into the fire-control system that would shortly be launching missiles at the intruders.

But already, smaller dots were emerging from the attacking planes as they released their own weapons. And on the screen, they could see their own ships firing at the Rigas in return.

"They did it again," a voice replied. "Increased speed after we had a solution." He was referring to the Soviet missiles that seemed to have a two-stage engine. The second stage, faster than the first, was a problem to a fire-control solution.

"Did you get that speed problem into the system the other day, Bill?"

"Right. I just hope it works." He pushed another button on his console. After studying the screen for a moment, he added, "I don't know, Admiral. We caught it but it delayed our firing time. We're shooting at those missiles on a new solution now." As they watched, a couple of the missiles fired from the Rigas winked out, but others got past the antimissile fire.

David looked at the screen. Two missiles seemed headed for the same ship. "Who's that?" He pointed at the apparently bracketed ship on the display board.

"*Halsey,*" Dailey responded instantly.

"Oh, shit, no!"

On board the guided-missile cruiser *Halsey,* her captain had already put the ship into a tight turn to present as little target as possible, but the missiles were closing at a tremendous speed. Men on the deck were deafened by the loud chatter of the 20-mm. close-in weapon system (CIWS), *Halsey's* last-ditch effort to bring down the attackers. Bursts of several hundred rounds were streaking out at the incoming missiles, the radar desperately tracking both the stream of uranium bullets and the targets to correct the aim. But it was too late.

One of the missiles might have been hit just before it came in contact with *Halsey,* for the explosion blew off both the fire-control radars on the stern, rather than going off inside the hull. The second missile exploded behind the bridge, after it had penetrated the ship's CIC, destroying the nerve center of the vessel and blowing the forward mack over the side. Her captain rushed to the starboard wing of the bridge to assess the damage visually. For a moment, he saw the aft section of the ship in flames, the damage-control party motionless on the deck. Then the smoke from the forward mack

covered the ship as the fires in the forward boilers burned out
of control. As it toppled from the superstructure, the forward
exhaust stack had forced a rush of air down to the fireroom.

Halsey was immediately ineffective, the forward fireroom
useless, the after missile system inoperative, and the control
center of the ship, the combat information center, destroyed.
She could neither receive information nor fire a weapon, and
she was already at half speed.

Julius A. Furer was a much smaller ship than *Halsey*,
smaller by 150 feet and over four thousand tons. Her captain
briefly saw the missile before it hit, possibly because he was
horrified watching the bullet stream from his own CIWS
system sweep forward as he unfortunately presented his
port beam to the attack. The explosion of the missile coupled
with that of the forward magazine were simultaneous as far as
the men in the aft section were concerned. Those up forward
were unaware of the bow breaking off about where the
magazine had been. The captain and his GQ team disappeared in a flash of white, along with most of the crew in the
forward section of the ship. *Furer* veered to starboard, already beginning to settle in the water, along with more than
one hundred of her crew.

When GQ sounded on *Blandy*, Quartermaster Third Class
Charles Goddard relieved at the wheel of the old destroyer. It
was not as if a junior man were taking such a great responsibility, since Goddard had been in the Navy for more than ten
years. He was one of the finest helmsmen in the fleet and a
good quartermaster when he was sober. But his liberty hours
were always spent finding trouble where others had already
looked. His escapades were legend on the ships he had
ridden. Even though he could talk his way out of trouble with
the civilian authorities, he too often found himself reduced in
rank by an unsympathetic commanding officer.

No matter how many times he appeared at captain's mast,
his lovable grin seemed to save him from courts-martial he
deserved. Only days before, the captain had threatened to
send him to the brig for his latest stunt and again he found
himself a third class for the fifth time. Now he was where he

belonged, at the helm of *Blandy,* as she steamed toward the enemy.

One missile was nearing *Blandy* when her 20-mm. shells contacted it. It exploded a good fifty yards from the ship, but the explosion and shrapnel showered the forward part of the vessel, killing most of those in the bridge area. Charlie Goddard, the only one left uninjured, was left in command of *Blandy* as she continued cutting through the ocean at high speed. The flying metal had torn through the pilothouse, cutting down every man but Goddard. The captain lay at his feet, a gaping hole in his chest. Those still alive were moaning or crying for help, but none were left standing. Goddard jammed the wheel in place just for a second and turned to the ship's PA on the bulkhead behind him. His voice boomed out over the ship as he asked the XO to call the bridge. He returned to the helm, a phone tucked under his chin. In a moment, the executive officer called him, learning of the loss on the bridge. Before the man arrived to take over, Goddard had already begun a zigzag course of his own, the headphones to main control lopsided on his head as he called for more speed. As the XO came through the pilothouse door, he found Quartermaster Third Class Goddard in control of the *Blandy* amidst the carnage of the bridge, grinning like a depraved elf as he often did when describing his exploits ashore.

The Rigas had dropped down almost to the surface to escape, and David could see them streaking through the formation. They were helpless, no longer armed, and maneuvering wildly to evade attack.

"For Christ's sake, isn't anyone going to fire?" David called out.

Silence for a moment. Then, "I can't yet, Admiral." The voice was Bill Dailey's. "They're still to close to other ships in the formation. They're using them to hide behind. We'll get them when they get out to the perimeter."

"Right . . . very logical . . . it's your baby. Bill. Sorry again."

"That's all right, Admiral. But that's not my biggest

problem. Look at that.'' He was pointing at the ASW board.
''Those leftover Forgers are going after the helos, trying to
free those submarines.'' He turned to a man behind him
speaking quietly into a headset. ''Vector some of those
Tomcats to help those helos. Goddamn, they're sitting
ducks.''

''Admiral, request permission to release *Valdez* to pick up
Furer survivors. She's sinking fast.''

Without looking up, Charles answered, ''Granted. Bill,
send some of those frigates out where the helos are going
down. Tell 'em to use anything they've got to fill the water
with high explosives. They're the ones who are going to be
firing at us.''

''Yes, sir. Perimeter ships have identified Soviet surface-
ship radar. They're getting into range, too.''

''We've got longer ranges. We should be attacking now.''

''We are, sir. We've already had some hits, but the group
commander reports that Russians are using something to
explode our warheads before impact.''

''Sub-launched missiles in the air!'' The report cracked
out over the enforced silence sharply. ''*Nimitz* is the target!''
As the report was coming in, an American Tomcat jet was
diving on one of the firing submarines, from the stern. Before
it could escape below the surface, the sail of *Virona* was hit
by two rockets. Fires in the sub's control room had incapaci-
tated its hydraulics and the crew was unable to keep their
craft from making a last furious, uncontrolled dive.

The Samson missile, an advanced version of the older
Soviet Shaddock, travels at speeds in excess of Mach 2 and
carries a warhead containing a thousand pounds of TNT.
This was how Kupinsky intended to soften up *Nimitz*. One of
the sub-fired missiles was misdirected to the wrong target and
managed to blow off the hanger and flight deck of the
destroyer *Moosbrugger*. The ship's LAMPS helos had just
loaded torpedoes and their detonation left her after section in
flames.

The two missiles that hit *Nimitz* created as much damage,
but it wasn't as incapacitating for the great ship. One hit near

the waterline up forward, blowing a tremendous hole in the hull, but this damage, which would likely have sunk a frigate, barely managed to impede *Nimitz'* speed. The damage-control parties easily isolated the flooding by sealing off the affected compartments. The second hit aft of the bridge, just below the main deck.

The staff damage-control officer soon reported, "No fires forward. Flooding isolated."

The second blast had been felt in flag plot. It had been much closer. "What about the hit aft," questioned Dailey, but he halted as he saw the man's hand in the air for silence.

He listened for a second. "Missile penetrated hanger deck just below and abaft the island. . . ." his hand still in the air, listening, ". . . radar tower hanging over the edge . . . no aricraft in the area at the time . . . small fires."

"That's what you call lucky," added Bill Dailey, but the DC officer's hand was still in the air as more damage was reported.

"After starboard elevator is buckled. Damage Control Central reports it inoperative."

"Not so lucky," Admiral Charles added.

"No, sir, but it could have been a hell of a lot worse if we'd been fueling or loading weapons in the area."

"You're right, of course, Bill." He grimaced. "But that's only the beginning, I'm afraid." He gestured at the status board directly in front of them. It was becoming more confused. The forward surface ships had been exchanging missiles since they had been within fifty miles of each other. The first ones were relatively easy to counter. As the ranges drew closer, there was less time to act individually if computer-controlled antimissile systems failed to do their job. The screen was a melange of blinking dots that would occasionally stop on the solid color of a surface ship.

What David Charles was pointing out to Dailey was the acceleration of missiles aimed at *Nimitz*. She was surrounded by ships whose sole duty was to protect the great carrier from just such an attack. The computer's target-designation system was doing a superb job, not to mention the unseen electronic war silently protecting *Nimitz*.

The first missile from a surface ship to hit the carrier landed on the forward part of the flight deck, penetrating into the chief's quarters. No one was there while the ship was at GQ. The second missile was not to be confused, nor was it ever intended to land on *Nimitz*. Instead, it settled, rather than fell, in the water less than a mile to starboard.

Nimitz' commanding officer wasn't fooled. Frank Welles was standing on the starboard wing while his OOD conned the ship. The lookout next to him saw it, too. "Torpedo to starboard, Captain."

"I see it," he answered shrilly. "Emergency port," he bellowed into the pilothouse.

"Emergency port, aye," came the instant answer.

But the giant ship was never designed to turn as quickly as they all hoped. It takes a long time for ninety-three thousand tons and almost eleven hundred feet of ship to turn, even in an emergency. A mile at sea is only two thousand yards and a high-speed homing torpedo travels that distance quickly. To Frank Welles it took an eternity for *Nimitz* to respond and an instant for the torpedo to arrive just forward of the bridge. It would have made little difference anyway, since it was a homing torpedo, set to explode at a depth of fifteen feet. Captain Welles's last impression before impact was the reaction on the lookout's face when he finally realized they would be hit. His eyes were like saucers, his mouth wide in an "O," his binoculars swinging from his neck as he dropped them to look down to the water's surface.

The detonation was felt by the whole ship's crew, and it was as if she had just passed over a reef. Those above it, especially on the bridge, felt their knees buckle. Then a column of water leaped well above the flight deck. As the geyser reached its maximum height, the noise rolled over them, again shaking the ship. It was the largest warhead the Russians could put on a torpedo and still fire it as a missile. The inward explosion was unlike anything anyone had ever read about, for there had never been one like it before. It had to be a new type of explosive. The hole torn in the side was

forty feet across and half as high, completely underwater.
The ocean poured in, causing the great ship to veer to starboard. Bulkheads weakened by the explosion fell under the
rush of the ocean. There was no fire.

In flag plot, David Charles felt the impact, not knowing
where the hit had been taken. Then the power went off,
followed by an ominous silence. Battle lanterns instantly
lighted the room and familiar sounds returned. "Engineering
spaces . . . torpedo." He looked at the ship's indicators on
the panel to his left. "Bad hit, Bill." He pointed at the panel.
"We've already dropped five knots, and we're going all over
the goddamn ocean."

In the pilothouse a white-faced sailor at the helm was
struggling to get his ship back on course. Captain Welles was
standing behind him, hand on the man's shoulder, "Just
relax. Tell me what she's doing."

"Pulling to the right, Captain. Whenever she starts to
come around, and I let up a bit on the wheel, she starts
shuddering and dragging to the right again. I can't hold her,
sir."

"Sure you can, son. We're still slowing down. It'll come
easier as we decrease speed." He had given the order as he
felt *Nimitz* veer to starboard, but it took a long time to slow
ninety-three thousand tons from the thirty-five knots she had
been doing. It was the only way to lower the pressure on the
bulkheads far enough from the explosion to hold back the
water. "Just keep fighting it, but sound off just as soon as
you feel anything different."

Reports were coming in from damage-control parties in
other sections of the ship with casualty reports, calls for men
and equipment, and reports of sections sealed off. Many men
had already died from the four hits *Nimitz* had taken, yet they
were a miniscule part of the entire crew. To a casual observer, it might even seem there was little damage to the ship,
but the torpedo had impaired her seakeeping ability for the
time being. It was impossible, at least now, to take evasive
action from further attack.

And then the report came from Combat. "Aircraft, port

quarter.'' The planes that Frank Welles whirled to find
through his binoculars were already on top of *Nimitz* as far as
he was concerned. They were miles away, but distance is of
little value when missiles are being used. But the planes
closed without firing. He couldn't understand why.

In flag plot, Bill Dailey reported, "Those are stragglers.
Don't know where they came from. They got through our
Tomcats.'' The screen they both observed showed three
Russian aircraft closing *Nimitz* with what were probably four
Tomcats in pursuit. The American planes obviously had no
missiles left and were probably firing machine guns at the
wildly maneuvering Rigas. The latter were trying to evade
both the weapons fired from the surface ships and the pursu-
ing planes. As they closed *Nimitz,* one was hit. Yet it kept
coming. Finally, as its maneuverability decreased, one of the
Tomcats concentrated its fire on the damaged craft. Beginning to lose altitude, it vainly tried to lift its nose, then
violently exploded into tiny pieces.

When Frank Welles saw that, he knew the Soviets were
carrying very heavy bombs. Now the two remaining were in
a screaming dive, growing larger and larger to the naked eye
by the split second. A second one was hit by gunfire from a
Tomcat. Its tail began to flake apart. The pilot was losing
control but he fought his craft, trying to will it toward the
carrier. As it became obvious to him that he would fall to the
side, he yanked back his stick, forcing the plane's nose
upward just enough to flip his bomb toward *Nimitz.* Then one
of his wings broke off.

As Welles watched, fascinated, the bomb glided lazily
toward the stern, too far away to hit the flight deck, but he
knew it might be close enough to cause damage as it
exploded. Suddenly his attention was riveted on the surviving Riga, the one making a picture-perfect attack and releasing its bomb. The Russian had been low enough and close
enough, and the flight deck made a perfect target. Welles
could not maneuver his ship.

The bomb penetrated just forward of the single elevator on
the port side. Experts would likely say it penetrated at least

two decks before it went off. When it did, in a missile storage area, the combined explosion was enough to blow the elevator straight up.

Frank Welles's initial impression was of a giant Roman candle. When the elevator reached its peak, flames shot past it hundreds of feet into the air. As the elevator descended, it was enveloped in fire. Then Frank Welles felt the impact as it tore more of the vital flight deck away. Only those deck personnel on the starboard side, awaiting the return of the first flight of aircraft, excaped the cascading flames.

Admiral Charles felt the main explosion in plot. This time the lights stayed on. The explosion had occurred above the waterline. But the impact, following so closely on the torpedo hit, told him that *Nimitz* was hurt. "I'm going to the bridge, Bill." Very little time had passed since the shooting began, maybe eight to ten minutes, yet hundreds of missiles had been fired by both sides, more than either of their computers could possibly defend against.

When David pushed through the door to the pilothouse, he was assaulted by a cacaphony of sounds, unlike the quiet, orderly flag plot. This is where the men were directing the fight to save their ship. Secondary explosions still came from the fire on the port quarter. Reports were too fast for Welles to assimilate. The ones picked out that were more important received an answer. The remaining helos were low on fuel and desperately needed to land. A Tomcat squadron was circling, hoping they would soon be able to see their landing field through the smoke. Then the smell hit David for the first time, a variety of odors of objects being consumed by the fire. He hung back, watching the ordered mayhem of a ship fighting for its life. No one recognized him, even though he was the only one without a life jacket or helmet.

David Charles inched his way out onto the starboard wing, picking up a pair of binoculars as he passed the chart table. Most of the damage was forward or on the port side, and the rear of the bridge was unoccupied except for a lookout, scanning the skies. David tapped him on the shoulder, "There's something I'm looking for over there." He pointed off the starboard quarter. "How about giving me a hand, see if we can find them together."

It was the same sailor who had watched the torpedo with Frank Welles, his eyes still like saucers. He simply nodded, too dumbfounded by the brass and terror around him.

"They should be about ten degrees abaft the beam . . . probably two or three of them . . . and they're pretty big. . . . See anything?"

"No, sir," then, "yes, sir. They look big all right, like tenders. . . . But those are the funniest looking ass ends on them, sir. I don't know what they are, sir."

"Well, we're even, neither do I." They stared through the glasses for a bit longer. "Now what the hell are they doing?"

The ships they were watching had slowed down. Their bow waves, standing out at high speed, had just as quickly disappeared. Then, first one, then another small craft appeared from their sterns. There were six in all, two from each of the large ships. They circled behind each of the parents for just long enough to get organized. Then David saw them lift out of the water, pointing their bows toward *Nimitz*.

"I'll be a son of a bitch." Before the sailor could ask what was going on David was into the pilothouse. Welles finally noticed him. "What speed can you make?"

"Well . . . Admiral . . . I . . . I imagine we could take her up to fifteen knots if we had too, but we're still shoring bulkheads up forward and I can't fan that fire on the port quarter." He thought more about the question. "For Christ's sake, why, David . . . Admiral?"

"Because you're about to come under a PT-boat attack, or something like that."

"Out here?"

But David already had a sound-powered phone in his hand. As he pressed the button for flag plot, he answered Welles, "Yes, out here. Only I don't know what the hell they're going to be like when they get closer." To the voice that answered on the other end, he said, "I want Dailey." He looked back at his old friend. "I don't know what they are, Frank. A little while ago we saw some odd-looking ships pulling up ahead of *Lenin*, and we asked for some pictures. Even then, we couldn't figure out what they were. Kupinsky wants this ship bad, Frank. Sinking *Nimitz* means everything to Gorenko. This is a symbol of what his navy has to do. If they can sink the most powerful ship in the world, then the world's going to know about it. And this is the damned worst time.''

He turned back to the phone. ''Bill, we got any fighters, or anything up there, that still have some ordinance?'' He waited, ''I don't give a shit if they're pop guns. Tell those pilots that if they want to land they're going to have to get every one of those small craft coming at us from the starboard quarter . . . . Yes, that's right. Those ships were some kind of amphib conversion. Two small craft in each one . . . surface-effect type . . . . They lifted right out of the water when they put the hammer down . . . probably carry torpedoes and rockets.'' He slammed the phone back in its cradle, and motioned Welles to follow him.

The sounds of the pilothouse hadn't changed. The reports were still coming in and were being barked out by talkers or written down in grease pencil by listeners. The sailor on the helm had found that the wheel was easier now at low speed. No more water was entering forward, and the reports coming to the bridge even indicated they were having luck with the pumps. The fire aft was under control, though it still appeared a conflagration to the inexperienced eye. In time they would be able to take aboard the helicopters, and perhaps even shortly be able to recover the Tomcats, although somewhat more slowly than usual.

''My God, look at those little mothers.'' The lookout, now sandwiched between the Admiral and the captain, was sure he hadn't heard right, but he kept his binoculars to his eyes, watching the high-speed approach.

''Right, high speed, most likely gas turbine, and . . . yup, I can see torpedo tubes, too.''

''And rocket launchers on the decks.''

David looked up at the sky. ''Where the hell are those jets?''

"You just called."

"They were supposed to be circling . . . waiting to land."

"Hell, they can't have much left in the way of ammo."

"Just their guns. That's all . . . expended on the rest of those Rigas."

"This is when I wish we had guns again, lots of 'em. Twenty mm. Forty mm. Three inch."

"It wouldn't do much good against those torpedoes."

"Nope, but that's what we've got to hope the jets screw up. I'd like to have guns to keep them from firing those damn rockets."

"Yeah, you're right."

The lookout hadn't said a word. But, he'd been listening and he was getting scared. His voice trembled. "What can we do about them?"

"Nothing." They both said the one word simultaneously.

"We just have to hope those Tomcats get here double quick," added Welles.

"Hard to tell their speed at this distance, Frank, but I'll bet they must be upwards of seventy knots."

"You're probably right, Admiral, but without a bow wave it sure is deceptive as hell." They had both dropped their binoculars to talk. "Give them three or four minutes at the most if they want a good shot, less if they try to keep their distance."

"Sir," the sailor declared, "they're spreading out."

"They sure are. Makes tougher shooting for us." David paused and turned to the young sailor. "What's your name, son?"

"Meehan, sir, Edward L., Seaman Apprentice, sir."

"That's all right, Meehan, relax. You're doing a fine job. Like the Navy?"

Without a moment's hesitation: "No, sir. Not now!"

"Good for you. Neither do I right now. It could be bad for your health. But don't worry. I've been in worse scrapes before, and I still look pretty good, don't I?"

"Yes, sir."

"Well, I'm glad you're in agreement. My wife would be upset if you didn't. Keep a close eye out for the enemy up here. I want to stay healthy too. You and I got to keep an eye out for each other. Right?"

"Certainly, sir."

"Good. We all have to do that. Why don't you just pass the word over that phone set of yours. Make sure the people on the other end get it on the other circuits too."

Meehan was staring back at him, binoculars in both hands at about chest level, mouth slightly open, questioningly, the phone strapped around his neck with the speaker jutting out under his chin.

"Go ahead, Meehan. You tell 'em that. I'll handle your sector here for a moment." And David brought his own binoculars to his eyes, scanning the area where the attacking boats were crossing. The amazed lookout had finally let his binoculars swing free on his chest and was now speaking rapidly into the phone, convincing others of his conversation with the Admiral. David saw the newfound trust in the young eyes.

As wise seamen would, the captains of each of the small boats were opening the distance between themselves. Their orders had been to provide as little opportunity as possible for surface ships or aircraft to get more than one of them at a time. They were all volunteers. Before the force had left the Maldives, Admiral Kupinsky had called a meeting of the entire squadron. He explained their mission and the chances of survival. It *was* a suicide mission, and he wanted to make that quite clear. When he asked for volunteers, the entire squadron had stood as one, as their fathers had at Stalingrad when their backs were to the Volga, or at Leningrad, Moscow, Kursk, Odessa, Sevastopol, Tallinn or any number of places where Russians had casually accepted death in battle for the Motherland.

Four Tomcats screamed out of the sky overhead, diving on the small craft, Gatling-type guns chattering. There were no missiles or rockets left, only 20-mm. shells. But their guns spewed a curtain of large bullets that would tear apart any small vessel. The pilots found that the trick was to hit these water bugs.

A surface-effect ship rides on air. It lifts out of the water. There is no drag. This allows it tremendous speed over water and it can turn on a dime. The first pass by the jets was totally unsuccessful. The Soviet craft easily evaded them, refusing to stay in one place.

On the second pass the pilots came in from behind rather than from the beam. This allowed more time to watch what the Russian craft were going to do, and they had a better chance to follow their own stream of fire up to their target. One of the pilots noted that the craft he was closing was too consistent in weaving from right to left. When he opened fire, he let the boat slew left. When it came back to the right, it fell right in his path. The 20-mm. guns began to rip it apart from the stern, tossing boat parts and men into the air as shells raced toward the small pilothouse. Flames broke out aft as the pilothouse and men in it were shattered. Then the torpedoes were hit and the boat simply blew up. The highly explosive fuel for the gas turbines had gone off at the same time.

"They're not even firing back at those Tomcats," said Welles.

"I imagine their mission is to get here the quickest way and not to worry about anything that might slow them down. We're the target. Any chance of putting helos up?"

"Not a one. They're either being refueled and rearmed, or they were shot down covering the subs."

"Look at that," whistled the lookout between them.

One of the jets was about to bracket a Soviet boat when it whipped around in a tight turn, going right under the Tomcat, then returning to its original course. There were still five of them. At about four thousand yards, two of them opened up with rockets while the others circled toward either end of the carrier, maintaining their distance as they sought to position themselves on the opposite beam. The rockets were like peashooters to the large carrier, yet their effectiveness cleared the deck as they found the range.

At fifteen hundred yards, the closest one fired its first torpedo. The boat did not turn away, but followed its fish directly toward *Nimitz*. The second one also fired a torpedo at the same distance as the first. Of the remaining three, one raced farther past to attack from the other side, while the other two bore in from bow and stern, waiting to see if *Nimitz* would turn to avoid the torpedoes. At one thousand yards, the firing boats put their second fish in the water. Welles had run to the pilothouse door and was vainly giving orders to the helm, knowing she would not begin to turn before they were hit.

The Soviet boat that had swung astern of *Nimitz* was hit in the same way as the first. It was so loaded with ammunition and fuel that it exploded under the concentrated 20-mm. fire.

The first two boats still followed their own fish, firing the rockets as they closed. The first torpedo exploded no more than fifty feet from the earlier one, buckling all the bulkheads that had been depended on to hold back the hullful of water, washing over the damage-control parties that had been working desperately to hold back the sea. The second one hit just under the bridge. The third exploded near the stern. A fourth miraculously dove under the ship.

"Bridge has lost steering control," cried the helmsman.

"Switch to after steering," shouted Welles.

They waited. No response. "No answer from after steering, sir."

"Call DC Central. Tell them we've lost steering control."

"The phone is dead, sir. I can't get anyone to answer."

A torrent of rockets shattered the pilothouse as a Soviet boat sped down the side spraying the upper decks of the island. David Charles, seeing the boat coming, had fallen to the deck. As the shelling stopped, he ducked into the open pilothouse door.

Stillness. No movement. There was smoke. Fire was shooting from exposed cables. His favorite bridge chair was torn and spattered with blood.

Frank Welles was sitting on the deck against the bulkhead, near the door David had just come through. He leaned over, jerking at David's pant leg. His face was pale, setting off the

blood that seeped from his scalp. He said nothing, just
pointed at the fallen sailor by the helm. David, understanding, grabbed the wheel, spinning it first one way, then the
other.

"Nothing," he said.

Then Welles found his voice. "Ship's speaker. Let DC
Central know we've lost control."

David did as Welles said. *Nimitz*' captain was in shock. A
Tomcat streaked over the flight deck in front of the bridge, its
guns chattering at a boat attacking on the other beam. The
pilot found his target. The boat exploded as it followed its
fish close in, but the torpedo also found its target.

David was about to speak into the mike when the torpedo
hit. He had been entranced by the shimmering path of the
torpedo. It was shallow running, and he couldn't believe it
was that large. The explosion, catapulting water high above
the ship, was followed by a second detonation of even greater
magnitude. Somehow, he determined afterward, the
warhead must have been armed with something that penetrated an avgas bunker. The flames from the second blast
surpassed the cone of water in height. The smoke that followed signaled trouble. Burning gas was difficult to fight
when a ship was still under attack.

David's voice boomed throughout the ship, "After steering, this is the bridge. We have no control. Steer course.
. . ." He looked for a course indicator, but that too was
shattered. "Belay that, left standard rudder. I'll tell you
when I want it amidships."

Smoke and towering flames, so intense that the heat could
be felt on the bridge, covered the flight deck. He had to get
the wind on the beam so the damage-control parties could see
what they were fighting. Slowly, too slowly, *Nimitz* began to
turn. The forward part of the flight deck came into view as the
smoke blew aft, then the midships section. But he realized
nothing would be able to land. The deck was a shambles. The
remaining aircraft would have to ditch.

He spoke again into the mike. "This is the bridge. Rudder
amidships." Now the after section of the flight deck came
into view. The port elevator sprawled halfway across, and a

great jagged chunk had been ripped out of the angled part of the flight deck. Burning hulks of planes were being pushed over the side by deck trucks. Hoses snaked over every part of its surface. Another explosion ripped upward from the fuel tanks, driving fire-fighting parties back to the safety of the island.

Looking forward, he saw the last of the Russian boats making a run on *Nimitz*. At a thousand yards, it fired a final torpedo at the after quarter of the ship. He knew there was no way to turn her in time. "Mr. Dailey to the bridge on the double," he shouted into the mike.

The boat followed its own torpedo in, raking the stern with rocket fire. Then, as the torpedo hit, it swerved for a run up the side. Even before they were fired, David knew rockets were coming at the bridge again. He dove through the port-side door as the first round exploded inside, blowing out the forward bulkhead. Incendiary shells ignited the pilothouse. David crawled back on his hands and knees, remembering Frank Welles still inside. He inched his way along the deck plates to the other side. But now Welles was hunched over on his side.

"Frank . . . Frank?" He rolled his friend's lifeless body over, lifted the eyelids for a fraction of a second, then let Welles slide back against the bulkhead.

Looking up, he saw the torn metal of the starboard bridge wing. Then, remembering, he leaped up, tripped over a body in his first frantic lunge, then crawled, choking on the smoke, through the starboard hatch. He was searching for the lookout he had been talking with a few short moments before. Nothing was moving. Then, peering through wafts of dense black smoke that had risen up to the bridge level, he saw Seaman Apprentice Meehan mashed against the bulkhead. He had taken a direct hit from one of the rockets. David closed his eyes tightly for a moment. He had not done very well looking after the sailor who had trusted him. He crawled back into the pilothouse, knowing *Nimitz* was now out of control. There were so many more of his sailors in the same state as his young lookout.

Suddenly he heard a steady banging sound through the

crackling of the flames. It came from the door behind him. It was partially open, but twisted metal kept the party on the other side from pushing through.

"Admiral, are you still out there?" It was Bill Dailey.

"Yes, Bill." He found a fire ax that had fallen from its place on the bulkhead. "Just a second. I'll smash the door open."

Gradually, he gained a few inches, enough so that Dailey and a sailor with him were able to squeeze through. Then Dailey realized they were the only ones alive on the bridge.

"Frank?" he questioned.

David nodded to the form on the deck plates.

"I'm sorry, Admiral." He hesitated for a moment, then continued, "I think you should consider shifting your flag, sir."

It was at that moment that David realized *Nimitz* was heeling badly to starboard. Looking out through the smoke he noticed she was in a continuous turn. He reached for the mike on the ship's speaker.

"It's no use, sir," Dailey shouted through the noise of the flames. "We have no steering control. The last torpedo jammed the rudder over. There is no after steering."

"The engines?"

"I'm afraid that would be useless, too, sir. We have only one screw now. And we've lost most of the power to the pumps. They're using portable billies up forward, but the flooding's way ahead of them. DC Central says they've lost pressure to most of the fire hoses." The rumble of more explosions reached the bridge. "It's pretty much hopeless, Admiral."

The heat had forced them back to the after door. "All right, Bill. Make arrangements." The giant ship gave an almost human shudder as it heeled more heavily to starboard. Its steady turn had almost ceased as *Nimitz* lost headway. Now the smoke again covered the deck. It was blowing through the bridge as they left.

In flag plot worried staff officers were quietly stuffing papers into their briefcases as Admiral Charles entered.

Battery-powered battle lanterns lit the room with an eerie glow. Already smoke from burning gas, paint, explosives, humans, and other flammables was adding an offensive scent to the air. Their grimy Admiral shocked them even more. His uniform was soot stained, his hat gone in his lifesaving dive through the bridge door. Welles's blood was smeared on his hands and arms.

David stared blankly at the carnage on the status board. Sunk: cruisers *Mississippi*, *Sterett*, *Worden*, destroyers *Farragut*, *Semmes*, *Hoel*, *Fletcher*, *Forrest Sherman*, frigate *Meyercord*. The last name brought a momentary flicker of recognition. That ship had been named after an officer in his squadron in Vietnam, a respected hero of the riverboat days.

"Have *California* stand alongside, Bill. I'll transfer my flag to her."

"I've already arranged to have her stand off, Admiral. But I'm afraid we can't make a direct transfer. It's too dangerous for *California* to move that close." His face was sad and serious. "We're going to have to go over the side, sir. She'll have her whaleboat nearby to pick us up."

"Fine, Bill. Thank you." Again *Nimitz* shifted more heavily to starboard as tons of water continued to pour into her innards. "Where is the XO?"

"He's standing by DC Central. He's waiting for your order to abandon ship. He doesn't want to give it until you're safely off."

"Then let's get the hell out of here."

"Do you want anything from your cabin, Admiral?"

"Yes, I guess I do. . . . No, forget it. Don't waste any time. The sooner we're gone, the sooner they can abandon ship. Tell the XO I definitely do not want him staying aboard. Give him orders to report to me on *California* as soon as every sailor is off." He paused for a moment. "I don't want her to have a slow death, and I don't want them to do it. We'll sink her ourselves."

There should have been joy aboard *Lenin*. They knew they had delivered *Nimitz* to Gorenko, that it was just a matter of

time before the great ship went to the bottom. But *Lenin*, too,
was hurt, badly hurt.

The concentrated attack on *Nimitz* had left the Soviet
carrier more open to the Americans that Kupinsky preferred,
but he had known that there was no choice, that they could
not achieve their objective as long as *Nimitz* was afloat. A
flight of Corsairs had been badly decimated before it came
within range of the Soviet carrier, but three of them had
gotten through with their missiles. One had actually been
able to deliver a five-hundred-pound bomb that knocked out
the forward missile launchers.

Of more importance were the American submarines
Omaha and *Groton*. Earlier in the day they had very quietly
maneuvered themselves into the line of advance of Kupinsky's force. They remained below the thermal layer, using
the sudden temperature change to camouflage themselves
from the aircraft flying protective ASW cover in front of the
advancing ships, Their torpedo tubes were loaded with Harpoon missiles, quite capable of accurately hitting a surface
target at sixty miles.

The submarines used their on-board computers to analyze
the sound signatures of the surface ships. Stealthily, they
isolated *Lenin* and the other major ships they wanted as
targets. No sound transmissions were ever exchanged. Earlier planning pretty much obviated that, and their CO's
realized it really didn't matter if they happened to hit the
same target. They would just be doubling the chances of
sinking it.

That was exactly what happened to *Marshal Grechko*, the
newest guided-missile cruiser in the fleet. *Omaha's* first
missile hit amidship, right at the waterline, ripping a huge
hole, tons of water instantaneously filling her engine room.
Groton's Harpoon detonated in a missile storage compartment, the force of the explosion slashing upward to smash the
bridge. Fires swept out of control through the forward section
as *Grechko* heeled rapidly to port. The flames were blown
back along the deck, driving the fire fighters amidship. One
of her radiomen had just begun to call for help when an

exploding magazine sent shells bursting into the space. He
never delivered his message. This explosion also forced the
men on the hoses back farther, though they hoped they might
gradually control the fires and move forward to help their
comrades trapped in the bow. The final blow was delivered
by a damaged Corsair about to ditch. Her pilot, as he streaked
low over the water, flipped his five-hundred-pound bomb
just behind the stack, destroying the engine room. Lucky to
survive the blast, the fire fighters now found themselves
with flames behind them also. Their only chance for survival
was a wall of water between them and the flames advancing
from the bow and the stern. And then the water pressure
dropped until there was only a trickle. In less than five
minutes, what remained of *Grechko*'s crew abandoned ship.

Zhdanov was also hit by an *Omaha* Harpoon, followed by
the first of the American surface-fired missiles. The leading
Soviet ships had more missile launchers than their attackers,
but not quite the range. With a lack of air cover to deter the
American ships, the Russians were forced to protect themselves before they could establish a surface-missile attack of
their own. The combined hits on *Zhdanov* were too much,
her midships' section burning fiercely and her rudder
jammed to starboard. Firecontrol parties were unable to halt
the flames as the circling wind blew from a variety of directions. Her bow was filling and crackling bulkheads signaled
the approaching end. A Kashin destroyer came close aboard
to take on survivors.

Groton was the first of the subs to hit *Lenin*. The initial
Harpoon struck aft of the bridge in the superstructure,
damaging the carrier's computer center. The second hit forward of the bow missile installation, just ahead of the
launcher bombed moments earlier. The detonation of
magazines was the first sign the *Lenin* had been seriously hit.

At the time, Svedrov had said, "Our attack on *Nimitz* is
progressing, Admiral. She has taken a number of hits, but I
don't believe any fatal ones yet. Do you want me to release
the torpedo boats for attack?"

"Yes, Svedrov, I think you'd better." They felt the rumble of an explosion in one of the forward magazines. "As you will note, they have not overlooked us."

Svedrov had the same feeling his Admiral did. Their fleet had more weapons than the Americans, but their sophistication and range might not be quite competitive. It was a necessity to sink the *Nimitz* to equalize the battle, but there was no point in being a winner if your own force was too decimated.

Alex Kupinsky watched the screens closely in front of him. His aircraft were inadequate to protect his ships. It was a matter of having more small carriers to spread over the ocean, for the airpower was still a controlling factor. He would have few aircraft or pilots left after this day was done. When he returned to Moscow, he would hammer home this lesson well. More shipyards would be converted to building many of the small VTOL carriers.

His own status boards reflected much the same information as David Charles's. Sunk: cruisers *Azov, Vasili Chapaev, Marshall Volorshilov, Admiral Izakov,* destroyers *Bravy, Bedovy, Zorky, Strogy, Smetlivy.* They were names etched in Russian hearts and minds, and their brave men would be missed. Countless statues would be erected in city squares to a new generation of heroes.

A third Harpoon plowed into *Lenin,* this time from *Omaha.* It hit just below the after section of the flight deck on the starboard side, exploding inside the hangar near the number-six elevator used for hoisting explosives. Ammunition was being loaded at the time, and that, too, began to detonate as the flames spread. If the explosions had been confined to a single area, the fires might have been contained, but rockets were being prepared at the time for the last flight of Forgers. Set off by the intense heat, they streaked wildly through the huge hangar, striking other aircraft and igniting their fuel. Damage-control parties were unable to enter. Bulkheads collapsed as explosions penetrated into adjacent spaces. Kupinsky was soon notified that the fires in the after hangar deck were out of control. The smoke filtering into his flag plot was already making breathing uncomfortable.

"Admiral, our reports indicate that *Nimitz* has been crippled. One more air strike will sink her."

"Svedrov, there is no doubt in my mind that you are correct. Yet, right now I can't launch another strike. We have almost no Rigas or Forgers left. We have fires in the aft section of the hangar deck that are out of control, and ammunition is exploding so fast that I could only arm the few aircraft I have up forward. The ammunition would have to be carried by hand, but we need every man available to fight the fires. We have succeeded with *Nimitz*." He took a deep breath. "She will either sink or David will torpedo her himself. But we are close to losing *Lenin,* also. And look at the losses already on that board. What have we won?"

"The Americans, too, have sustained heavy losses, including three cruisers."

"Admiral?" Kupinsky turned to another voice by his shoulder. The man had been trying to attract the Admiral's attention, but he was vying with the low rumble coming from the hangar deck.

"Yes, what is it?"

"We have just received a plain-language message from Moscow, sir. Intelligence reports that the American carrier, *Constellation,* has passed through the Strait of Malacca."

Alex turned back to Svedrov. "You see, strength in numbers. The Americans have lost a great carrier, but even before they knew it, they were directing another with equivalent airpower in our direction." The phone by his elbow buzzed. He picked it up, muttered his name into the mouthpiece, listened for just a moment, and hung it up without a word.

He stared intently at the displays framing the dimly lit plot, looking at but not seeing the lights and symbols that kept track of the battle. Finally his eyes stopped at the board with the list of ships' names, the ones already lost. "That was Captain Scherensky. He is concerned about *Lenin*. He feels we may want to shift our flag to another ship, or at least make plans to do so."

Svedrov's eyes dropped. The heavy eyebrows and stocky body gave him the appearance of a bulldog. There was still a lot of fight in him. "I see." He said nothing for a second. "I

will contact the *Admiral Senyavin*. They have the capacity
for our staff.''

''She has also been badly damaged, Svedrov. Our cruisers
have been excellent targets today, just like the American
cruisers. Perhaps we shall have to pick one of the destroyers.''

''I will see to it, Admiral.''

As Svedrov was uttering those words, the fate of *Lenin*
was being sealed. While the Aegis ships had sector positions
to maintain to protect *Nimitz,* the little frigates and destroyers
had continued directly into the Russian line of advance. They
were, as they had been in earlier wars, expendable. In this
case, they were literally the only ones to see the Soviet force
with their own eyes.

The brash, young commanding officer of *Capodanno,* one
of the smallest of the frigates, found himself watching the
burning *Lenin* through his binoculars. He asked a messenger
to find the pilots of the ship's LAMPS helicopters. Ensign
Steve Young reported to him in less than a minute, fully
dressed to fly and quite out of breath. ''I'm sorry, sir, we
have only one helo left. Bob Kerner didn't come back.''

''I'm sorry. I hadn't been informed.'' The captain handed
the young officer a pair of binoculars, then pointed to the
wing of the bridge. ''Come out here with me, Steve. I want to
show you something.''

They leaned together against the windbreak, their elbows
on the edge to steady their glasses. Wherever they looked
ships were racing to unknown positions. Ships were firing
missiles. Ships were burning or sinking. But the CO of
Capodanno centered his binoculars, and the young ensign's
as well, on the burning Russian carrier on the horizon.

''Your torpedoes can be set to run shallow?'' It was a
question and a statement at the same time.

''Yes, sir. I guess so, although they're designed to home
on subs.''

''I know that. But could your torpedoman set them to
maybe run a thousand yards and sink that carrier?''

''I don't think the people in Washington had that in mind
for the Mk 52, but we can sure take a shot at it.''

"Okay. You get on that phone," he pointed at one by the chart table as they stepped back into the pilothouse, "and get that man up here on the double."

The Mk 52 could be set for shallow running, and the torpedoman was sent back to the hangar to arm the helo. Over the chart table the captain spread photos and drawings of *Lenin* from almost every imaginable angle. He pointed out to the young pilot where the 76-mm. and Gatling-style guns were located. The helo was to fly up on the Soviet carrier from the starboard quarter, hugging the water. It would be hard to pick up on radar, and likely would not be seen by lookouts until very close. He would have to judge for himself when to release his fish. The guns were radar controlled, the Gatlings used more as a last ditch antimissile weapon. Perhaps their fire-control radar couldn't lock on him, but the minute they did, there would be little time. Once the torpedoes were launched, he was not to turn back to *Capodanno*. Simply put his bird in hover and jump into the Indian Ocean.

Rezvy, a relatively new Krivak-II guided-missile destroyer, had been selected by Svedrov. It could not take the entire staff by any means, but its communications system would allow the Admiral to regroup his force and maintain tactical command. As they prepared the last of their materials for transfer, the American LAMPS helicopter from *Capodanno* had succeeded in closing to less than a mile from *Lenin*. Because of the interior communications problems caused by the fires, the lookout on the stern could not immediately get his siting message to the bridge. It was finally relayed by a unique jury-rigged system that is the mark of sailors in every navy.

But by that time, the helo had positioned itself on the starboard beam of *Lenin*. Normally, there are two pilots and a systems man to coordinate the search-and-weapons section in the helo, but this time Steve Young had been selected to pilot the craft with his torpedoman flying shotgun. *Lenin* brought the 76-mm. guns to bear, but the fire-control radar could not isolate the helo. The mount captain put the gun in

local control, and his crew began the process of firing short
bursts to pinpoint their target.

The first torpedo was released for a straight run at the after
section of the ship at a fifteen-foot depth. The helo then
shifted its position slightly to direct the next one at the bow.
That caused the gun crew to shift their own sights slightly,
and allowed that extra second to release the second fish. The
helo was in hover. Ensign Young pushed open his door,
nodding to the other man to do the same, and together they
jumped.

As they came to the surface, the two Americans found
their attention divided. The first torpedo had struck about one
hundred feet from the stern of *Lenin*, sending a tower of
water skyward. At almost the same time, *Lenin's* guns found
the helo. The 76-mm. shells caused the machine to falter for a
moment before it began to dip. Then the Gatling guns found
their target tearing it apart before it hit the water. The explosion of the second torpedo, just forward of *Lenin's*
superstructure, riveted their eyes on the big ship. *Lenin* was
definitely heeling to starboard. What they didn't know was
that the first fish had exploded inside the after engine room,
buckling the giant shafts. Her motion was simply the movement of a ship coasting. Afraid to inflate their life raft yet,
they watched fascinated as more secondary explosions
racked *Lenin's* hull. She was beyond saving.

In *Lenin's* flag plot Alex Kupinsky felt the torpedoes
through the deck before the sound ever reached him. He no
longer was in contact with Captain Scherensky, and he did
not know where the torpedoes had come from. He simply
knew that today he and David had exchanged carriers.

It was too dangerous for *Rezvy* to put a line over to *Lenin*.
She stood off a few hundred yards and put her whaleboat in
the water. Alex Kupinsky departed his flagship in the same
manner as David Charles. He leaped from the lowest non-
burning deck into the Indian Ocean, inflating his life pre-
server as he surfaced. The whaleboat was quickly beside
him, and Admiral Kupinsky was hauled aboard just as soak-
ing wet as Admiral Charles had been. As the boat made a

wide turn away from the burning ship, it was Alex Kupinsky who sighted the two men in the water and directed the boat to them, assuming they were Soviet sailors. It was also Alex who was the first to offer a hand to the youth, whom, he noted immediately, was wearing American pilot's gear.

The ensign had no idea who the man was who had offered him a helping hand, just that he had seen him recovered from the water also. In English, Alex inquired, "Where is your aircraft?"

"Shot down."

"You are from the *Nimitz?*"

"U.S.S. *Capodanno.*"

The Admiral shook his head curiously. "I do not know that ship."

"FF-1093."

"A frigate?" Curiously, he asked, "You are a helicopter pilot, out here?"

The ensign simply nodded.

"What was your mission before you were shot down?"

Again no answer. The young man simply pointed at *Lenin*, now dead in the water, smoke pouring from every section of the ship.

"Those torpedoes were yours?" Kupinsky asked in awe.

The ensign's head again bobbed up and down a few times, agreeing with the Russian's questions.

Kupinsky turned to Svedrov. "We have both learned something today, my friend. That boy flies American helicopters off the fantails of those little frigates. Today, *Lenin* was sunk by a tiny helicopter." He halted his thoughts momentarily, then looked back to his Chief of Staff. "Just as we sunk their capital ship with tiny little boats, they sunk *Lenin* with a helicopter."

They were speaking in Russian, and the ensign had no idea what they were saying or who they were. Then the older of the two turned back, pointed at him, and said something else before taking a seat in the bow of the boat. He thought perhaps they were sealing his fate, but what Admiral Kupinsky had said was, "See that they are well taken care of,

Svedrov. They are both brave men, just as our small-boat captain were.''

The midday BBC report in London was somber.

TODAY, (the commentator began) has been a day of carnage in the Indian Ocean. Two powerful task forces, both with greater firepower than the world has ever seen, confronted each other head on. The reasons for this sea battle are as yet uncertain. Claims and counterclaims from Washington and Moscow have fallen on deaf ears at the U.N. Both countries have been implored by the Secretary General of the U.N. to impose a cease-fire. The earlier claims by the Party Secretary at the Kremlin yesterday concerning land-based American offensive weapons in the Indian Ocean have been denied in Washington. While the President has said little, the Secretary of State, Thomas Jasperson, has stated unequivocally that the island of Islas Piedras is a Trident supply base only, and that the missile system that has been established on the island is only for security of those countries in the Indian Ocean sphere who wish an umbrella of security to allow them to go about their ways peaceably. The Soviets still claim the island's missile system has not yet been completed and that their intentions are to halt aggression in the Third World, before the United States forced these poor countries into an untenable position. Lack of communications between the two countries, apparently as a result of satellite destruction by both sides, has brought all members of the U.N. to beg for a ceasefire. The Secretary General claims that only world pressure on the two superpowers will avoid many other countries being drawn into a world war as a result of treaty obligations. . . .

CHAPTER
FOURTEEN

THERE was absolute silence in the Oval Office. They had been entranced by the words of the newscaster who stared back out of the screen, seemingly at each of them. The President and the men about him were visibly tired, their faces drawn, pouches expanding under their eyes.

. . . and we still have no direct statement from the White House concerning this apparent slaughter of American sailors in the Indian Ocean. The Pentagon remains quiet also. It is known that the Chief of Naval Operations has remained with the President and that Secretary of State Jasperson has been commuting between the White House and the office of an Assistant Chief of Naval Operations.

The information that has come from the Indian Ocean remains spotty at best. No commercial flights have been allowed over the area. Available reports have come from merchant shipping already in that part of the ocean. They indicate that sporadic aerial duels, unlike anything since World War II, have taken place with heavy losses on both sides. Huge forces of American and Soviet military ships have maneuvered back and forth between the Seychelle Islands to the east and the Maldives to the north, with the controversial Islas Piedras as a pivot point. These reports also indicate vast amounts of wreckage and oil in the ocean and some downed pilots from both nations have been picked up, although none of them have as yet been able to explain satisfactorily what is happening.

To this reporter, it seems time that the American people were given a report by the President they elected. Not since the Battle of Leyte Gulf in October 1944 have there been any naval forces of this magnitude in opposition to each other. From what we can gather, perhaps there has never been such loss of American fighting men—and for a reason that none of us know . . .

"Turn it off!"

"Yes, sir," said one of the President's assistants, and the screen suddenly became blank.

"Tom, are you with me, or agin' me?" The Secretary of State turned to the President, but was unable to answer as the man continued. "You heard that. For all the people know, I may be leading them into a nuclear war. And all they get is silence." The Secretary opened his mouth to speak. "And furthermore, we're feeding more reporters than I've seen since my predecessor conceded. They're waiting out there like buzzards, circling and waiting. And I'm insulting the Secretary General of the U.N. by not reutrning his last call."

The President of the United States was exhausted. His hands never stopped moving, crawling and grasping like crabs, scratching imaginary itches that the man himself was unaware of. He was unable to sleep, and he knew he wouldn't be able to keep food in his stomach. Those close to him competed with each other for his attention, yet each contradicted the previous one. Many changed advice with the latest news or the predominant feeling at a given time. Only Jasperson was firm, and he understood the President better than any of the others in the room.

"Mr. President, I am aware of the increasing pressure, and I appreciate it. You may even have to give in to it." He couldn't resist that inference. "What I still need is the remainder of the twenty-four hours you promised me yesterday. There are about eight left."

The President's eyes crinkled as he squinted back at Jasperson. He rubbed them, then said, "I don't know why I ever gave into such a damn fool promise. My first instinct was to get right on that little red phone to the Kremlin and settle this like gentlemen." This time he rubbed his eyes, hard, with both hands. "I'm afraid I'm going to be remembered as the President who killed more people than Lyndon Johnson." He looked very hard at the Secretary of State through narrowed, tired eyes. "You are absolutely sure this Admiral Charles can hold off the Soviets until we can finish that base?"

"We hope so, sir. Please remember we didn't promise. No one can promise the outcome of any military engagement. But we are taking the most logical course of action considering all political and military factors."

The President was wavering. Jasperson had known him long enough to know the man could change his mind as easily as his pants. If he wavered to the other side now, he would be remembered as the man who gave the remainder of the world to the Russians. He had only to mention that to the man, as he had sixteen hours earlier, and he knew he could be guaranteed the remaining eight. But the President's Chief of Staff had been so enraged with that tactic the last time that he thought he'd wait until it was absolutely necessary. This was no time to start family arguments.

"No need to worry about unauthorized use of nuclear weapons?"

"Not unless you order it for our forces, sir." And then Jasperson decided to add, "I doubt you have to concern yourself with that. Admiral Charles has never been an advocate of such weapons unless the country were in danger, physically."

"I can't get over how you have such trust in one man."

At this, the Chief of Naval Operations, who had been at the President's side constantly, added, "My assistant, Sam Carter, feels that we have absolutely the best man considering the situation, Mr. President."

"Perhaps," the President nodded at the CNO, "you should be with Admiral Carter, rather than here."

"I think that it is wise that the Admiral remain here, with you, sir," remarked Jasperson. "This is a sea battle, and any decisions or future statements should come with the CNO at your side. Please be assured that Admiral Carter and I can adequately control the situation from the Pentagon."

"I concur, sir." The CNO wasn't about to leave the security of the White House. This was where civilian appointments came from, and he would soon be retiring.

There was a buzz from the President's intercom. He depressed the button, "Yes, Cindy."

"Captain Hogan from Intelligence, Mr. President. He has the photographs you requested."

"Please have him brought in."

No sooner had his finger left the button than an aide escorted the Navy captain into the room. Hogan looked around at those present, his eyes blinking rapidly. Either he's very nervous, thought Jasperson, or he's having problems with his contact lenses again, remembering his meeting with the man a few hours before in Carter's office. Sam Carter had a way with people, and he had also known Captain Hogan from earlier days. To put him at ease, Sam had kidded him about the day he was a check-fire observer in a five-inch gun mount during target practice. It had been on the old *Bagley* and one of Hogan's contact lenses had fallen out inside the mount. Carter told the story of how the exploding shells had begun to close the aircraft towing the sleeve. The pilot had broken off the exercise immediately, remarking that he wasn't about to be shot down by his own people. Sam had called the mount captain and learned that Ensign Hogan was on his hands and knees in the mount looking for his contact. Why wouldn't he tell the gunnery officer before they scared that poor pilot to death? The mount captain explained that when Mr. Hogan had gone down on his hands and knees, he had taken off his sound-powered phone because the wires were caught around his neck.

"I put him in hack for two weekends for that," Carter had said.

"Captain Hogan, you look exhausted. Please sit down," Jasperson said. The man sat in a proffered chair, clutching an overstuffed briefcase as if it were a case of beer. Jasperson briefly introduced him to the men around the office.

What he had in the briefcase were detailed photos of the latest engagement in the Indian Ocean. They had been blown up for those present, and they left no doubt about the destruction that had just taken place. Detailed photos of the attack on *Nimitz* showed much more than the earlier films relayed by a commercial TV unit. There was again silence around the room. The pictures told a story of horror that none would have imagined. Even Jasperson was momentarily taken aback, although he had known of the results of the battle earlier than anyone else in the Oval Office.

"She won't last, Mr. President." This was the CNO looking at pictures of *Nimitz*. If she doesn't go down on her own, Admiral Charles will have to sink her himself."

The President said nothing. He was unimpressed with the photos of *Lenin's* destruction. His concern was with the American losses. The President rose from his desk and strolled over to the window behind to look at the garden for a moment. He could see himself in the same corner as Lyndon Johnson, his ego shattered. He didn't want to have to make a similar speech to the people, because he wanted to run again. How could the United States possibly be bluffing the Russians that the Islas Piedras installation was complete? Soviet intelligence was supposed to be equally as good as his own. Maybe he should contact Simpson right now in Moscow and tell him to throw in the towel. No, negotiate was a better word. Jasperson was confident that this Admiral Charles could protect the island and drive the Russians back long enough to allow them to finish it. So far, all the photographs indicated was that the Russians were just as stubborn as the Americans and they were willing to take as much punishment to prove their point. There were too many inconsistancies in his mind, and the uppermost was how all this would affect his career.

He turned to the Secretary of State. "Tom, I can't allow you eight more hours. There's no telling what the world will think of us."

"Perhaps they will think badly of the Russians, sir."

"Perhaps they will, but I don't think I can take that chance any longer. My position will be significantly weakened if the Soviets can get to that island and show just exactly what we're doing."

So that's what's bothering him, thought Jasperson. He doesn't want to take any blame. "Mr. President, we have marines in the air now, from that exercise we had been conducting off the African coast." He knew the President had been informed that what might be Russian troop-carrying submarines had been detected closing in on the island. "I doubt the Kremlin is aware of their presence. We had them out there specifically to protect any offensive challenge to the island's integrity. I assure you they won't capture Islas Piedras."

It was Jasperson's strongest argument, the United States ability to keep the Soviets off Islas Piedras regardless of the finality of the sea battle. He didn't want to use his last personal argument with the President yet, not in front of his advisers. They would jump down the Secretary's throat at any inference that the President would be giving away the country or anything else. But the answer was obvious to Jasperson before the man spoke. His left hand squeezed the fingers on the right one until the knuckles were white. He had made the decision not to make a decision.

"Four more hours. That's all, then!"

The events of the past few hours had also made their impression on certain people in Moscow. The elation caused by the sinking of *Nimitz* had been short-lived for Gorenko. The loss of *Lenin* followed the first report by only moments.

Casualty reports were equally as hard to take. The Americans were just as tough as Alex had told him they would be. Stubborn was the word. They had developed some weapons of their own that had surprised the Russians and the unexpectedly heavy loss of ships was devastating. Gorenko wondered almost aloud to himself if maybe Admiral Collier's cockiness was based on a completed Islas Piedras missile installation. No, it couldn't be, he tried to convince himself.

They had been following the construction too long. How could the Americans have built everything underground without intelligence showing this happening? They weren't moles! And there was no way they could sneak the missiles in. That was pure fabrication on Collier's part. Although, if Gorenko could design troop-carrying submarines, why couldn't someone develop cargo-carrying submarines?

Ridiculous, he decided. The only way they were going to prove what the Americans were really up to was to take that island and show the world that the Americans were building a missile system that would perpetrate aggression in the Third World. It was time to send them home.

He pressed a button on his desk and, when an aide entered, he gave the order. United States defenses were minimal on the island. The Americans, he knew, had never projected the possibility of an attack that would not come over the water. Those submarines contained a specially trained force of marines, some of them the sons of those fine soldier/sailors he had commanded so many years ago against the Germans. They would encounter little opposition in securing Islas Piedras.

While Gorenko was issuing these orders, Bob Collier decided that he would have to contact Admiral Carter directly, in plain language, to find out what had transpired. Too many hours had passed since his last meeting with Admiral Gorenko. There must have been more action in the Indian Ocean. Since there was no change in the guards outside the embassy, he had to assume it was still a stalemate. But he could do no more until he learned what David Charles's forces were accomplishing. The fact that Gorenko's people would be listening to the conversation no longer bothered him. They would be as aware of the casualty reports, and he already knew enough of the events preceding the confrontation. He could follow his own intuition from that point on. But he must be sure whether one side or the other was gaining an advantage. The short conversation that ensued answered the questions he and Ambassador Simpson needed to know.

And in another part of the Kremlin, where political decisions are made, the Party Secretary had decided to call Admiral Gorenko. It was to authorize the orders that would move the submarine that was in the Strait of Hormuz. It was the one that had puzzled David Charles before any of the conflict had begun. It was conventionally powered, seemingly on an independent patrol to nowhere, well away from the forces that had clashed. He had no idea at the time that it was an integral part of the Russian strategy, and even Alex Kupinsky had been unaware of its existence. It was a mine layer, and it was fully loaded with the most advnaced mines known to man. They could be activated by radio and controlled by an operator far away, or they could be left on their own, preset for various depths and activated by passing ships.

In this case, it was the latter, since Gorenko had convinced the Secretary that it would be more impressive and would automatically halt traffic. And it was an easy way to enhance the idea of the Americans as aggressors. Washington knew about the sub, obviously, but their denying it as their own would be hard for the United Nations to swallow considering the Secretary's speech and the fact that the United States did control Islas Piedras and did have a vital interest in the OPEC nations. Gorenko and the Secretary knew this was their trump card. The Strait controlled the Gulf of Oman and the Persian Gulf. Lining these waters were such places as Kuwait, the Federation of Arab Emirates, Bahrain, Saudi Arabia, Qatar, Iran, and Iraq. Loss of this supply by the United States and its control by the Soviets would shift the balance nicely. Quietly their orders were carried out.

While the Russian subs were quiet, they found no reason to try to surprise the Americans completely. They knew that the Islas Piedras defenders were aware of their presence, and possibly even knew that the subs were probably there for offensive purposes. But they never suspected that American intelligence had known about the development of these troop carriers. Impressed with American ingenuity in lifting combat troops to just about any part of the world on short notice, Gorenko had decided that submarines were an excellent method of getting his marines into position for small forays. He did not plan to police the world, but Russian marines should be able to get to trouble spots unobstrusively, particularly when that trouble spot could be planned well in advance.

They were nuclear powered and large, an offshoot of the missile-carrying subs. Their purpose was to carry a large number of marines with their weapons, but without the heavy equipment required for prolonged operations. These were shock troops, hit and run. They were to hit a beach, accomplish a mission, and get out. If that objective had to hold for a longer time, then regular troops would be brought in.

On receipt of their orders, the subs raced in at high speed from their position approximately one hundred miles off the island. This allowed the marines just enough time to ready themselves. Periscope investigation showed no signs of preparation on the Americans' part. The subs literally grounded themselves after surfacing, bringing the marines as close to shore as possible. From a number of hatches in the hull, squads of marines emerged to leap into automatically inflated rubber boats, bringing with them small high-powered motors to quickly propel the small craft to shore.

At about the time the boats were reaching the beach, the helos that had been waiting on the other side of Islas Piedras rose to assist the U.S. Marines who now appeared, as if from nowhere, to meet this attack. If the two forces had met each other head on in a ground situation, it would have been difficult to say which might have been the victor. Both were superbly trained for this type of action, professionals who enjoyed testing their skills. But the American helicopters were the reason that the Russians never had a chance.

There had not been reports of many helos by Soviet intelligence, let alone of trained marines. They were gunships. Combined with the marines on shore, they offered more fire power and maneuverability than the Soviets could handle. The boats not already on shore were strafed. The troops that had made it to the beach were hit with rocket fire from the air and a variety of small arms from the defenders.

It was over quickly. When the major in charge of the marine detachment was sure his men could clean up the remnants of the Russian force, the helos were released to chase the submarines that had brought the landing force. But the silent black boats had slipped away as soon as they saw there would be nobody to bring home.

Upon receipt of the proper signal from Moscow, the submarine on the southeast of the Gulf of Oman had proceeded on a north-northwest course to the Strait of Hormuz. On arrival at a preset location, it carefully seeded the Strait with its new mines. No ship could now enter or depart the Persian Gulf.

During all this efficient operation, there was only one item overlooked. A junior communications officer was to have notified all ports in the Persian Gulf that Russia suspected an American sub had seeded the Strait. Later investigation seemed to settle on the fact that an announcement the next day at the United Nations would be time enough. No one bothered to check ship departures.

The S.S. *Prince of Peace,* of Liberian registry, was one of the two largest ships to ever sail the oceans of the world. When fully laden, she contained 750,000 tons of oil spread equally in her five giant tanks. She was over 1,400 feet long, more than a quarter of a mile, and her beam measured 240 feet, only twenty yards less than a football field. Her most impressive statistic was hidden when she was fully loaded, for the *Prince of Peace* spread below the surface of the ocean like an iceberg with her 100-foot draft.

She was truly a supertanker in every respect, and her full capacity of oil could have supplied all the energy needs to sustain a substantial city for more than a year. Her oil rode in the forward 95 percent of the ship, while her after 5 percent housed her small crew in absolute luxury. Her pilothouse was as spotless as an operating room and as automated as the Concorde jet.

The *Prince of Peace* had taken on her oil fifteen miles out from the port of Bahrain, simply because she could get no closer to the city. Safety experts had agreed these supertankers should be far enough away to avoid endangering the population. Resupplied by helicopter, she stood out into the Persian Gulf the morning before the mines were slipped below the surface of the Strait of Hormuz. Giant propellers bit into the warm water, but her sheer weight prevented the ship from gaining her economical cruising speed of fourteen knots for the better part of half an hour. While her speed through the water was unimpressive compared to the faster military ships, an urgent attempt to stop her would still cause the ship to remain in forward motion for over six minutes.

First light was just coloring the sky as the *Prince of Peace* was passing through the coral reefed strait toward the safety of deeper water and open ocean. The tremendous vibrations of the hull passing through the water activated two of the mines. The navigator had just appeared on the wing of the bridge to take his first star sight when the initial explosion shattered number-one tank in the bow. From one hundred feet above the water's surface and over thirteen hundred feet astern of the explosion, the navigator was fascinated most by the amount of time it took the sound to arrive. Before he could ponder the physics of the problem further, the second mine detonated under tank number three.

Enough volatile gas had collected in the few air spaces in the tank to instantly create a secondary explosion far beyond any that the designers of the mine could have comprehended. The navigator was never aware of the secondary blast, nor were any other members of the crew. The force buckled the hull, lifting the central section up, the weight fore and aft snapping the ship in half, the hull for a moment resembling a cracked egg.

Then a fireball rocketed skyward, fueled by the gases generated by intense heat. As it rose, more oil was sucked up with it, both from the number-three tank and those on either side as they ruptured. The first streaks of dawn were instantly changed into midday on the coasts on either side of the strait. The heat that arrived shortly after the light was so acute from its point of origin that for a moment it was as if the midday sun had stalled.

Steam from the ocean followed the fireball as it soared skyward, helping to intensify the winds now developing in the vortex of the flame. While the *Prince of Peace* was already settling in two vast, partially melted sections, the oil from all five burst tanks was now burning furiously. Where hardly a breath of air had existed a moment before, winds were now increasing in a circular motion, fanning the flames and drawing more oil and oxygen into the fire. Not a minute had passed before this firestorm had developed hurricane-force winds, encouraging a blaze unlike any man had ever thought of creating, beyond even Dresden or Hiroshima.

Later in the day, the dense, smoky, oil-laden clouds would drift eastward, creating a black rain that would cover the southernmost tip of Iran, reaching across the border into Pakistan. There would be little fishing for years to come and the blackened shores on both sides of the strait and the Gulf of Oman would reflect the disaster for an equal amount of time.

The loss of a freighter, or even a small tanker, might not have created as much furor around the world as this one unexpected mistake in communications. Within hours, the nations of the world—First World, Second World, Third World—were clamoring for a halt in this sudden war between the two world powers, a war over a misunderstood plot of guano in the Indian Ocean.

The concept first appeared on wall posters in Peking only hours after the loss of the *Prince of Peace,* which had followed on the heels of the unfortunate Soviet landing at Islas Piedras. There was no longer concern about security of communications either in Moscow or Washington. Their losses had been tremendous. The world was only too well aware of the danger that now existed. The wall posters stated:

A blatant message had been sent to the peaceful nations of the world that the two superpowers are willing to go to any length to establish superiority over the other, including hazarding the hegemony of Third World countries in their own affairs. If they are not willing to come to the peace tables within twenty-four hours, then it is time for the remainder of the world to bring them to their knees.

Peking saw the chance. Once and for all, Russia would be established as a dangerous aggressor. And the United States would have to listen to China now, instead of assuming a big brother role.

While other world leaders might not have interpreted Peking's basic reasons, they were willing to add their names to the list. Moscow and Washington were overwhelmed by the anger directed at them.

FROM THE LOG OF
ADMIRAL DAVID CHARLES

I HAVE WON. They will not get to Islas Piedras. Alex has won. He proved that the Soviet fleet can stand against us, toe to toe. Nobody has won. We have simply proven that we can hammer each other into a surreal state without the use of nuclear weapons. Maybe if we had used the atomic warheads and hit the other's capital ships first, there would not have been such unacceptable loss.

I feel like Chief Joseph. He was correct. He should be considered the great American, and maybe he would be if people had only listened to him. He said he would fight no more. He was a man of wisdom. He was also shouting into a hurricane, for his words were carried away before he could be understood. He knew.

Apparently we have to prove it to ourselves each time, just in case something might be balanced in our favor. I know how hard it is to turn the other cheek. We were well prepared, and I suppose we can say the day is ours. But is that what they're saying right now? I think so.

I wouldn't be sitting here now, making this entry, if I hadn't gone to the captain's cabin to borrow some clothes. The only item I took with me from *Nimitz* was this log, wrapped in the old watertight case that Maria gave me. I remember her card: "To the next Mahan." I had the log under my arm when I came in here, and decided I had to write even as I sit here in my skivvies. It just hit me. Who won and what was won? I kept staring back at *Nimitz* engulfed in flames. Over and over in my mind, I kept thinking of Chief Joseph as we pulled away.

I've made my decision. It's time for new warriors. The old ones are tired.

Tasha, my love,

There is a loneliness in command that goes beyond what any book has ever been able to describe. I cannot put it into words myself, but you would know it if I were beside you now, for my eyes must be telling that awful truth. Most of all, I want my father to know, even though I am not sure he would understand.

You must insist that my father tell you what has happened here on the Indian Ocean. You will not be able to read it thoroughly in the papers, but I want you to know my part in it. Briefly, we have fought over a period of a few days a vast sea battle, possibly one of the greatest in history. It was against the Americans, and my enemy (even briefly in my own mind, I think) was David Charles. I say "briefly" for that arrogance on my part passed quickly. I believe I have accomplished much for my country, but I am not sure what I have given up to do so. While we have proven to the world that in less than half a century we have been able to stand up to the greatest seapower in history, I find little to take personal pride in. The person that I had been trained to think I was is no longer me. While written words can't describe these feelings, perhaps you, in your own special way, will understand when I return.

The only way I can describe the feelings I have is to remind you of that American politician David told us about once. The man probably lived in the wrong era, for when asked what he wanted to do after literally giving his waking moments to his country, he said, "I want to sip red wine and watch the people dance," or something to that effect. He died before he could ever achieve that dream, and I don't want to. I want to sip the wine with the people, and I want to dance with them.

I count the moments until I am home with you and can give the love that has too often been bottled up inside me. Tell Peitr that he, too, is constantly in my thoughts.

With love,

Alex

DEAREST MARIA,

It is entirely possible that by the time this letter arrives, we may already be together again. You will have read in the newspapers and watched on television what I have been involved in. Whatever is twisted by the media can be corrected by Sam Carter.

I have always felt a deep pride for my Navy and my own small contribution to it. There is now a deep, deep hurt that will forever dig at me for my intensity in trying to destroy Alex's force and even Alex himself. There is something ingrained in most of us from childhood that brings out love or faith in country, an abiding nationalism perhaps, that I now know takes precedence over friendship. I have been increasingly concerned about that the last few days as I led my men directly at the Soviet force. Beyond Sam Carter, Alex, a Russian naval officer, may be one of the men I am closest to emotionally and intellectually. I can't describe it beyond that, and I don't know if I will ever be able to describe such a feeling to you.

Should anything happen to me before we are together again, I want you to know I am ashamed of nothing I have done. While the Navy may say what I am about to do is contrary to my oath, I followed orders and served my country as best I could. To me, choosing the military as a career never meant that I was choosing war—that I accepted, if there was no other alternative. While I may have some misgivings as I write this note, I can say with certainty that my concept of duty will eventually overcome any self-doubt.

You have been able to understand me when I can't express myself well, and feel what I feel when I say nothing. Then you know as you read this how you and the children are with me always, and that our own love becomes stronger each day.

With love,

David

CHAPTER FIFTEEN

A HAGGARD David Charles listened to Bill Dailey's casualty reports. The Chief of Staff was subdued, his eyes more tired than ever before, his shoulders a bit more rounded, his voice without its normal crispness.

". . . fuel for gas turbine ships is dangerously low. We were unable to top off each one when we spent the night in the Seychelles, and some of the small boys have been operating at flank speed since then. They haven't got more than a day before it's critical."

Dailey was continuing with the report, but David was hearing only what shocked him most. The personnel casualty reports were the items that stummed him particularly. Too many burn cases from *Nimitz* needed shore care. So many ships had been sunk that those still afloat were unable to provide adequate medical care or food for the survivors and their own men. Loss of his *Nimitz* had been a catastrophe, but the number of smaller cruisers, destroyers, frigates, even the stealthy submarines, that were lost was staggering.

He wondered if any other naval leader had ever suffered such losses as Dailey continued, ". . . it doesn't look like we can save *Texas* . . ." He had forgotten her. She had taken two missile hits, the second penetrating forward magazines between the missile launcher and her five-inch gun. Personnel losses had been exceptionally high from exploding ammunition, yet her crew had never given up fighting the fires. Now that her damage-control parties were gaining, her captain had just reported that he might have to abandon ship. He conjured up a picture of Larry Waterman and his family. Before he had been given *Texas,* he had lived in the same neighborhood with David and Maria Charles. Their children had played together and gone to the same school. The wives had been in the P.T.A., and the two couples had gotten along well, backyard barbecues and that sort of thing. When Larry had received orders for *Texas,* it was the Charles family that had thrown the celebration and good-bye party, for the Watermans would be moving to the ship's home port.

Texas was down by the bow, still taking on water too fast. "Captain Waterman says he'd like to stay on board *Texas* with volunteers, that maybe they can hold their own if some-one can get more pumps to her. . . ."

David held up his hand. "What is the exact casualty count among the men?"

David looked up from his notes. "I can't say exactly, Admiral. Some ships don't know how many men they have left to operate. And it will be another four hours or so before we can start to get an accurate count of survivors picked up by other ships."

"This is all crazy, Bill." David Charles stared at an invisible spot on the bulkhead before he turned to the other to continue. "We were out here for a display of power," his hands raised in despair, "a military show of force to back up a political decision." He shook his head and repeated, "It's all crazy, Bill. We were supposed to dig a couple of trenches out here to keep the Russians away while we finished the work on that island. This wasn't supposed to be Trafalgar or Jutland or Midway or Leyte, yet this was probably the largest sea battle in history . . . after surface battles were supposed to be finished." He stood and paced the tiny stateroom that the cruiser *California* called the admiral's cabin. "Christ, Bill, say something. Don't stare at me like that. Don't you think the whole thing is crazy, this wholesale slaughter, this,

this . . ." He shrugged his shoulders, searching for the right words.

"I don't quite know what to say, Admiral. I didn't expect this either." He stopped to gather his thoughts, could think of little to say, then, "But the Russians have taken tremendous losses themselves. It's not all on our side."

"That's just it, Bill. Each of us has clobbered the other. Why? What have we got to show for it? I don't even know if Alex is alive to know or even perhaps be pleased with what he's done to us." He turned to look directly at Dailey. "I'm not proud of what we've done to him." He jammed an index finger at his chest. "Not me. Hell, I'd have to show something for it to be proud. A victory. Or whatever the hell you call it these days." He raised his brows, wrinkling his forehead. "But what do I have to show for it, Bill?"

"I'm afraid I don't know what to say, sir. We've heard so little from Washington the last few hours. I assume they've had everything relayed to them."

There was a sharp knock on the door.

"Come," David called out.

A sailor with a message board entered, saluting as he shut the door with his other hand. "Two emergency messages, sir."

David took them and scanned the contents, frowning. Initialing them, he passed the board to Dailey. "I guess things can't get any worse."

Dailey's jaw dropped perceptibly as he read first about the loss of *Prince of Peace* and then the ill-fated invasion of Islas Piedras. He shrugged his shoulders and shook his head slightly, his brows raised in a what-the-hell-do-we-do-now look.

"I'm going to get hold of Alex."

"Sir?"

"I'm going to contact Alex. For Christ's sake, Bill, we've reached a stalemate. He can't get through to Islas Piedras, so we'll probably be able to finish the work there. But, on the other hand, Gorenko seems to have secured the Middle East. It's a trade-off!" The expression on his face seemed to say that it was all so simple now. "We get Africa. They get the Arabs. We protect the South Atlantic. They get their warm-water port."

"Don't you feel we should wait for further orders, sir?"

In a voice very unlike his usually conservative demeanor, David replied, "Shit no, Bill. Those sons of bitches in Washington must be so goddamn scared of what everybody's saying about them that they're going to worry about saving their own hides. Sam Carter won't be able to get a word in edgewise. Shit, when he mentions us, all those scurvy politicians are going to say, "Who?' When it comes down to your neck, they could care less what's happened out here." He was pacing more rapidly now in the confined space. "Same with Alex, I'll bet." For just a moment, he returned to the Admiral Charles of the previous day. "Hell, Bill, I'll put five on it right now the Party Secretary won't even let Gorenko talk about Alex's ships. After that great speech about protecting the Third World from American aggressors, he's only thinking about how he's going to explain an armed invasion—that didn't work—and that goddamn tanker. Christ, Bill, anyone in the world who isn't white ought to be pretty happy now. For once, we didn't drag everybody else in. We just blasted away at each other, which must have made them feel damn good." He stopped, looked at Dailey politely listening, and sat back down.

"Want me to go on, Bill?" He grinned.

"If you'd like, sir."

"Forget it. I guess everybody in the service feels used at one time or another, but we've been drawing pay for years just for this day, haven't we?"

"You could put it that way."

"Well, that's why I'm going to call Alex. We could continue to shoot at each other, and we probably might once we get finished licking our wounds, so I want to stop it before it starts again. Why should we kill any more Russians?"

"And why should we let them kill any more of us?" The Chief of Staff looked thoughtfully at David. "Point well taken . . . especially mine."

"Okay. Step number one, Bill. Issue orders to anyone

afloat that they are not to fire unless fired upon first. Number two, get one of your comm officers up here on the double. I want direct voice contact with Alex somehow. Number three, get a message off to Washington that we feel Islas Piedras is safe for the time being, and that we are dropping back to regroup. Tell 'em casualties are extreme, just in case they've forgotten, and that if they want to fight anyone, they'd better get some more ships out here fast. And see if you can find a fresh set of whites my size in this ship. Like the lady said, 'I don't have a thing to wear.' ''

"Aye, aye, sir. I'll get that comm officer for you first."

Svedrov was crushed, emotionally exhausted. The first message that his Admiral handed him simply stated that the landing on Islas Piedras had failed. It had come from the submarines, not from the landing force. The second slip of paper he had picked off the deck, where it had slipped from Alex Kupinsky's hands. It told of the *Prince of Peace*.

"I will contact David."

It had been a simple statement, not a question. Svedrov knew his advice was not being asked but that a response was necessary. He would continue as Admiral Kupinsky's alter ego, to act both as a right arm and as the royal opposition, whatever the occasion required.

"Why do you say that? We have won!"

Alex whirled. "Won what, Svedrov? Tell me what we have accomplished today."

"Why . . . the Americans have been badly beaten. *Nimitz* is sunk."

"*Lenin* is also."

"We have destroyed so many of their ships, we could launch an attack on Islas Piedras this instant."

"With what?"

Silence from the other.

"We have used two air groups. The Maldives force is decimated. Gorenko can send us nothing. It is more likely that he is right now trying to explain what happened to that supertanker."

"Admiral, we now have the warm-water port we have

needed for so many years.''

''And I think, my friend, that Islas Piedras may soon be completed.''

Again there was silence from the Chief of Staff. Svedrov did not know what more he could say to his Admiral, a man he revered. He could not comprehend the fact that, after such heavy losses, a task-force commander could look like Kupinsky. To inflict damage, you must accept losses yourself. It was doctrine. But perhaps the older man was right. They could not go on.

''I sincerely believe, Svedrov, that only David Charles and I can avoid any more death. It must stop.'' He slammed both hands hard on the table in front of him. ''We cannot afford to lose any more ships or men, or we will have nothing left to sail into that warm-water port of yours. And, if Islas Piedras is completed by the Americans, we must have a strong fleet in the Indian Ocean.

''Svedrov, is there anyone on this little *Rezvy* who can contact the Americans for me? I will talk to David myself.''

The other raised his hands in despair. ''I will find out.''

''And, I also want you to inform all units that they are to drop back and to use their weapons only to protect themselves.'' He raised his hands, keeping Svedrov from speaking right away. ''I do not think, Svedrov, that we will receive any orders from Moscow. Admiral Gorenko is probably trying to explain right now why so little has been accomplished today.''

''But we have done so much.''

''And so have the Americans. What do you think is going on with Admiral Charles right now? He is probably waiting for orders from his seniors in Washington, who are trying to explain all of this to their politicians. Can you imagine what the U.N. is saying to the Americans right now? Can you imagine what the whole world thinks about both our countries? Think, Svedrov, what might have happened if either of us had been the first to use atomic weapons.''

There was only silence from the other. Svedrov understood. It was just so hard to take when so many ships had been lost, and so many friends he had known from the days at his Higher Naval School. He had not told his Admiral about his brother. He had been made captain of *Boiky,* before they sailed. *Boiky* had been lost in the wolfpack attack.

David Charles sat in the bow of *California's* whaleboat, a craft much smaller than his own admiral's barge. Try as he would, the young coxswain could not keep the water out. At first he attempted to steer around the ocean chop, but that was impossible in such a breeze. Then he had the engineman throttle down, hoping the speed could be raised and lowered to make the ride drier and more comfortable for the Admiral. But that was impossible also. David had told them to proceed normally, not to worry about him. They would see the other boat they were to meet soon anyway.

It had been a most unusual conversation with Alex. *California's* comm officer had suggested one of the international-distress frequencies. Most ships would be guarding it anyway with so many aircraft down.

"I want to speak with Admiral Kupinsky." He had used Russian and identified himself. The pause was momentary.

"This is Admiral Kupinsky."

The voice had come back too quickly, he thought. Again he identified himself and asked for the Soviet Admiral. As he released the key, the other voice came back instantly.

"This is Admiral Kupinsky." again in Russian. Then, in English, "This is Admiral Kupinsky."

There was no way to identify a voice over the air, but there was no mistaking the familiar accent. Charles then said first in English, then in Russian, "Alex, this is David Charles. It was necessary to call you."

"Yes. I recognize your accent, David. I intended to speak with you also. That is why I was nearby."

"We should talk, Alex. We know from listening to your radio circuits that you have no more contact with Moscow than we do with Washington."

"We realize your problem also."

"I can sink the remainder of your force if I have to, but I feel we should talk first."

"It doesn't really matter who could still sink the other,

David. Rather than concern ourselves with that, let us attempt to save the remaining lives, if that is at all possible. But, I will not come on board one of your ships.''

"Nor I yours. I have asked my ships to drop back. If you will do the same, I suggest we use small boats and meet by ourselves in between.''

"I have already asked my ships to reform, David. Let us bring our flag ships within five kilometers to limit the distance traveled in small boats. Then we will have them fall back ten kilometers. Do you agree?''

"Agreed. Will you come alone?''

"Yes. But two other men are necessary to handle the boat.''

"I hadn't thought of that, but yes, you're right. No weapons?''

"I see no use for them at this point.''

"Alex, do you have any of your good vodka aboard?''

There was a different intonation in the answer, a lighter one. "When will you Americans ever modernize your Navy?'' There was a pause and a voice in the background as the key was held down. Then, "No vodka. But, David you are in luck. We happen to have some of that good Georgian brandy that you like so well. Compliments of the Soviet Navy!''

"I will accept them. It is now 1420. Could you be there at 600?''

"David, I had my whaleboat readied half an hour ago.''

So, there was no question about it. They had both had the same intentions. "I'm sure our chart positions may be slightly different. I believe that a point three five zero degrees true, one hundred fifteen kilometers from the center of Islas Piedras, will be pretty much equidistant between our two ships right now.''

"I believe so. I can assure you there will be no firing as the ship you are riding approaches that point to put over its boat.''

"I assure your safety also.'' They had never for a moment said what either wanted to talk about. It had been understood.

He thought of that conversation now as he saw the coxswain ppoint just off the bow and shout something that drifted away with the breeze. He stood, looking over the canvas, and saw the other boat, no bigger than his own, working its way toward him. It was having equal difficulty with the developing chop that came with a stiffening breeze.

Again, he thought how strange it was that two small boats were approaching each other in the wake of a battle that had involved some of the most powerful ships in the world only hours before. He held tightly as they lurched to starboard. Then the wave that had slapped the bow covered them with water.

As the other came closer, he could see the Admiral's flag in the bow and the hammer and sickle in the stern, both diaplayed as he had also directed his boat be decorated. David had ensured that his sailors were in their full dress uniforms. Now soaked, he still wanted to show them off as the pride of the American Navy.

As the other drew abeam of him, he noted that the Russian sailors were dressed the same way. And Alex, too, was in a dress uniform similar to his own. What do you know, he though, a formal ball on the high seas. I wonder if his is borrowed, too?

There was no time for further daydreaming. The coxswains had brought their craft within hailing distance.

"We will come about and throw you a line," shouted Alex. "We will ride together into the wind?"

"All right."

The Soviet boat came around smartly, as much to avoid the seas as to exhibit seamanship. Its coxswain held the tiller between his knees briefly as he bent to pick up a heaving line. Already prepared, he had only to throw the hard ball of the monkey's fist over and grab the tiller again to maintain course. A second line, from the bow, was heaved to the Americans and secured forward. Now it was only a matter of seconds as the two boats were brought slowly together, protective fenders dropping over the sides when they were close. Once the enginemen were sure they had the same revolutions on their propellers, the two boats rode as one, taking the swells together.

The two men eyed each other for a moment. They seemed to notice the other's hand tentatively moving at the same time. Then they saluted each other smartly, as much for the watching men on the ships in the distance as anything else.

"Will you come over here?" Kupinsky was the first to speak.

"I'd be more comfortable if you joined me."

"I brought the brandy." Alex bent down and picked up a bottle which he displayed in his right hand. "The least you could do is join me for a drink." He smiled then for the first time.

David grinned, the first these sailors had seen. "Why, of course. I forgot my manners. I'd be happy to join you. But may I suggest that perhaps we should exchange one of your men . . . to keep an equal number in each boat, and to keep them," he gestured first at his own ship, then at Alex's, "from getting worried."

"I had thought of that." He pointed at his engineman, explaining that he was to board the American boat. Then Kupinsky said, "Wait." He brought out another bottle, handing it to the man. "You will share together." He again used his hands to point to all four sailors. His gesture was answered with grateful smiles.

Alex carefully undid the seal and opened his bottle. "Sorry, I forgot the snifters," he said with a wry look on his face. David accepted the proffered bottle, sniffed at the contents, and nodded approvingly. He lifted the bottle to his lips, taking a deep swallow, then wiped his mouth with the back of his hand.

"Excellent, vintage, my friend." He handed it back to the other, who also drank deeply.

The Russian ran a forearm across his mouth. His eyes were watering slightly. "I'm not used to drinking like this, I'm afraid. Too much sea duty."

David coughed slightly as the potent liquid brought a flush to his cheeks. "I couldn't agree more, Alex." Then he gestured at the four sailors who were generously passing the other bottle among themselves. "They don't seem to have any language barrier."

Kupinksy's face instantly became serious again. "David, you and I have no language barrier, nor any others that I know of. It has hurt me deeply that we were forced to do this to each other . . . this death . . . this destruction . . . ." His hands, which had been making sweeping gestures as if to show the extent of it all, dropped to his sides. "I never intended this to happen."

"Nor I. It was supposed to be a tough show of force, very tough. But this wasn't supposed to occur. I guess perhaps it was the loss of communications . . . we didn't know what was happening in Washington."

"I was out of contact with Moscow," Alex added helplessly.

David reached again for the brandy. "I had no intention of using nuclear weapons, without orders from the President."

"Neither did I. We would have had to be insane." The bottle was passed back to its owner.

"Did you really feel Islas Piedras was an aggressive action?"

"I don't know, David. I am aware only of what I received in the messages. . . . Was it?"

"I don't think so. I guess I knew as much as you did."

"Is the missile installation indeed completed?"

"Probably." Then he looked at the Russian. "No. I don't know whether it is or not." They sat thoughtfully for a moment, each again taking a turn with the brandy, this time in smaller quantities. "Did you plan to sink that supertanker?"

"I don't know anything about it. Probably communications again. Maybe we'll never know?"

"They think I'm crazy, I suppose. They want to destroy you."

"You don't?"

"I never did," sighed the Russian.

"Wouldn't it be nice to be back in London?"

"Lovely, with Tasha and Maria . . . and our children."

The last phrase brought silence for both of them.

"We would be crazy to continue this slaughter," said David. "We are too even. They must settle this across the tables."

"Perhaps that's where Gorenko has won, my friend. Thirty-five or forty years ago, this would have been impossible. Even, he smiled, "back in 1962, we could not match you. Today we did. You and I are even, my friend, and perhaps my old father has finally made his point."

"We could argue that forever, but we must stop this, now."

"Have you received any instructions from Washington?"

"No. Any for you?"

"Nothing." He pulled on the bottle and handed it to the other.

"I suggest that we might radio our governments directly and tell them we are withdrawing."

"Perhaps we should inform them of our meeting."

David pointed skyward without looking up. "I'm sure they're aware of it right now."

Kupinsky knew he was referring to the spy planes, high up out of sight. They would be relaying accurate pictures of the meeting if the proper satellites were functioning. They continued their conversation, discussing directions of withdrawal, safety measures, and the countless items that had to be considered. And all the while, the eyes of Dailey and Svedrov were glued to their binoculars, waiting for the slightest hint of trouble.

But when it came, it developed where it was least expected. From deep in the Indian Ocean, deep enough so that there was no light, it began stirring, like a great wounded creature, not quite dead. It had broken away from its mother ship, *Mendel Rivers*, when that boat's pressure hull began to break up. By all rights, it should have gone to the bottom with the stricken submarine, but the pressure had somehow cracked the hull in an odd enough way so that the great black fish bumped and crashed and finally tore out of its lair. Its engine seemed to catch for a moment, then died, but the torpedo was caught in a strange undersea limbo, neither diving nor surfacing, its engine occasionally sputtering.

For hours its electronic brain searched for a reason to activate its internal mechanism and finish the mission it was designed for. A great battle was fought overhead, but nothing that passed near the fish on the journey to the bottom was able to stimulate it. Then, when all was quiet, a message was passed from one segment of its brain to another, perhaps activated by a shift in ocean current that caused it to roll ever so slightly and bring damaged circuits into contact for just an instant.

The torpedo came alive, its engine humming evenly. But it was much too deep. The nose pointed straight upward. Rapidly, it headed for the surface, no active target in its memory cells since it had never been programmed for a specific target. Its sensitive acoustics picked up a faint noise and relayed a directional change to the fins. Slowly, as graceful as a shark, it turned toward the sound, locked on, and then raced toward the source.

Both Dailey and Svedrov noted the intitial reports from their sonar, and both paid little attention. Their binoculars never left their eyes. They may have heard the frantic reports at the last instant that the noises were high-speed torpedo screws in the vicinity of the small boats, but there was little they could do.

They saw the boats lifted into the air, the occupants dislodged briefly from their positions, but only for a split second before the explosion. Then there was nothing. Remnants of the boat were visible on the surface of the water, and perhaps even parts of a human being, as the spray cleared. There was no fire. There was nothing to burn.

The glasses fell from Svedrov's grasp, swinging from his neck. His jaw relaxed and his mouth fell open. He turned to the Captain of *Rezvy* to say something, but nothing would come out. His eyes blinked involuntarily.

''Shall I give orders to attack?'' questioned the captain, his face contorted in anger.

Svedrov shook his head, the bushy eyebrows knit together. The other looked questiongly at him. The Chief of Staff shook his head again and muttered, "The torpedo report a moment ago. That must have been it. But there are no submarines in the area. No one has fired . . . it must have been loose in the water . . ." he pointed down to the surface from their spot on the bridge, ". . . it was an accident." He was trying desperately to find a reason for this loss.

Then the Chief of Staff's face hardened. "He was right. We must stop this." He turned to *Rezvy's* captain, "Set a course for the Maldives, and give the order to the force." And at the look of concern from the other, "I will contact Gorenko myself." Then he quickly turned toward the sea so no one would see his face.

On *California,* Bill Dailey's eyes misted for a moment. Then he lifted the binoculars to his face to search the spot again. His mind raced. He heard someone push the general quarters alarm even though, for all practical purposes, they had remained in that status. He remembered the report from sonar, torpedo near the small craft. Then he had watched horrified as the blast eradicated his Admiral and the Russian in an instant. He tried to remember which boat seemed to have been hit first, but then he realized it was impossible to tell, even if he had been taking a picture. And what did it matter anyway?

Then he sensed *California's* captain at his side, waiting for orders. The bell was still clanging. His mind raced. They couldn't do anything foolish. He must stop them. "Captain," he called "Set a course for the Seychelles. Give that order to all ships." It was time to stop this insanity. That's what Admiral Charles had gone out there for, he thought, to make sure no more lives were lost. He allowed no one to see his eyes as he left the bridge to prepare the message he would send to Carter.

Gorenko had the driver stop when they were halfway up the driveway to the dacha. The trip from Moscow lasted less than an hour, but it was the most agonizing hour of his life.

The driver saw in the rearview mirror that the Admiral sat stone-faced. No expression crossed his face. He appeared emotionless.

But his heart had been torn from his body when he saw the tape of that explosion. Tears would not come for the loss of the man he had found as a boy in a little village on the east bank of the Volga. But the inner pain was pure agony. He knew immediately he would have to go to Tasha. He had sent her to the dacha a few days before, far enough away for her and the child to be safe.

Now as he looked out the car window, he saw the boy running across the snow-covered yard. How much like his father, thought Gorenko. The Admiral had also arranged for his grandson to be released from his Nakhimov school to be with his mother. The Navy could do without him for a few days. He swung the car door open, and the boy leaped excitedly in, then, in respect to the other, extended his right hand to shake the old, gnarled paw of his grandfather.

It was then that Gorenko broke down. Tears came to his eyes silently. There was no sound. The boy did not notice it until they swung around by the front door. When he saw his grandfather sitting perfectly erect, face forward, the tears streaming down his cheeks, he ran into the house to get his mother.

Tasha Kupinsky bent slightly as she came out of the door to look into the car. She hadn't understood her son. But when she came to the open door and looked in at Gorenko, she knew.

She extended her hand to the suddenly very old man, whose shoulders were now slightly rounded. He looked up at Tasha. Her great sad eyes looked deeply into his and said they understood the pain, and she gestured with her other hand for him to come inside with her.

The moisture did come to Sam Carter's eyes. At first they were tears of rage as he stared at the picture before him in disbelief. The pencil in his hands snapped. One of his aides had just left the room, and for a moment he was alone with his terrible knowledge, the scene riveted in his brain. He rose from his chair, knocking it over, sweeping the papers on his desk to the floor as he strode across to a window.

With the realization of what had just occurred, the tears of rage changed to tears of anguish. The angry young ensign who had returned from a Cuban beach to shout at his captain was now gone. All of the emotion he had held back for years suddenly welled up from inside. He knew he was losing control, and he fought back.

At that moment, his secretary entered, following her usual method of pushing through the door as she knocked. Sam Carter heard the sound and turned. Stopping dead in her tracks, she mumbled an inaudible excuse and pulled the door shut behind her. She had never seen an Admiral cry.

He wasn't sure how much time had passed since he had stared at that picture of horror. That instant was still vivid in his mind. Now, he was at Maria's door in Virginia. He turned to look back and saw his car in the driveway, the chauffeur sitting respectfully at the wheel. He knew why he had come. He had to be the one to tell her.

He couldn't remember if he had pushed the bell. He reached for the button again, but the door was already swinging open, and there was Maria, looking as lovely as he always remembered her.

She looked out at Sam Carter and saw only the ghost of the man David had always loved. She saw it all in his eyes, and knew right away why he was standing on her doorstep.

"Please come in, Sam."

He removed his hat and stepped up into the foyer. He looked deeply into her eyes and opened his mouth to tell her, but nothing would come out.

She put both her hands out and grasped his, squeezing them tightly, and said, "I know why you're here." Then she stepped forward and put her head on his shoulder. She was crying for her sailor, who would not be home from sea.